IN PLAIN SIGHT

RICHARD JOHN THORNTON

IN PLAIN SIGHT

DEDICATED TO THE RICH AND FAMOUS

PROLOGUE

The age of celebrity.

Public acclaim is a facet of life that has steadily become an ever more indispensable commodity.

In any field of notable achievement, whether it be politics or sport, entertainment or indeed crime, public analysis of such right and wrong doings is now deemed part and parcel of everyday existence.

Yet the subsequent attention ensures that those found wallowing in their fifteen minutes of fame, unwittingly tread a fine line between fanatical reverence and equally enthusiastic rejection.

For the great majority of individuals that run the gauntlet of success and its associated trappings, incessant media coverage and the accompanying luxuries rarely promote cause for concern, as they willingly stomp new ground in the quest to uphold their newly acquired status.

But for a proportion of those wide-eyed souls suddenly subjected to such exposure, natural curiosity from their observers can sometimes evolve into hardened resistance.

And occasionally, hostility.

And a once harmonious situation can swiftly become eclipsed by malice.

Yet at the outset, it is perhaps a given rarity for those riding the wave of acknowledgement, to ever consider the consequences of a potential downturn in their popularity.

When this negative reality eventually dawns, it is typically far too late in the game.

Only then, do the subjects of scrutiny wish to retreat from the spotlight they once coveted.

Only then, when opinion has switched, and they are bombarded with the inevitable scorn and derision, do the innocents begin to regret that their dream ever came true in the first place……

ONE

Twenty-Twenty-One. The Thirty-First of May. Monday.

It had been fifteen months. Over a year of uncertainty. Over a year residing in fear. Over a year of watching the world become crippled by suspicion and then in turn rankled by increasing frustration.

Finally, after over a year of waiting, the rabid desire for that concept called normality, was to be sated once and for all.

Ashley Griffiths had just about coped with the enforced policies that had put lives and livelihoods in limbo. He had employed patience and respect for authority. He had, like many millions of others, been an exemplary law-abiding citizen.

The theory behind being Furloughed seemed a promising novelty initially. In practice it was agreeable for a while. But the overwhelming truth eventually overshadowed the optimism.

The truth being that it was a fallacy. Being paid *not* to work and to be confined at home only encouraged the personal deception. It wasn't a realistic long-term prospect. And once that penny dropped, Ashley's tolerance of the situation swiftly began to wane.

Eighty percent of salary going in the bank each month was all well and good in principle. But for those many souls in the country who took their occupations seriously and never for granted, the Government's pandemic response engineered existence to be balanced on a tightrope.

After all, there was no endeavour required in being awarded a wage for doing nothing. No skill set to be called upon. No sense of responsibility. No actual earning of one's income. No daily routine to oblige. No experience and qualifications to substantiate.

Just a generally and genuinely confused mindset that eventually supplied a sense of unease and maybe even guilt, for being on the end of the Government's apparently incredulous generosity.

Not unlike most other workers in the hospitality trade that been left suspended in animation by the raging threat of Covid, Ashley had inadvertently discovered new strings to his bow to pass the time on hand.

He had become a fanatical jigsaw enthusiast.

At least one new thousand-piece puzzle arrived in an Amazon van for each new month of his particularly effective, lockdown survival strategy. And as the puzzles were duly completed, they were dismantled, replaced in their boxes, and stacked up in the cupboard under the stairs.

Ashley pledged to himself in earnest that they would eventually be supplied to a deserving charity at the most convenient opportunity.

Gardening had also unexpectedly entered his realm. He had long realised that simply owning a lawnmower could never truly be counted as a qualification in possessing green fingers.

Having not so much as turned a border in his life, suddenly buying seeds and compost online had resulted in several potted displays of industrious beauty. Flourishes of pink, red and purple sat proudly around the tightly manicured greenery of the rear lawn and extensive decking area.

And Ashley had also convinced himself that talking to plants was an acquired talent that did indeed promote and encourage flora to bloom.

Binge-watching had also become an adopted alternative to the endless stream of propaganda, media analysis and ineffective nightly lectures from Downing Street.

Stranger Things, Peaky Blinders and The Walking Dead provided a much more stimulating agenda for the brain to absorb.

But months and months of wallowing in the murk of such a fabricated secondary lifestyle were about to come to an end. And Ashley Griffiths was perhaps the most relieved man on the planet, as he stood before the bedroom dress mirror and studied the image in the glass.

He had forgotten how it felt, to not only *wear* a suit, but also the feeling of empowerment it evoked. The tracksuit and running shoes had become an increasingly despised necessity during his time out of work.

But such garb wasn't truly him.

The thinking being that if he looked like a slouch, then it stood to reason that he almost certainly would *feel* like one.

He had the poise and figure to carry a good cut of cloth.

And it was with immense contentment that he could acknowledge today as his first official day back at the helm donned in full occupational regalia.

Ashley's particular domain of authority being Operations Manager of the nearby Hernwood Hotel.

The Hernwood was one of a chain of reputable hotels performing under the umbrella of the chief ownership company, Ultimate Inns Limited.

Over the previous fortnight, Ashley and his equally excited members of staff had been back on site supervising all manner of preparatory missions in readiness to re-open the doors and welcome back the public.

But he'd been performing this daily supervision attired in the aforementioned leisurewear. Not his preferred outfit for duty and certainly not a combination that allowed him to stand out as The Operations Manager.

But there was little point in overdressing during the previous days as he had spent a good proportion of each shift being hands-on with the frantic spruce up.

Or occasionally even on hands and knees to assist with the very specific final inspections of every completely sterilized guest room. Of which there were two hundred spanned across four floors, with each needing to comply with five pages of cleanliness requirement forms.

And Ultimate Inns Limited had only afforded each site two weeks' notice to action the sanitation plan before the Big Day.

Suffice to say, this element of preparation was behind schedule somewhat.

Even with the current official Covid figures supposedly exhibiting a virus in decline, hospitality and retail nationwide had taken the biggest hit by far since March of Twenty-Twenty. And now, even with lawful permission to recommence daily business, the parameters of hygiene were to be strictly adhered to at all costs.

Cost being the operative word.

Ultimate Inns Limited had not been one of the chains required to assist with the accommodation of NHS staff and as such had been languishing longest in its apparent operative redundancy.

But all that was history now. The future was the only thing that counted. And that future began today. To say the least, Ashley Griffiths was raring to embrace the next chapter with every ounce of his acumen and expertise.

'Ash! Your tea and toast are going *cold*!'

Ashley straightened the knot in his tie as the voice of his ever-loving long term partner Carl resonated up the stair well. If Covid had proved nothing else, it had established that Ashley's four-year relationship with Carl Davis was resilient and enduring.

Ashley was forever thankful to have found a considerate, affectionate, and reliable companion. Even Marjorie, Ashley's very studious and suspicious seven-year-old long-haired tortoiseshell cat, had instantly taken to Carl when he moved in six months before the first Lockdown. So, Ashley was now fortunate to boast *two* considerate, affectionate, and reliable housemates.

Throughout all the self-doubt and innate concern that manifested through the pandemic, Ashley could always count on his co-habiting confidantes.

'Okay, thanks. I'm on my way down!'

Ashley checked his wristwatch. Nearly six a.m. If he left home by half-past, he could be on site by seven with most of the team. His mind had thought of little else during the previous few days and today was last chance saloon.

The final walkthrough and box-ticking inspection of the entire premises before it could be deemed ready for public admittance.

Every key employee at Hernwood had been officially removed from The Furlough Scheme and would be at their posts in anticipation.

Sadly, from Ashley's perspective anyway, a few members of the team had opted to leave the hospitality trade during the extended closure of the hotel, as Furlough payment didn't cover their needs.

This entailed a rapid recruitment drive for, among other positions, a new bar manager, two gym supervisors and an overnight duty manager. But thankfully most of the staff had retained the belief that business would bounce back, and that their employment prospects would remain relatively secure.

From chefs and kitchen hands, through to the laundry operatives, cleaners, and security officers. And of course, the front-facing end of the business - reception and foyer services.

All departments needed to pass the internally conducted assessments with flying colours.

Besides all this, the necessary national Covid guidelines would need to be instigated for the safety of all that passed through the building and surrounding grounds.

It was a tall order, but Ashley upheld his managerial faith that all would be functional and in readiness for resumption of trading.

The sooner everybody shook off their fifteen months of accumulated depression, rust, and cobwebs, the better.

Staying at home for one's income was now a chapter for the history books. And there was secretly no man on Earth more invigorated by the fact than Ashley Griffiths.

Carl on the other hand had found himself to be in a rather more prominent and prosperous position than many.

As a professional freelance website designer, he had quickly become inundated with commissions during both lockdowns. With months at home to indulge themselves, the I.T. and online communities nationwide created a spike in demand for graphically produced software. Indeed, the surge in the industry's popularity was unprecedented.

Carl was no slouch when it came to showcasing his talents and networking his business. Now weighed down with a hectic and sometimes overbearing schedule of deadlines, his working shift usually consisted of a dawn start and a dusk finish.

Whilst Ashley had been looking to fill his time with plants and puzzles, Carl was considering opening a petition for thirty-six hours in a day as opposed to the standard twenty-four, such was the clamour for his abilities.

He was in typically effervescent mood as Ashley finally entered the kitchen *sans* suit jacket and seated himself at the dining table.

'I've fed Marjorie. She's gone out already. She couldn't wait for you.'

Ashley sampled some of his tepid tea whilst scrutinising the scene beyond the kitchen window.

'Thanks. My hero! Looks like a nice day too. Shouldn't think the cat will be back until her tummy's rumbling again.'

Marjorie was christened in memory of Ashley's maternal grandmother.

Like most felines of distinction - and indeed in similar fashion to Ashley's late grandmother - she was an astute judge of character and would readily express her distaste concerning any aspect of the house that she veritably ruled from top to bottom.

Luckily for Carl he was on her acceptance list almost immediately and he had become as much of a human father to Marjorie as Ashley was. Indeed, as Carl once described it, Marjorie welcomed his arrival with wide open claws.

Sitting himself opposite Ashley, Carl glanced across the table as he tipped cornflakes into a bowl.

'How are you feeling about today? Nervous? Excited? Dreadful?'

Swilling more tea, Ashley did not need long to deliberate on the answer to a question he had not been asked for a very long time.

'Not concerned at all to be honest. Everyone should sail through the drills today. They are a great squad. If anything, it's probably *me* that's forgotten how to do his job properly!'

Carl chuckled as he applied milk to his cereal.

'It'll go like clockwork! Take more than Covid to stop my man in his tracks. I'm sure you've got a well-oiled machine in place.'

A moment for reflection befell Ashley as he spread butter on his toast.

‘I’m quietly thankful that we didn’t have to stay open for the doctors and nurses. Sounds terribly selfish, doesn’t it? But we’d have struggled badly trying to run the show with a skeleton crew. Can you believe some hotels were fully occupied with NHS, yet chain owners wouldn’t retain the staff numbers to cover it? I think Ultimate got off light.’

Carl nodded as he crunched his first mouthful.

‘Well, if the Government were paying to keep them at home it’s a no-brainer, isn’t it? Not costing employers a penny. How many guests are you expecting this week?’

‘Oh, about fifty rooms are booked from tomorrow. Plus, any passing trade now people are venturing out to work again. It’s a suck and see thing, I think. No one is sure how our business will fare. Makes you realise how the pandemic might have really messed economics up for a lot of places. Before Covid we were at full occupancy most weeks. That’s less than two years’ ago. Now we might have to pull strangers in off the street and *beg* them to spend the night!’

Both men laughed at the ridiculous yet telling scenario.

Ashley pointed out a critical factor in events.

‘The problem is that most office-based workers are still at home. They were our mainstay. Must be a strange way of life after all the mad commuting and city hustle and bustle.’

Carl looked open-mouthed at Ashley in feigned astonishment at what he had just heard.

‘Yeah right!’

‘Yeah right, what?’

‘These bloody office workers. Having a tough time? Logging onto their laptops and watching daytime TV all day? Sounds ideal to me, Ash!’

Ashley grimaced at the very thought.

‘Oh no! I couldn’t think of anything worse! I know I’ve watched a lot of stuff through box sets, but I couldn’t watch the shit that’s broadcast on mainstream telly every day. I’d have turned into a zombie by now.’

'So, I take it you're ready to jump back into things, then?'

Ashley observed in amusement as Carl drank the remains of his breakfast straight from the bowl.

'I most definitely am! I've missed the team. The interaction, you know? I've missed meeting members of the public for the first time and seeing them again for the second and third times. I'm ready again to give them great service in a top establishment. It's been a bloody weird period in life. Fingers crossed the worst is over now. Anyway, enough about me, what about you? A lot going on today?'

Carl rose gingerly to his feet and yawned loudly.

'I should have started already if truth be known but your enthusiasm to finish off that bottle of red last night kind of slowed me up a little this morning.'

Ashley raised his eyebrows in mock astonishment.

'Oh, so your hangover is *my* fault, is it? And here's me recalling my suggestion of an early night before you came in the lounge and opened that *second* bottle? At least you haven't got to drive anywhere, even if you do feel a bit ropey.'

Carl stood to attention and raised both arms with his palms facing outwards.

'Touché! My bad! Guilty as charged your honour! Dare I ask what time you think you might be home tonight?'

Grimacing as he finished the last piece of toast, Ashley looked to the ceiling and closed his eyes as if in meditation.

'Honestly? Today is going to be at least twelve hours. If I'm back through the front door by eight it will be a minor miracle.'

Carl moved position to embrace Ashley from behind and nuzzled into his neck.

'No worries. I'll aim to finish by then too. Lasagne for supper. I'll get salad and garlic bread, yeah?'

'Might end up being a midnight feast!'

'Doesn't matter, Ash. Just come home smiling. I've got my fingers and toes crossed for you.'

Ashley felt very touched by Carl's attentive nature.

His enthusiasm to display support for Ashley's return to routine was heartening and soothing.

'How can I *not* come home happy knowing you'll be waiting here for me? And the lasagne of course. That's the real deal maker.'

Ashley turned and hugged Carl tightly.

The feeling of being loved was something Ashley cherished dearly.

He never thought it would ever happen to him.

And for a time, Ashley's parents had given up hope of their son finding a partner and settling down. Especially when they first learned of his sexuality.

It was not an announcement that inflated them with billowing pride, considering he was only eighteen when he told them. But time hopefully cures most issues of any initial discomfort.

Now at the age of forty-two, Ashley figured he had spent more than long enough doubting his own destiny.

Checking his watch once more, Ashley swallowed the remnants of his tea mug.

'Right, Carlos…teeth and a wash and a dab of man scent and I'm out of here.'

Carl set the dishwasher in motion and retreated upstairs to his makeshift office. Starting up his graphics tablet and PC he then studied the noticeboard for the day's priorities. There were dozens of them, such was the demand for his expertise.

Within five minutes he was downstairs once again, hanging from the frame of the front door watching Ashley place his suit jacket, briefcase, and laptop in the back seat of the car, before returning to Carl to say goodbye.

The two kissed on the lips and looked longingly at one another.

'Right Carlos…wish me luck!'

'When you're a real-life super-hero luck doesn't come into it. Knock 'em dead! Missing you already. I'll keep an eye out for Marjorie to make sure she gets her lunch.'

Ashley gave a thumbs-up before slipping behind the wheel. Turning the ignition key, he chuckled to himself as Marjorie suddenly appeared on the garage roof as if to bid him a farewell of her own.

Leaving reverse and finding first gear, the overwhelming sensation of fulfilment washed over Ashley Griffiths as he guided the car away from home.

Normality beckoned.

At long last.

TWO

A definitive joy accompanied Ashley for the duration of the journey to work. The route felt strangely unfamiliar although he had driven along this path so many times in the past. But today was about embracing a renewal of old and faithful habits. And the opportunity to again sample such forsaken pleasure was strangely intoxicating.

The landmarks along the way were never truly acknowledged in the days pre-Covid. Yet the buildings, flyovers, parklands, and precincts formed a vaguely representative guard of honour as he navigated through town towards his destination.

The wrought-iron hotel entrance gates beckoned him inward and instigated an increased heartbeat. Once today's final audit was completed, all sites in the Ultimate Inn chain would be in position to declare their premises open to the public.

And Ashley found himself to be quietly ecstatic about the prospect.

Locating the car in the space reserved solely for The Operations Manager, he gently applied the handbrake and disengaged the engine. The upbeat sensation of earlier was now suddenly competing with a pang of trepidation.

Glancing into the rear-view mirror, Ashley observed his reflection. The image depicted a face exhibiting determination and stature. The manager of The Hernwood Hotel was back, and despite Covid and its associated restrictions, he was perhaps in his finest fettle.

And if he were honest with himself at that moment of contemplation in the mirror, Ashley would readily acknowledge that the business still had a veritable mountain to climb despite the positivity surrounding its long-delayed resumption.

Fulfilling the post-pandemic criteria was an unavoidable hindrance, and certain aspects of the new guidelines might well prove to be stumbling blocks. But he was adamant his team would reclaim what had been denied them over the previous fifteen months with the utmost professional gusto.

And then a prevailing wind of euphoria once more eclipsed the fleeting shafts of doubt.

The challenge was set for the entire staff of nearly forty employees.

The reward would be indeterminable, yet the initial target would be to attain the levels of success achieved prior to the lockdowns.

And Ashley Griffiths took immense pride in the fact that he was designated as the person to lead the charge.

Carl was always telling him to blow his own trumpet far more often.

So, on today of all days, Ashley pledged to take that advice on board.

He looked the part.

He felt the part.

And an albeit slightly rebranded sense of tenacity would arm him well in facing the mission head on.

Fully inflating his lungs, his attention was diverted to the main glass entrance doors. Security operative Lee Pinder stood outside just beyond the hotel reception area.

A bright yellow sandwich board sported bold black lettering. Information indicating the protocols to access and egress around the foyer. The first placating sign for Ashley that new health and safety regulations were being undertaken.

And although only employees were permitted on site today, it was gratifying to observe that the groove was being adhered to already.

The booking system for guests went live last week with tomorrow being the first day of customer entry. Sanitary procedures were already being practised as habit by the team. Covid Safe was the new soundbite in the hospitality sector. Whether that could practicably be maintained remained to be seen.

Ashley alighted the car and retrieved his suit jacket from its hanger over the back seat. Pulling out his computer and briefcase, he secured the car and readied himself.

He walked slowly across the tarmac to be greeted by a sheet of golden sunlight that had swiftly determined that dawn's grey clouds were to be banished for the day.

The horizon was looking bright.

Brighter than it had looked for many a month.

'Morning, Lee. A beautiful one on the cards by the look of it.'

The young security guard exhibited a broad smile as Ashley skipped up the four steps to the entrance.

'Morning, Ashley. Not long now.'

'It's been *too* long though, hasn't it, Lee. *Far* too long.'

The discomforting new Government directives still dissuaded people from shaking hands if it was deemed practical to avoid the gesture. Being very much a 'people person', Ashley knew he would instinctively struggle to accommodate this strand of policy.

Engaging with Lee Pinder without any physical interaction felt odd, and perhaps even ill-mannered but needs must, he supposed.

At least the wearing of face masks was now reduced to participation only on a voluntary basis as opposed to being mandatory. And with the vaccine rollout underway, the transition from previously accepted custom might not be too diverse or painstaking.

'It has for you guys. Security hasn't had any time off, though.'

'Lucky you.' quipped Ashley. 'Lockdown is *so* overrated, believe me. Honestly its crap!'

Lee chuckled as he checked a large set of keys.

'Well, no rest for the wicked, is there. I'll have to take your word for it that being Furloughed was painful. Although days and nights here on this job dragged like hell with nothing to look at.'

'Yes, I can well imagine. Why on Earth did they keep you working when the hotel was closed?'

'All about insurance, isn't it? Them policies still exist even if Covid kept everyone away.'

Ashley turned to study the smattering of vehicles in the car park.

'Sounds crazy to me, Lee. Bloody legislation. Don't worry, though. This place will hopefully soon be buzzing again starting tomorrow. Should make your walkabouts more stimulating, eh?'

Lee nodded in approval of the suggestion.

‘I never thought I’d hear myself say this Ashley, but I think I’ve actually genuinely *missed* seeing people, you know.’

Now it was Ashley’s turn to laugh.

‘I’ll come back to you this time next week and ask if you still feel the same. Have a good day, Lee. Make the most of the remaining peace and quiet. I know I’m going to.’

‘Cheers, Ashley. Let’s *do* this!’

The large tinted double doors had been crudely wedged at the bottom to ensure they remained open. Whilst allowing Ashley to stride confidently into the reception hallway, he couldn’t help the feeling that the measure, although temporary, looked very cheap and amateurish.

‘This is going to be fun for you in Winter, Jeanette.’

The supremely experienced Head of Reception was instantly distracted from her computer screen and undeniably delighted to witness the oncoming vision of Ashley Griffiths.

She pulled down her face mask and smiled broadly from behind the clear plastic screen that had been screwed to the countertop. In typical Jeanette Morris style, she upheld the pretence of proverbial cynic for the entertainment value if nothing else.

‘If they don’t get that sensor put it place, I’m going to be sat at my desk in hat and scarf by October. It’s going to be a bit difficult inputting online bookings and taking phone calls if I’m wearing mittens!’

Ashley and Jeanette welcomed the resonance of one another’s mirth, which was another relic of the recent past making a swift and pleasurable return.

Although only a few years older than Ashley, she embraced his younger zest and relished the chance to play his comedy foil at every given opportunity.

It was a working chemistry that had historically offered a much-needed mutual kick start every morning.

‘Nice to see you’re dressed for business for once instead of cross country. Now you’ve got your suit back on does that mean we have to behave ourselves?’

'I told you the scruffs were for getting dirty in. Back to normal now, Jeanette. Ruling with a rod of iron again and all that.'

She mockingly looked him up and down.

'Very dashing! I forgot how suave you look in a suit. *Very* James Bond!'

Ashley let his attention wander around the foyer and on to the guests' recreational seating area.

'Flattery will get you *everywhere*. How are the barracks looking? All ship shape and sparkling?'

Jeanette sat back in her chair and removed her headset.

'Well, all is in good order on *this* side of the desk. All guest reminder emails have been sent.'

'Splendid. So, what's happening or *not* happening on my side of the desk then?'

She shook her head as a mark of partial despair.

'Well, I'm bringing a flask to work because the rec room coffee vendor is out of order, and we aren't allowed to make our own drinks on site yet.'

Ashley presented an expression of completely feigned sympathy.

'Oh, it's a hard life isn't it. And all because of a silly thing called Covid!'

Jeanette didn't offer a reply as he continued to scrutinise the array of pandemic safety posters and hand-sanitising stations.

'Bloody eyesore, isn't it? Same for everyone though I suppose. Any more trouble at mill I should be warned about? Besides your flask issue?'

The Head of Reception rolled her eyes and pretended to cough in advanced exaggeration of potentially negative news.

'The cleaners are about two days behind schedule due to sickness absence, but all rooms needed for current bookings are ready. But on the bright side the full replacement stock linen delivery is in the storage compound.'

'Okay. Well, the behind-the-scenes crises we can deal with. Just keep on top of the bookings and liaise with the room staff as and when

necessary. Speaking of which have I got access to the booking portal yet because it was playing up in my office last week?'

'Already been sorted, Captain Griffiths. Up and running, sir.'

'Jeanette Morris you are just too good for this world of ours.'

She blew on her fingernails and rubbed them on her lapel in jest.

'Kitchen staff scrubbed up, okay?' he enquired.

'On their marks ready for the get-set-go. They've done their own hygiene audit apparently. Assuming we are allowed to serve food to the public, that is. They're just pleased they haven't got to cook with these bloody masks on.'

Ashley shook his head in genuine compassion this time.

The grey areas were the ones requiring most urgent attention.

'Yes, but I need to confirm the situation for the table staff though. Bloody complicated, isn't it?'

Jeanette raised a hand to add one more point to the agenda.

'M.D. Derek will be here later today, which I'm sure you are already aware of.'

Ashley pursed his lips in disdain.

'Yes, thank you, I knew he was paying each site a visit these next few days. I don't want any loose ends fraying when he gets here to sign us off, so I'd better get my arse into gear sharpish, hadn't I.'

Jeanette replaced her headset and began scanning her email inbox.

'Nothing else pressing for you to concern yourself with, Ashley. I suppose any creakiness will iron itself out once we get the public back on the premises. Oh, there was an issue with the hotel Wi-Fi, but maintenance have been on to it and done some random signal checks.'

'Far too technical for me to worry about. I'll leave them to it, I think. Not long now then, Jeanette my little cupcake. I bet they've missed your welcoming smile too!'

Once more she purposely opted not to respond as her eyes flickered up and down the monitor screen.

'By the way did you go up and give my office a good dusting and polishing? Perhaps a scented candle here and there?'

Jeanette decided to accompany her dismissive glare with a covertly exhibited middle finger before replacing her face mask.

'Thought not. No matter.' he murmured.

Ashley could not help but emit a fit of the giggles as he walked toward the elevator.

It felt so good to be back in the saddle.

THREE

The day endured with relative success. Several hurdles were navigated with aplomb. Concerns and quandaries quelled and overcome. And then, just as he sat back in his office chair with the time approaching four p.m., Ashley received the call from Jeanette that the Managing Director of Ultimate Inns - Derek Evans - was on site and had set up camp in the small conference room.

The Operations Manager, as fully expected, had been summoned.

Striding along the corridor, an alarming thought crossed Ashley's conscience as he briefly inspected the shine on the toes of his black leather shoes.

Despite the best efforts to ensure the hotel could hit the ground running tomorrow, this imminent encounter might well prove to be the biggest obstacle of the lot.

Ashley opted not to knock on the closed door of the meeting room, instead deciding to enter with a flourish and a beaming smile of positivity. He was a little surprised to see *two* people in the room as opposed to just the M.D.

'Afternoon, Ashley. Do come and join us. Please make yourself comfortable. There's tea and coffee on the side there.'

It had been a few hours since he had sampled caffeine, and his throat was begging for liquid refreshment. But he decided that he would much rather get this encounter put to bed and then perhaps reward himself with something a little more potent once home later that evening.

'I didn't think we were allowed to. I'm fine thank you though, Derek. Nice to be in such auspicious company on this very important day.'

Derek Evans glanced briefly toward his female companion before exhibiting an engaging if slightly expectant stare. Ashley sank into a chair opposite. Evidently, he had failed to completely conceal his nerves about the pending final sign-off.

'The drinks making issue is sorted. We're covered.'

‘Well, I don’t want to be breaking the law before we’ve even started, do I?

‘Relax, Ashley. I’ll get round to the audit soon enough. Not that I’ve any prior quibbles. I’m sure all is in tip top Bristol fashion.’

A statement that did little to abate Ashley’s unease.

‘This little get together is a bit more impromptu and I needed to be here at Hernwood to talk to you directly. Have you met Wendy before? She is our Marketing and Promotions consultant?’

Ashley repositioned to his feet and offered a hand of greeting. Then realised such an act was not yet within bounds of Covid safe practice. The woman looked to be in her mid-thirties. Brown shoulder length hair and stylish spectacles were an impressively striking combination atop the navy-blue business outfit. Quite the contrast with Derek’s grey suit, white head of hair and slightly overweight features. Her expression instantly gained a friendlier glint as she spoke.

‘Hi Ashley. I’m Wendy. Wendy Parkinson. It’s my first visit to Hernwood, so I doubt we’ve crossed paths before today.’

They had never been formally introduced, but Ashley found her to be vaguely familiar from a previous occasion. Then the light bulb flickered into life.

‘Were you at Sholton when I did my media relations course?’

‘Yes, yes, I was. Good memory, haven’t you?’

‘*Knew* I’d seen you somewhere. How’s tricks with post-Covid recovery going, then?’

Wendy smiled and raised her eyebrows.

‘Funnily enough that’s *exactly* what we are here to discuss. And I can instantly see why Derek suggested you.’

Derek Evans observed the puzzlement spreading across Ashley’s features. He leaned forward with elbows on the tabletop.

‘Sit yourself down, Ash. I’ll cut to the chase. What with the pandemic having a tremendously negative impact on our industry and many other industries of course, I felt it was an appropriate opportunity to make the most of re-opening our doors to the paying customer.

After some brain-bashing with the owners and shareholders, myself, and Wendy, we all agree that the time is right for a re-brand. Something new and different that might alleviate the problems caused by enforced closure and offer security going forward.'

Ashley still had no inkling of what the M.D. was talking about.

He scratched his forehead in a genuine reaction of wonder.

'Okay. Good strategy. But why did you need to come and discuss it with me? I haven't much experience in the art of championing causes and flying flags.'

Derek and Wendy exchanged knowing looks before both centred their attentions back on the Operations Manager.

'Well, for a start you can stop scowling and flash that smile again.'

Derek Evans broke into a giggle at his own comment, rendering Ashley no further forward in his search for the answer to his very fair question.

'Flash my very *best* smile? Like *this* you mean?'

'Perfect!' boasted Wendy. 'Absolute knockout!'

Derek let Wendy Parkinson take the floor with her pitch.

'Even before Covid came along, Ultimate was lagging behind its chief competition. Not by much, but by enough to be noticeable and warrant addressing. Which seemed at odds with the fact that our amenities are more upgraded and modernised than other rival chains.'

Ashley retained his patience and listened to Wendy with due courtesy as she steadily homed in on the crux of the matter.

'We are re-thinking the general look of every aspect of the public-facing side of the business. Same name but in a different guise. New logo. New livery. New uniforms. New signage in and around the hotels. New website design. New literature. It all needs a makeover. And those are just the starting points.'

Ashley was still clamouring for clarity as he gazed at the two officials seated the other side of the table.

'All sounds very uplifting. A very forward thinking and positive scheme. But I still don't see where me or my best smile fit in to the grand plan.'

Derek Evans sipped his coffee for a few contemplative seconds before slowly replacing the cup on the saucer. His eyes never left Ashley, and they widened with excitement as he continued to explain.

'The campaign is already at the green light stage. But Wendy feels that the chain would benefit by adding a more personal touch. A visual bridge between the customer and the service they will be anticipating. A bright, obliging image that will front up and assist the re-marketing thrust. A representative badge that the public will readily relate to. A welcoming connection that will encourage confidence and hopefully increase our standing in the trade. A face with automatic appeal.'

The penny was now edging ever closer to the drop zone.

Ashley digested his superior's buoyant vision and sat up in his chair.

'A *face*? You mean…*my* face? You want *me* to be part of this re-branding strategy?'

Derek Evans was veritably shaking with enthusiasm as he saw his most competent manager slowly beginning to get a handle on what they were proposing.

'Wendy here has been tasked with total renovation of Ultimate's label. We can easily sort the logistical side of the operation. But the critical piece of the jigsaw is still missing. Yes, a face to be centrally associated with the entire campaign. But not just *any* face. We need a person with direct and strong links to our business. An employee of accomplishment and repute. Someone who not only fits that bill from our point of view but someone who is also willing to become the company insignia.'

At last, Ashley realised the purpose of this unusual congregation.

And registration of such an idea was not an easy process.

'Let me make sure I'm reading you both correctly, here. You want a poster boy? And you think I'm the boy that would be most suited to adorn your posters?'

Derek shook his head and sat back.

Evidently, he was a little reticent to be so exact about the scheme.

‘I don’t particularly like that phrase, Ashley. Sounds far too *American.* But I suppose that we are asking you if you would embrace the chance to do this on behalf of the company.’

‘Do *what*? Become the poster boy?’ Ashley smirked.

Derek Evans appeared mildly concerned.

‘Yes! Yes okay, Ashley. We are convinced of the potential success of this campaign, but it really hinges on *your* participation. What do you say?’

Ashley couldn’t conjure even a semblance of optimism and conveyed his pangs of reservation about the project.

‘Don’t you think you might need someone a little…well, a little *younger* than me? I mean, I’m a bit long in the tooth to start modelling. Surely there are other more suitable candidates within the business? I think the public might look at my mug and suspect I’m a bit past it for the glamour game.’

Wendy Parkinson didn’t hesitate to interject.

She had evidently targeted Ashley for specific reasons.

‘On the contrary, you are *exactly* right for this. We need the image to convey expertise and a sense of welcoming reliability. Trust. Warmth. Assurance to guests. Kids can’t offer that. But I am absolutely convinced beyond any doubt that you possess *everything* we need. You encapsulate the entire feel of the thing. You do understand where we’re coming from with this, Ashley?’

It was a surreal sensation if very flattering. Ashley shuffled from buttock to buttock whilst trying to think on his feet.

‘Okay. So, say I agree in principle. How is this campaign of yours actually going to be put in place considering we have no time left before occupancy begins again tomorrow?’

Now it was Wendy’s turn to place her elbows on the tabletop and appear sternly persuasive.

‘It’s very simple really. Like we said the structure is in place already to implement most of the changes. If you agree to be part of things, we will submit you for a studio photography session. You know, suited and booted.’

‘Oh…the proper costume?’

‘Call it that if you like, yes. Company blazer and such. Chain logo on the lapel. You get the drift. Once we get you caught through the lens, we will then decide which images will be suitable for literature, posters, and the like.’

Ashley’s inert sense of showmanship was beginning to simmer under the surface. But he remained tight-lipped as Wendy continued to divulge the plan.

‘We would also really like to get advertisements placed on several billboards here and around our other sites. Off the link roads and motorway junction and further afield. You’ll catch eyes instantly if we can pull this off. It’s a very bold yet inherently simple approach. We’re a little behind the times with a lot of competitors in terms of public placement but I’m certain once you are plastered around the community they will come in their droves.’

Ashley left his chair and poured himself a very necessary coffee.

His previously undisclosed inner glee at the prospect of participation was now on full display as he chuckled to himself.

It might have been fair to say that the proposition was directly pandering to his ego, although he would never admit to having an ego.

‘You don’t have to creep, Wendy. But I’m liking your faith in me!’

‘It’s vital that you buy into the campaign whole-heartedly, Ashley. You will be a key component in the short-term and long-term future of Ultimate Inns. The public will associate the chain with your image. Those already familiar with you and the hotel will lap it up. But it’s the first-time guests that we want to entice. You will portray the whole advertising package, in effect. You will be the standard bearer of the business. A critical role.’

Ashley nodded as he turned away from the percolator, swiftly becoming wrapped up in the theories of the Promotions consultant. She was a very insistent saleswoman.

And her pitch hadn’t yet concluded as he reclaimed his seat and sampled some caffeine.

'We want customers to be attracted by *you* and by what *you* will represent to *them.* It's almost as if they will check in to the hotels expecting to see you in person. Which many of them will, of course. If we implement the campaign in the right manner, it could be incredibly effective very quickly. The post-Covid link needs to be forged with customers again. They need to feel confident. Psychology is *everything* now. They want peace of mind, and we want them to know that Ultimate is the best possible supplier to ensure they get it. So…now I've bent your ear for ten minutes…what's your thoughts?'

This was certainly a string to his bow which he never envisaged. Whilst no one could ever accuse Ashley Griffiths of being a wallflower, being plinthed for public scrutiny was a mildly daunting premise.

He adored being around the guests in person and making sure their needs were tended to. But having his image portrayed out in the unknown was a practice Ashley had never previously contemplated.

Until now, that is.

But he could not fail to be bowled over by the forthright common-sense argument that Wendy Parkinson had so professionally enforced. She had foresight and drive. She had belief and conviction in her role and what she might achieve for the company.

Derek reclaimed the stand once again.

'The back end of the pandemic had rendered hospitality open to a level playing field. Striking while the iron is hot is pivotal if Ultimate are to take advantage of the situation. The marketplace is unsuspecting and ripe for this kind of promotional assault. We need to get our noses in front. For everyone's sakes.'

Ashley's lurking hesitancy had all but been obliterated by the last statement of the M.D.

He placed his coffee cup on the table and exhibited his award-winning grin once more.

'Okay, Derek. Okay, Wendy. I'm game. I'll do it!'

Both the M.D. and the Marketing consultant clapped their hands in evident delight. Wendy continued with her own personal round of applause before standing and deliberately shaking the hand of the new face of the business.

'Absolutely splendid, Ashley. I assure you that this is a great move. One that you won't regret, I promise. There were no other candidates for this. We pinned all our hopes on you. This campaign hinged solely on your agreement. You can make this work so well in so many ways.'

Ashley laughed out loud as Derek patted him on the shoulder.

'No pressure, then!'

He lifted his drink from the table and toasted the two visitors.

'Now I've said yes, I'm getting quite excited about the idea. I appreciate the opportunity, guys. Thank you both. I can't wait for it to happen, actually. It will give me a much-needed lift too, I think.'

A very jovial vibe descended on the room. It hadn't taken long for Ashley's cautious reservation to be enveloped by vigorous zest toward the whole concept.

Wendy was very keen to get the ball rolling.

'Okay, Ashley, now that we've bagged the star of the show, I'll set up a plan of action with the photography studio. I hope to get this arranged and completed swiftly. The sooner we nail the prime images the sooner our designers and printers can work their magic.'

'Wow! Fame at last. And I thought my fifteen minutes had passed me by! Next stop *Hollywood*!'

The M.D.'s expression conveyed sheer relief as he again offered his congratulations.

'Well, it will certainly get you noticed. Wendy and her team are second to none. She's got all the contacts needed to make this work. And you are the biggest and final piece of the plan. I'm really pleased, Ashley.'

'I take it I wait for the nod to see when the camera studio wants to see me?'

'Don't you fret, Ashley…' smiled Wendy. 'When the appointment is booked, you'll be the first to know about it.'

The trio shook hands once again before Ashley departed the room.

Closing the door behind him he gazed along the corridor not quite believing what he had just agreed to.

But it felt positive.

And if it was going to encourage positivity then that was enough inspiration in itself.

Ashley Griffiths had no real self-image to feed as such, but the thought of being a public attraction definitely held appeal.

Even if it was only for the hotel trade for the time being.

The movies would just have to wait their turn.

FOUR

'WOW! Who's a clever and pretty boy, then?'

Ashley was claimed by a fit of the giggles as Carl delivered his response to the news.

'I'm not a bloody parrot, you know. But yes, it does seem that I am deemed to be a very clever and pretty boy. I agree.'

Carl offered a tight embrace of earnest appreciation.

'You've worked so hard for that company. You more than deserve a bit of recognition. And just think what *fun* it will be. About bloody time your efforts were acknowledged by the big bosses.'

Ashley filled the kettle and retrieved two mugs from the cupboard.

'Well, it was put to me that business needs a boost after the lockdowns. They must be short for inspiration if they've asked *me* to come to the rescue, eh?'

Carl's expression rapidly altered from one of earnest glee to one of abject disapproval. He sternly waved a forefinger in Ashley's direction.

'Oi, Griffiths! Don't put yourself down. It's not an attractive trait. They want you because of your work ethic. Because your heart and personality shine through in what you do. I know already that the posters will look absolutely fantastic!'

'Really? And just *how* would you know that, then?' smirked Ashley.

Carl presented a loving gaze across the kitchen island as the kettle began to hiss.

'Because my man will be in it. Front and centre. Just where he belongs.'

Laughter resonated around the room, prompting a belated appearance from Marjorie, who peered through the cat flap to greet her human parents. Slivering through the clear plastic portal, she stared directly up at Carl and silently informed him that she was hungry.

'I think I'd better feed her before she starts eating the furniture. It's the first I've seen of her all day.'

Reaching under the sink for a sachet of cat meat, Carl filled Marjorie's bowl to an appreciative accompaniment of loud purring. He couldn't contain his buoyant anticipation for Ashley's imminent venture.

'So, when are you up on the catwalk then?'

'Wendy said as soon as possible.'

'Really? *That* soon? We'll have groupies at the door day and night.'

Ashley was mildly distracted by Carl's last comment.

Whilst obviously made in jest, the thought was a little perturbing.

'Christ! Do you think so?'

Carl stifled his will to mock.

'No, stupid head. It's a bloody hotel advert not Milan fashions. You're not quite up to supermodel status just yet.'

Ashley finished making the drinks and the pair moved into the lounge, leaving Marjorie to dine in peace. Reclining next to one another on the sofa, the joviality soon returned.

'I've thought for years that your role at the hotel is undervalued. You were practically living there before Covid hit. It's a nice feeling for me to think that someone has actually been observing your contribution. Shame they didn't chuck a pay rise in as well for nominating you Hernwood hunk of the year.'

Ashley couldn't help but snigger at Carl's cutting appraisal, which then veered into generous overdrive.

'It must be a weird feeling knowing you will be on show across the whole southwest. I think it's a fantastic opportunity, Ash. You should milk this for all its worth. I'm even a little bit jealous of you, you *cow*!'

Ashley mirthfully spluttered coffee down his shirt.

'Now Carlos that does not surprise me in the least. But I can't see what you have got to be jealous about.'

'The attention you'll be getting! Your problem is you're far too humble to accept how handsome you are.'

'Whereas you'd be giving it the big swirls and dancefloor shapes?'

Carl giggled quietly as he held his coffee mug to his lips.

'Dead right I would! You'll need a proper haircut, though.'

Ashley pretended to rock under a wave of feigned indignation.

'Cheeky git. What's wrong with my hair?'

'Nothing drastic, love. But if you're going national you need to jazz things up a bit.'

'*Jazz things up a bit*?'

'Yes, darling. A bit of the cosmopolitan needs to be flashed. You need to appeal to the masses. Not just lorry drivers and IT consultants that need a bed for the night.'

Ashley found himself at odds with Carl's flamboyant overview of the situation.

'What a load of tosh. The boss says he wants me because I'm the genuine article. No heirs and graces. They say I represent the manager that all guests should want to be dealing with. I've got honest eyes, apparently.'

Carl's playfully sarcastic reaction echoed around the lounge as Marjorie squatted in front of the settee and began to wash her face.

'Well, I take it all back. Your boss must need his bloody eyes testing. Don't judge a book by its cover I always say.'

Ashley shook his head in amusement.

'You'll be *wearing* that bloody drink in a minute.'

Carl sat forward and placed his hand on Ashley's knee.

'In all sincerity Ashley, I am *overjoyed* for you. This couldn't have come at a better time and could be a real turning point in your career.'

'Well then, I'd better get myself down the barbers for a crew cut, hadn't I. Being as that is what my promotions expert of a boyfriend has advised.'

Carl observed Ashley from under a furrowed brow.

The preparatory silence endured for a few seconds as he studied Ashley's head and conjured another quip.

'Just needs a trim. Nothing over the top. And some decent shoes. Not your usual winkle pickers. They're scuffed up to buggery.'

Ashley's smile broadened once more as he engaged with the eyes of his partner.

'My shoes are fine. You know something…I wonder why you love me so much if there's so much you want to change about me. Have you got a thing for tramps?'

'Of course, I love you. Just look upon me as your occasional fashion guru. You can thank me later. But if my man is going to be the subject of a professional photo shoot then I want the world to know that even if *he* hasn't got any sense of style, then at least the public will see that he's taken sound advice off someone that *has*!'

Ashley shook a clenched fist in mock anger.

'So, you think I'm making the right decision by agreeing to take part in this thing then?'

Carl nodded determinedly.

'Like I say…I'd snap their hand off. Go get 'em girl! I've got your back all the way. You'll smash it hands down. And at the end of the day, what have you got to lose?'

Ashley could not help but agree with Carl's ever reliable and straightforward logic.

'You're right. I don't know what I'm worrying about. No harm can come from it. In fact, I might forget this coffee and open that bottle of white in the fridge.'

Carl moved closer on the settee and voiced agreement.

'Indeed. We need to celebrate. A toast to new beginnings.'

'Yes, Carlos. To new beginnings. Which reminds me…we've got to see my folks tomorrow. Looking forward to that. Hope the element of surprise works on them.'

FIVE

Ashley had been very careful not to subject his parents to any unnecessary social contact during the previous year or so. As with all families, the enforced segregation that prevented offspring from indulging in physical proximity with their loved ones had been adhered to.

However, patience was now wearing thin on both sides of the fence. Face to face communication thus far had been infrequent, brief, and necessary, but attitudes had steadily evolved from upholding a firm obligation to the law, into a renewed approach to the virus that could perhaps be best described as casually dismissive.

The wholly unexpected vision of her only son at the lounge window filled Elaine Griffiths' heart with utter joy. She had missed him so much in recent times. Occasional shopping errands did not compensate in any way for the despair she felt at his prolonged absence.

She had seen him of course, but the invisible - if mandatory - wall of separation had become an upsetting aspect of recent guidelines.

Elaine had longed for the moment she could engage with her son without a pane of glass or a nearly closed door between them. She had long become despondent with the repetitive lack of closeness via telephone conversations, too.

Neville Griffiths heard his wife's exuberant holler as it resonated up the stairwell. Interrupting the search for his slippers, Neville shuffled to the top landing and called down.

'Is that our Ash's car out front? Lovely! It feels like it's been a lifetime.' he concurred, descending steadily step by step in his socks.

Elaine met her husband in the hallway and now beyond excited she veritably yanked open the front door.

Ashley and Carl stood before them, grinning in the porchway, adorned with a pack of Neville's favourite beer, a bouquet of Elaine's favourite flowers and a box of biscuits that they would both enjoy tucking into.

Ashley's broad and infectious smile preceded his opening line.

'Hi, Mum! Hi, Dad! You can let us in now according to Boris. Thought we would come and bother you properly for a while being as it's all legal and above board again.'

Gently squashing her son's cheeks with the palms of her hands, Elaine kissed Ashley full on the lips in a maternal eruption of emotive impulse.

She pulled away, tears beginning to seep from her blinking eyes.

'Oh, it's so lovely to see you both. It seems so long. What a wonderful surprise. Absolutely lovely.'

Carl too was the deserving recipient of Elaine's genuine affections.

Nearly crushing the bouquet in her efforts to exhibit her heartfelt relief, Ashley giggled as his mother released Carl's shoulders and endeavoured to calm herself.

'I brought you these lilies, Elaine. Ashley assures me you won't have anything else in the house.'

'Bless your kind soul, Carl. So thoughtful. Such a darling.'

Neville too engaged in warm embraces with both visitors before ushering everyone into the lounge. The reception was tender and genuine, and much belated. It came as no small relief to Ashley that their unannounced arrival at his parents' home had been deemed an immediate success.

His father had taken a long while to become accepting of - and then eventually become accustomed to - Ashley and Carl's relationship. Neville Griffiths was initially of the opinion that his old-fashioned ways were inflexible. Now at the age of sixty-six, he had thankfully mellowed in his opinions slightly. Perhaps recent retirement had allowed him some time for reflection.

Subsequently, Ashley had generally kept his private life just that. His genuine concerns were borne out, however, with the introduction of Carl to the family several years ago. It created a detectable undercurrent that was perhaps inevitable. The bond between father and son became mildly estranged and slightly fractious for a while.

But Ashley was quietly appreciative of the fact that the situation was becoming gradually easier for all concerned.

In fact, considering the way *everyone's* lives had been altered during the previous twelve months or so, Ashley beheld the current responses of his father and was quietly overcome with appeasing waves of contentment.

Neville Griffiths was visibly delighted to be welcoming Ashley and Carl back into the fold. If truth now be told, Neville was proud of his son for the manner he had conducted himself and his career.

And Carl was now regarded by Neville as a reliably permanent fixture in the family set-up.

And if ever pressed on the issue, Neville might even admit to feeling rather ashamed of his initial bigotry and prejudice.

Neville relieved Ashley of the bottles of brown ale and expressed his heartfelt gratitude through a beaming smile.

'Goodness me I have been spoiled! I can't see this little lot lasting until the weekend. Look at this Elaine.'

As always when guests arrived, Ashley's mother turned her attention to the kitchen and filled the kettle, before re-joining the merry throng in the lounge.

'Yes, you are a very lucky father, aren't you. I'm sure you don't deserve it, either. I've got a pot of tea coming, boys.'

'Thanks Mum, I'm parched. So how are you both? I know I only saw you a few weeks ago passing bread through the window, but I don't really count that as quality social time.'

Neville laughed out loud at the comforting sound of his son's ready-wit and charm. Ashley lit up the room. There was no denying it. In fact, he brought light into *any* room he walked into. Neville also noticed the loving gazes of Carl as Ashley spoke.

Perhaps once upon a time not so long ago this would have made Neville feel very uncomfortable. But no longer did he oblige the natural urge to cast doubt.

All in all, the lockdowns had encouraged a refreshment of attitude.

And despite the craziness of the previous fifteen months, the renewed allowance of normal everyday connectivity was now infinitely pleasurable to be part of once more.

Elaine perched herself on the arm of Ashley's chair.

In between clasping her hands in elation, she couldn't desist from affectionately touching her son's shoulder every few seconds.

'We're doing fine Ashley. Thank you. We've had our second vaccinations last week, too. Apart from that we've not been far or seen much. But we still go for our daily walks. But we're not going mental with cabin fever just yet, are we love?'

Neville laughed.

'You speak for *yourself*. I've *always* been mental. Nobody would know the difference with me. Got me company pension sorted out last month though, which is a big relief. I can officially relax now.'

'So pleased you've had your jabs. That's great, Dad. I suppose the pension would have been sorted long ago if it wasn't for Covid?'

'November of Twenty-Nineteen I first asked for a settled quote. Finally getting it paid in now. Right palaver, too.'

Elaine was becoming slightly impatient. She knew all about her husband's financial hurdles. Lord knows he'd been bemoaning them to her for long enough.

But it was her son's affairs that she was now keen to be updated with.

'So, how's things with the hotel? Are you glad to be back? I bet it's been hectic, hasn't it?'

'Bedlam today, Mum. Not enough notice to get organised to be honest. But we got the big thumbs-up from the Managing Director yesterday as you know. And our doors opened to the public for the first time in over a year, today. I think I preferred being on Furlough.'

Elaine humorously pointed toward her son.

'Now I know you don't mean that. Bet you're loving it already.'

Ashley sat back in the armchair as his mother grasped at the fingers of his hand as if ensuring he were truly there and not some mirage.

‘If I’m honest, it is *great* to be back in the place. Long days ahead, though. That’s why we are late tonight, cos I got delayed. We aren’t up to anywhere near capacity yet, but I’ve missed seeing people and making sure they are okay. I’ve missed the team, too. Got some vacancies to fill sharpish, as well. A headache I could do without, to be honest.’

Neville intervened.

‘Have some people left during the lockdowns, then?’

‘Sadly, yes, Dad. They couldn’t afford to lose twenty percent in wages. Even though Furlough payment was generous, some were struggling before all that, anyway. So, I’ve got to sift through HR records finding out where we need to recruit. Lost some good people, too.’

Elaine reclaimed the inquisitive honours from her husband.

‘That’s such a shame, isn’t it. This bloody pandemic really has put the cat among the pigeons. How about you, Carl? Have you had the call to go back into the office?’

Carl suddenly sat up sensing the spotlight was on him.

‘Erm, no not yet. But I didn’t get Furloughed. We just started working from home. Most of my assignments are freelance anyway so I already had the office set up. Funnily enough I seem to get more done in the spare bedroom than I ever did going out to work. Weird, isn’t it?’

Neville continued with the enthusiastic questioning.

‘I can’t see any offices opening again, can you? The internet has really proven itself to be invaluable to a lot of businesses now. Who wants to leave the house and commute when you can log on and sit in your pyjamas all day?’

Carl chuckled in agreement at Neville’s perhaps overly simplistic appraisal of matters.

‘Well, it’s okay to a point. I get called in now and again to oversee new clients and new projects. Perhaps the odd meeting if we aren’t doing it by zoom. But yeah. Basically, I’m left alone to get on with it. If I meet the deadlines and the customer is happy, then all is good in the hood.’

Ashley covertly observed his mother’s features as she watched Carl and Neville converse. The lockdowns had aged her somewhat.

Not so much in her physical appearance, but more in terms of her demeanour and mannerisms.

Whilst obviously overjoyed that lives might just be returning to a recognisable state after such upheaval, he sensed an edginess to her. As if she were in anticipation of something negative.

And he had also noticed her tics. She smiled readily yet nervously.

And every few seconds she would wring her hands together or be interlinking her fingers.

Habits which Ashley had focused attention on since the beginning of the year, albeit during his occasional and fleeting visits.

In this, his first sustained contact with her for many months, the tics were quite notable. Although at that moment, he wouldn't be so impolite as to bring the issue to the forefront of the group's conversation.

His father on the other hand looked in impressive fettle for a man in his seventh decade. A lifetime driving lorries for a wage had not diminished his general fitness, and the supreme spring and now early summer sunshine gave him a golden glow and had even bleached further his already white hair. This of course did not apply to the tan-brown circle of his scalp.

Neville Griffiths' face carried a healthy hue and the whites of his blue eyes popped bright and sharp. No doubt the recent reunification with the local golf course after the second lockdown had assisted his general health no end.

From Ashley's personal perspective, it was no small relief to acknowledge that his mother and father had emerged through the pandemic, so far unscathed and still thriving.

As he himself could testify, Covid was not only deemed a threat to physical health, but also wellbeing of mind. Yet his parents did not appear to have succumbed in either capacity to any concerning degree.

Elaine tended to the tea pot and brought in a tray of crockery. As she opened the box of biscuits, Carl thought it appropriate to nudge Ashley into revealing the latest development with his career.

He watched proudly as Ashley began to chomp on a chocolate digestive.

'Hey, Ash...you haven't mentioned to your folks about your imminent media celebrity status.'

Elaine and Neville stared at their son as he instantly ceased crunching his biscuit and feigned a wide-eyed grimace toward his partner.

Suddenly Elaine appeared to be relaxed and she excitedly leaned forward to inspect her son's reaction from a closer vantage point.

'No, Ashley you *haven't* said anything. What's happening then? Are you going to be on the telly?'

Ashley felt duty bound to swallow the morsel of crumbs in his mouth and laugh out loud.

With Carl's instinctive prompt, he could no longer keep the secret from them.

'Calm down, Mum. I'm not quite at global superstar level just yet.'

He relayed to them the details of the meeting with Derek Evans the previous day. It was another ray of light shining into the lives of his parents, who reacted with undiluted glee.

Elaine Griffiths was particularly elated.

'Wow! Oh, that's *brilliant*. You must be so proud. I think it's wonderful that they've chosen you. Oh, I think I want to cry with pleasure.'

Neville shook his head as he glanced at his wife.

'Don't be so soft, Elaine. Well done, son. A lovely gesture from your boss and no doubt well deserved.'

Ashley dunked another half biscuit into his tea and duly crammed it into his mouth.

Although hindered, he tried to respond coherently.

'Thanks, Dad. Means a lot. To be honest I've still not got any idea what the crack is going to be. The photo shoot was confirmed today. Its next Wednesday with our marketing lady. It will be a half-day off work and a giggle if nothing else. I'll be plastered on local billboards, too.'

Neville sat and observed his son admiringly.

'Only *half* a day? Tight buggers!'

'Well, they can't let me take my hands off the helm for too long, Dad. Anything could happen in a few hours.'

'You've proved your worth to that company many times over, my lad. About time they saluted your efforts. I do take it you're getting a bit extra for giving them your image rights and free advertising?'

Carl laughed out loud.

'That is exactly what I asked him, Neville. You know what? He's getting absolutely nothing at all.'

Neville shook his head and sighed.

'I repeat…tight buggers…'

Ashley now found it to be his turn to laugh.

'It's part of the job so far as they're concerned. But they did ask me very nicely, though. The way I figure it, I'm way overdue a bit of fun and only something good can come from it. So, I'm plunging in feet first and not even holding my nose.'

Elaine dropped a sugar lump into her teacup and began to stir as she focused proudly on her son.

'So, when do we see the twelve feet tall version of you, then?'

Ashley shook his head as he finished his drink.

'According to the Chief Exec, everything is in place waiting for my fizzog to be printed on it. Then they can give it the green light. I don't know how long it might take for the printing and distribution to get sorted though, Mum. No idea at all. If anything, it will put guests off seeing my ugly mug on the front door as they park their cars!'

Elaine Griffiths was quick to shoot down her son's self-deprecation.

'Oi you can stop all that nonsense, now. You're a beautiful and handsome man. Thank goodness you inherited *my* looks and not your *father's*!'

Feigning indignation against the backdrop of chuckles, Neville eventually laughed along with his wife's gentle quip.

It was sating for Ashley to observe his parents still bouncing off one another.

‘It’s lucky I’m not the sensitive type isn’t it. I like to think Ashley has been blessed with the best of both of us.’

Elaine rolled her eyes as she sipped her tea.

‘Yes, dear. Whatever you say, dear.’

Carl ventured some further support for the pending star of the show.

‘I’ve already told him off last night for being so self-critical. I’ve told Ashley he will knock ‘em dead. I’m very interested to see how the hotel’s new website looks, too. The old one was a bit prehistoric, to be fair.’

Neville volleyed in with his own positives.

‘*You’re* qualified to revamp that for them aren’t you, Carl? I’d have thought Ash would have chucked your name forward to sort that out.’

Ashley didn’t get the chance to defend his position on the matter.

In all honesty, the option hadn’t occurred to him.

‘I probably could, Nev, but the hotel chain will use their own people. It’s likely there’s someone already employed that looks after it. Besides, I’m expensive, you know.’

‘*No shit*!’ blurted Ashley, succumbing to a fit of the giggles.

Amid the relentless banter, Elaine could not stop grinning at the prospect of her son becoming a real-life marketing tool.

‘Ooh I think this is all so very exciting. There was nothing like this when I worked in retail. I’m bursting for you, Ashley. Made my year this has. You’re doing so well again after all this Covid mess.’

Ashley presented a very humble posture and expression.

‘I put it down to brilliant parenting, myself. The gold dust has rubbed off to the next generation.’

‘Hear! Hear! Couldn’t agree more!’ Neville chipped. I knew my genes would become destined for something greater than long-distance haulage one day.’

Elaine offered a disparaging glance to her husband before offering some sensibility to the arena.

‘It’s lovely that after such a miserable year we all have something to look forward to. Especially when the person at the centre of it all is my lovely son.’

Again, Ashley found himself studying his mother as she spoke.

Her possible nervousness of earlier had seemingly calmed over the past half hour. It was evident just how much enforced isolation had affected her emotionally. But she was swiftly returning to her old self once again.

In just thirty minutes she had been reacquainted with feelings of old.

Her inert quandaries and unfounded fears that had naturally manifested themselves during the lockdowns were rapidly evaporating.

Perhaps, just perhaps, this visit was significant to everyone as a marker that typical routine was being embraced once again.

*****

Ashley felt incredibly thankful as he stood in the hallway with Carl in preparation to depart.

His mother moved toward him, once more on the verge of tears.

But happy ones.

'Let me know when the photos are done. I want first approval of everything. That's my right as your mother.'

Ashley stooped and kissed her on the cheek.

'Don't worry, Mum. I know you're the boss. I'll be straight round with the negatives.'

Carl gazed in humorous astonishment.

'*Negatives*?'

'Shut up, you. I know there's no such thing anymore.'

With farewell embraces, Neville and Elaine watched their son and Carl wander down the driveway.

With swelling hearts, they waved the pair off until the car vanished from view.

Neville closed the front door and turned to his wife.

'He's done well, that boy. And it sounds like he will continue to do well. He's a credit to us.'

Dabbing her moistened features with a tissue, Elaine nodded to her husband.

'Nothing to stop him now, love. No one to stand in his way. I think he's going to have a good year ahead of him. I'm just pleased we can share it with him again. And he knows we'll be behind him all the way.'

SIX

'Essentially, we want to try and capture the character and personality of Ashley Griffiths. We'll get as many shots as we think will cover all bases. Even if there's nothing perfect that materialises, we can always doctor it slightly with photo-shop.'

Ashley stared in mock astonishment at Wendy, who tried not to smirk in response to the photographer's commentary.

But Ashley could not resist a gentle retort.

'Christ Almighty, Missus! Don't make me feel good about myself whatever you do. You just continue raining on my parade.'

Wendy Parkinson now relented and creased up at her midriff. Some glamour shoot this was going to be. Amusingly, it seemed that Ashley's concept of what would transpire in front of the lens was a little removed from the brass tacks of reality.

'I'm sorry, Ash. Don't feel deflated.' Wendy giggled. 'I know this is your big day. Tits and teeth on show then! Chest out. C'mon!'

With a furrowed brow, Ashley centred his focus on the young lady named Catherine who would be catching him in all his glory from behind the camera.

'And I suppose *you* just want me to stand here and smile, do you?'

Catherine Marchant simply continued to fiddle with her equipment before altering the position of the spot lamps.

She was representative of a very reputable business in the area, but even she could not muster the will to sugar coat the occasion for her indignant subject.

'Well…if I'm totally honest, Ashley, we can do so much processing through publishing software these days that you won't even need make up.'

'*No make-up*? Well, I'm sorry but that's the deal breaker, then!' Ashley chuckled, as Catherine checked her camera once again.

'I just want to get a certain expression from you that sums up the message the business wants to convey. And I won't even know what that image will be *myself* until we check afterwards. The eventual stills always portray a different story to the shoot.'

Ashley rolled his eyes and exaggerated his tone of disgust.

'And here's me fretting that the camera never lies. What a load of tosh that turned out to be, then.' he quipped whilst briefly inspecting his reflection in a wall mirror. 'I may as well have just given you my passport snap, save all this messing around, eh?'

Wendy could not conceal her endearing amusement.

Ashley's devout pretence of disappointment was almost convincing to the uninitiated.

She tried to soften his mood.

'We just want you to enter into the spirit of the occasion. So, straighten that tie and broaden that smile for Catherine. There's a good boy. Your public awaits you.'

Ashley glared at Wendy without expression for a few seconds before mouthing the words '*piss off*'. This did little to quieten her as he again checked his image in the tall glass.

'Okay darlings. I think I'm as perfect as I'm ever going to be for my age. Let's get the punishment over and done with, then we can all get back to work.'

After all the anticipation and expectation, the entire photography session only endured for just over forty minutes. Catherine declared her contentment with the shoot.

'I think that will be fine for the purpose intended. Thank you, Ashley. You're a natural poser. Would you like me to take a final snap of you and Wendy together as a memento?'

Now grinning from ear to ear, Ashley's enthusiasm to observe the results was rejuvenated as he took up position with Wendy in front of Catherine's computer monitor.

'No thanks. Let's get on with sorting *me* out! *That's* the most important job.'

The lady with the camera pressed a few buttons and supplied some comforting words of appraisal.

‘We took fifty-four shots. I’m always a firm believer that the ideal one will leap out at us. The specific one required will be in here, Ashley I’m sure of it.’

‘Are you certain? It didn’t seem to take very long. You wouldn’t have had time to get the right one, surely?’

Wendy intervened.

‘Trust me, Ashley. Besides, we don’t have time to debate the thing all afternoon. This campaign needs to get into first gear.’

‘Well, no doubt *you* will be making the choice, anyway. I don’t suppose I will have much say in matters. You’re the boss on promotional stuff. I’m just the whore who happens to be on show and being used for company profit. Anyway, I thought you said we would need to take some photographs at the hotel, too?’

Wendy shook her head in feigned dismay.

‘We haven’t time. Derek wants this nailed. These will have to do.’

‘Well, that’s typical. Any point me saying any more?’

Wendy sniggered again.

‘Oh, such a drama queen. On the contrary, *your* input is vital, now. The three of us need to reach common ground on the decision today, so if you object then shout up. We can’t really go into print unless you are one hundred percent confident with it.’

‘Very considerate of you, dear.’ chuckled Ashley, as his attention became focussed on the screen of Catherine’s laptop.

It took nearly an hour to progress through the process of elimination. Fifty-four stills were scaled down into a final three.

Wendy was rapid in casting her vote with an eager yelp.

‘This is the one for my money. It’s a great shot from the waist up. The Ultimate logo pops off your blazer, too.’

Ashley slowly shook his head as he studied Wendy’s choice.

‘Yeah, never mind the face look at the badge. Forget what’s above the collar line, eh?’

Both women exploded with laughter at Ashley’s abiding sense of self-mockery. Wendy reinforced her convictions.

‘I’m sticking with number three. I’m sold on that one. Like it or lump it.’

Catherine expanded the image a little.

‘Yes, I can see why. The eyes are bright. The features are symmetrical. The smile is warm but not totally cheesy. What do you think. Ash?’

‘You’ve just put me off number three. I mean...*cheesy*?’

Wendy sniggered again as Ashley pondered further.

‘Let me study number one again please, Catherine.’

The photographer obliged with a single click of the mouse.

‘There you go. Opinions, people?’

‘I’ve gone off that one, now.’ blustered Ashley. ‘Get rid of number one, please.’

But Wendy was having none of it.

‘But why? It’s lovely!’

‘*Why*? Because I look like a bloody game show host. That’s *why*! A bloody *smarmy* game show host, at that. No! No! No! Delete, delete, delete!’

Wendy giggled uncontrollably.

‘Now you mention it, you do, yes. He’s right, Catherine. Get rid.’

The entertainment continued to echo around the studio as Ashley declared his final, absolute favourite of the entire fifty-four.

‘Okay...drum roll...I’m going for number two. End of. Sorted. No debate necessary.’

Wendy scrutinised the second of the three finalists.

‘You know something, Ash. I agree. Number two is perfect. One and three can go in the bin Catherine thank you. Two is the winner.’

Catherine sat back in her chair and asked for confirmation.

‘You both quite sure I can press delete on the others?’

Wendy looked in open-mouthed vacancy at Ashley.

Ashley looked back at Wendy with a real light of enthusiasm in his eyes.

They both nodded simultaneously.

‘What’s the timeline for the literature samples?’ Ashley enquired, the adrenaline of anticipation now coursing his veins.

Wendy was genuinely aghast at his query.

‘We haven’t got time to look at *samples*, dear boy. The image is off to the printers today. The word has been given. There’s no time to waste. Derek wants this out of the blocks as soon as possible.’

‘Crickey! So, the subject doesn’t even get final approval of his work, then? So, the next time I see that photo of me it will be doing the rounds across the length and breadth of the southwest?’

Wendy nodded in excitement.

‘Yep. Every site reception. Every foyer. Every lobby. And a few motorway billboards thrown in just for good measure. Ashley my darling, you are going to be the talk of the town within a fortnight.’

Ashley stared into space as the thought registered.

‘I suppose I should say, *lucky me*, should I?’

Wendy placed a very sobering hand on Ashley’s shoulder.

‘You can say what you like, but it is happening, now. No regrets. You’ll be lapping it up once folk start commenting about it. You should feel very positive about this idea. It will be great for the company and I’ve a sneaking suspicion it will be great for you, too.’

Ashley suddenly felt himself becoming distinctly reticent about the whole thing.

‘You think so, Wendy?’

‘Trust me. It’s a winner all day. Ashley Griffiths…your audience is waiting. And they will love you.’

SEVEN

Wendy Parkinson exhibited an expression of unbridled joy as she opened the Operations Manager's office door to let him re-enter. As Ashley stepped out of the corridor and back into the room, he also noticed the comparatively unreadable features of Derek Evans.

Although the Managing Director did immediately offer his most accomplished employee a very assured handshake, which belied the momentary uncertainty of his demeanour.

His follow-up statement certainly evaporated any trace of doubt.

'Close the door, Ashley. I think we've hit the jackpot with this. The printers have done a supreme job. Exceptional, in fact. You've never looked better.'

Ashley couldn't prevent nagging pangs of concern as he hovered around his desk and glanced at Wendy. She had deliberately obstructed his view of the wall side table, on which were arranged several different sized stacks of what appeared to be publicity material.

She issued her own pronouncement through a very noticeable tone of enthralled anticipation.

'Get ready for these, Ashley. You're going to be seen in a lot of places. And let me just say…what a gorgeous devil you truly are.'

Ashley stared in turn at his colleagues before delivering a time-honoured morsel of humour.

'I take it photoshop worked its magic, then?'

Wendy pursed her lips and presented a serious side for once.

'Believe me…Catherine altered nothing at all. It's all you as nature intended and in full glorious technicolour.'

Ashley tried to conceal his swelling excitement as he peered over Wendy's shoulder.

'I take it that the piles of stuff behind you are the new promotional bits and bobs. Oh my God. Let's have a butchers then. No more teasing. Let the dog see the rabbit.'

The atmosphere was pensive yet teetered on celebratory.

Wendy playfully shuffled position to ensure that Ashley was still unable to fully set his sights on the bounty of glossy literature that adorned the tabletop.

'I think you will be happy, Ashley. Derek and I are *definitely* satisfied.'

Ashley's infectious giggle broke loose.

'Do I need a stiff drink before I inspect the results?'

The M.D. was most generous with his summary.

'You've done us proud, Ashley. This is just what I envisioned. You were very kind to agree to be involved but I know our faith in this idea will pay off very quickly. Huge congratulations, to you. And on behalf of Ultimate…our heartfelt gratitude, too.'

It wasn't appropriate to offer his boss any sarcasm.

So, as a rare alternative, Ashley's sentiments were conveyed in earnest.

'High praise indeed, Derek. Thank you.'

'No, no. Your thanks aren't necessary. No other chain is providing this kind of post-lockdown exposure. You could be a game-changer for Ultimate Inns. Mark my words.'

The upbeat views of the M.D. did little to settle Ashley's stirring trepidation.

He attempted to acquire full control of his doubt once again.

'Can I grab a coffee before you give me a look at my wonderful self? I need something to concentrate on whilst I panic in silence.'

Ashley filled a cup from the percolator behind his desk whilst attempting to glimpse a little of what Wendy was trying to conceal.

'Oh, come on, Wendy. Put me out of my misery, will you?'

Wendy Parkinson had always found Ashley's humour instantly infectious. But she would not push her luck with his patience. She had picked up on the fact that he was genuinely becoming uncomfortable with the hiatus between photo-shoot and revelation of the end products.

If he had been generous enough to give this much of himself, then it was only correct that she treated his perfectly natural anxieties with the respect they deserved.

Even if she battled to keep a straight face whilst doing so.

Hernwood had been unofficially declared as being the tentpole site of the entire Ultimate chain. The promotion campaign had successfully comprised all requisite ingredients.

Ashley had made his contribution very effectively.

Now it was Wendy's turn to display her professional acumen.

'Okay, Ash. I will go through each piece of literature for you. First off…this will be the foyer point of entry board. This will feature in every reception area. Obviously, the text will differ for each hotel, but the basic completed design is here.'

Wendy picked up the four feet by three feet poster and reversed it in her grasp to allow Ashley his initial response.

'This will be rendered onto card and fixed to metal point of entry stands.'

Ashley stared at himself, for once being stunned into a silence that was indeterminable to Derek and Wendy. He sipped some coffee.

Then that famous smile emerged.

'Oh…my…GOD! Wendy…are you sure that's really *me*?'

'Of course, it's you. Who *else* could it be?'

Ashley's tone became almost wistful.

'But…but…he's *beautiful*.'

Wendy chuckled as Ashley placed his coffee on the desk and ventured closer for further inspection. He began to clap his hands in genuine appreciation of the finished article.

His emerging delight at what he was being faced with quickly eclipsed any pre-conceived dread.

Derek observed Ashley's reaction and was desperately relieved that the eventual result of their endeavours had been fully endorsed.

'I take it you are a fan of the design, Ashley?'

He never imagined he would enjoy looking at a photographic reproduction of himself. But he had to admit that the designers, under Wendy's adept guidance, had performed a brilliant task.

'I love it. And thankfully you caught my best side.'

'*Best* side? It's a frontal portrait?' queried Wendy.

'Yes. That's what I mean.'

Laughter resonated around the room. Ashley's pleasure shone through his expression, as he wallowed in the emerging sense of accomplishment.

Wendy turned back to the wall table to select another piece.

'Okay…this next one will be rendered onto plastic boarding and will be at the entrance to every site car park in the chain. Again, the text will differ, and it will be a lot bigger. But you get the drift?'

Ashley was now riding on a crest of undiluted enthusiasm.

'Brilliant. Really…really, good.'

Wendy rolled her eyes at Derek and pretended to talk to the ceiling as if addressing a higher mortal with her heartfelt thanks.

'This next image will front a four-page information leaflet that will be available at every reception desk and in each individual guest room.'

Ashley scanned the print quickly, his eyes darting back and forth to his image.

'Getting better by the minute, Wendy. You'll be due a pay rise when all those customers come rushing back through our door wanting to meet their hero.'

Striving for a witty reply, the M.D. stuttered before offering a strained snigger.

But Ashley wasn't going to let him off the hook quite so easily.

'*Yes*, is the word you're looking for, Derek. As in *yes*, Wendy does deserve a big pay rise for being a marketing genius.'

Amid a discomforting and soundless pause, Wendy opted to move swiftly on with the next piece of advertising.

'This next one will be in all our restaurants on the menus and such. Any meal deals will appear around your midriff and are of course prone to change each month.'

Ashley slowly nodded in approval.

'Good thinking, Batman. Always changing are those pesky meal deals.'

Wendy then held up a printed ream of A4 paper on which was represented the home page of the re-vamped company website.

'This interface is what potential customers will use when they log on the check availability and such.'

Ashley homed in for a close view as Wendy continued the pitch.

'Instead of a boring picture of a hotel front they get a wonderful host and manager parading before their very eyes. Why would they *not* want to stay here knowing *you* will be greeting them?'

Ashley cast his gaze toward Wendy.

She was very convincing at times.

In fact, she was very convincing all the time.

'Oh yes. Far more enticing. I can hear those keyboards rattling out the bookings from here. And hark…is that the first of the convoy I detect cruising into the car park beyond?'

Obviously amused, Wendy set down the sheet of paper, clasped her hands together and faced Ashley square on.

'Right…I've saved the best until last. The piece de resistance. The ultimate advertisement for Ultimate Inns. The billboard layout…'

Ashley positively gleamed with anticipation.

'Yes…this is literally the big one. Hit me with it then, girl.'

Wendy turned and reached under the desk for an A3 sheet of card, on which was exhibited the sign that in theory would attract customers from all over the country.

'This will be at the nearest available motorway junction to each site in the chain. We already know when and where Hernwood's will be going.'

Ashley teasingly fingered his chin.

'Let me guess…retail park…at the roundabout?'

'Yes, Ashley. Spot on! How do you feel about this? Because this is really the ace up our sleeve. This could clinch so much passing trade. This in my opinion is the genuine crowd puller. All the other literature will of course be in-house. So, this baby is pivotal in reaching out to people beyond the site boundaries.'

Ashley continued to study the billboard design and the other samples on his desk. He envisaged their positions and their purpose. He imagined driving in from the motorway and being confronted with an enormous rendition of himself.

After a few seconds, the self-analysis ended.

And the smile re-emerged.

'Wendy…you and your team have done a superb job. I cannot fault a single aspect of this project. I honestly can't.'

Now was the hinging point for Wendy Parkinson as she secretly crossed her fingers.

'So…you're telling me you're giving this campaign the thumbs-up? That we can use you?'

'Yes! Go for it! You have my full blessing. Let's take the public by the horns and get them in here.'

'Even the billboard idea? You're good with that, too?'

'Of course. Why wouldn't I be?'

'Well, some people might be a little wary of being placed so high and mighty in the community. But you're not exactly a shrinking violet, are you?'

'Not at all. The very notion! Get me out there. Loud and proud. If it benefits the chain, it benefits us all.'

Wendy turned to Derek Evans, who had remained rather subdued during the preceding minutes.

'I'll set the logistics in motion this afternoon. I hope to have everything in place on each site by this time next week. Done and dusted.'

Once again Derek shook Ashley by the hand.

'Thank you. The chain is investing a fair amount of capital into this, and we are absolutely convinced there will be a great return on it. Recovery from the pandemic is already in motion, I can sense it.'

Ashley raised his coffee cup as if to toast the moment.

'Bring it on Derek. I'm ready for anything and anyone, now.'

EIGHT

'Well, well. Three times in three weeks. I am honoured, Lord Evans. And of course, Lady Parkinson, esquire.'

With smiles at the ready, Wendy and Derek stood by the reception desk as Ashley approached through the main doors of the building.

Jeanette was most grateful to be positioned on the front row as the performance played out.

Wendy vocalised a pre-emptive contribution.

'Here he comes…Hernwood's answer to Robbie Williams.'

Ashley floated elegantly toward the unexpected visitors. Evidently pleased to see them, he stopped his stride and placed his knees together and clicked his heels before taking a comical bow.

'At your service, ladies and gentlemen.'

Derek chuckled and fired up the banter.

'I hope your newfound superstardom isn't going to your head already, Ashley.'

'Have no fear, Derek. Jeanette has been keeping my feet firmly on the ground.'

Jeanette shook her head as her lips formed a smirk. She was suddenly aware that Ashley's reference required her response. Under such esteemed scrutiny, she felt compelled to participate with the light-hearted conversation.

'Don't concern yourself, Mister Evans. Rest assured that Ashley was already full of himself long before he managed to get his photo glued all over creation.'

All four laughed in unison before Ashley made his very predictable enquiry.

'So…what can I do you lovely people for, today? You know I do love on the spot random visits by powerful executives. Especially when I'm in the middle of my morning check list.'

Derek placed an affirming hand on Ashley's shoulder.

'If only every site manager was so astute.'

'Well...one tries one's best, sir.'

'I wish I could say the same about your counterparts. One or two have already let the side down this week. But I know you will be flying the flag of standards highest as always.'

To further accentuate the need for humour, Ashley placed his head in his hands to feign embarrassment.

'Aww shucks. Thank you, your worshipfulness.'

Once more the trick worked.

A purposed and important visit was reduced to a comedy routine, with everyone enjoying the moment.

Ashley's consistently upbeat charm was instantly infectious.

Even for the Managing Director.

'Don't you *ever* behave seriously, Ashley?'

'I did once, Derek. But it scared me. So, I stopped immediately.'

Waiting for even a veiled sense of responsibility to return to proceedings, Derek gestured toward the lift doors.

'Shall we go upstairs to your office, or would you like to remain down here in the foyer? I'm easy.'

Ashley glanced toward the corner seating area.

'Down here is a splendid option. The sun is streaming through the windows. Glorious. And Jeanette will arrange for some tea and biscuits to be brought over, won't you darling?'

The subject of his last comment did not divert her eyes from the computer screen as she muffled a reply.

'Yes, sir. Of course, Jeanette will. Tea and biscuits, sir. Three bags full, sir.'

Ashley leaned toward the plastic screen fixed to her desk and whispered in a husky, semi-romantic voice.

'Thank you so much. I *love* your biscuits...'

Jeanette could not conceal her slightly motherly affection for Ashley.

'Don't get cocky. I'm not your slave just yet. Take a seat everybody. I'll let the kitchen know.'

Ashley followed Derek and Wendy over to the designated table, as his M.D. offered a commendable observation.

'You're very fortunate to have such an obliging and friendly team here. We've not witnessed this kind of camaraderie on many other sites.'

The trio seated themselves as Ashley conveyed his ever ready repost.

'I'll let you into a little-known secret, Derek. It's my *team* that's lucky. Lucky to have *ME*.'

*****

The informal discussion covered the usual fundamentals. Ashley Griffiths ran a very tight ship and was renowned for possessing a never-ending stream of practical solutions to anything untoward that might arise in debate.

Derek Evans did not hold back with his praise.

'You've got an eye for responding to and dealing with the unanticipated. Traditionally, any upcoming problems are usually embraced with gusto and handled with professional ease.'

'One does one's utmost.' grinned Ashley in response.

'However, the issue of Covid has dealt the entire globe an unsuspecting blow. Like many trades and industries, hospitality is in the race against time to recoup losses and restore reputations. Consumer confidence had taken a battering. Efforts to restore faith needed to be stringent.'

'I agree, entirely.'

Judging by the positivity heaped on Ashley during the conversation, it appeared that his contribution to Wendy Parkinson's endeavours had been received with enormous enthusiasm throughout the entire chain.

The seed of inspiration was rapidly bearing fruit.

Derek Evans veritably beamed his appreciation across the table as he stirred his tea.

‘So far, the guests are evidently willing to oblige any Covid protocol they are being asked to comply with. Sanitisation points are part of our liability insurance policy now. It’s an unavoidable measure but tolerable, it would seem.’

Ashley nibbled on a shortbread as he prepared a reply.

‘Well, we’ve only had the doors open a couple of weeks, but I’ve heard no complaints here, Derek. In fact, I’d say that the implementation of the one-way system and hand wash stations have given cause for our guests to feel more comfortable as opposed to feeling infringed upon.’

‘Yes, Ashley. That’s my hope. Whilst we intend for our services to return to normal eventually, there are going to be occasional teething problems.’

Wendy dropped sugar in her tea and reached for a biscuit as she ventured opinion.

‘On a lighter note, the reports from other sites this week suggest a real thumbs-up for the promotion campaign. Numbers are rising steadily. It’s very early days yet, too.’

Ashley was modestly sceptical.

‘How do you work that out then, Wendy? I mean…I know I’m a dreamboat, but it can’t just be my handsome fizzog that’s pulling them in off the streets, can it?’

Derek set his cup down and interrupted.

‘Don’t undersell yourself, Ashley. And don’t underestimate the power of advertising. Your face represents everything about the company. When the public think of you, they think of Ultimate Inns as being their choice. It might only seem like a few new fliers and posters, but they do work. The current business quarter is already looking very promising against forecast.’

Ashley leaned back into his chair and interlinked his fingers behind his head.

‘It must be a massive help to us when tourist attractions and pubs are also opening again with minimal restrictions. All pissing in the same pot, aren’t we?’

The M.D. fully appreciated Ashley's wise overview.

'Yes of course, Definitely. That's why I was keen to strike while the iron is hot. If this chain didn't respond to its own predictions for potential returning footfall, then other chains would gladly dip their bread.'

Wendy nodded avidly.

'As things stand…and I'm not blowing my own trumpet, here…but stats suggest we have our noses in front of our nearest competitors. If we are pinching custom whilst the campaign has barely begun, then just imagine the long-term results.'

Ashley sat forward again and emptied his cup.

'So, what now? Carry on as we are?'

Derek Evans' eyes widened as he gave some guidance as to the next stages of the promotion.

'Hernwood, as expected, has already set the bar with this. You've already got standards in place that none of the other sites can hold a candle to. But they are going to have to play catch up fast. We can't pin all our hopes on one hotel carrying the other twenty-eight.'

Ashley couldn't fully convince himself that the new marketing scheme was having such an immediate impact.

'Do you think Hernwood's current increase in business is simply because people know I work here?'

Derek would not tolerate the thought.

And Wendy was not about to allow Ashley's mild pessimism go unnoticed, either.

'There you go again, Ashley. You are the chosen one for a reason. If you get the public back in here, then they will follow suit and return to the other hotels in the chain. I'm convinced of it. You're our business model. Literally and figuratively. You should have more faith in what you are aspiring to achieve. We will breed success through association. The public will be ultra-confident in Ultimate. You'll see. We envisage things that bookings may get to a stage where we are barricading the doors because every site is full. Now wouldn't that be the ultimate dream for Ultimate Inns?'

Wendy's words were prophetic and genuine.

Derek promptly changed the subject.

'Have all of your staff been recalled from the Furlough scheme, yet?'

'No, not quite. I thought it best to feather them back in as duties and demands dictate. Too many cooks and all that. Just thinking of the company coffers. We don't want people back in the workplace and being paid for doing nothing, do we?'

'I appreciate your concern, Ashley but let *me* worry about the money side of things. If you can cope for the moment that's fine but ideally, I'd like all contracted employees back to work as soon as possible.'

'I don't think we will have to wait very long. This site looks busy again?' Wendy intervened.

Derek appeared to be quite content with his findings.

'Any other business you can think of while we are here, Wendy?'

The Marketing and Promotions consultant shook her head slowly whilst checking her works' diary.

'No. Nothing obvious. Hernwood ticks all boxes. We should get over to Fleeting, now. Apparently, the promotions packs never arrived there. Bit of a mystery with the delivery times. And they are *still* waiting.'

Derek rose to his feet and briefly surveyed the foyer and reception areas.

'I have to say, Ashley. Its spick and span in here. Very sharp and welcoming. Enticing. Really good.'

Wendy and Ashley joined the M.D. as he ambled across the carpet.

'Well…if you're happy Derek, then we can all sleep better at night.'

Once again amused by Ashley's supply of wit, the two visitors ventured to the check-in desk, alerting Jeanette to their departure.

'Thank you for the tea, Jeanette. See you very soon.'

Ashley didn't hesitate.

He was awaiting his opportunity.

Jeanette did not look at him on purpose.

'She's a whizz when it comes to mashing a brew, is our Jeanette. By the way Derek, did you want to take some shortbread with you to Fleeting? If they're struggling for guests, they might not be able to provide you with such a treat. Not the chocolate ones, though.'

Derek wasn't quite sure whether Ashley was jesting or if his offer was serious.

'I think we'll manage, Ashley. Thank you for the offer, anyway.'

'Bye-bye both. Speak soon!' Ashley grinned, as Derek and Wendy exited the main doors.

Jeanette could only stare with incredulity at the continual clowning that her manager exhibited.

'I don't know how you get away with such cockiness, Ashley Griffiths. I really don't.'

The Operations Manager spun on his heels to convey a suggestion in a very convoluted and indeterminable quasi-continental accent.

He simultaneously blew on his fingernails and rubbed them on his lapel.

'Madam Jeanette…it is 'cos I is *untouchable*. It is cos I is de best manager dare is.'

Now she finally relented and burst into a giggle fit as he sauntered toward the elevator.

'One of these days, Ashley. One of these days.'

'I know, I know. I'll meet my match one day. I know.'

NINE

In light of Wendy Parkinson's positive overview, Ashley himself had to admit that he had not truly anticipated such a positive response from the public.

During the month since the campaign launch, the feedback and footfall had been unprecedented. The stream of positivity around Hernwood was tangible.

The vibrant change of mood among the staff was refreshing and gratifying. Especially for a manager who had harboured conviction that Covid might just have put the lid on the industry for the foreseeable future.

Seventeen other Ultimate Inn hotels had contacted Ashley to commend him on his efforts and in the same breath his fellow site managers were asking for advice on emulating his methods.

Ashley felt like a man in control again.

A leader. A person to inspire.

And if he could do it whilst raising smiles along the way then all the better for everyone.

The shadow of the pandemic was visibly retreating. Ashley had studiously checked the performance figures for the entire chain. All sites were gaining momentum. But Hernwood was streets ahead.

Perhaps he did deserve the special plaudits after all.

Ever the professional, he acknowledged the appreciation from his colleagues with good grace and hoped to encourage others to raise their game where needed.

The sense of collaboration was a most welcome addition to his current working day.

He had a spring in his step again.

It was a tried and tested policy that if he was bouncing around the place offering good will and plaudits, then it should start rubbing off on others rapidly. Everybody benefits from seeing a happy boss.

At least, that was the theory.

His contemporaries at other sites were perhaps sometimes wary of Ashley's modern approach to steering the ship. He was relatively young to be at the helm. Many managers in the trade were a decade older and decidedly more reserved in their demeanour.

Ashley's age may have belied his status, but he got results.

The progress was visible in all quarters.

In all honesty, his counterparts knew they could not hold a candle to him in terms of the current promotion. He carried the photogenic appeal that none of the others possessed. Not their fault, of course. But it ensured that any perceived rivalries or potential jealousy was eradicated from the outset.

By default, Ashley was the only man for the job. And no one could deny the company had made the correct choice. Especially considering the subsequent effect it was having on business.

But despite being nudged toward local celebrity status, the nuts and bolts of the job still always required prior attention.

It was around four p.m. one particular Thursday. Late June. When Ashley was summoned to the laundry room. A discrepancy over the linen delivery looked to leave a potentially disruptive shortage. A polite yet persuasive phone call ensured that a second delivery would be on route first thing the following morning.

Swift. Decisive. Effective.

Such trifling issues were of course all part and parcel of running a hotel. Most routines were attuned to a very similar schedule across the industry.

Yet there was a definitive change in the air since Hernwood had effectively become the tent-pole site for the entire chain.

Ashley was finding that responses to his requests were more in depth and rapid than in the days pre-Covid. The mechanic of putting a face to the name seemed to facilitate a far smoother transition of most aspects of the operation.

In short, Ashley was becoming identifiable as the man who will make things happen, whatever the situation may be.

People were enjoying dealing with him on a daily basis.

Both staff and customers alike felt confident in his presence.

Image was key, indeed.

But that shouldn't have detracted from his natural flair for making amiability appear simple. No one and nothing would perplex or frustrate him. He had a clear understanding of his role and responsibility.

He was paid to manage. And he could manage people and any associated problems with inherent aplomb.

With the laundry anomaly solved, he then ventured to the restaurant.

The currently sparse catering crew needed more hands due to several key departures during both lockdowns. Ashley fully understood the problem, but the recruitment budget had been frozen for the time being.

Subsequently, with the new evening menu about to go live, it was a scene of frantic activity as the staff prepared for incoming guests and their rumbling stomachs.

As he strode through the dining room and entered the kitchen, he hoped a cheery greeting might lift spirits before the imminent shift commenced.

Everybody in his eyeline would receive a heartfelt smile and a verbal acknowledgement. Chefs to pot washers. Waiting staff to front of house. Bar attendants to buffet servers. All were highly valued cogs in the machine.

He entrusted the members of his culinary team to perform their hourly hygiene inspection, but it was not unusual for them to observe him making a personal appearance in the kitchen every couple of days.

The actual back-room kitchen staff currently consisted of just six. Busiest times were at breakfast and evening and so preparation was key behind the scenes. And with Hernwood at nigh-on full occupancy once again, no oversights could be afforded.

Demand had to be obliged at all times, to the customer's complete satisfaction.

Despite most viewing Ashley as a comparatively informal superior, there was always the opportunity for him to trip somebody up should an oversight slip through the net.

But Ashley would not view them as failings.

He liked to term them as missed opportunities to retain excellence.

An impromptu check on the kitchen provided one such instance.

'Scott…that fire door shouldn't be open. In fact, if the glass bolt is broken it should have been reported to maintenance.'

The second chef, Scott Wainwright, knew exactly why the safety bolt was missing. An uncomfortable silence endured as Ashley nudged the fire exit wide open with the toe of his shoe.

He then peered through the doorframe and had suspicions confirmed. The presence of the two porters was betrayed initially by the stench of their fruit flavoured E-Cigarettes. A pungent fragrance that polluted Ashley's nostrils immediately.

Then the smokers' secret location was identified by two billowing plumes of vapour rising from behind the refuse skip enclosure.

Ashley opted to take a little walk over and surprise the culprits himself.

To say they were startled was something of an understatement.

'Josh and Ray, isn't it? Come on, lads. I don't mind you having a fag break, but I do care *where* you have it. No smoking on site. You *know* that. Only permitted beyond the site perimeter. Good lads. See you soon.'

The young porters instantly switched off their vape machines and followed Ashley back into the kitchen to resume their duties.

In the meantime, Ashley engaged in a quick phone call to maintenance.

'Hello, George? Can you investigate replacing the security bolt on the kitchen fire door please. As soon as possible, please. Thank you muchly.'

Ashley replaced his mobile phone into his suit jacket pocket and offered Scott a discerning glance which needed little further explanation.

Then came the unexpected bonus comment.

'Apart from *that* little matter…excellent, Scott. Top marks. Keep it up.'

The second chef breathed a sigh of relief, glaring at the two young porters as the Operations Manager exited the kitchen.

*****

Ashley's phone bleated into life once again as he strode through the ground floor of the building. He scanned the caller display and answered.

It was his most favoured Head of Reception.

'Hi Jeanette. All good in the hood?'

Passing the large function room, Ashley's concentration on the call was disturbed by the thumping beat of loud music from within the vicinity.

He poked his head through the door of the main suite to be greeted by the sight of the Zumba class just about to commence their early evening session.

Satisfied all was well, he continued to converse with Jeanette.

'A *visitor*? You mean…to see *me*? I haven't got any appointments scheduled.'

Jeanette confirmed this to be the case and that the visitor was prepared to wait.

'Okay, I'll be five minutes. Just been watching the pensioners and their aerobics class. What a sight for sore eyes that is!'

He heard Jeanette chuckle as he ended the call.

Zoe the Zumba instructor gave a wave to Ashley as she prepared her warm-up routine for the group. All heads turned to him. The vision of two dozen elderly gym members being put through their sweaty paces to a never-ending dance track was not on his bucket list.

Subsequently he blew Zoe a kiss and made a speedy exit from the hall much to the amusement of the class.

*****

Jeanette Morris was an indomitable lady. A wondrous adversary of worth. And Ashley adored her. She had been Head of Reception at Hernwood for nearly twenty years. Previous to taking the post she had amassed two decades of clerical and logistical experience in the industry.

What she didn't know about running hotels frankly wasn't worth knowing.

Ashley approached the front desk with a smirk that conveyed nothing less than totally affectionate respect.

'My dearest, Jeanette. How is our foyer vibe this afternoon?'

Jeanette rarely took prisoners with her often forcibly doleful act.

But that is all it was - an act. Ashley was one of those few individuals who could trick her into dropping her façade.

She very nearly smiled back at him through the large sheet of clear Perspex as he put his elbows on the desktop.

'Hello, Mister Griffiths, sir. All is good here. No second post. I've forwarded all relevant emails to you just now. And over your shoulder in the corner of the foyer area by the drinks machine, there is a lady with a very nice coat and a blonde bob haircut, that claims she would like a word in your shell-like.'

Ashley raised his eyebrows to feign a sense of horror.

'You're *kidding*? What have I done to the poor creature?'

Jeanette furrowed her own brow in response.

'She didn't give the impression she's here to complain. I've not seen her before. And I would recall her face if she had been here during these past few weeks.'

Ashley stood up straight and saluted.

'Okay dokey, Mrs Receptionist. I shall go and tend to the lady visitor's whims, forthwith.'

Jeanette shook her head in mock dismay as Ashley performed a semi pirouette and veritably waltzed across the foyer.

The lady with the nice coat and blonde bob haircut was dwarfed by the large leather armchair in the bay window. She did not sense Ashley's approach until he engaged her attention by conveying a typically warm welcome.

His smile, posture and mannerisms combined with flawless persuasion.

'Good afternoon to you, Madam. And what a glorious one it is too. My name is Ashley. I am the Operations Manager of this hotel. How can I be of assistance to you, today?'

The visitor glanced up at Ashley and fixed her studious green eyes into his. Steadily rising to her full height, she was little more than five feet tall. Ashley estimated she may have been in her early forties. She was attractive enough. She was certainly well presented and carried herself with a certain poise. And he noticed the designer label jacket, too.

Jeanette was spot on. A very nice coat, indeed.

A striking smile emitted a low, soft tone as the female stranger offered a hand of greeting.

'Oh hello, Ashley. Forgive me. I'm a little nervous.'

Slightly puzzled by her opening statement, Ashley attempted to brush off her concerns with professional courtesy.

'*Nervous*, my dear? Come, come, whatever *for*? Absolutely no need to be shy. You're among friends now.' he chuckled.

The lady beamed a broader expression of pleasure in response to his customary charm.

'This is going to sound so *silly*...but...I just wanted the chance to meet you in person.'

Ashley played along with her and applied a generous dose of comedy.

'Well, you can tick that box now, because here I am. In the flesh!'

She continued to study his features intently as she composed another thought to convey.

'Like I say...I'm a little anxious. I've never met a celebrity before.'

Ashley's good manners afforded him a polite reply.

'Oh right! Yes! The posters. Well, I must say I'm honoured to finally meet my first ever groupie! I thank you very much for hunting me down!'

The diminutive blonde was no longer smiling.

She appeared somewhat bemused by Ashley's line of patter.

She maintained her focus on his face and an awkward silence ensued.

Swiftly changing the conversational gear, Ashley opted for a more purposed approach.

'Did you have a room booked with us this evening, Madam? I can assist you with checking in if you wish?'

'Oh no. I'm not staying. I just popped by to say hello.'

Another hiatus followed as Ashley conjured another suitable reply.

This was a first - even for a manager of his broad experience.

'Oh right, okay. Have you stayed with us prior to today, then? Or indeed at any other of our hotels in the chain?'

The woman appeared to be caught in a daze and was obviously awe struck to a degree.

It occurred to Ashley that she had indeed only entered the site on the off chance of engaging with him in person.

Her next statement confirmed his suspicions.

'No, I'm not familiar with your hotels at all. I was just driving through town earlier and saw you on the billboard near the railway station. You are even more handsome in real life, aren't you?'

Ashley's confusion was slowly evolving into a mild wariness. Having now performed his usual ritual to get customers onside, he himself was now struggling to identify the deeper motive for her presence in the building.

There was certainly limited scope for continuing the conversation, but he endeavoured, nonetheless.

'A drink, Madam? Tea or coffee? On me? Whilst you look around?'

She contemplated his offer as her attention dropped to his suit and then down to the floor at his feet.

He persevered as she held back her response.

'It will be a complimentary drink of your choosing. Being as you have been so complimentary towards me.'

The blonde clutched her handbag with both hands and fidgeted on the spot.

'No, nothing. Thank you. I'd better be going. I just wanted to meet you, Ashley. That's all. It's been very nice, though. Short and sweet but very nice. I'd better let you get back to managing the hotel, hadn't I.'

Now suitably perplexed and even slightly embarrassed, Ashley offered a hand in farewell.

'Well, on behalf of Ultimate Inns I wish to thank you for coming by and talking to us. It's nice to know I've been noticed. Who knows…maybe one day we will cross paths again.'

The short woman with the blonde bob haircut, nice designer coat and startlingly green eyes shook Ashley's hand.

Her intensive stare was unwavering.

And gradually, unnerving.

'Yes…I would like to think so. By the way, please excuse my rudeness. My name is Pauline. Pauline Braithwaite.'

'Well, Pauline Braithwaite. It's been a pleasure. You take care, now. Hope to see you staying with us here at Hernwood in the near future. If not sooner!'

The visitor nodded without further comment.

She turned on her two-inch heels and exited the reception area. Ashley thoughtfully observed her departure down the foyer steps. She appeared respectable in demeanour and presentation.

But there seemed to be more going on behind her front cover than one brief encounter would allow him to determine.

Jeanette had covertly witnessed the episode from the front desk.

Ashley walked slowly toward his Head of Reception, exhibiting a mask of bewilderment.

'Well…that was definitely *different*!' he gasped.

Jeanette giggled without restraint and nodded toward the main doors of the building.

'I take it you weren't previously acquainted then, Ashley?'

'Never laid eyes on her in my life. And I think that strictly between you, me, and the gatepost, I won't be too bothered if I don't lay eyes on her ever again.'

Jeanette's mood turned mildly serious.

'Why would you say that? She seemed friendly enough from where I was sitting. Lovely looking, too.'

Ashley glanced around before tapping his right temple with his right forefinger.

'I'm not entirely sure she was firing on all cylinders. Perhaps a sandwich short of a picnic. I could be wrong.'

The Head of Reception adopted a stern and disapproving air.

'Oh right, so now you're a superstar you want to pick and choose your fans, do you? Typical reaction. If you're public property you must take the rough with the smooth.'

'*Rough* being the operative word! Anyway, I'll be in the office for an hour if any more nutters come looking for autographs, okay?'

Jeanette wanted to smile but refrained.

'Okay, honey. I'll try to get them formed into an orderly queue.'

*****

Outside in the hotel car park, a visitor sat motionless behind the steering wheel of her three-door silver Fiat.

It had been nearly an hour since her first introduction to the Operations Manager.

Acclaimed hotelier and public figure of repute that he was now purported to be.

She was not disappointed.

Far from it.

Subsequently, as per his suggestion, she had already decided that she would indeed be making another visit.

Pauline Braithwaite turned on the ignition and cruised away from the premises to mingle with the amassing rush hour traffic.

As she navigated the car through town, she reflected on her very successful and encouraging afternoon.

She deliberated on the date of her next impromptu appearance at the hotel.

Perhaps it might occur tomorrow.

Maybe next week.

Whim would dictate.

Now she was assured of the warmest of welcomes, any reservations regarding her initial acquaintance with Ashley Griffiths had completely evaporated.

He had unwittingly passed her test with flying colours.

He would definitely be meeting Pauline Braithwaite again.

TEN

They embraced tightly in the kitchen. It had been a very hectic few weeks for Ashley. Carl was absolutely delighted with the positivity surrounding the rapid return to something like normality.

'You must be so relieved, Ash. I know you really struggled in the lockdowns. But you've come off the ropes swinging. I'm so happy for you.'

It was just after eight p.m. Another thirteen-hour shift for the Hernwood Hotel Operations Manager. But the red wine was already going down a treat. Ashley swilled the contents of his glass as he rested his chin on Carl's shoulder.

'I'll be honest…I thought the hotel game was up the spout. All those months away from the place left me feeling I'd never get back there.'

The men parted and Carl poured himself a drink to match Ashley's.

'I know! But just look at you now! The single-handed saviour. A real knight in shining armour, aren't you.'

Ashley couldn't prevent a broad grin of acknowledgment, which evolved into a fit of the giggles.

'You can laugh, Ash. But your public are still out there and wanting to see you again. They just needed that special reason to forget Covid and become confident. The place will be deluged long term, now. You mark my words.'

Ashley nodded in worthy agreement and sampled some wine. It was a soothing reward in the circumstances.

He chuckled once more as another thought entered the fray.

'I actually went online the other night for the first time in weeks and changed my profile picture to the promo one. It must be going to my head, Carl. It's had so many likes from friends. The response to the campaign all round has been phenomenal.'

'Well why shouldn't you? I've told you. Blow your own trumpet. Nobody else is going to. It's been a long time coming. And I'm not surprised about all the pats on the back. You're a popular and well-respected man, Ashley Griffiths. And don't you forget it, either!'

The pair relocated to the comfort of the lounge and duly topped up their glasses.

'It's not just down to me though, Carl. The staff are fantastic. They more than play their part. More than me, sometimes. They wanted to stay open for the nurses, but Derek said it would entail massive issues with Furlough. He knows best I suppose. But he would have surely been worrying more than even I was.'

Carl observed Ashley from the other end of the settee and shook his head disapprovingly.

'There you go again. Putting yourself at the back of the queue. Derek knew the future lay with you and he was proved right. But *without* you he'd be sunk without trace. Believe you me.'

Ashley raised his free hand in mocking acceptance of the telling off.

'Okay, Okay. I take the hint. I'll try my best to be big headed from this point onwards. To be honest the guests we've had so far seem fairly impressed with the operation. We are definitely raising the bar in terms of customer satisfaction, I think. Even had a personal vote of thanks today from a lady that hasn't even stayed with us before!'

Carl shuffled his backside along the sofa and clinked his glass against Ashley's.

'Good. Let them keep coming and showing their gratitude. Here's to life without Covid. And the next time you get a thank you in person, give them a hug and thank them back. And give them a hug from me too. What harm can it do?'

Marjorie entered the lounge and sat quietly on the hearth rug.

Awaiting her evening meal, she would, however, need to display some patience.

As her two human parents looked toward the promising horizon spanning out before them.

ELEVEN

The fourteenth of July. A Wednesday.

Jeanette departed the hotel at approximately seven p.m. Her regular duty cover for overnight reception was a new employee. A very capable young woman named Martine.

She had settled in for the evening and confirmed whether there were any scheduled late check-ins due to arrive. According to the computer system, there were no new guests expected that night.

Martine attuned her mindset in anticipation of an incident free twelve-hour shift.

The security operatives had also just handed the baton over. Lee Pinder was to oversee the premises until morning. He had just commenced his first walk round to inspect that all was well on site.

Ashley retrieved his suit jacket and briefcase and locked the office. He was more than ready for the journey homeward.

Pizza and a film night lay ahead.

On exiting the elevator at reception level, he checked on any issues with Martine before wishing her a good night.

Nothing out of the ordinary was predicted.

All seemed normal within the walls of the Hernwood Hotel.

*****

Nearly two hours into their shift, Martine had just finished making a coffee for herself and for Lee. She placed both mugs behind the reception desk and hoped to catch Lee's eye if he passed the foyer entrance.

He would not be far away. He casually mentioned that he needed caffeine and would back in five minutes after checking the car park.

It was a quieter week compared to the frantic activity of late.

She double-checked the occupancy.

Just over one hundred and fifty rooms filled for the evening.

Nearly half of which would be vacated by ten a.m. next morning.

All in all, there was very little for Martine to attend to. Guests had occasionally passed by on route back to their rooms and bid their goodnights. Boredom was setting in as she opened a puzzle book to commence a new wordsearch.

So long as she was on the end of the phone and available to respond to any guest room queries, her mission for the duration appeared to be looking very straight forward as she began to count down the hours.

Lee appeared through the now fully automated main doors and made Martine jump a little as he disturbed her concentration on the puzzle book. He generally wasn't one for small talk but made attempts to be vaguely sociable.

'Thanks for the drink. Gonna be a long one by the looks of things. Ring me if you need me. I'm off checking the fire doors are shut. Won't be long. Then we'll do a crossword if you want.'

'Okay Lee. See you in about twenty, then.'

The security officer vacated the scene and relative silence swiftly resumed.

Martine hadn't been keeping close eye on the time, but it was certainly after nine o' clock when the lone woman appeared outside at the entrance to the foyer area.

A short lady with blonde hair cut into a bob style.

Martine observed that she was small in stature but displayed a stern, unnerving grimace. The glass doors opened as she made her approach and invited the woman's entry toward the reception desk. She seemed rather tentative as she clutched her handbag and made a little progress across the carpet.

Despite her apparent uncertainty, she was no stranger to the place.

Stopping her stride, she studied the life size point-of-sale cut out of Ashley Griffiths, as he grinned back at her in a display of integrity and earnest motive.

She gradually altered her downcast facade and began to smile to herself. A full minute elapsed as Martine observed the woman, before finally feeling compelled to enquire if she could be of any assistance.

From behind the plastic screen, she adopted her most hospitable guise.

'Good evening, Madam. You look a little unsure. Are you staying here or perhaps looking to book with us this evening?'

The visitor now fixed her full attention on the night reception cover.

The harshness instantly resumed pride of place in her features as she made a measured advance toward the check-in counter.

Then once more as if at the flick of a switch, the woman's expression adopted its previously friendlier gloss. Her voice was almost too soft in tone for Martine to decipher, as if it was purposely whispered.

'Good evening. I know its late and I'm afraid I haven't a reservation. Would you be able to accommodate me tonight?'

'Yes, Madam. Of course. Let me access the system for you? Just a room for yourself, is it?'

'Yes please. But I'd like a double if possible. I don't mind paying the extra.'

Martine was naturally bemused by the relatively untypical request, but rightfully complied with the visitor's wishes.

'Okay, room four-four-four is available this evening. That would be ninety-two pounds for the one night. Check-out is ten tomorrow morning. Do you require breakfast at all?'

The woman gazed around the foyer area before centring her concentration back to the booking clerk once again.

'No, thank you. No breakfast. I'll likely be gone before the sun rises. Just a flying visit.'

'Okay, that's just ninety-two to pay then please. Will you be paying by cash or card?'

'Cash…thank you.'

Martine quickly inputted the information onto the system and confirmed the arrangement.

'Have you stayed with Ultimate Inns before, Madam?'

'No, it's my first time. Looks very nice, though. I saw the billboard poster near the motorway junction. Very inviting. I'll be sure to put a review online afterwards.'

Whilst the new guest appeared pleasant enough, Martine could not help but sense an element of strangeness about the episode.

But as always, professional compliance ensured that all customers benefited from the same courteous treatment.

'Can I take your full name please, Madam?'

'Yes. Its Braithwaite. Pauline...Braithwaite. In fact, I've changed my mind. I'll pay by card. It's easier all round, isn't it.'

'No problem. Madam. The card machine is ready for your transaction. If you are contactless just hold it over the panel.'

'No, I'll have to put my number in, sorry.'

Pauline Braithwaite diligently used the keypad. The silence across the desk was a little unsettling for Martine but she could not decide why that should be.

'Okay, Mrs. Braithwaite. That transaction had gone through. Here is your room card. Just place it in the slot on the door handle and the green light will flash to confirm the door is unlocked.'

The latest arrival took the small envelope and inspected the door card.

Martine completed her ritual introductory speech.

'The bar is open until Midnight. If you should require anything, please contact reception using the phone in your room. The number is one-one. Do you need any help with luggage, at all?'

Pauline Braithwaite shook her head appreciatively as she placed the door card and her purse back in her handbag.

Martine observed the woman shuffle toward the lift doors and offered one final instruction.

'Fourth level. Room four-four-four. Thank you, Mrs Braithwaite. Enjoy your stay with Ultimate Inns.'

Pauline Braithwaite de-pressed the button to ground the lift.

She turned back to Martine with her own parting shot.

'Thank you for squeezing me in.'

'My pleasure. Have a good evening.'

Martine continued to watch covertly as the newcomer entered the lift.

The steel sliding doors finally enclosed her.

It struck the night receptionist as odd that the new guest had no baggage with her, whatsoever. Not even a small overnight case.

Still, she was a paying customer and that was the only priority.

Lee the security guard suddenly entered the foyer area and checked the two fire exits.

'Ahh, the wanderer returns!' quipped Martine with a smirk.

'Don't tell me I've missed something exciting.'

'Nothing at all Lee. Are you making us both another drink? Then we can attack this crossword.'

TWELVE

'Morning, Ashley!'

Jeanette's welcoming tone was always a reassuring token of Hernwood's professional standards. The Operations Manager approached the booking desk. His eyes ever scanning the vicinity for potential lapses.

'Hi there, my favourite ever receptionist in the world. How are you on this fine sunny summer morning?'

Jeanette's smile was a rare delight and it encouraged Ashley to place his elbows on the counter and lean closer around her plastic screen as she responded.

'I'm very well, thank you for asking, my favourite hotel manager in the history of hotel management. And may I say how very dapper you are looking today. *And* that you're not supposed to be seen breaching this screen.'

Ashley grinned as once again he observed the sparse foyer.

'Well, one does like to make the effort occasionally, doesn't one? Where is everyone? Have we had the place evacuated?'

The Head of Reception followed her manager's gaze.

'Well, it is only after seven. Not quite breakfast time yet.'

'Many new additions last night? I did check before my zoom meeting yesterday afternoon. We seemed a bit thin on the ground after a bumper start. Just shy of a hundred and fifty rooms taken, wasn't it?'

Jeanette promptly checked the system for verification.

'Well…it was up until…let's see, hang on…yes up until I went last night. Then night cover took a booking for an extra one at nine-fifty.'

Ashley's attention switched directly to Jeanette.

'An extra room or an extra person?'

'One and the same, isn't it? But a bit weird this. Single occupancy of a double room. Room four-four-four. And they weren't here long because according to the system Martine checked them out again at five-thirty-eight this morning. That's got to be a record.'

Ashley didn't pass up the chance to jape.

'Perhaps they found the sheets were itchy. Even so…eight hours beginning to end? And they were alone? Oh well…none of our concern so long as they paid and didn't leave a dirty protest.'

Jeanette simply shrugged her shoulders and chose the similar standpoint of indifference.

Ashley confirmed the time on his phone.

'Okay, dokey. I'll be in my office for thirty minutes then out on my rounds before I phone Derek at ten. Anything to report from front end? Cleaners and maids, all good?'

Jeanette scrutinised her monitor.

'Eighteen emails forwarded to your office since you left last night. The usual spam, I think. Some envelopes are *still* in your pigeon-hole that you forgot to take up yesterday, which I shall pass to you now to ensure I witness you taking ownership of them.'

'You're a slave driver. But thank you for looking after me. Right, I need coffee. I'll be upstairs in the boudoir should anyone shout for help.'

Jeanette giggled at the reference.

'Oh…don't forget…the group health and safety inspector will be here mid-morning.'

'*Shit*! I did forget! Mind you it's only a pre-brief. Our pants aren't pulled down properly until next week.'

The Head of Reception glanced in disgust.

'Thanks for that image, boss. Made my day, already.'

Ashley grabbed his mail and his briefcase before venturing across the foyer to the lift doors.

'Always happy to help, darling. See you shortly!'

The lift panels glided open just as there was a holler over his shoulder.

'Morning, Ash. Glad I caught you.'

Turning to ascertain the source of the call, Ashley was surprised to see the day shift security operative, John Bonsall, making strides toward him.

John was a lumbering timed-served veteran of the field.

And as an ex-policeman, he was automatically deemed the unofficial supervisor of the security team.

'Hi, John. How are you? Is everything okay?'

The steel doors of the elevator began to separate.

'Yes, Ash. All is good. No problems at all. I just wanted to catch you first thing. When Lee finished earlier, he handed me this.'

Ashley observed the small package which was about the same size as a packet of cigarettes. It was wrapped very neatly in red foil cellophane. His puzzlement was immediate, and John was evidently none the wiser as to what the parcel contained.

Ashley broached the inevitable query as he stepped into the lift.

'Not Christmas yet, is it?

John eyed the article at close quarters and wrinkled his bulbous nose.

'No idea what's in it, Ash. Lee said a female guest checked out first thing this morning. Reception was dealing with somebody upstairs apparently, so the guest left her door card on the desk and told Lee she was off. She gave this to him and asked if he would pass it onto you in person.'

Now more than a little intrigued, Ashley took the splendidly covered item from the security guard and shook it gently next to his ear.

'Thank you, John. How strange?'

'I didn't see the lady in question of course but Lee wondered if you might have been expecting anything today.'

'No…not at all. I'm as much in the dark as anyone. I'll have a look once I'm in the office. Thank you again, John. And thank Lee for me just in case I don't see him.'

The lift doors closed once again, allowing Ashley to ascend and enjoy the privacy of his own office for - he hoped - at least the next thirty minutes.

*****

The caffeine tasted heavenly and soon worked its magic. For some reason the coffee at work always seemed to have a far more potent effect than the first one of the day which he religiously sampled at home before leaving.

It certainly alleviated the laborious nature of checking emails and opening envelopes full of junk. Hernwood had very quickly become the focal point for the entire chain and fellow Ultimate Inn managers were relentless in tapping Ashley up for tips and advice.

This was a very flattering and novel aspect to his working day, but as time went on, each daily set of requests for guidance from his counterparts was taking longer and longer to sift through.

He double checked the arrangements made with the site insurance representative and the accompanying health and safety box ticker. Counting fire doors and extinguishers was going to eat into most of the day, but they weren't due on site until eleven so there was plenty of opportunity to comb the relevant areas for potential black marks.

Then he remembered the small package handed to him by security.

He picked it off the tabletop and admired the perfectionist wrapping. Expertly done, indeed. Not a seam or a crease in sight. Tender loving care had been applied to concealing the gift.

Curiosity finally defeated him, so Ashley commenced peeling off the paper.

Curiosity that rapidly evolved into complete bemusement.

The gift was a bottle of his favourite aftershave.

Eau de cologne Aramanda.

Two hundred and fifty millilitres of it.

Even cheap end it would cost in the region of seventy pounds.

Ashley furrowed his brow and drained his coffee cup.

First instinct suggested that the gift must have been from Carl.

But security declared that it was a lady guest that had deposited it with them. Ashley's brain then moved naturally though the gears as the moment digested.

Why would somebody staying on site do this?

And how would they know what his favourite balm was?

A card of thanks from guests was a very occasional gesture.

But something so personal to him?

The mystery was afoot.

*****

Before commencing his daily visit to the linen store, Ashley ventured back down to reception to find Jeanette amid a telephone conversation.

She spotted his approach and dutifully brought the call to a conclusion.

'Hello again, sir. Missing me already?'

Ashley appeared unusually pensive, and she noticed his attention flitting around the foyer as though looking for someone.

'Are you okay, Ashley?'

Finally, he focused back on her. But the expression on his face suggested that the customary humorous banter was not on the agenda for once.

'I think so. Jeanette, can you do me a favour, please?'

'Of course. Name it.'

'Can you check the log and see who checked out at first light this morning? John on security said the key card was left on this counter. I just want to confirm a name.'

Jeanette promptly scanned the system. She checked departures records for a few tentative seconds.

'A Mrs Pauline Braithwaite. Checked in last night at nine-fifty-one. Room four-four-four. The room was recorded by Martine as vacant at five-forty-nine this morning. The only way we can check precise departure time would be to look on the camera footage.'

Ashley quietly pondered Jeanette's findings.

'No, thank you. No need. That's fine. I'll sort it from here.'

A rather perplexed Jeanette observed Ashley's rather purposed stride outside beyond the main doors.

A minute or so later, he re-entered the building accompanied by John Bonsall. They both accessed the lift together.

'What's this about again, Ashley?'

'I just want your help in checking the footage from first thing this morning. That package you gave me. I'm keen to identify the person who left it here. I've got a name, but I need a face to go with it.'

The lift doors slid open, and the two men entered the corridor leading toward Ashley's office.

'Do you think the person is familiar to you, then?'

'Well…yes and no. Not familiar in the strict sense of the word. But I believe I've met them, yes.'

John was asked to sit at Ashley's desk and bring up the CCTV footage on his computer, from between midnight and six that morning.

A period of silence ensued as John forwarded through film of the early hours. Finally, the departing guest was visually confirmed approaching the vacant reception desk and duly leaving the key card on the counter as reported.

Ashley stood and deliberated.

It definitely looked to be the same woman that visited the other day.

Short in stature. Blonde bob haircut. Steely stare.

Yes. It was her.

But it didn't make sense for her to have any motive to stay over.

One night alone.

Unless it was specifically to leave him the gift?

Ashley failed to register the potential reasoning behind her actions.

'Okay, John. That's fine. Thank you for your help.'

At that moment his mobile phone rang.

'Yes, Jeanette?'

'Your insurance man and fire inspector are on site, captain. Shall I tell them you will come and collect them from reception?'

Ashley's thoughts were decidedly elsewhere.

'They're *early*! I'm not *ready*. Nowhere *near ready*! Okay. Yes. I'll be down in five minutes.'

THIRTEEN

'I tell you something, Carl. I'm not a big fan of social media as you well know. Too many negative arseholes spouting what they like and hiding behind their keyboards. And they get away with it, too!'

Carl smiled knowingly as he set down a mug of tea next to Ashley's laptop.

'You look to be doing okay. Though. Got a right little fan club brewing online now. Not that I'm surprised. Your fame is snowballing.'

Ashley sipped and blew his drink as he maintained attention on the computer screen.

'Well…I wouldn't exactly deem it a fan club. But it is lovely to see so many genuinely positive comments about the campaign. I didn't really anticipate the responses of people that truly know me. I just thought of it as part of the job.'

Carl couldn't help but laugh out loud as he stood over Ashley's shoulder and scrutinized the monitor.

'That new profile photo alone has netted four hundred and forty-eight likes in the space of a month. I'd say it was *you* that folk were keen on - not the bloody promo campaign.'

Carl continued to study the long feed of appraisals as Ashley pondered on another thought.

'Do you think it really *is* about people liking *me*, then?'

'Well, what do *you* think? But I suppose if you can't handle all the public love and kisses then you'd better tell everyone to stop it this instance. I mean, who needs compliments in this day and age? How very old fashioned. How very Twentieth Century. How very dare they be happy for you?'

Now it was Ashley's turn to chuckle.

Carl's sarcasm had hit a nerve.

'You know what I mean, though. I've got nearly a thousand friends on here. Most of which I never see from one month to the next. Or even one *year* to the next.'

'Yeah. So?' grinned Carl.

'To be honest I'm blown away by the time and consideration they have taken to write a nice message to me.'

Carl scratched his forehead in mild despair.

'It's not a *coincidence*, Ash. People like to see what you are up to. They will have been overjoyed to see your new photo. Besides…isn't that why you put it up in the first place? So that your friends can respond?'

Ashley feigned a glare of scorn in Carl's direction and shook his head.

'Oh, shut up, then. Go and do some housework if I'm boring you.'

'Too late for housework. It's gone ten p.m. There's a neighbourhood curfew for hoovering, you know.'

Despite their playful bickering, the pair remained absorbed by the ready flow of good will that exhibited itself on the screen.

'In all seriousness though, Ash. I'm bursting with pride for you. It was such a brave thing to do. Not many in your position would fancy the idea of being displayed in full colour at motorway junctions for a stretch of over two hundred miles.'

Ashley nodded thoughtfully as he slurped his tea.

'I'd not really analysed it on those terms to be honest. I was more worried that the actual photo would look okay.'

'Oh yeah, of course. Well, I mean, you look a right scruff, don't you. *And* you didn't get your hair cut like I told you too. Don't be so bloody coy cos it gets on my nerves. You look *amazing*. You love the camera. The camera loves you. What's the term…naturally photogenic?'

Ashley could not disguise his swelling self-belief any longer.

'There's no kidding you is there, Carl Davis?'

'Damn right there isn't. Not when it comes to knowing *you*, anyway. Oh, I say…by the way…it looks like you've got a brand-new fan club member waiting in the wings to join the celebration.'

Ashley glanced at the laptop display.

'What do you mean?'

‘There look. On your friends’ notifications. Somebody else wants to jump on the publicity bandwagon by the looks of it.’

Ashley concentrated on where Carl pointed.

‘The red circle with the white figure *one* in the centre.’

‘OH…I wonder who that can be?’

Carl simply stared back at Ashley without word.

‘What have I said now?’ asked Ashley in all innocence.

‘Christ Almighty! How old are you…*ten*?’ Carl quipped.

‘I can’t be because you have to be at least thirteen to have an account on here, so there.’

‘May the lord preserve us. No wonder I deleted my profile. The whole things a load of crap.’ barked Carl.

‘You’re just jealous, that’s all.’

‘Oh, of course I am. Green to my gills with envy. So come on, then. Who is the latest groupie you’ve acquired?’

‘I didn’t think you were that interested? I thought you said it was a load of crap?’

Carl failed to hide his smile.

‘Just show me for fuck’s sake. Then I’ll leave you alone.’

Ashley’s mirth also got the better of him as he moved the cursor over the red circle and clicked.

A hushed anticipation enveloped the room as Ashley and Carl simultaneously digested the name of the requester.

Carl, inevitably in the circumstances, was the first of the two to make vocal his response.

‘Who the hell is Pauline Braithwaite, then?’

Ashley suddenly became distinctly unsettled in his chair.

He continued to reserve his right to remain silent.

Carl leaned in to gain a closer, much keener view.

‘Well? Are you accepting or not? Do you even know her? I’ve not heard you mention her before.’

Still without word, Ashley felt under certain duress to comply.

Carl’s impatience was unwittingly pressuring Ashley into action.

'Well, click on her, then! Let's see who Pauline Braithwaite is and what she looks like.'

Ashley did as he was asked.

Then he lied to the man he loved.

And as soon as he had done so, he regretted it.

'I'm not sure who she is. Her name isn't familiar.'

Carl swiftly reached for humour.

'Well…I'm not surprised. Another distant admirer to add to the growing list of hundreds.'

Ashley's next step was performed without prompt.

He clicked on to her profile page.

Carl's frustration quickly got the better of him.

'Well, a fat lot of good that is! You say you don't know her. Not giving us much to go on, is she? No photo and no information whatsoever. Why do people open accounts and leave them like this?'

Ashley was backing himself into a corner. He needed to think and act fast. He screwed his nose up and rubbed his temple in attempting to concoct a believable thread.

'I suppose I should know the name. It's ringing a vague bell, now.'

Carl, however, was now under submission to his own sense of dismay.

'This is why I stopped doing social media. People can hide too easily. Knackers you up for offering a reply if you don't even recognise who she is?'

Ashley continued to blankly observe the screen as recent history flashed through his conscience.

The recollection was decidedly uncomfortable.

Especially as Carl was now fully informed of her existence.

But Ashley couldn't bring himself to dismiss her out of hand.

'Well, like you say, I'll just file her away with the rest of my adoring fan base. She's been nice enough to make contact and I've been nice back. Having her on board can't rock the good ship too much, can it?'

Carl suddenly shifted position around the table and faced Ashley directly.

'Are you raving *mad*? Even infants are taught not to talk to people they don't know. Get rid of her. Now.'

'But you just told me to accept her?'

'Yes…that was before I realised that she is a complete stranger, and you don't have a scooby-doo who it is!'

'Well…I suppose I must have crossed paths with her at some point. Probably though the job. She obviously knows *me*.'

Carl nearly spilled the remnants of his tea mug over the laptop.

'Half of the southwest of England knows who you are, *now*!'

'Look. She's bound to turn up on a photo somewhere.'

Once more, Carl interjected with a cautious observation.

'Well…I don't know if you've noticed, Ash…'

Ashley's eyes darted across and around the computer screen.

'Noticed what?'

'She has just become your nine hundred and forty-third friend.'

'Yeah…so?'

'And you, Ashley, have just become her *first*.'

'Don't be silly. She must have more than just me. The friends window could be set to private?'

Carl put his face ever closer to the screen and scrutinised further.

'No…just one. Just you.'

'Maybe she only just started her account?'

'Yeah…like…in the last ten minutes by the look of it.'

Ashley yawned as fatigue took hold.

He checked his mobile phone for any work-related messages.

'Well, at least I can say I did my good deed for the day. Made myself a friend to a lonely woman. And I am ready to hit the sack.'

'Right oh. Shut that PC down and let's get up to bed. We're both on an early start tomorrow.'

Ashley grinned knowingly.

'Okay, boss. Whatever you say.'

Giving little more thought to the movements online that evening, Ashley switched off the lounge lights and followed Carl upstairs.

Marjorie had conveniently decided to vacate the bedroom.

She momentarily observed her human parents before venturing downstairs and out though the cat flap.

Where the unknown wilderness of night awaited.

FOURTEEN

It had proved to be a particularly testing day. Ashley had almost forgotten how tricky organising rotas had become. Having polled every employee on their post-pandemic return to the workplace, he was now faced with trying to please them all as best as possible.

Democratic shift coverage.

An unenviable mission with unavoidable collateral.

Having spent most of his time making phone calls and dispensing pleasure and pain in varying quantities, he decided he was ready for home. Any loose ends left untied could be sorted tomorrow.

With the time marching toward seven-thirty, his exit was already a belated one. Carl was preparing his mystery speciality for supper. Ashley's phone call declaring his probable late arrival was hopefully the final piece of troublesome news he had to deliver for the day.

Emerging from the reception lift he was very surprised to see Jeanette still at the check-in desk. Unsurprisingly, she too was in the process of bemoaning a drawn-out finale to her very long shift.

'The night cover is running behind. So that means *I'm* now running behind.' she griped.

Ashley could not help but smile and he offered not a jot of sympathy for her position.

'Well, my dear Jeanette, that is the game we are in. We cater. We cater again. And we cater some more until everything, and everyone, is catered for.'

She offered a glare of disdain.

'Fat lot of good *you* are. I think the post Covid bookings are on the rise again. We had a bit of a lull lately but looks like edging towards full occupation the next few weeks.'

Ashley sighed noticeably.

'Oh great. That means Derek will be moving the goalposts soon then. Now we are just about used to the current schedule.'

Jeanette's smile was a very rare and beautiful event.

'Well, I can only put this frantic activity down to your handsome face, Ashley. I mean in all seriousness, what else could be attracting them to us so readily?'

Ashley laughed out loud at Jeanette's wily cynicism.

'Flattery will get you everything but that elusive pay increase that you're after. But I suppose it's preferable to be busy instead of bored?'

Jeanette rubbed her eyes underneath her reading glasses.

'I agree in principle, but a seventy-hour week is not something I really want at my age. The place will kill me off. Apart from anything else, pretending to be pleased to see the general public for such a stretch is going to prove impossible.'

The conversation was observed by the incoming night security operative, Mohammed. With a slightly stooped gait, he shuffled through the glass doors and toward the check-in desk.

Ashley offered a typically warm greeting.

'Hi, Mo. How have you been. Seems ages since we laid eyes on one another. How's things here for you?'

'Oh yes, Mister Griffiths. No problems. I'm off on my first walk round. Just saw you and thought I'd say *hello*.'

Jeanette supplied an opinion as she watched Mohammed waddle off toward the other end of the foyer.

'Now there's a man who always seems to be happy in his work.'

'Unlike you and I, you mean? I wonder what his secret is?'

'I've just remembered. Somebody phoned up this afternoon requesting details on hiring the large function room for a wedding reception.'

Ashley was quite astounded by the revelation.

'*Really*? Do guidelines allow us to do that yet? I thought gatherings were limited.'

'I told them to put it in writing to you. I'm sure you'll enjoy finding out where we stand on parties. It seems enthusiasm to regain total normality has finally hit. Oh, thank goodness. Martine is here, at last.'

Ashley checked his phone once more.

Thankfully, close of play could finally be declared.

'Right then, Jeanette. I'm off. See you in the morning.'

*****

It was just approaching eight-fifteen when Ashley eventually walked through his own front door in Harrogate Close. The aroma of Carl's bolognaise sauce was instant ecstasy to the senses.

The creator of the wondrous fragrance peered around the lounge doorway to greet his man.

'So sorry, Carl. Mare of a shift. Suppers not ruined, is it?'

Carl sauntered up to Ashley and hugged him.

'Not at all. The secret is in the simmer. White wine?'

'My hero.'

'Problems at the hotel I take it?'

The pair reconvened in the kitchen as Carl pulled two glasses from the cupboard.

'Not problems as such. Just time-consuming and boring chores. Rotas. Costing. Recruiting. Anyway, that's shop talk. I say we empty this bottle between us then eat.'

'Great plan. Get your feet up in the lounge, Mister Hotel Manager of the Century.'

*****

'You're not checking your online fan club again, surely?'

Despite hearing Carl's mocking enquiry, Ashley didn't avert his gaze from the screen of his iPad.

'Just a quick check-in before lights out. I'm very tired and it all starts again in seven hours. Just replying to a few of today's well-wishers. Then I'm following you up. I promise.'

'Come on, it's gone eleven.'

Marjorie opted to join Ashley on the sofa to attract some attention her way.

It worked momentarily.

'Hello my fluffy. Has she been fed this evening, Carl?'

'Yes, about seven-ish. She can go out when we go to bed. And I'm locking the flap too. Half three this morning she was on the landing squawking her head off.'

Ashley engaged with the discerning stare of his long-furred feline and began to gently rub the top of her head with his fingertips.

'Oh, you're getting older though now, aren't you Margie. You can't help it can you?'

'I think she's going senile too. That is actually a medical cat condition, you know. Feline *nuttiness*. Very common.' Carl commented.

'I think we're all on a slippery slope regards mental well-being, to be honest. Covid has sent us all a bit bat-shit.'

Carl craned his neck around the lounge doorway.

'Right. I'll see you in Bedfordshire.'

'Yes! Five minutes more and I'm up there with you.'

As Carl made his weary ascent upstairs, Ashley yawned and confirmed the time to be eleven-seventeen. He was just about to shut off his iPad when his focus was drawn to a little red circle giving notification in the corner of the screen.

Without deliberation he opened it up, fully anticipating it to be work related.

It was a private message.

From his latest friend - Pauline Braithwaite.

Again, he thought little more of it and commenced reading it.

Her words were concise, direct and she had obviously put thought into the way it expressed.

It was sent nearly twenty-four hours ago.

Just after he had accepted her friend request the previous evening.

Having read through it once, he analysed it a second time, reading it in a soft whisper to encourage registration in his brain.

Dear Ashley,

Thank you for accepting me as your friend. It means so much. As you've probably gathered already, I'm new to this social media game. But it was necessary as I would never have had the confidence to ask you in person.

When we spoke a while back at the hotel, it confirmed to me that you are indeed as lovely and charming as your photograph suggested. I was very nervous to meet you but I'm so glad I found the courage.

Now that we are friends, I'd like to take things to the next stage.

Would you be agreeable to meeting me for a drink somewhere? You don't have to see it as a date as such, but I'm going to even if you don't.

You can choose when and where.

Just so long as you say yes, I don't really care what we do as a couple.

Looking forward to seeing you again very soon.

Yours always

Pauline xxx

Ashley resumed breathing and felt the cold clamminess of the skin on his back, buttocks, and palms.

The situation was beginning to expand into something unwelcome.

He realised he needed an instant solution to this potential dilemma.

Disappointing people was not usually in his life remit, but Pauline Braithwaite was firmly in line to being let down like a lead weight.

He should have felt slightly flattered, of course.

Yet instinct was causing an undeniable wariness.

But the sense of urgency regarding dealing with her in a courteous and convincing manner was paramount.

The response needed to be forthright yet gentle.

But now was not the time to reply.

He shut the iPad down and turned off the lounge lamp, before resigning himself to grabbing maybe five hours slumber.

That's if he managed to sleep.

Observing her master's departure, Marjorie sat contentedly in the kitchen, gratified that she had not in fact been locked out as per Ashley and Carl's plan.

She might decide to wake them from their dreams unexpectedly in the dead of night.

Then again, she might not.

She would make her choice later.

FIFTEEN

As with most other outlets falling under the nationwide umbrella of hospitality, the gradual resurgence in post-pandemic business was not without its teething problems.

Ashley had again been forcibly encamped in the office for most of his morning, combatting all manner of supply issues. From continuing linen shortages, misplaced catering orders, and a plea for spare furniture, through to a non-attending window cleaning company and decidedly late deliveries from the brewery.

All this aside from persevering to resolve the staffing rota conundrum and organise further recruitment.

Hernwood's status as current champion of the Ultimate Inn chain wasn't so much under threat but was taking a few unforeseen sucker punches to the ribs. This was causing knees to wobble behind the scenes.

Ashley Griffiths was however determined to iron out any potential hindrances.

He remained quietly adamant that the threat to his crown would not endure for long.

It was very frustrating that so many variables came into play to meeting the latest company criteria.

Power usage efficiency was now required for weekly record.

Box ticking for the site insurers was becoming beyond a joke.

Derek Evans now demanded weekly statements on occupancy trending in a sustained effort to maintain and upgrade Ultimate Inns' standing in the marketplace.

And aside all this, Ashley had scores of guests to personally oblige.

It was tough at the top, as some inciteful soul once said.

There were a lot of factors to balance, but despite his lack of practice lately, Ashley felt confident his personal acumen would prevail.

And his superiors evidently felt confident in him, too.

Subsequently, Ashley hadn't had much chance to invest any real thought into the issue of the date request from Pauline Braithwaite.

Work had consumed his brain space for most of the day thus far.

So, when he did finally afford himself opportunity for a quiet coffee and sat back in his chair to contemplate the issue, it couldn't have been coincidence that his office phone bleated into life.

He had mentioned the private message to no one.

It needed careful handling.

Even though his response was already set in concrete.

There was nothing to consider regarding the suggestion.

A case of thanks, but no…thank you very much.

He hadn't checked his online account before leaving the house that morning but hoped in very probable naivety that his lack of a response might help convey the seed of his feelings to her.

Sending the message - without sending a message.

Absorbed in thought, he completely forgot about the droning handset on his tabletop. He glanced idly at the caller display.

It was Jeanette.

'Yes, my dearest and most affectionate subordinate. How can I help you, now you have awoken me from my doze?'

Jeanette proceeded to snigger down the line.

'Sorry, Ashley. I know you said do not disturb three hours ago, but I had no choice. I thought you would like to know that you have a visitor downstairs in the foyer.'

He swiftly checked his desktop diary and a couple of windows on his computer.

'I've no appointments for once. It's not that blithering idiot from the window cleaning firm, is it? He's let us down once. He's shot it. Full of false promises. I bet he doesn't even own a bloody ladder!'

There was a troubling silence from Jeanette's end of the exchange.

Eventually, the Head of Reception decided to speak.

'No…it's not Mister Clearpane. But the lady in question is quite adamant that she needs to talk to you. I've set her up in the foyer with a coffee. How long shall you keep her waiting?'

Ashley's heartbeat instantly increased.

Alarm bells in the recesses of his conscience grew ever louder.

Surely not.

Surely it wasn't *her*?

But it must have been.

It wouldn't be anybody else.

It couldn't be, *could it*?

'Is it the same lady from a month or so back? Blonde bob? Short? Attractive?'

'It is, indeed, Ashley. The very same. Very astute guesswork.'

His bodily responses were confounding.

Why on earth should he be feeling a sudden sense of vulnerability?

Why were his hands shaking?

Enough of this ridiculous deliberation.

Time for the professional to kick in.

'Okay, Jeanette. Tell the lady I'll be down in two minutes.'

'Will do, boss.'

Placing the handset gently back in the cradle, Ashley noticed that he was beginning to perspire.

He stood up and adjusted his tie in the mirror. He returned to the desk and from the top drawer retrieved the unopened bottle of aftershave and slipped it into his jacket pocket.

He was now in little doubt that the gift was from her.

He decided he wasn't going mad after all.

Two and two did still equal four in the real world.

Nevertheless, as he exited the office, marched along the corridor, and pressed the relevant button on the lift panel, any slant of feigned assuredness began to desert him.

He was strangely fearful.

Ever so slightly concerned.

If only the visitor could have been the rep from the vending machine company. Or perhaps the bride-to-be wanting to inspect the function facilities. Oh, how he so wished it was the insurance man.

Anybody in the world would have sufficed.

Anybody but the person he thought he was about to confront.

The lift ground to a halt at reception level.

The steel doors slid aside for Ashley to make his reticent entrance into the foyer.

He glanced across to Jeanette who covertly guided him with a directional forefinger from behind her plastic screen.

He mouthed the words to her; *thank you.*

With absolutely no truth in the sentiment whatsoever.

But Jeanette remained blissfully ignorant of the current predicament facing her friend and colleague.

Ashley sincerely hoped it would stay that way as he stared unenthusiastically at the source of the problem.

No more than twenty yards away perched the disregarding figure of Pauline Braithwaite. Sipping her complimentary coffee and gazing at the summer sunshine that streamed through the windows.

Ashley strived to swallow a lump of trepidation as he commenced his light-footed approach.

Yet he sensed that she was somehow already aware of his proximity, as though she possessed eyes in the back of her head.

He gulped dryly again and through a very parched mouth delivered his opening gambit.

'Excuse me. Mrs Braithwaite? You requested to speak with me?'

Pauline Braithwaite did not immediately react to Ashley's presence. Her movements were measured - almost as if rehearsed.

She took another sip of her drink before gently setting down the cup and saucer on the table in front of her.

Then after a few seconds of grating indecision, she suddenly turned in her chair to face him, and displayed the widest possible, even forcibly exaggerated, smile.

'Hello again, Ashley. Now you *know* you shouldn't have to keep on calling me that. *Mrs Braithwaite*, indeed. Makes me sound like a schoolteacher! Please, Ashley. It's *Pauline* from now on. We are officially friends now, after all.'

Ashley grinned nervously in response.

Even though his instinct was instructing him to fight every single inherently natural reaction that might be summoned.

His habitual pleasantries needed to be suppressed in dealing with this delicate matter.

Her emerald eyes were almost mesmeric as she engaged him.

'Did you wish to take a walk with me, Ashley? Perhaps a drink somewhere more…private?'

This was beyond strange.

This was downright, off the chart, other-worldly.

'I can't really leave the site, I'm afraid. I'm working. We can chat here. In fact, here will be just fine.'

He was taken aback by her misguided familiarity.

Her use of *his* first name wouldn't have been an issue in any other scenario. After all, they barely knew each other.

But her presumption that he would just slot her into his schedule at a moment's notice was mildly annoying. She was not a client. She was not a supplier. She was not a paying guest.

And to all intents and purposes she was certainly not a friend.

Whether requested and accepted or otherwise.

He was under no obligation to interrupt business and accommodate her. Yet he understood that politically it was probably the wise move.

'To be absolutely honest with you, Mrs Braithwaite, I'm a little tied up with things upstairs. It's been a frantic day and doesn't look like letting me off the hook in any hurry. Perhaps you would prefer to liaise with reception, and they can make you an appointment time to save you waiting today?'

Pauline Braithwaite's features dulled significantly. Her eyes lost their sparkle as they narrowed. Pursing her lips, she clutched her handbag and rose to her feet. Her glare burrowed into him as she unloaded her reply through a gritted hiss.

'Come along now, Ashley. Friends shouldn't need appointments to see each other. You should always make allowances for social visits.'

Ashley's unyielding determination to avoid any unpleasantness was gradually being eroded by the irrefutable presence positioned before him.

But despite a simmering temper, he quickly regained perspective.

Diplomacy must rule in all disputes.

'Okay, Mrs Braithwaite. Would you prefer to come up to the office for a few minutes to discuss things? We can talk privately in there.'

With a nod of self-gratification, she obligingly followed Ashley away from the public rest area toward the lift doors.

Jeanette had been observing the encounter from her position behind the check-in desk. She was fully acquainted with the covert hand signal that Ashley exhibited to her just as he entered the lift.

Four fingers and his thumb splayed apart signalled that a rescue plan would be needed within five minutes.

A phone call and a fabricated excuse to extricate him from an uncertain circumstance.

This was unprecedented for everyone.

The Head of Reception watched with dubious concern as the lift doors enclosed her manager and his mysterious companion.

She commenced her personal five-minute countdown and alerted security to be on standby, dearly hoping that they would not be required to intervene at any point.

*****

Ashley entered the e-lock combination and pushed open the door to his office. Now feeling anxious at what might transpire during the pending encounter, he somehow maintained a façade of decorum.

'Please, do go in and take a seat, Mrs. Braithwaite. Can I get you a drink of something? Tea or coffee, perhaps?'

'No. No need, Ashley. Thank you. Just had my free one.'

She began to let her eyes wander around the room and its contents as Ashley shut the door.

'So, this is where you come and play when not in public view, is it? Very swish! Not many hotel managers get to enjoy an office of this size, you know. They are normally crammed into a box room behind reception somewhere.'

Ashley observed warily as she nimbly placed herself in the chair across the desk from his own. Her unnerving smile had returned.

Perhaps he had made the right decision taking her upstairs to the inner sanctum away from unnecessary scrutiny.

'I can see why they chose *you* as their poster boy. All looks very orderly and efficient. Proper little manager, aren't you?'

Her impish giggle made him squirm as he tentatively placed himself in his seat and rested elbows on the desktop.

He was in no mood for banter of any degree at that moment.

He took a decisive deep breath before attempting communication.

'Mrs. Braithwaite…'

'Erm…last warning…its *Pauline.* No more of this silly formality, Ashley. I told you. Now we are friends we can drop the barriers.'

Pretending to be amiable with her was a discomforting premise.

But Ashley figured that compliance might just do the trick in reaching a swift resolution to matters.

'Okay…*Pauline*…I'm afraid you have me at a distinct disadvantage.'

She continued to exhibit the incessant forced smirk.

But as her hypnotic eyes locked with his, he thought he detected the truth behind the mask.

'But why, Ashley? Whatever do you mean?'

He was already on the verge of allowing his brewing despair to brim over. It was clear that her troublesome act was something she was willing to sustain.

'Can you explain to me what exactly it is that you came here to discuss with me, today? Because you see…I haven't got the slightest idea of what it could be that we need to talk about?'

He felt his heart pounding against his breastbone as he watched her.

Pauline Braithwaite placed her handbag on the desktop, pressed her back into the leather guest chair, and in an obvious gesture of feminine suggestion, she slowly crossed her legs.

'This room is so relaxing! I'm not surprised you like it up here. So…what is it, in *particular*, that is confusing you, Ashley?'

He had already decided to abandon the policy of cordiality.

It was blindingly evident that it would cut no ice with her.

'Do you wish to lodge a complaint about the hotel?'

Her indulgent eyes widened in feigned surprise.

'What? Of course not, *silly*! I stayed here you know. One night. Two or three weeks ago. I forget the date. It's very nice. No…there are no issues from me about the place, I can assure you of that much.'

Ashley's jagged mindset was evolving with every passing second.

Confused anger of two minutes earlier had been eclipsed by an inner desire to escort her out of the premises forthwith.

And never to set eyes on her again.

To say he found Pauline Braithwaite to be odd was the understatement of the very odd year so far. Nevertheless, he was tasked with bottoming out this nonsense as soon as possible.

'You left me a gift?'

Her expression adjusted to convey puzzlement.

So, he persevered once again with the pragmatic approach.

'The *aftershave*? The aftershave you gave to security that morning when you checked out?' That *was* you, wasn't it? Why would you do that?'

Pauline Braithwaite giggled quietly and put her hand to her mouth as if suddenly assailed by embarrassment.

'Well…I didn't want to just leave it lying around. And the receptionist wasn't at her station. So…'

Ashley's demeanour switched again, from a polite tolerance to suppressed fury.

He leaned further across the desk.

'No! I mean why would you buy me a gift in the *first* place?'

'Well...to show my heartfelt appreciation, of course. I knew which scent you liked. I detected it on you the first time we met downstairs.'

Ashley was now bewildered by inner frustration.

Either she was a very commendable actress, or she was a stark raving lunatic. She evidently saw nothing unusual in her conduct. It briefly occurred to him that perhaps he himself should put on an act.

A front of warmth and gratitude, so to speak.

'Don't tell me I picked the wrong one. I can change it if it's not your favourite, Ashley. They are all so similar these days. I've still got the receipt. It's no trouble, honestly.'

The conversation was digressing toward the very territory Ashley was determined to avoid. The dialogue needed reining in if possible.

But she was no fool.

She knew her game.

Ashley only wished he was aware of the rules, too.

'Don't get me wrong, Pauline. It was a lovely gesture. Much appreciated. But you didn't have to. Guests aren't obliged to buy their hosts gifts. And besides which, I'm not allowed to accept it, anyway. Gratuities aren't permitted in my contract.'

Now it was her turn to evolve the mood.

She uncrossed her legs as mild scorn etched itself into her visage.

'*Gratuities*? Hell, Ashley. It wasn't meant to be received as a *tip*, for Christ's sake. It was a token of affection. Friend to friend. That's okay, isn't it? Or does your contract also prohibit you from having friends that want to buy you nice things?'

Her apparent misconception of accepted sociability was now bordering on being a real cause for alarm.

Yet Ashley summoned the wherewithal to uphold his pretence of calm.

'Yes, of course it's okay. But Pauline...you and I...we don't really *know* one another as friends. Connecting online doesn't qualify us as bosom buddies to any degree, does it?'

If any line should adequately ruffle her feathers, it would be that one.

She now leaned across the desk toward him, her mask of disapproval now accordingly adjusting with elements of apparent hurt and rejection.

'Well, Mister Ashley Griffiths...I seem to have misinterpreted matters. But I believe that I have seen and heard enough of you to want to count you as a friend. So, sue me for liking you? I'm very sorry if you don't feel the same way.'

The very last thing he wanted to do was cause the upset that seemingly now transpired before his very eyes.

Ashley shook his head and raised his hands as a motion to plea.

'Okay. Let's draw a line under what's already happened. But we are going round in circles. I ask you once again...can you please tell me why you are here today?'

Pauline Braithwaite seemed on the verge of tears.

But Ashley was already convinced that any portrayal of distress she exhibited was likely to be false.

'Well...to find out where we are going, of course.'

Ashley was now perplexed once again as her demeanour suddenly lurched back to one of positivity.

'Where we are *going*? What...you mean *we*...as in the two of us?'

She cackled as her green eyes rolled toward the ceiling and then engaged back with Ashley's.

'On our *date*, silly! I messaged you to pick a time and place for a drink. I know you saw it. But you haven't replied yet. So, I thought I'd better pop along in person to finalise arrangements with you.'

Ashley was succumbing to the grip of mental and physical tension. It was like being trapped in a spider's web. Every time he went to make an evasive manoeuvre, she would ably pounce and corner him.

He observed her contorting features. The rapid changes in her disposition were way beyond normal. Almost at the flick of a switch, she could become someone else with a different persona.

And now, unfortunately for him, she donned the guise of a woman bursting with unwarranted excitement.

Whilst his own position was becoming more untenable with each passing second.

'Pauline…I don't know what it was that gave you the impression we would be going out on a date but I'm pretty certain the signals haven't come from me.'

Her perfect teeth gleamed as her scarlet lips then puckered.

'Now, Ashley…don't go all coy on me. You're just keeping me hanging in suspense you little tease. So…where shall we go? Your choice. What night are you free? Tonight?'

Ashley left his seat and perched on the corner of the desk nearest to her. His dilemma was now seemingly multi-faceted. His dual reserves of compassion and humility were being swiftly drained.

How was he going to put her fire out without becoming overtly objectionable in the process?

And even if he did employ a sterner approach, would it solve the problem, anyway?

She became visibly enticed by his physical proximity.

The simple act of getting out of his chair was already proving to be another piece of bad judgement on his part.

'Listen to me, Pauline. A date involving you and I is totally out of the question.'

Despite his hopes, the commencement of the bombshell news did not serve to deter her in any way.

She raised an interruptive index finger. Ashley briefly focussed on her immaculate pink nail varnish before he re-engaged with her reply.

'I understand you might be nervous, Ashley. Hell, I know I am! I haven't been on a date for years! But it will be so perfect. Just the two of us…getting to know one another even better than we do already.'

The eerie and constrictive atmosphere was suddenly disturbed by the drone of Ashley's desk phone. Jolting to attention, he moved to his seat once again and lifted the handset.

Pauline Braithwaite patiently observed, fully aware of the charade being performed for her benefit.

'Okay Jeanette. Yes. Thank you.'

He tentatively replaced the receiver in its cradle before reverting focus to his unwelcome companion.

'I've got to go down to the restaurant. There's a problem needs my urgent attention.'

Pauline Braithwaite smirked as her gaze rested on the sun-drenched scene beyond the window.

'Come on, Ashley. You can't kid a kidder. That wasn't the chef, was it? That was your pensionable receptionist complying with your prior instruction to hook you out of here. Luckily for you...I'm not offended. She's mutton dressed as lamb, by the way.'

Ashley had now lost patience with the disconcerting, presumptive and frankly rude woman seated opposite.

'There's no need to be like that, is there? I *do* need to be in the kitchen. And I need to go there *now*.'

'Yes, Ashley...whatever you say. So...this date of ours...'

Ashley rubbed his forehead and gritted his teeth amid a moment's contemplation.

'Pauline...it's not going to happen. I have a long-term relationship with my partner and I'm very happy. I'm sorry. Okay?'

Far from feeling rejected, she now adorned her features with a hint of mischief.

'Don't apologise, Ashley. We can work around this. I'll be your other woman. Your...bit on the side. Casual? No strings? She won't even know I exist.'

Ashley had now had his growing suspicions affirmed.

His realisation had been thankfully swift.

This woman was an absolute, undeniable, misguided, crank.

He had tolerated her ridiculous gibberish for far longer than was justified.

Tempers both sides of the line now began to fray.

'No...you don't understand. Even if I was single, you wouldn't be my type.'

His voice wavered as he prepared his scuppering revelation.

Her tone suddenly developed a sharper edge.

'Why? What do you mean by that? Am I not attractive enough? Too old? I can have a makeover. I'll make it my mission to impress you so you can't resist me. You can't wriggle away that easily, Ashley.'

There was seemingly no stopping this deranged and deluded individual.

Surely once he delivered the pivotal final detail then she would have to accept that her crazed venture is at an end.

'I'll spell it out for you, shall I? Before you leave my office, once and for all. I'm gay. Okay? You can't interpret that any other way than its original form. I repeat. I'm *gay*. So, heterosexual relations with *anybody* are automatically deemed out of the question. A date with you…is out of the question. Us ever meeting again…is out of the question. Is the picture clear enough for you now…*Mrs. Braithwaite*?'

Her face instantly converted into an ice cold covering for her misplaced mindset.

Seconds of silence ensued as she considered Ashley's statement.

For his part, he now felt undiluted embarrassment at having to fend off a stranger's interest with such a revelation about his personal life, but it was seemingly his last means of defence.

Nearly half a minute passed as he allowed her time for registration of the undeniable facts.

And then, she put the striking smirk back in place, before retrieving her handbag from the desktop and rising to her feet.

Ashley remained unsure of what kind of conclusion he should expect to their impromptu conference.

His discomfort was eased slightly as she turned smoothly and made her way to the door.

He remained rooted at the desk.

Mistrust was his only guardian as she reached for the handle and predictably began to offer her parting shot.

She did not look at him as she spoke.

'How…incredibly foolish of me, Ashley. I do apologise for placing you under such pressure. I feel awkward and slightly ashamed of myself.'

Ashley now shifted position to join her by the exit and escort her away from the place as soon as possible.

'It's quite alright. Let's chalk it up as a simple misunderstanding, shall we? Let me take you down to reception.'

Pauline Braithwaite pulled open the door and stepped into the deserted outer corridor.

Her display of discernible disappointment remained fixed in place as she finally turned once again to engage with him.

Her tone was now meeker.

Almost humble.

'No need to hold my hand, Ashley. I'll find my own way out. You'd better go and find out what the chef wants…hadn't you…'

A surge of cleansing relief washed through Ashley as she strutted steadily to the lift doors and pressed for the ground floor.

'Yes…yes, I had. Well…take care, Pauline. And for what it's worth, I'm glad you paid a visit today and that we had this conversation.'

The lift doors slid apart.

She entered the compartment and promptly spun on her heel, before removing her smile and throwing Ashley an ambiguous farewell.

'That's quite alright. It was good to talk. I'll be seeing you sometime then, Ashley.'

A chill went down his spine as he observed her become enclosed by the elevator doors. To be assured of her departure, he watched the elevator's digital read-out drop to the reception floor.

He leaned back against the wall of the corridor and stared vacantly into space. His mind traced her potential steps as he breathed slowly.

She should be out of the lift by now.

She would have passed the check-in desk.

And within ten seconds she would be outside in the car park.

And then be off site.

Hopefully, for good.

He returned to the office and closed the door.

His skin felt damp under his shirt.

Feeling the weight of the aftershave bottle in his jacket pocket, he pulled it free and studied it in his hand. He had fully intended to give it back to her. But now, its seconded destination would be the waste bin.

A symbolic gesture of finality.

He sat down behind the desk with only one prevailing thought.

Lifting the handset, he punched in the number for reception.

His contemplation of the madness just experienced was interrupted by Jeanette on the end of the line.

'Yes, your Highness?'

Her voice was instantly calming.

'That lady I took to my office. Has she passed you by, yet?'

'Your visitor has indeed left the building. Are you okay?'

Despite his voice being slightly laboured, his mind was gradually re-aligning to rationality. He struggled to summon the appropriate response to Jeanette's concern.

Finally, he conjured a reply to abate the naturally protective Head of Reception.

'Yes, Jeanette. I'm fine. Thank you.'

'Tell me to mind my own business if you want, but who is she?'

What did he do now?

Lie? Concoct a story to a dearly respected colleague?

He felt at that moment there was no other option.

'Just a sales rep. Pitching a new cleaning contract. I've told her we are quite satisfied with the cleaning team we currently have. So, I don't think she'll be back anytime soon.'

The pause in the dialogue hinted at Jeanette's digestion of Ashley's explanation.

'Okay, Ash. Here if you need me. As always.'

He listened to her hang up as he set the handset back in its cradle.

And then quietly stared into a disconcerting, uncertain space.

SIXTEEN

'I've been over to speak to her, but she insists she doesn't need any assistance with anything. And I can't ask her to leave because she is on a public footpath.'

Security operative Lee Pinder pointed across the car park toward the entrance gates.

Ashley squinted in the suggested direction as they both observed from the foyer main doors.

The identity of the woman who had been loitering all afternoon soon became worryingly clear.

If nothing else, Pauline Braithwaite was persistent in her quest.

Whatever that quest was remained a mystery known only to her.

And it was painfully obvious that the message she had received on her previous visit forty-eight hours earlier, had not been undertaken.

Unlike the outfit of leggings and t-shirt the other day, she was now attired to impress in a short black dress, matching heels, and cream-coloured jacket.

Ashley became nervous as he pondered the options.

Which at that moment were minimal.

'Well Lee, you've done all you can. Just leave her be. She's not breaking the law or anything. Not much else we can do, is there?'

The security guard looked at his manager quizzically.

'Bit weird though? It's the same woman who left the present for you a while back, isn't it?'

'Indeed, it is. Maybe she's waiting for a friend.'

'I've been watching her, Ashley. She keeps looking toward reception as though she's expecting someone to emerge. At least three hours she's been there. She'll disappear for a bit, then come back. She perhaps wants to speak to you?'

Ashley checked his watch.

Nearly six-thirty.

Both men were due to depart site soon.

'Who is on incoming night security, Lee?'

'John Bonsall, this week.'

'Is he likely to be here, yet?'

'I haven't set eyes on him, but he might have come in the back way and be in our changing room.'

Lee's understandable fascination with the woman beyond the gates continued.

'Maybe you should go and have a word, Ashley. If you think it's *you* that she is trying to contact. I tell you what though…she's lovely looking. A real stunner.'

There was little scope for Ashley to contribute to a debate about her looks. But maybe it would be a potent idea to go and communicate as a measure of courtesy, if not appeasement.

And then sanity prevailed.

His most recent encounter with Pauline Braithwaite ended on a particularly sour note. He had no intention of fanning the flames of her dubious curiosity if possible.

It would have been akin to an act of cruelty.

'Leave her alone, Lee. Let's get ready to ship out of here. If she does need help, then she can come into reception.'

*****

It was pushing seven-forty-five when Ashley finally accomplished his last missions of the day and shut down his computer.

Tomorrow's linen delivery was confirmed.

The stock check in the kitchen was completed and the order submitted to the wholesalers.

A zoom meeting to discuss advertising varying operative vacancies had been rather fruitless. The maids' team was woefully short-handed. Derek Evans didn't seem to grasp the basic point that a skeleton room service crew on daily overtime was proving a far costlier exercise than recruiting more bodies. Never mind the subsequent backlog.

It was particularly frustrating for Ashley as Derek was simultaneously critical of the overtime requests being submitted by Hernwood. He didn't seem able to marry the two issues together.

Derek had pledged to review the situation at the 'earliest opportunity'.

Which was French for *don't hold your breath*.

It was no small relief to be vacating the building.

Not the best of days at the office.

Ashley needed to get home and would hopefully be in time to rescue another sublime supper that Carl had lovingly prepared.

*****

He bid a good evening to the night receptionist, Martine, and passed John Bonsall on his return from the first evening walk around.

All seemed in good order as Ashley descended the steps and made his way across the car park. Although barely into September, Autumn's early shroud seemed relatively potent that evening as rapidly diminishing daylight encouraged a stiff breeze.

The security lamps cast an intermittent amber glow as Ashley placed his jacket, computer, and briefcase in the boot of the car.

He instinctively turned his head to scrutinise the site entrance gates.

The sun had cast its last rays and the wrought-iron gates looked to frame a comparatively bleak and lifeless main road beyond.

His chest thumped as he continued his determined observation.

There was no sign of her. Relief descended around him.

He hoped she had become bored.

It seemed appropriate to refrain from telling the security team her possible reasons for standing at the entrance all afternoon.

To depict her as an unwanted admirer was not something Ashley desired to become common knowledge.

It may have bemused the young security guard, but Ashley saw through her presence immediately.

She was there purely for the purpose of intimidation.

And there was nothing anyone could do about the fact.

Ashley slipped behind the wheel and started the engine.

His eyes still scanning everywhere as he selected first gear.

He navigated with certain caution between the rows of guests' vehicles until reaching the exit and applying the brake.

He employed an indicator as an approaching car sped into, through and out of the beam of his headlights. It wasn't yet completely dark but the illumination from the car was necessary.

He looked left.

He looked right.

He looked left once more.

And it was at that moment when he prepared to lift the clutch that she revealed herself once again.

Emerging from the dancing shadows across the street, Pauline Braithwaite posed with her mobile phone in hand, as if in position to take a photograph of Ashley's departure.

His pulse began to race, yet the crumb of comfort came in the knowledge that whilst he could clearly see *her*, Pauline Braithwaite could not ably detect his reaction of sheer horror due to the glare of the headlamps.

As acute fear crept over his shoulder, he looked left once more.

Then looked right again.

Then he released the clutch.

As the car entered the main trunk road the headlights lit up the tarmac in front, narrowly avoiding the chance of portraying her in all her threatening glory.

But inevitably, his attention was drawn to glimpse her as he passed by.

Only briefly, but the image was disconcerting enough.

She carried a haunting expression in the encroaching darkness.

Almost as though she felt gratified by the perceived sense of panic she had induced in her target.

Ashley pressed the throttle to the floor and sailed away from the scene.

Such was his desperation to escape the moment, he mistimed the gear change. The engine growled and screamed in opposition as he quickly arrived at the next junction of traffic lights.

He brought the car to a juddering halt and selected neutral.

Ashley's next instinctive move was to study the rear-view mirror.

But this proved to be a futile exercise.

It was getting too dark to properly ascertain shapes and movement.

And if she had chosen to pursue him on foot, she would be free to do so undetected, as a car following Ashley's dazzled its blinding main beams into the glass of the mirror.

He desperately crunched into first gear again as the traffic lights evolved to green.

He was liberated once more. But only in the physical sense.

He was still shackled by his thoughts.

And the one prevailing worry now, was that the apparently rational and concise discussion he shared with Pauline Braithwaite only two days ago, had not been absorbed by her in the manner he had hoped and anticipated.

She had obviously not been dissuaded from her dubious mission.

Not one iota.

In fact, Ashley's noble effort had only served to ramp up the game.

She had determinedly refused to accept the sentiment he had clearly explained. And it was becoming steadily obvious that she would require a more stringent method of persuasion if the current situation was to reach a sensible end.

Not to mention eradicating the now regular signals of stress and strain that were welling with increasing regularity in the mind and body of Ashley Griffiths.

The twilight horizon evolved from orange grey into a sinister blackness. And accompanying the blackness, clouds of foreboding began to swirl in the conscience of Ashley Griffiths.

SEVENTEEN

Up until this point, Ashley had been determined to keep his own counsel regarding his most unenviable personal conundrum.

But the private burden was steadily becoming overbearing.

The drive home had gone some way to cement the conviction that it might be time to confess the situation.

The prospect of involving Carl had weighed heavily on Ashley's mind for a couple of days and he wasn't even sure how to begin unveiling such an unpleasant scenario.

As emotive as it might prove for Ashley, coupled with this was the concern regarding Carl's potential response. The quandary was uncanny. Entering Harrogate Close instilled him with dread.

He reluctantly locked the car and had no sooner reached the front door of number thirty-nine when it was duly opened by a very cheery greeter.

'Well hello at last, Mister Hollywood! I was about to phone Interpol to start a search. How was your day in the land of high living?'

Ashley's heart sank as he entered the hallway and forced a smirk in response to Carl's buoyant quip. Yet his nerves were already getting the better of him as he kissed Carl on the lips and took off his shoes at the bottom of the stairs.

A prompt avoidance of discussing his day was summonsed but was highly unlikely to hold out.

'Something smells good. Could that be your fantastic beef chilli floating under my nose?'

Carl chuckled affectionately.

'It is indeed. With extra garlic and herbs. The sauce is done. Just got to cook the rice when you give the nod. Poppadoms too!'

Ashley stood in his stockinged feet and the pair embraced.

'Wine first, then. I'm ready for a drink.' muttered Ashley into Carl's shoulder.

*****

The salient points of each other's day were exchanged on the settee as the bottle of white was readily quaffed. Ashley still had reservations about how to commence his pressing admission.

The intake of Dutch Courage did absolutely nothing to ease his trepidation as he entered the kitchen and observed the saucepan of chilli on the hob.

'How long until we can eat, do you think?'

'That depends when you want to, Ash. Its nearly nine-thirty. The rice will only take ten minutes.'

Ashley duly retrieved more wine from the cooler and reclaimed his seat next to Carl and peeled the seal from the new bottle.

'Okay. I need to talk to you about something before supper.'

Carl offered an exaggerated squeal and hunched his feet up under his knees.

'Ooh, this sounds exciting.'

Ashley re-filled their glasses.

'Yes…well…you might change your mind in a minute when I've told you…'

Marjorie had entered the fray and in obliging her typical feline instincts she parked herself next to the cooker in anticipation of some exotic treat.

However, having seen her human parents reclining in the lounge, she then opted to join them, figuring any potential morsel might be a while in coming yet. She promptly curled up on the hearth rug and kept her ears firmly open.

Ashley was now overcome with crawling anxiety.

Carl detected the air of concern that had enveloped the room and figured that humour was best left on the back burner for the moment.

'Ash…you look worried about something. And by default, that means *I'm* worried. What's wrong?'

Ashley stared hopelessly at Marjorie and gulped a mouthful of wine whilst pondering the next sentence. Marjorie simply stared back, offering absolutely no assistance whatsoever.

'Cast your mind back, Carl. Three weeks. Perhaps a month.'

'Crickey that's a test, in itself! Give us a hint...which subject are we veering towards?'

Ashley sampled more from his glass. They had been overindulging in the demon drink of late. But alcoholic lubrication was pivotal in loosening Ashley's stifled demeanour.

This conversation was already proving even more uncomfortable than he had expected it to be.

'Some weeks after the promo campaign went live at work. I got that friend request online.'

Carl chuckled and conveyed a mistimed jibe.

'You must have had twenty messages a day this past two months. Narrow it down for me.'

Marjorie stretched and rose onto all four paws before retreating to the kitchen once more. A symbolic gesture of desertion if ever there was one. Ashley continued despite wanting to kick the cat.

'We were here at home. I had just changed my profile photo to the works' promo image for a laugh. It was the only friend request I had that day.'

Carl's features screwed up into a mask of concentration before his eyes widened with pleasure that the power of memory had not evaporated altogether.

'Yes! The woman with no history or images. Mrs. Nobody. I can't remember her name off the bat. Did you accept her? I can't recall you mentioning her since that night.'

Ashley did appreciate his partner's inherent inclination toward light-heartedness, but unbeknown to Carl, making a joke of the matter was certainly not appropriate.

'Pauline...Pauline Braithwaite.' Ashley muttered with considered reluctance and a large pinch of distaste.

Carl jovially pointed upward to the ceiling in mock celebration of familiarity with the name.

'Of course, it was! How is the old dear? Has she started your fan club, yet?'

Ashley squirmed inside as he realised how close Carl's quip had come to the mark.

No going back now. Carl deserved to hear the whole story in full.

'Let's just say to cut a long story short that she got carried away with a crazy idea of her own invention.'

Carl was understandably puzzled but was keen to listen.

'I don't want the cryptic version. Give me the whole works.'

'Are you sure you want to hear the full version?'

'Listen…if you don't hurry up and spit it out, we will be having chilli for *breakfast*. How bad can it be? I don't grasp how there can be a problem and I don't get what this woman has got to do with anything. So, from the top if you will…and make it snappy cos I'm starving. And so is Marjorie.'

Ashley figured he may as well get straight to the point in the vein belief that Carl might see the funny side and it will be dismissed as a load of childish nonsense.

There was no way of predicting Carl's reaction, and yet there was only one way to find out what that reaction might be.

'I think…well…I know for a *fact*…that she has taken a bit of a fancy to me…'

Carl stared at Ashley with absolutely no giveaway clue as to how the revelation would hit ground.

Expansion on the details was going to be required.

'She's been to the hotel…to see me at work. She messaged me online. She wanted a bloody *date*!'

Carl continued to divulge nothing aside exhibiting slight confusion and a delivering mocking question.

'A *date*? What? With *you*, you mean?'

'Well, who the hell *else*? Yes! *Me*!'

Carl adjusted position on the settee and reached for his own glass.

'Wow! How did you jump *that* little hurdle, then?'

Ashley observed Carl's growing mirth. Perversely it was a source of relief to see the response of barely concealed amusement from the man he loved.

But for Ashley, the funny side of the issue remained somewhat elusive, to say the least.

'Look…it's no laughing matter!'

Now straining to contain his giggles, Carl ventured the supposedly natural query.

'So, big boy…what did you say to her?'

'Well…I had to let her down very gently, didn't I.'

'How very gallant of you. Then what happened?'

It was quite obvious that Ashley's partner of five years was now verging on a bone-shaking fit of hysteria regarding the very concept.

Pauline Braithwaite was in theory a rival to Carl in vying for Ashley's affections. After days of earnest worry about disclosing the episode to the man he trusted more than anybody in the world, he was now being sniggered at.

'She even stayed the night at the hotel and left me a present the next morning before I got on site. That bloody aftershave I wear! She guessed the brand just from being near me! My favourite Cologne that you get me every Christmas!'

Finally, Carl's mischievous grin dispersed at hearing about the gift.

But humour was still lingering in the air.

And Carl was doing his level best to extract the funny side.

'Well, she'd give Columbo a run for his money, that's all I can say!'

'Yes, she would! But it was only on her *third* visit that she admitted to it!'

Carl reached down for the fresh wine bottle and pulled a face of disappointment on seeing it was already less than half full.

'*Third* visit?'

'Yes! *Third*! She pitched up two days ago wanting to know why I hadn't replied to her message and why I wouldn't go on a date with her. So, I explained in simple terms that she was barking up the wrong tree.'

Now Carl let his chuckle resonate freely around the room.

'Well. She sounds barking alright. So, what's the problem? She now knows you are ring-fenced. Surely the issue is solved?'

Ashley was momentarily distracted by Marjorie's return from another impatient kitchen inspection. It was only now, after offloading the subject onto someone else, that it dawned on him how farcical it all was.

A bizarre encounter that was likely all done and dusted.

For Ashley, the penny had only just dropped.

He suddenly felt he had been worrying for nothing.

About…*nothing*.

'The thing is, Carl, she wasn't prepared to accept no for an answer. In fact, she became quite offended by the harsh facts of the matter. As though being attracted to a gay man was something she felt aggrieved about. As if I had invented it specifically to infuriate her.'

Carl hunched his knees back under his chin and gazed into his glass.

'I think you're overthinking this whole damned silliness. Trust me, Ash. She'll have got the message that you're a no-go zone. Most women would give up the ghost straight away. She made a mistake. Pure and simple. Probably very embarrassed if truth be known.'

Ashley leaned closer to Carl and engaged with his deep brown eyes. It wasn't very often that such a serious natured conversation took place between them. But Carl could detect Ashley's authentic concerns and was appreciative that he had been privy to them.

'Well, yesterday I would have agreed with you totally. But get this. She was hanging around the hotel all afternoon.'

'*Today*, you mean?'

'Yes. And she was still there when I left. Out on the street. All dolled up ready for a party. It was getting dark for Christ's sake!'

'What was she *doing*? Why would she not get the message? You've been polite enough by the sounds of it. Some blokes would have lost their rag or got the coppers involved.'

Ashley nodded sullenly. His glass now empty, again.

'I can't predict her, Carl. To be honest it's given me a few sleepless nights.'

'Has she tried to speak to you since getting the brush off?'

'No. She hasn't been back inside the hotel. I might start parking round the back so she can't see I'm at work.'

Carl stretched out his legs and sat back on the sofa with the zaniest expression on his face. Ashley still couldn't decipher how seriously his partner was taking the disclosure. But the next exchange of words would surely put his responses to the test.

'And so exactly how long have you been whittling yourself about this shit, Ashley?'

'I wasn't really worried at all until the last couple of days. Then when it got up close and personal in my office I started to buckle. I knew then I needed to tell you.'

'Sounds to me like you've handled her superbly. I mean, what else *could* you have done?'

'Look…I know I've got all the managerial training and all the charm to turn on when it matters…but I must have missed the class that dealt with how to control freak-head fanatics.'

Thankfully, Carl emitted a genuine belly laugh at hearing Ashley's last remark.

He turned to his man and donned a serious expression.

'If it's any consolation…I'm *glad* you confided in me. And I hope you feel much better for having done so.'

Ashley reached across and grasped Carl's left hand in his right.

'Do you really mean that, Carl? You're not angry with me?'

Carl shuffled across the settee into Ashley's space and put his arm around his shoulders.

'What are you like, Ashley Griffiths? Of course, I'm not *angry*. None of this is your fault, is it?'

'No. I know. But if I hadn't agreed to be part of the bloody hotel campaign then…'

'Ahh…no! I will stop you there! You made the right decision about the promotion campaign. And it's been a *brilliant* success so far. Hundreds of lovely people had told you how great you are. It's the law of averages that dictates one negative experience out of all those, isn't it.

One nutter out of a thousand sane folk shouldn't make you doubt yourself.'

Ashley felt protected within the loving arms of Carl.

He no longer carried the weighty depression of earlier.

In fact, it was almost as though the problem had never arisen in the first place.

'I suppose I've made a mountain out of a molehill, haven't I?'

'Well, you wouldn't be *you* if you hadn't started panicking. Come here you daft bugger.'

They hugged one another tightly on the sofa. Contentment had been fully restored within the walls of number thirty-nine.

Carl drew away and offered further words of solace.

'No more worrying. And if this woman persists on being slow on the uptake, then that's *her* problem. Not yours. Okay?'

They kissed firmly and meaningfully.

'Yes…you're exactly right. As you always seem to be. Thank you for understanding and thank you for being my rock. What would I do without you, Carl Davis?'

There was a pleasant pause in the conversation before Carl added a final thought.

'I tell you one thing I *have* learned in the last hour.'

'What's that then?'

'I can see now why movie stars have to use bodyguards everywhere they go!'

At last Ashley unleashed a pent-up bout of liberating, glorious laughter.

'Right then, Carlos.'

'Right then what, Ash?'

'Better get that rice on. Its nearly bedtime.'

*****

Outside in Harrogate Close, the swelling breeze began to dispatch leaves from branches.

The resulting fall eventually gathering as small clumps in the darkest corners of the estate.

The amber glow of the streetlamps formed alternate patches of light and shadow, playing their trick on the eye of the unwary.

The warmth and unity emanating from the house containing Ashley, Carl and their cat named Marjorie, was enough to brighten even the grimmest of temperaments.

The street was a scene depicting nature's whim, yet aside the squall of the wind, movement was seemingly nil.

And yet, in the most blackened, unseen reaches of the neighbourhood, life did indeed stir.

Nocturnal activity was about to commence, with scavengers embarking on their ritual search for scraps.

And unknown to the typical nightly troupe, an unfamiliar addition was silently poised.

Like them; concealed within the gloom.

Like them; a predator on the prowl.

Exercising patience and tenacity.

As she deliberated on her motive for causing wanton, emotional intrusion.

Within the walls of number thirty-nine, the familial contentment was about to be disturbed.

As the hunter lay in wait.

EIGHTEEN

Carl straightened Ashley's tie before withdrawing a couple of paces. He scrutinised the finished article and presented an affirming thumbs-up.

'Will I do, then? smirked Ashley, glancing briefly at the dress mirror.

'Ten out of ten as per usual.' Carl beamed, as he brushed some imaginary dust from Ashley's shoulder before planting a farewell kiss on his lips.

'It's the big meeting today, isn't it?'

'It certainly is. Post pandemic recovery appraisal. Derek and all his operations managers. And no doubt a few other big wigs to stir the pot along the way. Though I hate zoom meetings. I always struggle to get the blessed thing to work. Technology always makes me arrive later than everyone else. Could do with taking you with me!' giggled Ashley, still preening over his reflection.

The sun continued to bless a fair ration of warmth despite it being late September. The forecast for an Indian summer appeared to be on the money so far.

Ashley unlocked the car and placed his suit jacket, laptop, and briefcase on the back seat, before strapping himself in behind the wheel.

Carl shuffled onto the driveway in his pyjamas as Ashley wound down his window.

'Right then, Carlos. I'll see you tonight. Could be anytime between five and eight. Probably nearer the latter. It will likely take me that long to link up to the bloody meeting.'

Carl laughed heartily as he observed Ashley's car reverse off the drive and head away through the estate. He stood and took note of the abiding surroundings that they had been blessed with.

The Maygreen Estate had only been constructed just before the pair became an official item.

Ashley bought the plot five years earlier before a brick was even laid. There was a certain stigma attached to newbuild residential areas, with critics citing lack of character, high prices and certainly a lack of internal space.

But over the recent years, it had developed into a very civilised and welcoming community. Families mixed with single occupants and retired couples. It was a most pleasant environment.

Carl took a few moments to absorb the scene and his good fortune, before retreating indoors to begin his own working day.

Never did it enter his head that the apparently hospitable exterior beyond would be harbouring a concealed and deranged observer.

*****

Having navigated his way toward the dual carriageway, Ashley joined the growling thrum of early rush hour traffic heading toward the city centre.

The old through road was flanked by acres of countryside which were a shimmering sight for sore eyes this time of year. Yet even in the depths of winter the rural vista beyond the car windows was a welcome tonic preceding the entry into urban territory.

Ashley fell in love with the location at first site. Home was far enough out of town to offer seclusion, yet close enough to amenities that avoided the potential sensation of isolation.

Plus of course, the journey to and from Hernwood provided obvious positives with the views.

The road began to widen as it accommodated the rapidly increasing volumes of cars and lorries. Multiple lanes split traffic either side of and through the middle of town.

Perversely, maintaining a gridlocked course on the one-way system was the most efficient way of reaching the hotel. Ashley found the tried and tested truth bemusing but taking either by-pass to get to his destination entailed a significant increase in the duration of the journey.

Whenever possible, he preferred the average thirty-five minutes behind the wheel, which meant taking the most direct route on offer.

The ring roads bumped the travelling time toward the hour mark.

Crazy times, indeed.

He could ably cope with the horns and the impatience of fellow road users, so long as he got where he wanted to be in the shortest span of time. This inclination to get to work sooner rather than later had reignited itself since his return from being Furloughed.

With former lockdown restrictions now being eased considerably, this new approach had taken him quite by surprise during the previous weeks. The vibe at work was upbeat.

The few pressures and constraints of resuming business were balanced out by the upbeat approach of his colleagues and paying public alike.

Most folk seemed to be singing from the same hymn sheet when it came to claiming back the familiarity of life that all had been accustomed to pre-Covid.

The recent positivity from staff and guests had been infectious and addictive. Though Ashley would only admit under extreme duress that the rejuvenation of the Ultimate Inn chain was possibly down to him. The reticence he felt at the outset soon evaporated as the wheels of promotion began to turn.

And despite the one obvious fly in the ointment, he had no regrets whatsoever.

The seven-a.m. radio station news bulletin brought a temporary interruption to the stream of pop and rock music. Ashley turned up the volume on the car stereo as he came to a stop at the first of four sets of traffic lights on route.

He could willingly tolerate the stop-start to the flow of driving in. He knew the hotel was only fifteen minutes away. He had time to spare.

As the car idled in lane his gaze was drawn through the windscreen and the rear end of a forty-foot container wagon. His attention took itself to the view through his own door window and then the passenger side.

There was nothing of note to catch his interest, aside white van man and a very precariously loaded scrap metal trailer.

The lights changed to green up ahead and the snaking line of vehicles began to shift forward.

Ashley selected first gear and found his bite point.

A perfunctory inspection of the situation in the rear-view mirror would ordinarily warrant a glance enduring for no more than a second or two.

Yet as he lifted the clutch and the engine drive engaged, his attention was suddenly alerted to the vision behind him.

The car found gradual acceleration and he shifted up to second, yet his focus was commandeered by the car to his rear, which had lagged somewhat with the flow of other surrounding vehicles.

Ashley stared intently into the small rectangle of mirrored glass as he tried to decipher what it was that had distracted him so. He studiously observed the small silver three-door as it maintained a few yards distance from his back bumper before then braking exceedingly close.

Unbeknown to him, there was another unforeseen delay to the flow up ahead, which swiftly trailed back through the lines of traffic and red lights illuminated all around once more.

But not on Ashley's car.

He had not detected the need to apply the brake at the same time as other drivers in the vicinity.

Reverting attention to the activity out front, he instinctively stamped down on the brake pedal amid instant panic.

The bonnet of his car ceased its unwitting advance just inches from the underside of the container lorry's carriage.

The engine stalled, requiring quick thought from Ashley as he dipped the clutch and turned the ignition key.

Moving forward again, he was naturally relieved to have avoided a collision.

Yet his concentration was enticed once more to the situation regarding the small silver car behind his own, which was persevering within very near range again as the traffic juddered to yet another stop.

Ashley let his gaze rest on the driver.

Despite his initial reaction to what he thought he saw in the rear-view mirror, his mind refused to perform the usual process of registration. Indeed, his mental faculties were seemingly trying to override the result of physical function altogether.

He briefly checked through the windshield once again to confirm that traffic wasn't likely to move forward anytime soon.

And then back he ventured to the unfolding mystery gaining momentum behind him.

As finally, his brain conceded defeat to his eyesight.

His faculties were indeed aligned and in full working order.

The driver of the small silver car was suddenly familiar.

In the worst possible way.

He engaged with her blonde bob hairstyle.

Before becoming entranced by her face.

A hard, unwavering grimace glared directly back at him.

And as mutual recognition dawned, Pauline Braithwaite then displayed her eeriest, most loathsome smile.

Ashley instantly plummeted into a pit of fearful confusion.

His wanton disbelief was losing in the contest against crystal clear, undeniable reality.

The traffic had been granted a green light once more and acceleration required second and then third gear.

But Ashley was now immersed in a dense mist of turmoil.

He needed this journey to conclude.

Utilising fourth gear, he maintained strict vigil on the silver car now some fifty or more yards behind.

But it remained fixed in his wake.

Through another set of traffic lights and through another round of gear changes.

Almost as if in pursuit.

Ashley steered out of the one-way system and slipped into the trunk road that would carry him directly to the hotel. He tried with all his might to retain total attention on the road ahead whilst attempting to obliterate from his conscience the insidious presence he had addressed in his mirror.

He entered the hotel car park and occupied the first vacant space that was identified. Disengaging the engine, he climbed swiftly from behind the wheel.

He curiously scrutinized the minimal movement of vehicles around him on site. He scanned the smattering of guests that emerged from reception or ventured back toward the main doors.

A sense of frantic urgency had compelled his desire to studiously analyse his surroundings.

For a full two minutes his nervous inspection endured.

The perceived silver vehicle and its driver were nowhere to be seen.

And once again, the self-doubt cloaked him.

Was his imagination running riot?

Could it *really* have been *her*?

Would she stoop to such a desperate measure as to begin stalking him? Was she truly so desperately sad and lonely?

Could she be sufficiently aggrieved as he had suspected?

Ashley reached into the back of the car for his suit jacket, laptop, and briefcase. As he did so, he ensured to keep attention locked on the vicinity for any potential sighting.

A further minute elapsed as he stood motionless amid his wildly blossoming astonishment.

If it *was* her, she had evidently given up the chase.

But as he locked the car and walked toward reception, another troubling thought crashed into his psyche without invitation.

Where her apparent pursuit had concluded, was suddenly not of chief importance. Ashley's rapidly prevailing concern was far more ominous as he strode through the glass entrance doors.

If indeed he *had* just seen Pauline Braithwaite tailing his journey to work, then there was now a wholly different question that begged him for an answer.

Where did her journey *begin*?

NINETEEN

Eight a.m. the following day John Bonsall, Lee Pinder, and Mohammed Ravek were seated opposite the Operations Manager in his office. It was unusual to convene all three regular security operatives simultaneously, but Ashley had decided that an increased measure of on-site vigilance was now deemed appropriate.

John Bonsall was on day shift roster. Lee Pinder had just handed the baton over after a tedious night shift. Mohammed Ravek had generously agreed to attend the meeting, although he was amid three rest days.

None of the trio had any authentic suspicion for the reason to be called in together. All they knew for sure was that such a request was highly irregular. But Ashley felt justified in taking the next course of action.

The only other colleague privy to his plan was his ever-trusted confidante and his Head of Reception, Jeanette Morris.

He studied the three faces of his security team. Each carried understandably vacant expressions as they cradled their tea and coffee.

'Thank you for coming in to see me, gents. Lee, I appreciate you staying on and Mo you're a gem for interrupting your break. I know this is odd, but I believe there is potential for a situation to develop which needs our keenest attention.'

John Bonsall responded with the hammer instantly hitting the nail on the head.

'Is this about that woman that was hanging around outside?'

Ashley considered his professional reply with due caution.

'It is, yes. It's a delicate and potentially disruptive issue at this current time. And I'm making you all aware of it at the earliest opportunity.'

Mohammed was not completely in the loop regarding recent history and naturally requested some expansion as to the nature of the problem.

'Is it the same lady that left you the present that night she stayed here?'

'Yes, it is Mo. The one and the same. But unfortunately, she seems to find it increasingly difficult to remain away from the place since her first visit some weeks ago.'

Lee leaned forward in his seat and looked Ashley directly in the eye.

'I've spoken to her on at least two separate occasions about loitering at the car park entrance, but she doesn't seem to realise she could be causing anyone any undue upset. But I've certainly heard no complaint from anyone else. What exactly do you want us to do about her?'

With the circumstances bordering somewhere between causing him unwarranted angst and personal embarrassment, Ashley himself wasn't entirely convinced how to proceed.

But he hoped his thoughts would convey to the others as sensible at the very least.

'On an absolute basic level all I ask is that should she appear, please engage with her, and insist she leaves. I don't believe she will persist in attempting to come on to the premises, but the possibility that she might be in waiting to pounce gives me grave concern for the welfare of staff and guests alike.'

Mohammed was now suffering under the weight of confusion.

'But if she is a member of the public, how can we rightfully refuse her right of entry? I'm not even sure what she looks like?'

Ashley obliged the prompt and slid three identical photographs across the desktop.

'This is Pauline Braithwaite. Forgive the quality of the image but it has been lifted directly from our CCTV. To cut a long story short, she befriended me online when the promotion campaign gained wings. She holds the severely misguided notion that she and I are a match made in Heaven. Giving her the brush off is proving very taxing.'

John Bonsall smirked respectfully.

'But...is she aware that you are...well, not available, so to speak?'

Ashley nodded and even smiled himself.

‘Yes John. She’s been informed of my persuasion. Unfortunately, that seems to have made things considerably more intense. It’s as though she’s adopted the perception that me being off the radar has awarded her more incentive to continue the chase. Mad as it sounds lads, I know.’

Lee adorned a mask of earnest sympathy.

‘Do you anticipate she has the potential to do something silly? Such as commit assault?’

Ashley addressed all three with a sullen glare and a distinct tone of acute authority.

‘This is the very crux of the problem, gentlemen. I don’t know anything about the woman. I don’t know her character. Her background. Her history. To all intents and purposes, she is a complete stranger to me. But she appears to have become fixated. Obsessed. Call it what you will.’

Mohammed also now carried a coarse grimace of anticipation.

‘Perhaps this should be a matter for the Police to deal with, Boss?’

Ashley sided with Mohammed’s suggestion.

The principle was just and correct. But not practicable at that current time.

‘The problem we have there, Mo, even though she is a presence in my life I could well do without, is that she hasn’t yet actually broken any law. The Police would file it and forget about it. Its only if she crosses a legal line that I would need to inform the cops. But I hope to avoid that, if possible. Aside from anything else, it wouldn’t be a good image for the business if a Police presence was stationed here every day, just on the off chance a loony might attack me.’

Mohammed countered Ashley’s opinion.

‘But surely, they should listen to your anxieties about her? And maybe have a word with her before something *does* happen?’

Ashley shook his head in appreciation of Mohammed’s supportive naivety.

‘They haven’t got the resources to do that, Mo. They can’t go around warning all *potential* criminals - only the ones that break the law. Unless she acts illegally, they won’t be interested.’

John interjected with a logical query.

Ashley was fully expecting to parry such honest questions.

'I'm puzzled, Ash. Why do you think something *might* happen? You've put her in her place. Why are you still worried?'

Ashley took a calming deep breath before selecting his words.

'Having spoken to her on more than one occasion, I have formed the view that she is not of a rational disposition. She is intuitive and clever. The aftershave she bought me was indicative of her astuteness.'

Lee intervened once more.

'Is that all she's done, though? Hardly enough to put the frighteners on you, is it?'

Ashley reinforced his fears with further evidence.

'She's had access to my place of work. She has followed me into work at least once as I'm aware of. Which gives me subsequent concerns that she now knows where I live. On the face of it she is keeping a lawful distance. But believe me, gents, she means business. All I can ask of the three of you is that you heighten your senses until this mess passes over. Can you do that for me, lads? For everyone's benefit?'

All three security operatives rose to their feet and shook Ashley's hand in a joint gesture of assurance.

'I'm on it right now, Ash.' exclaimed John Bonsall.

Mohammed also conveyed his alliance to the cause.

'Rest easy, Mister Griffiths. She won't make a move without me spotting it.'

Lee Pinder was the last to offer words of encouragement.

'I've seen her up close and personal. She won't get near you, Ash.'

Ashley swallowed nervously and tried to smile about circumstances as he showed his colleagues to the door.

'Thank you so much for your assistance with this, gents. It's a headache we can all do without considering how much else we have got to cope with at the current time.'

Having seen the trio out, Ashley closed the office door and resumed his seat behind the desk.

Alone with his thoughts once again, he checked his mobile phone for any missed calls or messages.

Satisfied he was not in demand for the next few minutes at least, he let his gaze rest idly on the grey clouds that gathered at a pace beyond the window.

And he silently wondered when the sunshine might return.

TWENTY

A Sunday heralding time away from work. The first official day of leave for Ashley since the re-opening of the hotel. However, his ambition for a long lie-in and the potential for breakfast in bed was thwarted somewhat before the sun even considered peeking over the horizon.

'Jesus Christ what the hell is that smell?'

Ashley craned his neck to look at Carl, whose head remained firmly entrenched in the depths of the pillows. The purposed attempt to rouse him had little effect and so Ashley opted to investigate alone.

The putrid fragrance was unlike anything Ashley had ever previously encountered. He hauled himself from under the duvet and pulled on his bath robe.

The invasive aroma grew in potency as he emerged from the bedroom and stood on the landing. Descending the stairs rendered his nostrils vulnerable to a full-on assault. By the time his feet touched the hallway floor, his stomach was considering rebelling, too.

And at very moment, the source of the problem became all too apparent. To the point where he nearly stepped in it.

At the base of the front door lay exhibited a small cluster of faeces.

Ashley screwed his face into mask of angered disgust.

'For fuck's sake don't say Margie's been locked in all night.'

He turned to view the scene over his shoulder and began to hunt the suspected culprit.

'Here, Margie. Where are you, girl? Silly Daddy locked the cat flap, didn't he?

Ashley's very audible disgruntlement had rumbled Carl into vague semi-consciousness. He turned over to see that the other side of the bed was vacant. It was enough of a prompt to venture upright and yawn loudly as he squinted down into the semi-murk of the stairwell.

He hollered down to Ashley who had vanished from view.

'What are you doing up at this hour? It's a quarter to five on Sunday morning! Where are you? Ash?'

Ashley heard Carl's call and duly returned to the scene of the crime with a roll of kitchen towel. He gazed up at Carl's bemused and weary expression that hung over the balustrade.

'Sorry for disturbing you. But this mess here is the reason I'm awake.'

Carl rubbed his eyes as he commenced a descent.

'What mess?'

'This bloody mess that I'm currently shovelling up! Can't you smell it? Marjorie decided to leave us a good morning present.'

Carl observed the clean-up operation that Ashley was performing on all fours. The Commander-in Chief of the mission issued a stark instruction.

'Carl, can you see where she's hiding whilst I shift this? She might be under the sofa or under our bed cowering in shame.'

A full minute elapsed as Carl checked the ground floor. He then trudged back upstairs and undertook a full inspection of every room. Finally, crouching down he quickly scanned the area beneath the bed.

'She's not up here either, Ash.'

Ashley's grimace remained in place as he completed the task at hand, flushing the offending items down the toilet and wiping the remnants from the hallway mat with a damp cloth.

The duo reconvened in the lounge.

Carl gestured toward the kitchen.

'I need a coffee after all that drama.' he giggled.

Ashley's mood had softened considerably as he scanned the darkened scene beyond the kitchen window.

'I wonder where she can be then?'

Carl filled and switched on the kettle before retrieving two mugs from the cupboard. His memory was beginning to return.

'I reckon we've got a phantom pussy cat, Ash.'

'Well, I can assure you that cat shit was not a figment of my imagination!'

Carl's memory suddenly retrieved a fact.

'It's coming back to me, now. I put Marjorie out last night. She wasn't keen but out she went. And I locked the cat flap. Look!'

Ashley reached down to confirm Carl's story.

'Yes...the flap's locked.'

His next move was to open the back door.

Within seconds Marjorie appeared on the patio.

She stared at her master in abject disapproval before yowling an understandable and possibly justified request for an early breakfast.

Ashley stared blankly at Carl, who spooned coffee granules into the mugs.

'You're right. She's been out all night. So, the question remains... who's muck have I just been cleaning up, then?'

Carl was also completely baffled.

A state that was given further credence by his next point of observation.

'Not *hers*! We would have noticed going to bed last night if she did it before being let out.'

Marjorie entered the kitchen and called up to her human parents once again for a supply of food.

'Of course, we would.' Ashley concurred. 'But it wasn't there then, was it? We would have nearly walked in it for crying out loud.'

Again, a squawk from Marjorie attempted to centre the focus on her empty bowl, with Ashley pulling a pouch of meat from under the sink and taking her back onto the patio.

Here you go, girl. But you can eat al fresco if you're going to start messing indoors.'

Carl expressed severe doubt about Marjorie's guilt as he put the milk back into the fridge.

'Well, all I can say is that if that mess *was* hers then she's a bloody good shot.'

Ashley returned to the kitchen and picked up his drink.

'Why do you say that?'

'Well, if everything *was* locked then the only way in is through the letterbox, isn't it?'

Ashley nodded in silence whilst he watched Marjorie avidly scoff her meal.

As Carl's presumably innocent last words slowly began to register with a resounding, dreadful thud.

TWENTY-ONE

It was a surprisingly pleasant change to be on site early for once. Ashley pulled on the handbrake and checked his phone. No contact from Derek Evans yet.

That was good, Today's meeting was likely to be lengthy and for the most part, tedious. These meetings seemed to be recurring every other day recently.

Fellow chain managers detailing their individual problems before a live zoom audience was not Ashley's idea of fun, but at least with the advent of visual conference calling nobody had to make a commute.

Still perched behind the wheel, a quick text message to Carl dictated his love. It was just after six a.m. Time for a few checks in varying areas before the zoom gathering commenced at ten.

Carl's reply was immediate and in the form of a kiss emoji. Such little gestures meant everything. Gazing into space, Ashley began to count his blessings that he had found such a caring, wonderful man to share his life with.

Typically, his joyous daydream was obliterated by a sharp knock on the window of the driver's door, which made him jump out of his skin. Ashley's head spun to view the vision of Mohammed the security guard staring with some intent back at him, his eerie profile half-lit by a large handheld torch.

Despite Mo's propensity to speak very loudly in all situations, Ashley thought it best to lower the window. Even Mo, with his unerring ability to shout, couldn't be heard through a pane of glass.

'You frightened the bloody life out of me! Are you okay?'

Mohammed Ravek was veritably jumping up and down on the spot.

Something was evidently due to be announced.

'Have you seen it, Boss? Have you seen it?'

Completely baffled by the urgent tone of the twitching security operative, Ashley could not help but smile at the guy.

'I've only just arrived, Mo. Whatever is the matter?'

Mohammed continued to gesticulate and pointed to the rear of the car as he shifted weight from foot to foot.

Such was his sense of desperation to unveil the mystery as soon as possible, he pulled on the handle of the driver's door to encourage Ashley's attention.

It worked. Ashley emerged from behind the wheel.

'What on earth is wrong, Mo? Calm down!'

Mohammed beckoned Ashley toward the back of the vehicle. First by waving his hand. Then by tugging at Ashley's shirt sleeve as he waved his flashlight erratically.

'This, Boss! Have you seen *this*? Bloody bastard vandals! That's what they are!'

Ashley observed his colleague steady the torch beam onto a spot just above the registration plate.

'This is crazy damage. No respect some people.'

Ashley's attention focused on the section of red metallic paint.

Etched into it, in roughly hewn three-inch high capital letters, was a word.

Then on closer inspection, Ashley detected that there were in fact *two* words scratched into the paintwork.

Carved right down to the metal base.

LOVE/HATE.

The hairs on the back of Ashley's neck stood on end.

He suddenly felt very cold. Even for early October.

His throat became dry as he attempted to summon a worded response.

'Christ! No, Mo. I had no idea this had been done. This looks to be an expensive job. You did very well to see it in this light.'

Mohammed himself put his face close to the damage.

'Big sharp screwdriver, Boss. This wouldn't have taken long to do.'

Ashley tried to remain calm as his heart pounded in growing horror.

'You need to report this. The police need to find the bastard! I'll check the CCTV for you now, Mister Griffiths. I've nearly ended my shift, but I'll sort this for you.'

Ashley continued to stare blankly at the indelible scrawl that now defaced the boot lid. He found himself in total agreement.

'Yes…please, Mo. If you get chance. Have a look for me. But I'm pretty certain this hasn't been done here on site. How did you manage to see this anyway its pitch black?'

Mohammed placed a hand of support on Ashley's shoulder.

'My torch, Boss. I was at the gates when I saw you pull up and thought I'd confirm it was your car. I'll get this person on film then we phone the Police. Okay?'

'Okay, Mo. Yes. You see what you can uncover. I'll ring my insurance company so they can no doubt tell me I'm not covered.'

Ashley observed Mohammed veritably scamper across the car park toward the security lodge, still with illuminated torch in hand.

He reacquainted himself with the damage from closer vantage.

In his heart of hearts, he hoped Mohammed might uncover the perpetrator.

But his head had already overridden such a premise.

The instigator of the message scratched unceremoniously into the car was at large.

And Ashley only had one suspect in mind.

His resilience in refusing to involve the law was now being slowly diminished.

She was gradually forcing him to respond with aggression.

He knew that soon enough the likelihood would leave him little choice in the matter.

And he needed to enable Carl's support now.

The situation was gradually spiralling beyond his realm of control.

And as the chronicle of torment slowly expanded, Ashley could only guess at what the next chapter might bring.

TWENTY-TWO

Carl emerged from the shopping centre feeling quite pleased with himself. Having purchased a pair of dark slim-fit jeans and white long-sleeved shirt, the sense of achievement offered a renewed bounce to his stride.

Despite his expectations, the crowds were relatively light considering it was Saturday afternoon. If nothing else, the lack of numbers afforded him more patience and longer browsing time.

He had decided that he would dress to impress that evening and he planned dinner out with Ashley whatever kind of day he might have suffered at the hotel.

But Ashley wouldn't be home for hours yet, which pretty much limited exactly where and what time the pair could go out later.

Hence, no table reservation had been made anywhere. But Carl habitually like to turn up to restaurants unannounced, just as a measure of customer service levels.

He waited at the four-way pedestrian crossing.

It was only just two p.m.

Plenty of time to kill.

Time for a sit down and a warm drink.

*****

Positioning himself with a large latte in the front window of the coffee shop, Carl settled into his chair.

It was social media catch-up time. Of course, being a global hobby nowadays, most people throughout the shop were staring silently at their phone screens, but for Carl in particular it was an engaging way on checking how his freelancing was performing and liaising with clients old and potentially new.

Carl had changed his profile image to that of Ashley in hotel promotion mode. He studied the photograph and smiled openly.

He was so proud of his man and the acclaim that had been garnered though Ashley's part in the Ultimate Inn campaign.

And Carl had no qualms about singing Ashley's praises to friends, either. He genuinely believed in Ashley's abilities as a representative of the national hospitality trade, and even quipped to Ashley's parents that their son was that good at his job he could sell ice cream to Eskimos, such was his charm and demeanour with the public.

The minutes passed as Carl quietly sipped his drink whilst being ensconced in the many varied and entertaining offerings of the internet.

So distracted was he by the plethora of videos and messages, that nearly an hour had endured before he adjusted position in his seat and looked around the coffee shop.

It had become decidedly busier since he entered the place.

His attention became briefly distracted by the scene beyond the window, and he quickly became lost in a daydream of sorts, simply staring through the glass at the activity floating past on the pavement.

Then, his momentary solace was interrupted by a voice.

'Excuse me…is this seat taken?'

Carl glanced up to ascertain the source of the enquiry.

An attractive lady of middle age faced him squarely and beamed a very striking smile his way.

'Forgive me. I wasn't paying attention. What did you say?'

The woman's expression broadened with amusement.

'Yes, I could see you were miles away. I just wondered…is it okay if I joined you at your table? It's a bit of a squeeze in here just now.'

Carl did not deliberate.

He moved his shopping bag and as all gentlemen should do, he pulled out the spare chair for his newfound companion.

'Please do. I'd be glad of the company. It will save me from nodding off to sleep if nothing else.'

The woman giggled to herself as she placed her tray on the tabletop.

Carl eyed the contents.

Tea for one and a lemon drizzle muffin.

He watched as she placed herself in the chair next to him and slipped off her coat.

'That cake looks nice!' he mused. 'I might have to go and get one for myself.'

The lady's inviting expression was warmly intoxicating and was accentuated by her short blonde bob haircut. She off-loaded the tray and placed it on the floor next to her feet.

'Feel free to share this one with me if you want. I don't think I'll eat all that, anyway. They don't look as big as this behind the counter.'

Carl was taken aback by her friendly and generous disposition.

He obliged her invitation with a lick of his lips.

'Okay…I tell you what…I'll do you a deal. I'll have a bit of your cake if you let me buy you another drink because my cup's empty anyway.'

The woman responded by widening her unusually green eyes and nodding avidly.

She projected a gesture of agreement.

'Okay! It's a deal!'

The pair shook hands and exchanged genuine laughter. She took her knife and gently cut the muffin across the centre as Carl returned to the table with his own plate and a fork.

Apportioning his piece of the cake to his plate, he observed the crowded shop.

'I think there are more people in here than there are in rest of the entire town. It was very quiet when I came in.'

The woman eloquently placed a small piece of muffin in her mouth and poured herself some tea.

'To be honest, I've only come out for a ride on the bus and do some window shopping. Just a change of scenery. Does one good occasionally, don't you think? But its cold today, isn't it.'

As she spoke Carl noticed her eyes fixing on his large designer label bag.

'I can see you've been brave and made a purchase, though.'

'Oh, yeah. Just a couple of bits to throw on later tonight. I'm taking my partner out for a good drink and a slap-up meal. He just doesn't know it yet.'

The woman nodded with a wry smile.

'I get you. That's very thoughtful.'

'Well, he deserves it. He's had a tough time of late with one thing and another.'

She added milk and sugar to her cup and began stirring.

'I think that's a very considerate gesture from you. Pardon me, but did I hear correctly? Your partner is male?'

Carl appreciated the refreshing honesty of her question.

'Yes, that's right. He's a workaholic so I'm giving him his orders when he finally gets through the front door, later. The pub it is! No excuses!'

The woman sampled her drink whilst maintaining her focus on Carl. She watched in mild amusement as he devoured his half of the muffin.

'That was delicious! Thank you.'

'Don't mention it. Share and share alike, eh? Does the man in your life have an intensive kind of job, then?'

Carl looked briefly across the room at the lengthy queue.

He was thirsty and in need of a refill.

'Yes, it's quite stressful. He runs a local hotel. Since the second lockdown ended it's been a bit mental really.'

The woman presented no obvious reaction to Carls' revelation about Ashley. The conversation flowed amiably.

'Yes, I can well imagine. I bet there's been a mad rush on bookings too, now that we are all allowed to come out and breathe each other's air again.'

'Dead right. Tea for one again?'

'Yes, please. Very kind of you.'

*****

It was a full ten minutes before Carl returned to the table with fresh drinks.

'Bloody line never seemed to get shorter. Got there in the end, though.'

His female companion popped her last morsel of cake into her mouth and sat back in her chair, her attention resting on the stream of pedestrians outside.

As he emptied the second tray and placed it next to the first under the table, Carl sensed she was mulling over another question.

And the question duly came.

And it was not one he expected.

'Well, forgive me for saying this but I think you are both very *brave*. Did you face much in the way of opposition when you first announced you were in a relationship together?'

Carl found himself a little aghast at the direct and personal nature of her enquiry but figured that she was affable enough to merit a reply.

An honest question surely warranted an honest answer.

'There was no real problem from our friends I don't think. Because of course it was no secret that we were gay. But Ashley's parents were pretty *anti* from the get-go. Well, his father *definitely* was. He really struggled with Ashley's sexuality for many years, so for his only son to finally declare his love for another man was not something that sat well. But I think he's mellowed to the idea, now. Well…I *know* he has.'

As he was speaking, Carl noticed his lady companion did not take her eyes from the activity beyond the shop window.

She did not alter her posture or even respond facially.

But she was evidently listening intently to every word.

'Sorry…did you say your partner's name was Ashley?'

'Yes, that's right. Here…I'll show you his picture.'

Carl retrieved his phone from his pocket and unlocked it. He did not notice her evolving grimace as she observed him put the pin code in.

She watched as he scrutinised his photo gallery, flicking through the album eagerly to find a suitable image to show her.

Finally, he made his choice.

'There you go. That's my Ashley. You may recognise him. He's on a massive billboard up near the viaduct as you come off the motorway. Handsome devil, isn't he?'

The woman took Carl's handset for a closer study of the photograph. She stared silently at the screen for seconds on end. She offered no feasible clue in her expression, maintaining a blank, unyielding glare.

Finally, she decided to supply a verdict.

'Yes, Carl. I can fully understand why you fell for him. He's a beautiful man. Every inch the perfect hotel poster boy.'

He heard her words and did not initially feel alarmed.

But then subsequent digestion of her last statement caused him to feel strangely ill at ease.

He watched dumbstruck as she placed his phone handset back on the table, almost as if she had suddenly become disgruntled about something.

The woman folded her arms and crossed her legs.

Exemplary defensive body language.

Of course, she needed to say no more.

Carl's brewing curiosity was gradually accompanied by pangs of concern. She would no longer look him in the eye.

And he hoped his steadily raging instincts were completely misguided in their responses.

But he had no choice but to ask the next question.

'Excuse me...how...how do you know my *name*?'

She refused to engage his attention.

She continued to focus straight ahead through the windowpane into the High Street.

The seconds elapsed before she finally replied.

'I'm sorry? Did I speak out of turn?'

Carl was now sensing a raging wave of trepidation that was about to engulf him.

'You know my name.'

'Oh. Do I? Well, what a coincidence!'

Tension gripped Carl's tone as he leaned forward.

'But I didn't tell you what my name was.'

Now she turned her head ninety degrees to face him and could not conceal her mask of gratification.

'Did I guess right, then? Well…lucky, I suppose?'

He rapidly took the implied confirmation as gospel.

'It's *you*…isn't it? You're the woman who has been hassling Ashley. It's *you.*'

She simply maintained her amused glare as Carl attempted to deal with the sudden realisation.

'Please…tell me I'm fucking dreaming. Or is this a true-life nightmare I've just entered?'

Finally, she disclosed her total pleasure at Carl's discovery.

A broad, striking, unequivocally attractive smile broadened across her features.

And for the second time, she held out her right hand.

'Overjoyed to meet you, Carl. Yes. I'm Pauline. Your powers of deduction are in good working order.'

She giggled quietly as the wholly unpleasant scenario sent Carl cold to the bone.

Wide-eyed, he observed the peculiar figure perched next to him at the table.

This person.

The supposed enemy.

For whom he had bought tea for one.

And shared cake with.

And she had upheld the bravado and the audacity to sit there and maintain the pretence.

She had totally duped him with her act of sociability.

In his head, a thousand thoughts cursed him as they correlated and collided.

Pummelling his conscience and giving sustenance to his instantly thriving regret. He wasn't yet certain of the response she intended to generate from him, but fury was the prime candidate as he grappled to place his thoughts in a semblance of order.

'You weren't in this coffee shop by coincidence, were you? You must have been tailing me all afternoon. Watching my every move. Jesus Christ.'

Pauline Braithwaite remained completely unmoved by Carl's visibly flourishing distress. Her inane grin remained in place, suggesting she was evidently garnering some sick thrill from the drama she had instigated and was willingly continuing to engineer.

Before, she was deemed only a minor nuisance.

Yet she had now portrayed herself as someone who gleaned satisfaction from watching others' sufferance. The starkness of the truth was causing real alarm for Carl, yet she retained an ill-fitting serenity that contrasted with his rabid inner quest to find an escape route from the insidious predicament.

And still the layers of descending reality had not fully settled as he bore into her visage with ballooning anxiety.

'I mean...*fuck*...I've been in town for about four hours! And you have shadowed my every step?'

And still she offered no willingness to contribute to a verbal joust.

Comprehension crushed Carl's spirit as he pieced the terrifying puzzle together.

'You must have followed me from the house. Otherwise, you'd *never* have found me in town.'

At last, she relented with a cackle and presented him with a small yet thoroughly alarming admission.

'You catch on fast. Much faster than Ashley. He still doesn't know what day it is half the time, bless him.'

Carl's chest drummed relentlessly now as adrenaline diluted his veins. He scanned the vicinity of the shop. There were plenty of people around.

Yet no witness could vouch for what was transpiring.

He was completely alone and rendered vulnerable to her incalculable whims.

'So, what the fuck do you want with *me*? And more to the point, why are you stalking *Ashley*? What's he ever done to deserve it?'

Pauline Braithwaite gazed to the ceiling of the coffee shop and laughed out loud in the face of Carl's frantic protestations.

'Stalking? *Stalking*? Such a Twentieth Century term. I much prefer the modern angle.'

Her dismissive arrogance was now fuelling Carl's disgust at his own apparent naivety.

'The modern angle? How does that quantify itself, then?'

She stopped chuckling and addressed him with a dead pan expression.

'Genuine curiosity. That's all. I liked the look of him. So, sue me.'

Her unflappable mannerisms served to depict her as even more crazed than Carl had already suspected.

He wanted to leave there and then.

But he also wanted answers.

'Why on Earth would you be curious about *us*? About *Ashley*? You have no connection to him, whatsoever. He's just a photo on a poster. Nothing more than an advertisement by the roadside. What's the *matter* with you, woman?'

Pauline Braithwaite remained utterly unmoved by the disquiet evolving across the table. If anything, Carl suspected a sense of glee emanating from his now distinctly unwelcome companion.

Almost as if she was sated by accomplishing her sick little mission.

Carl became immersed in dread as he deliberated on making a quick exit or ringing the Police.

'Of course, you know where we live. After all, it was *you* who keyed Ashley's car, wasn't it? It was you who put the shit through the letterbox, wasn't it? You're off your fucking head, woman!'

He reached for his phone and searched through his contact list.

Pauline Braithwaite was unflinching as she observed him.

Aside from casting a black cloud to overshadow his intentions.

'Going to tell him, are you? Going to ring him and tell him you've been sitting in a coffee shop with his obsessed female fanatic, are you? That you bought me a pot of tea and shared my table and my lemon muffin? Here and now? This very minute? Whilst he's slogging away managing his hotel? Think for a moment, Carl. This might not look good on you.'

He scowled at the haunting presence that now goaded him.

He hissed a proclamation in her direction.

'I've got nothing to hide from Ashley. We don't have secrets. He's told me all about you. If I phoned him now and told him what had happened, he'd believe me. And I might just ring the law as well.'

Pauline Braithwaite rocked back in her chair and emitted the now familiar, almost spectral chortle.

'Oh really? And what exactly would your complaint to the Police entail? That you willingly had a drink and with a complete maniac that you think is stalking your boyfriend. I think you need a rethink, Carl dear.'

It was of little comfort for Carl to immediately accept the futility of making the intended calls.

And salt in the wound was also liberally applied, as Pauline Braithwaite leaned forward and painted the daunting bigger picture for him through a sinister whisper.

'And whilst we are on that theme…some more advice you should heed. You can allege anything with my name attached. But you have no proof of any criminal activity involving me. It will be your word against mine, every step of the way. And where there is black and white evidence, it only confirms what has already been established. That I stayed one night in the hotel. Oh yes…and had a friend request accepted by the supposed victim in all this. Think on, Carl. Think on.'

He felt completely boxed in by the confounding logic of her statement.

She was, sadly, completely correct.

Pauline Braithwaite, in the eyes of the law, would be guilty of nothing.

'My God. You've really worked all this out, haven't you? A mad scheme from a twisted mind. So, what's the motive? Jealousy? Are you medically insane? Have others in your miserable past crossed paths with you and suffered the same treatment?'

Pauline Braithwaite suddenly rose from her chair and put her coat on, before picking her handbag off the table. Carl could not believe how tranquil the woman was as she stood among the scene of her disorder.

But his anger was desperately fighting to breach as she began to move to the door.

'So, you think you can just get up and walk away from this? Are you so deluded that you think there will be no repercussions?'

She threw him an almost brutal glance of smugness as she scanned the scene outside.

'You know you can't do anything, Carl. Neither of you will be capable of stopping me. I admit I may be a little out of the ordinary for your liking, but I will always be three moves in front of you. Never forget that. You won't *ever* outthink me. Make sure you convince your buzzing little brain of that much. No one will stand in my way. No one.'

She shuffled to the shop doorway and pulled it open to allow an elderly couple to enter. The instant contrast in her demeanour was almost eerie as she expressed the epitome of good will to the pensioners.

With one foot in the street, she offered one final thought to Carl before departing. She nodded to the tabletop and donned a crooked smirk.

'By the way…thanks ever so much for the tea. Finish the pot off if you want. I bet you're thirsty now. Oh yes…and I hope you and Ashley have a really good night out on the tiles later. Ciao!'

With that, Pauline Braithwaite was gone.

Merging instantly with a thousand other shoppers.

Once again transforming herself into an ordinary Saturday afternoon browser about town.

Carl looked at his phone in desperation.

Maybe now was not the right time.

He would wait until Ashley came in later.

It wasn't fair to interrupt his working day with this episode.

He purposely spent a few minutes scanning the vista beyond the coffee shop window before convincing himself the coast was clear.

With composure now frayed, he picked up his shopping and headed for home.

TWENTY-THREE

It was an unusually mild Autumn Tuesday morning. Ashley had left Carl dozing and rose early to sample his first coffee of the day. Being mainly a freelancer, Carl could often dictate his own daily schedule, although weekday lie-ins were not typical.

Since working from home became the norm, his average logging on time was eight a.m., despite his claims to the contrary about 'starting early.'

Ashley sampled his drink and studied the rear garden's gradual process of illumination through the kitchen window. The thought occurred to him that he might welcome a return to remaining at home himself.

It would be infinitely more rewarding than the imminent meeting with the new toiletry suppliers and undoubtedly more satisfying than the enquiry he would have to broach with the food wholesalers about their inconsistent order picking.

Considering all current circumstances, hotel management was not quite living up to expectation in any aspect. But if Ashley was totally honest with himself, he knew where his true talent lay, and it would not likely enjoy being perched in front of a graphics tablet all day.

Even Carl himself had made the proclamation some time ago that he was perhaps the quietly creative half of the partnership, whilst Ashley was far and away the more personable of the two.

But with the shadow of Pauline Braithwaite looming large across both their lives at this time, neither Carl nor Ashley felt particularly comfortable in their own skin.

Their previously reliable and smooth routines had developed a succinctly jagged edge. The seemingly ongoing issue with her had certainly levelled the playing field for them both.

As Ashley finished his coffee and set the mug down on the draining board, a movement in the rear garden caught his attention. Something was stirring in the semi-darkness between the shed and the line of conifers.

With his curiosity provoking an investigation, Ashley secured the belt of his bath robe, and in his slippered feet. he opened the back door to inspect the scene.

Even when halfway along the garden path, the poor light made it difficult for Ashley to identify what it was that was provoking his interest.

On finally reaching the shed, Ashley squatted down and cleared his vision with a rub from his index fingers. He suspected it was most likely to be a hedgehog snaffling for scraps.

On his haunches, he shuffled forward to allow closer scrutiny.

It was Marjorie.

Ashley's initial disbelief was swiftly eclipsed by acute distress.

And then he instantly evolved into horrified panic.

'JESUS FUCKING CHRIST! CARL!'

Ashley immediately bounded into a very uneven stride back along the garden path. He crashed through the kitchen door and scrambled an ascent to the bedroom, where Carl remained dead to the world under the duvet.

Carl felt a sudden shove in the shoulder which proceeded to shake him into semi consciousness. He retained a controlled tone as Ashley offered verbal encouragement to speed up the process. Carl eventually opened his eyes and squinted toward the cause of his awakening.

'You've got to wake up. Marjorie doesn't look well. She's under the trees near the shed. Wake up for fuck's sake! You need to come and look at her.'

Having stirred momentarily, Carl assimilated Ashley's desperate request.

He needed no further prompt.

In only boxer shorts and with bare feet, Carl jumped downstairs in two leaps and followed Ashley's frantic lead into the back garden.

Both reached the shed and observed the scene.

There wasn't much scope for conversation.

Certainly, no necessity for any lengthy contemplation.

Carl conveyed his conclusions.

'She needs the vet. And I mean *now*. I think she's eaten something she shouldn't.'

Ashley managed to stem his verging upset at the sight of their struggling, defenceless feline. Carl got down on his knees for a more definitive examination.

Marjorie detected that she was under the deeply concerned scrutiny of her human parents. She switched the angle of her head to engage her focus onto them.

'My God, Carl. I've never seen her like this.'

'Right, Ash. Keep calm. We'll get dressed and get her in the car.'

'But the vets won't be open, yet.'

Carl retained his composure as Ashley began to break his.

'I'll phone them. Come on we need to get going. Hurry!'

*****

Carl entered the bedroom as Ashley fought back tears.

'Okay, Ash. I've just rung them. I've explained the symptoms. The emergency vet will see us immediately. We don't need an appointment. But she says time is at a premium. I'll get the carry-box from the loft.'

Having swiftly dressed himself, Ashley resumed vigil by Marjorie's side next to the shed.

'There, there, baby. Daddy will look after you and get you better. Don't fret, darling. We'll take you to the cat doctor and he'll give you some medicine. You'll be back home in no time, I promise. My beautiful fur baby. You'll be right as rain soon.'

As Ashley fought gamely to keep his upset under wraps, Carl returned to his side with the carry box.

Ashley stood back and rubbed his eyes.

'You'll have to lift her, Carl. I can't. I'll get the lid off the carrier and put the towels in it.'

Carl nodded before offering a reassuring smile and moving into position.

Gingerly ascertaining Marjorie's body position, he managed to slip both palms securely under her so as not to cause any further distress.

He carefully elevated Marjorie from the undergrowth.

Ashley put a hand over his mouth as he watched Carl back step away from the shed with the furry little patient.

Thankfully, within seconds and without further drama, Marjorie was securely in the carrier.

'Come on then, Ash. You need to put your foot down.'

*****

It was approaching seven-thirty when Ashley, Carl and Marjorie pulled into the tiny car park. Occasional meows resonated from the back seat, contrasting with the fearful silence in the front.

The emergency veterinarian opened the rear door to the surgery.

She was a very young-looking woman yet sported an assuring manner. She spoke in a sympathetic tone through her face mask. Inviting Ashley and Carl into the consultation room, she observed the carry box whilst donning white rubber gloves.

'I'll get told off for allowing you inside along with your pet, but it looks as though Covid rules will have to go down the priority list for this little one. She sounds like she needs some urgent attention.'

Laying blue paper towel on the examination table, the nurse then took the carrier box from Ashley and placed it on the countertop before removing the top half. Carl introduced her to the vet.

Much to Ashley's relieved amusement, Marjorie poked her inquisitive head over the rim of the carrier on hearing her name. Her curiosity appeared to have eclipsed her discomfort to a slight degree.

'Hello, beautiful!' smiled the nurse. 'My, aren't you a pretty one. So, gentlemen, please fill me in on what's happened this morning.'

Ashley and Carl informed the nurse of events so far. They watched with raw trepidation as she then carefully lifted Marjorie out of the box and set her to rest on the paper towels.

The cat seemed a little calmer to the uneducated eye, but unbeknown to her hopeful human parents, her condition was now critical.

The professional commenced a brief examination. Her concentration did not flinch as she gently felt areas of Marjorie's stomach and hind with the tips of her fingers.

'From what you have told me and from what I can deduce, there is a significant probability of poisoning. And with these symptoms having classic association, I would predict that she has ingested coolant or antifreeze.'

Both Ashley and Carl listened with mouths agape as the nurse probed them with a question.

'How likely is it that your car is leaking or how likely is it that she might have inadvertently accessed such material at home?'

Carl shook his head in utter bewilderment.

'There's no chance. There's no leak. And we certainly don't have any antifreeze at home.'

The nurse exhibited a sterner brow as she continued to try and assess Marjorie.

'Well...there is little other household substance that can induce such a symptomatic reaction in cats.'

Ashley interjected with a valid point.

'It's very rare she ventures beyond the property boundary, to be honest. She's very comfortable within her own territory.'

The nurse temporarily halted her inspection of Marjorie and focused on Ashley with a very demoralising suggestion.

'If that is the case, then we must consider the possibility that someone has specifically tempted her with food that had been purposely contaminated. She wouldn't be deterred from temptation. Antifreeze has quite a sweet attractive aroma. Even a relatively small quantity sprinkled on meat or biscuits would cause an instantaneous reaction in her gut.'

As they watched Marjorie search for fuss on the tabletop, the emotional impact of her sufferance began to hit home. It was impossible to reconcile the prospective conclusion to her ordeal.

In trembling tones, Ashley asked the nurse what needed to happen to get Marjorie back to health.

The nurse faced both men.

Her voice now carried both authority and an edge of urgency.

'Okay…this is what I propose to do over the course of the next twenty-four hours. Marjorie will undergo all relevant bodily fluid tests. If we are in time, we hope to prevent the substance from penetrating her vital organs.'

Ashley shook his head in shock.

'Can't the poison simply be passed through?'

'I'm afraid not. If the kidneys become affected, they may fail her.'

A dreadful silence greeted the stark prognosis.

Ashley and Carl gazed at one another, both grasping for a handle on reality. This was a despairing situation. The potential repercussions had not registered with either of them.

Carl ventured a reluctant query.

'So…if her kidneys fail…she could *die*? Is that what we are talking about, here?'

The vet resumed her examination of Marjorie's abdomen. The cat was now quite content to let her tummy be prodded as she lay exhausted on the table.

'That is a possibility we should be prepared for, yes. Time is of the essence. But if her tests come back reading as we would like, then she should have every opportunity of a complete recovery. The problem is we don't know how long the poison has been in her system. But you did exactly the right thing by getting her here. She's in the best hands, now.'

Ashley wiped his eyes and could not refrain from asking the one question he did not want answered.

'What are her chances?'

A pained quiet descended on the room once again as all three humans gazed down at the tormented little animal.

Her very life now apparently in the hands of fate, should medical expertise not prove sufficient.

Wisely, the vet declined to speculate.

'We will start the procedure immediately. She will be very carefully monitored. You have my word we will do everything in our power. She needs to be weighed and moved to the treatment room where we will get her on a drip.'

Ashley and Carl stood rooted to the spot as though they had not heard the nurse speak.

She attempted to give them a verbal nudge.

'There is really nothing more you can do for her. If you kindly go to the reception desk, we will take all your relevant details there. Including any insurance references. We will contact you without delay if there is any deterioration in her condition.'

Ashley wiped his eyes again as he caught Marjorie staring directly at him.

It may have been a feline communication to say thank you.

Or to say goodbye.

'Can't we stay here with her?' Carl pleaded.

'I'm afraid that isn't possible, sir. I've already flaunted current surgery policy by letting you inside the building. But I promise if you leave your contact number at the desk you will be regularly updated on her progress.'

Both men sullenly observed their little fur baby and gave her a farewell stroke and kiss atop her head.

Obliging the vet's request, they entered reception to confirm the relevant information before returning to the car park.

The mutual and tearful desolation was inevitable.

Back inside the treatment room, Marjorie was placed into a bed and hooked to an intravenous line. She clawed at the vet's assistant in protest at the whole inconvenient episode.

Both colleagues eyed one another with their sorrowful suspicion that successful retrieval of the situation was already highly unlikely.

*****

Marjorie passed away within the hour.

On receipt of the news, Ashley's legs buckled, and he dropped his phone, before dropping to his knees on the lounge floor.

Inconsolable.

Drowning in grief.

Carl picked the phone from the floor and assumed control of the dialogue with the surgery.

Ashley forced himself to calm down as he listened intently to each one of Carl's responses to what he was being told.

'Okay…I understand.'

'Acute renal failure.'

'Yes, it was obvious she was suffering.'

'You did your best for her I'm quite sure.'

'Yes, I'm glad she went peacefully.'

'We all tried our best, yes.'

'No…we will fetch her. We can come now if that's okay.'

'Yes, we would much prefer her here with us at home.'

'Thank you so much for trying, nurse.'

'Yes, we are sorry too.'

'See you shortly.'

Ashley's focus shifted instantly as Carl disconnected the call.

Yes, the vet was so sorry.

Yes, he and Carl were so sorry.

And the unspoken pledge was taken.

A pledge declaring that nobody would be as ultimately sorry, as the merciless bastard who had committed this act of cruel, heartless, savagery.

And from the depths of Ashley Griffiths' psychological torment, the likely suspect had already emerged to the forefront of his mind.

TWENTY-FOUR

Marjorie's burial was a swift and solemn affair. Carl had lined a makeshift cardboard casket with her favourite snooze blanket from the bedroom. He also performed the honourable duty of blessing her before placing her inside.

A suitable location in the rear garden was selected, so they would always be able to see her, even from the kitchen window. Underneath the Jasmine bush. So sweet smelling and beautiful in bloom. Next summer when the plant flowered the setting would do her true justice.

Both Ashley and Carl conveyed a silent prayer as Marjorie was laid carefully into the ground. The unenviable process of covering her over with earth was left to Carl. Ashley understandably declined the opportunity with a snivelling shake of the head.

The plot was marked with a large painted stone which was a gift decoration seconded from an indoor pot plant.

The entire process of bidding farewell to a much-loved pet was typically arduous for her human parents, but mercifully short.

Ashley and Carl held hands and crouched down together to say goodbye to their little one, both acknowledging the affection and humour that Marjorie had brough into their lives.

With oversight of her painful departure concluded, Ashley rose to his feet as bleak thoughts now relentlessly bombarded his conscience.

His stern visage betrayed a stirring mindset. And a now drastically altered outer demeanour. Carl observed his partner's grim mask of disdain. Wondering what feelings might be stirring behind that moistened, wandering gaze.

During the previous hours, Ashley had sensed an enforced shift within his soul.

Violent thoughts now occupied his psyche.

Sinister misgivings now muddied the once crystal-clear waters of his existence and indeed, his personality.

Noxious demons had invaded his once impenetrable disposition.

His was now a concerning state of mind.

He could not previously bring himself to talk of such an evolution to Carl. The time had not been right, before.

But the pain weighed him down so heavily.

They wandered slowly along the path back toward the house.

Ashley felt a sudden urge to divulge.

With a furrowed brow, he turned to the love of his life and freely confessed about the torturing phantoms that now plagued him.

The declaration was no longer laced with the strain of loss.

But with the hint of intention.

'You know something, Carl. I've always believed I was born with an earnest approach to fellow man. I always thought I was blessed with a hearty and forgiving moral stance toward people. I always see the best in folk. I never see fit to speak ill of anybody. Even with probable just cause.'

Filling the kettle, Carl was understandably a little puzzled by Ashley's unexpected sentiment.

'Bit deep and random for you, Ash. Where you heading to?'

With a resonant sigh of remorse, Ashley leaned back against the kitchen worksurface. His attention unavoidably drawn through the window to Marjorie's final resting place.

A few seconds elapsed before he expanded on his initial remark.

'I suppose what I'm trying to say is, that if I wasn't such a kind-hearted and genuine person, then I would logically only come to one conclusion about who killed our pussy cat.'

Carl was listening as he spooned coffee and sugar into two mugs.

He was very intrigued to hear where Ashley's train of thought would eventually take him. And he supposed it might well be the same destination he himself had already arrived at some hours ago.

'We know how she died, Ash. She ate poison.'

Ashley's focus switched from the garden and firmly on to Carl.

The fierce expression etched into Ashley's face was one Carl had never witnessed before.

As if despair was actively eating into his features.

Yet Ashley's eventual disclosure proved their minds were aligned in deducing who the perpetrator must be.

'It was *her,* Carl. I'm convinced of it. It's got to be *her.*'

The kettle completed its steaming tantrum as Ashley's words ghosted around the kitchen walls and ceiling. Carl struggled to digest Ashley's conclusion, knowing full well his partner's presumption was automatic, and justified.

The facts fitted the theory.

Carl now felt he had little choice but reveal the details of his encounter in the coffee shop a couple of weeks earlier.

He wasn't expecting Ashley to react positively. But if nothing else, Carl's personal exchanges with Pauline Braithwaite only served to fuel the belief that she might just be capable of something so despicable as murdering the family pet.

He handed Ashley his drink.

Friction in the house was a highly unwelcome sensation, but the currently downbeat atmosphere was about to descend even further.

'Ash…there's something I should…well, I *need* to tell you. And I should have told you the day it happened, but I didn't want to ruin our night out.'

Ashley offered a few light blows to the top of his mug and took a sip. His eyes then fixed fully on Carl, who was now swimming against his own powerful tide of simmering fury.

'I'm all ears, Carl. Fire away. Today can't get any worse, can it?'

Carl paused in contemplation.

A hiatus that only served to ramp up the festering tension between them.

'It's about this Braithwaite woman. I crossed paths with her. A week last Saturday, when you were working, and we then went out and got sloshed and fell into the curry house.'

Ashley's eyes widened like saucers and his attention was now rabidly centred at Carl.

He set down his mug and folded his arms.

'You...*crossed paths*? With Pauline Braithwaite? Please explain.'

'You'd had a long day at work, and I didn't feel it right to speak up at the time. But considering everything that's now happened...I feel now that I've got no choice.'

Ashley shifted position around the kitchen island to get closer.

'Carl...stop beating about the bush and tell me what the fuck you are talking about, please.'

The coffee shop episode was recalled clearly and concisely, without any intervention from Ashley as the very captive audience.

Carl finished his recollection and pensively awaited the eruption. But to his immense relief, Ashley was calm and considered as his reaction unveiled itself.

'So...she must have tailed you? She must have been watching our front door. Then observed your departure. Then shadowed your movements in town. Then had the brass neck to sit next to you for a coffee?'

Carl's plea of innocence carried a grim authenticity.

'Well, I didn't know it was her, initially. I didn't even know what she looked like, did I? I'd never set eyes on her before in my life.'

It was no small relief for Carl to see that Ashley was adopting a rational and ordered process of response. There was no explosion of temper. In fact, he was displaying a surprising level of empathy towards Carl's predicament.

'If you were anticipating me losing my shit, then I can tell you I'm not going to. It's not your fault, Carl. None of this is down to either of us. I'm impressed with her tenacity. I must admit that much. She means serious business with us. Well...*me*. That's obvious, now. And to declare to you that nothing will stop her? That takes a dangerous state of mind.'

Carl moved to embrace Ashley.

Relief quietly washed through him.

'You understand why I didn't mention it before? She scares me, Ash. She's off her head.'

Ashley nodded as his chin rested on Carl's shoulder.

The question begged: *now what*?

'So far as I can see, she's left us with no option, Carl. We've got to tell the Police about her. About everything. Too much has happened, and we can't brush it under the carpet any longer.'

The pair drew apart and engaged with one another's moistened eyes.

'Thank you for not being angry at me, Ash.'

'Angry at *you*? Listen...I've had enough of her. She might be a deluded nutcase but the law's the law. And she's going to find out soon enough that even *she* isn't immune to that.'

Carl now felt strangely agitated on hearing Ashley's implication.

'But surely the Police won't be interested just because we have our suspicions? It's like she said in the coffee shop. We've got no proof that links her to anything vaguely criminal. In the eyes of the Police, she's squeaky clean.'

Ashley's tone adopted an edge of resilience.

'That's not the point. If we have concerns, then we have every right to get them logged on record. Then, when she does drop the ball and we do get proof, we can refer to our original claims.'

Carl's concern about the plan was painting itself across his visage.

'How long do we wait, then? Until the next time?'

Ashley did not hesitate.

'Finish your drink. We're going to the station right away. I'll phone Jeanette and tell her I'll be in late.'

*****

Ashley and Carl departed the Police station with decidedly mixed emotions.

Intense frustration combined with unavoidable cynicism.

Anxiety shackled itself to wary expectation.

Currently, the problem called Pauline Braithwaite was still at large.

And in the eyes of the authorities, she would remain unacknowledged as a potential threat. She would indeed remain at liberty to expediate the imminent next stage of her toxic campaign.

The journey home was endured in silence as Ashley and Carl tried vainly to convince themselves of vindication.

But as the consulting officer of the law glumly confirmed, without any evidence of a legal breach, they have no power to intervene.

As the pair trudged disconsolately into the hallway at Harrogate Close, the time was pressing towards midday.

Ashley tried to make light of an infinitely depressing morning.

'Well, aren't you the lucky one staying at home. I've got to get my backside to that bloody hotel or Jeanette will have my guts for garters.'

Carl kicked off his trainers and sighed wearily.

'Fuck working. I'm not up for so much as logging on today. I can't even be bothered to check my business phone. I dread to think what the backlog looks like.'

'Sadly, I haven't the luxury of such a choice. I'd better get my glad rags on.'

Carl placed a caring hand on his man's shoulder at the bottom of the stairs.

'Ash…we did the right thing. Even though the cops' hands are tied for the time being. We did right by making a statement.'

Despite Ashley's former enthusiasm to go to the Police, the anticipated apathy projected by the local constabulary had only served to tarnish his earlier conviction that they had made a positive move.

'I'm not so sure we did the right thing if I'm honest, Carl. Especially now we've been and done it, you know. That Sergeant Sanders or whatever his name was made me feel we had rudely interrupted his break time. He would have been more captivated if we had gone in and read out the weather forecast, I reckon.'

Carl smirked and nodded in agreement.

'Yes Ash. I noticed. But it was still the correct course of action. Whatever happens in the future at least we have some back up. We're not alone with this issue anymore. And when she slips up, the authorities will come down on her.'

Ashley sniggered as he began to sidle up the steps.

The doubter within him had been given good cause to surface.

'You watch too much telly, mate. I've not got faith in the system like you have. I don't think my brain can absorb much more what with one thing and another. It's going to explode cos of all this stuff going off. I'm getting a tad fed up now.'

Carl followed Ashley up the stairs until they halted halfway.

He seemed quite angry.

He was also insistent.

'Hey you…Ashley Griffiths. We *will* get through this! And you need the day off, today. It didn't start well with saying goodbye to Marjorie. Then the Police visit was demoralising as we both thought it probably might be. Stay here at home and relax.'

'I can't relax. I need to work to take my mind off all the crap. But yes, Carl…I'm sure we will win the war in the end.'

'It's a blot on the landscape of life, Ash. A blip on the radar. We will beat the enemy together. Do you hear me? And when you've gone to work, I'm going to order one of those camera doorbells that links to our mobiles. At least the coppers offered some decent advice on that score.'

Ashley's half-smile did little to convince either of them that there would be a resolution to the current episode in the ongoing drama.

'Okay, Carlos. Whatever you say, captain. You're in charge.'

'Yes! Whatever I say! Now get upstairs and get your suit on. And then get your chin up. Promise?'

Ashley finally made it to the top step before turning to blow Carl a kiss.

'Yes, dear. I promise.'

TWENTY-FIVE

Elaine and Neville Griffiths fully understood that their son was a busy man. Both at home and at work. But they also recognised the discrepancy revealed by his minimal communication with them of late.

Since the second lockdown restrictions had been completely lifted, Ashley had only visited them once with Carl.

There hadn't been a phone call for over two weeks, either.

Elaine had expressed her pangs of maternal concern as usual.

Neville had attempted to explain to her that Ashley's particular industry was now under duress to recover from Covid's grasp.

They both resided in the knowledge that for the foreseeable future, the hotel would likely be occupying most of their son's schedule.

So, when Ashley eventually *did* appear at their front door out of the blue one evening for the first time in over three months, his parents were initially overjoyed that their justified concerns might no longer be warranted.

But it soon became inescapably obvious that their only child's demeanour was not typical.

He seemed distracted and fatigued.

As though his natural verve had been dampened somewhat.

Sure enough, the usual routine of warm engagement in the hallway was ably performed at the outset, but once the formalities had been ticked off, the atmosphere shifted from buoyant to bleak within minutes.

Parental instinct is one of the most potent powers in the universe, and for Neville and Elaine Griffiths, they would at least take slight comfort in learning that their prior misgivings were founded after all.

The radiant if manufactured expression on Ashley's face only briefly belied the fact that upsetting and disturbing revelations were imminent.

Mothers and fathers know when their offspring is off kilter.

Elaine and Neville were not yet aware of the details, but they knew there was a problem.

And that the problem in question was the reason for Ashley's unannounced visit. Fortunately, Ashley's relationship with his parents was close-knit, warm, and honest. This factor was to prove an infinite blessing, as he showed precious little reservation in cutting to the chase as they sat in the lounge.

Depicting how his life had adopted a gradual downturn in recent times was no easy admission, but in the space of an hour, Elaine and Neville had become suitably acquainted with the menacing existence of one Pauline Braithwaite.

Every sinister chapter was adequately illustrated by their son, albeit accompanied by pauses for angry outbursts and emotive intermissions were required from both sides.

It was excruciatingly painful for Neville to observe his singular child, crouched over and whimpering into his mother's lap, as he tried to speak candidly about the final hours of Marjorie's life.

To the point where Neville's own emotions were verging on physical symptoms, and he felt dutiful in moving behind a quivering Ashley and placing comforting paternal arms around him.

The family trio swayed amid their storm of sorrow, until finally it passed over and prompted re-positioning of themselves to their seats.

Neville gazed at the floor, as he attempted to decipher the torrid diary of recent history that Ashley had just relayed.

'My God, Ash. I can't even begin to think of a response to it all. I can't imagine how stressful things must be for you.'

Ashley reached for the box of tissues.

'The thing is, Dad. We *know* she's behind it all. But she's clever and elusive. My complaint to the Police felt like a waste of breath. Unless we catch the bitch red-handed, they won't be interested.'

Elaine could not escape the horror of poor Marjorie's demise.

Through a watery gaze she could only muster woeful sentiment as her contribution to the debate.

'It's pure evil. To think that a human being could willingly inflict such treatment on a defenceless animal. It's beyond belief. It really is.'

Neville leaned forward in his armchair and directly engaged with his son's starkly desperate expression.

'And you believe that she is doing all this out of *spite*? Because you turned her down for a *date*?'

Ashley rolled his eyes in despair.

'Yes, Dad. There can be no other reason. But what I believe or what I think about any of this is irrelevant to the Police. It's only what I can *prove* that will make them sit up and take notice.'

Ashley's father pushed himself to his feet and he shuffled to the bay window. He faced the wholly unappealing Autumn vista beyond the glass. Grey skies above were buffeted along by powerful gusts. Dead leaves danced in the gutters. Bare tree limbs were throttled by the frigid air.

He never suspected he might ever be in the situation where he would be powerless in attempting to conceal his distress. Fathers should never let their children see them upset. At least, that was the way he was brought up.

Yet Neville Griffiths would uphold that staunch tradition at all costs. He would remain stoic for his only child and as such, he hesitantly attempted to lighten the subject matter as he turned to face his family.

'I know you probably wish you'd never agreed to get involved in the blessed thing, but how's the hotel promotion been doing for business?'

Ashley appreciated the opportunity to talk about something distinctly more palatable.

'Apparently the chain is doing better than forecast. Brilliant, in fact. The feedback to the hotels and to me personally has been fantastic. Well, apart from the obvious problem, of course.'

Elaine supplemented her husband's interest and attempted to bolster Ashley's evidently flagging mindset.

'Well, that is excellent! At least the great majority are on your side. You should be very proud of yourself, Ashley. You went beyond your comfort zone for this campaign and I'm glad the positives far outweigh the negatives.'

Despite her appraisal, Ashley wasn't totally appeased by his mother's rose-tinted view on matters.

'It's all well and good in theory, Mum. But the reality is this. My cat has been murdered. My car has been vandalised. And I'm being hounded by a stalker who went on a date with my boyfriend after I gave her the cold shoulder. And those are the harsh truths regarding my life at the current time.'

Neville wasn't overly impressed by his son's flippancy, but nevertheless appreciated the motive behind it.

'Now then. Ash. We're on *your* team. And I know that it has been a very testing time of late. But I get the feeling this problem will get bored if you ignore it for long enough. She can only play her game with a willing opponent. So, if it recurs, simply keep taking a step away from it. You'll be fine.'

It was intensely frustrating for Ashley to keep hearing and heeding the same repeated dictum.

Wilful toleration of Pauline Braithwaite was not a policy that he held much faith in any longer. And the prophecy that she would magically vanish was not convincing, either.

Confronting the issue head on was Ashley's preferred choice.

But that was a non-starter as things stood.

'You know Dad, I'd really like to respond to her whilst carrying a baseball bat. I wouldn't get bored of clouting her all day.'

Elaine glanced in sheer disbelief at her husband. Such a sentiment was extreme and dramatic to be heard coming from her son's mouth.

Neville was swift to give concurrence to his wife's shocked reaction.

'We've promoted better standards in you than that, Ash. You weren't raised to think in such terms. This family doesn't do violence. Never has and never will. Besides which, there is more than one way to skin a cat…oh my…that's a terrible reference…I do so apologise…'

Ashley allowed his father's last statement to digest.

He could not help but peek at the humorous side to it.

It wasn't so much the slip of the tongue, but Neville's immediate subsequent embarrassment that tickled Ashley's funny bone.

Much to his father's instant relief, Ashley began to laugh.

'I'm so sorry Ash. Forgive me. Me and my mouth.'

Ashley's chuckles had at least lightened the mood.

'It doesn't matter, Dad. Honestly. You've put a smile on my face. Not many have managed to do that lately. I should thank you for it.'

Elaine mockingly shook her head in feigned disapproval of the comment, before presenting another subject that she felt required some expansion.

'And how was Carl after bumping into the Devil Woman in town? I bet he was worried about telling you, wasn't he?'

Again, Ashley sniggered, this time at his mother's choice of reference.

Comedy was in the room.

It felt cleansing to be immersed in it.

'He was very worried, yes. More worried about my reaction than anything else, I think. But Carl is very strong for both of us. He's not a ditherer when it comes to making his mind up. I can run a hotel, but my brain goes to mush when it comes to decisions at home. We complement each other very well. He's always got my back. He's my rock.'

Neville too felt oddly intrigued by this particular example of Pauline Braithwaite's dedication to her mission.

'And Carl had literally no idea who he was sitting next to in the coffee shop? She's got some bloody front, whoever she is.'

'Not just sharing a table, Dad. They shared a lemon muffin, too! And she got him to buy her a pot of tea! How much more brazen can a psychopath get?'

A few seconds elapsed before all three members of the Griffiths clan succumbed to a fresh bout of mirth.

And as the laughter resonated, the mutual anxiety was temporarily blunted.

Ashley felt infinitely more at ease having confided in his parents.

A visit that he had not initially relished, had surprisingly supplied an uplifting conclusion.

'Another cuppa, love?' chipped Elaine from the kitchen.

'No thanks, Mum. I'll be getting off. I'd better go and see Carl. It's been a long day. And I supposed I'd better check that the roof of the house hasn't been set on fire by her ladyship, too.'

Further guffaws accompanied Ashley's departure.

As parents embraced their son on the driveway, they felt mildly disappointed that he couldn't stay a while longer. They watched as he walked to the car and pulled open the driver's door.

Neville thought it apt to offer some parting advice.

'Promise you'll keep us informed, Ash. Anything and everything. You don't have to shoulder all this alone. I know you've got Carl, but me and your mum would like to be kept in the loop, too. One way or another, this trouble will be ended.'

Ashley nodded and expressed his sincere gratitude.

'I will do, Dad. Let's see what tomorrow brings, eh? Love you both. Speak soon.'

With a final wave and a chuckle, Ashley slid behind the wheel and was soon away.

Elaine Griffiths followed her husband back inside the house and closed the front door.

As she stared at him in the hallway, she quietly observed the unrestrained anger that had now manifested itself in his face.

She knew when her husband was furious.

She attempted to bring him down to earth once again.

'Come on, love. Ashley's a big boy. He'll be okay. You'll see.'

Neville Griffiths entered the lounge without response, as unhealthy distraction began to pollute his mind.

TWENTY-SIX

'Why won't this bloody thing connect me?! I thought the Wi-Fi had been sorted!'

Ashley set his coffee down on the desk as he observed the more than familiar notification of another failed attempt to join the daily business update meeting.

As with most other aspects of modern technology, online conferencing remained a completely baffling exercise to him. In such a case, he would invariably plead for the assistance of his Head of Reception.

Yet of late, instead of coming to his rescue, Jeanette has been playfully refusing to rescue the Operations Manager, probably out of some twisted sense of amusement.

Strangely enough in this instance, his ritualistic notion to ring her for some help was intercepted by his desk phone.

She was ringing *him*.

He lifted the receiver to his ear with the obvious quip ready in the barrel.

'You must be telepathic…either that or you heard me swearing my head off again at this bloody software.'

Jeanette did not respond in kind.

There was a pause that endured for several seconds.

When she did eventually speak, her tone was most odd.

No sarcasm. No humour. No mockery.

Her opening statement was absent of any of her typical workday traits.

'Ashley…sorry to interrupt. You erm…have a couple of visitors that would be obliged if they could come up and speak to you.'

He checked his onscreen diary.

No one was scheduled in until that afternoon.

'Is it the landscape company? They're early. Why can't people stick to appointment times? That's the bloody point of appointments, isn't it?'

Jeanette offered no interruption to his mini tantrum.

'Well, I'm trying to connect to a conference call at this moment but having precious little luck. I could do with your expertise in such matters.'

Once again, Jeanette paused briefly before responding with a solemn declaration.

'I don't think these particular visitors require an appointment, Ashley.'

Now totally confused by her cryptic announcement, he demanded some clarity.

'So, it's not the landscapers, then? It's okay…I'm on my way.'

Her next reply was issued with firm intent.

'No, Ashley. It's probably best for all concerned if I bring them up to your office. They say it is a matter of importance.'

His patience, already fraying due to the internet issue, was now in danger of being fully relinquished.

'Who is *they*? Who's itching to talk to me?'

She did not need to accentuate the revelation.

The phrase alone carried its own innate levels of foreboding.

'Ashley…it's the Police.'

*****

Jeanette felt incredibly tense as she ushered the two male Police officers into the reception lift. Her own heartrate began to quicken as they ascended in total silence.

If there was trouble expected on the horizon, Ashley would ordinarily give Jeanette the heads-up, so she was prepared when the visitors in question entered the premises.

Yet today, he had mentioned nothing. Which immediately suggested to her that he was not anticipating their visit. Which further prompted the implication in her own mind that the matter could well pertain to Ashley himself and have no concern with the hotel whatsoever.

The lift stopped and the doors opened. Flanked by the silent constables, she reached his office door and gently knocked three times.

Ashley was primed for their arrival and with his practised smile welcomed Jeanette and the two officers, who were both wearing facemasks. It was a pleasant surprise to see the pair obliging hotel protocol, even though staff were now exempt.

'Please, gentlemen, the facemasks can come off.'

As the officers removed their masks, it was also notable that neither had removed their headwear, which struck him as a little rude, let alone not conforming to their own protocol.

They were also an unerringly striking vision. It wasn't every day that Ashley's office was besieged by burly gentlemen adorned in peaked caps, black uniforms, and fluorescent vests.

Both constables carried indeterminable expressions, which was perhaps to convey as little clue as possible regarding the motive for their presence on site.

And the fact they requested to speak in private suggested that this was not a routine post-lockdown check-in, which many other chains of hospitality had been privy to during the previous months since re-opening their doors.

The broader, shorter officer had a deep suntan and finally removed his hat. He continued to refrain from smiling. He simply stared into Ashley who had now reappointed his position behind the desk.

Disconcertingly, Ashley was prompted to broach the inevitable question with the slightest strand of humour.

'Good morning to you both, anyway. You're a sight for sore eyes and no mistake. How may I assist you?'

There followed an uneasy and overlong void of silence.

It quickly dawned on Ashley that this meeting was not likely to be termed under the heading of social call.

The taller, paler of the two officers now also removed his headwear but did not utter a syllable. His stouter colleague eventually deemed it appropriate to commence proceedings.

'Are you Ashley Griffiths, sir?'

Ashley swallowed a hard lump of trepidation.

Now he *knew* the nature of matters was serious.

'I am, yes. I am the Operations Manager of the hotel. Is there a problem?'

The shorter officer glanced to his colleague before continuing.

'We've been dispatched to talk to you about a certain matter sir. And if possible, we would like to speak with you…alone.'

Now the group's attention fell directly onto Jeanette, whose feathers were also adequately ruffled due to the sudden mystery.

She took the hint and pledged to leave the room.

'If you want me Ashley just ring.' she declared, closing the door behind her.

More momentary uncertainty prevailed before Ashley decided to play the amiable host.

'Please, be seated, lads. Would you like tea or coffee?'

The squatter officer with the orange face did not even acknowledge Ashley's good manners and moved immediately to the nuts and bolts of business.

'My name is P.C. Standring. My colleague is P.C. Wainwright. We are here to investigate a formal complaint from one of your recent guests.'

Despite combatting his better instinct, Ashley was not dissuaded from applying further humour to the exchange.

'I *knew* that Gorgonzola was off! I did tell the chef, your honours. Honest!'

The two officers remained rooted to the spot with their headwear under their arms. They were evidently unimpressed by Ashley's inclination to make light of the situation.

Their blank, callous visages registered only tedium and growing frustration.

Ashley opted to dispense with the stand-up routine and changed his approach.

He also decided to sit down.

The constable with the fake suntan spoke again.

'Mister Griffiths…can you recall where you were on the evening of Wednesday the fourteenth of July this year. Between the hours of seven p.m. and seven a.m.?'

Ashley's first thought was that the Police were now having the laugh at his expense. Although by his own admission the date did ring a bell for some unknown reason.

'That's *weeks* ago? Months ago, in fact. How am I supposed to remember *that* far back?'

The glint in the eye of the officer with the browned hue suggested that Ashley's response was deemed overtly unacceptable.

'It would be in everybody's interest if you could think clearly and accurately, sir.'

'Well, it isn't long after we re-opened, is it. Few weeks, perhaps. I can tell you that much. About *three or four* weeks after I think, but I can confirm. I know I went to the cinema in July because me and my partner love the movies and we obviously hadn't been for absolutely ages. Or it could have been the night me and my partner visited my parents? But in either case I would have been home for nine and in bed for ten or eleven. And if neither case applies then I suppose I would have been home after work. But I'm normally away from here around seven, anyway.'

Still the two officers stood unmoved and without word.

Both with thumbs hooked in their yellow vests.

Both rigid in mind and body.

Ashley was now getting a little bored with the conundrum.

'Excuse me if I'm sounding dumb…but you haven't given me any single indication of what your visit is specifically concerned with. Is it too much to ask for some expansion. Please? I'm not trying to be flippant. I am genuinely confused by your unexpected appearance in my office. Is it wrong of me to be wondering why you're here?'

Finally, the broader, tanned officer prompted the conversation further towards unveiling a little detail.

Ashley quickly wished he hadn't requested it.

He was caught completely cold by what was depicted.

'There has been an allegation, sir.'

Ashley swallowed dryly again.

He suddenly felt extremely vulnerable.

'An *allegation*? An allegation of *what*, exactly?' he quivered.

'Do you know a woman by the name of Pauline Braithwaite?' asked the shorter officer.

Under the desk, Ashley's legs began to tremble.

Over recent times, the mere mention of that name had acquired the acumen to reduce Ashley to a bundle of nerves. Yet when spoken by an investigating Police officer, it carried an insidious vibe that could capably crush his very spirit on the spot.

In any context, referencing Pauline Braithwaite now ripped mercilessly into his core.

Ashley strived to retain composure as he conjured up a valid reply.

'Yes. I know *of* her. Well…I know who she is at any length. She was indeed a guest a while back. Checked in very late and checked out very early. I didn't happen to be present on site for her arrival or indeed her departure. It's *her* that's making the allegation, I take it?'

Both officers shuffled their weight from foot to foot and altered position, moving slightly toward Ashley.

Whilst not being physically surrounded, Ashley's reactions were now undergoing a crisis akin to claustrophobic proportions.

It was now clear that the taller officer was simply a witness to how the exchange might transpire. He observed whilst his smaller colleague continued to be the mouthpiece.

'How well would you say you know Mrs. Braithwaite?'

Anger was now simmering within Ashley as he continued to try and keep his temperament on an even keel.

'We've…erm…indulged in a few conversations since first meeting here. In reception downstairs, in actual fact. To be honest, I'm disappointed that you didn't do your research before making the trip here.'

'Research, sir?'

'Yes, officer. *Research.* She's become a real problem of late. Well…more than a problem to be honest. She appears to have developed something of an obsession with me. Even to the point where I made a statement at the station about her over a month ago. Did you not view it on your records?'

There was no visible reaction from either lawman.

As if Ashley's words had fallen on totally deaf ears.

And it occurred to him at that point that the conversation already seemed very one-sided. He was now becoming enthusiastic to get to the crux of the matter.

After what felt like a yearlong period of indifferent quietude, the Police officer blessed with the authority to communicate finally muttered another question.

'Would you say you know Mrs. Braithwaite well enough to spend the evening with her? Overnight, perhaps?'

Ashley's unease forced a cold chuckle of disparaging disbelief.

'Are you *serious*? Did you not register what I just told you? Are you asking if I would ever be in a position to *sleep* with her?'

The officer simply nodded with lips firmly pursed together.

'NO! Not at all! It is a frankly ridiculous and offensive question to put to me. She has become so much of a pest that I wish I'd never heard of her. But if you'd have done your homework before jumping in your car with the blues and twos going, you would be fully *aware* of my opinion and official standing with Pauline Braithwaite. She is a menace. She is capable of anything. As I suspect I am about to find out yet again.'

Ashley's very agitated and impassioned claims cut no ice.

It was now obvious the officers were on their own separate mission and would not be diverted from the task at hand.

However relevant and conscientious Ashley's valiantly expressed mitigation might be.

The next utterance from the supposed law enforcer was even more confounding.

‘Well, sir. I’m not in any position to comment on whether what you have stated is connected to this matter in any way.’

The indifference in the faces of both policemen was most discomforting.

Ashley could feel himself losing self-control by the second.

‘What *matter*? Why are you even *here*? What is supposed to have happened on Wednesday the fourteenth of July? Enlighten me.’

Yet another unwelcome and now brooding hiatus of tranquillity elapsed around the office.

From Ashley’s perspective, the exchange had already surpassed the point of ridiculous and was now verging on the realm of total farce.

But unbeknown to him, the officers were playing their game to suit.

Biding their time.

Awaiting the pertinent chance to pounce.

The perfect moment to strike.

‘Look, gentlemen…I’m sure you’ve got bigger fish to fry and I’m a very busy man trying to pull this place out of the gutter thanks to Uncle Covid. Can you be forthcoming about why you are here, or can you please vacate? Either way, can we do it in the next thirty seconds or so?’

Still, they stood. Still, they did not speak.

‘I’ve got to ring my receptionist to set me up on a conference call and I’ve already missed the start of that meeting playing silly beggars across this desk with you two. What are we doing?’

The broader, shorter, olive-skinned officer looked to his colleague again and they both nodded to one another. The younger, taller, paler of the two then unclipped a set of handcuffs from his utility belt.

He then walked toward Ashley and motioned for him to turn around.

Ashley’s reflexive response was laced with desperate concern.

‘What the hell is going on? What am I supposed to have done? Please will you tell me why you are here?’

The officer who had led the conversation from the off stood in front of Ashley as his colleague took hold of Ashley’s wrists and applied the handcuffs.

‘Ashley Griffiths. I am placing you under arrest on suspicion of the sexual assault of Pauline Braithwaite on the night of Wednesday the fourteenth of July. You have the right to remain silent. Anything you do say can and *will* be used against you in a court of law. You have the right to a legal representative. If you cannot afford one, a duty representative will be appointed for you.’

Aghast with horror, an already fragile and despairing Ashley quickly escalated into being frightened out of his wits.

Incredibly, externally, he remained composed.

And offered one request to the constables.

‘Please…I don’t need cuffing. I’ll come willingly. This is embarrassing enough without traipsing me through the hotel bound up. But you’ve been duped. She is a born liar and mentally ill. You’ve made a big mistake.’

Nothing more was said.

The handcuffs were duly removed.

With a very heavy heart, Ashley accompanied the two officers out of the office and along the corridor to the elevator doors. As the lift descended to ground level, Ashley’s sense of dread engulfed him.

Aside from this latest dilemma, he could not envisage a more damaging scenario to the image of the hotel. After all the work he had put into the promotional campaign and the effort to attract custom back through the doors.

And here he now was, about to be herded past the guests in the foyer and past his Head of Reception like some accosted convict.

He pushed back his trembling upset and stared into the mirrored wall of the lift cubicle, just to confirm that it was him, that he was there and that he was not in the middle of a fictional nightmare.

He was there alright.

There was no waking up from this disturbing turn of events.

Unbeknown to him, when Jeanette observed her immediate superior and two police officers marching across the foyer carpet to the exit doors, she had no foresight or inkling as to what might have transpired.

‘You okay, Ashley?’

He turned and glimpsed her intrigued expression.

And even in such testing circumstances, he found humour.

‘Yes, Jeanette. I’m just nipping out for a while. Hopefully I won’t be too long. But at least it got me out of that bloody conference call.’

Despite his fear of witnesses being privy to the unfolding events, it was no small relief to get into the back seat of the Police car and eventually manoeuvre away from the hotel site.

At least the episode hadn’t evolved into the public spectacle he feared that it would.

But now, for Ashley Griffiths, the unknown awaited.

Rendered seemingly defenceless at the unfathomable mercy of Pauline Braithwaite’s disturbed imagination.

A most unenviable prospect that chilled his blood, whilst he kept vigil on the view through his passenger window, as the journey unfolded through town and onto the dual carriageway.

And unbeknown to the three occupants of the Police car, behind them a small, silver, three-door Fiat maintained a fixed, yet covert pursuit.

TWENTY-SEVEN

Carl eyed the investigating officer with nothing less than abject distaste. Since receiving Ashley's permitted solitary phone call, he had been enshrouded in a fog of dismay.

Having arrived at the police station on foot and then absorbed the severity of the accusation, his desire to extract Ashley from this tumultuous mess was all consuming.

Carl's role was simple from his perspective. To supply an alibi that might just be as conceivable as it was casual in its detail.

He was a more stringent personality than Ashley was when under pressure. Their whereabouts on the date in question was on the face of it impossible to deduce due to the time that had elapsed.

So, just like Pauline Braithwaite, Carl employed some fabrication of his own.

And, unlike the Police, he also did some black and white research before entering the station as per his appointed role. In a positive twist of fortune, Ashley's phone call had not been proficiently supervised as per the protocol in such situations.

He had been able to leak the date in question to Carl, who then proceeded to formulate a cut and dried rescue operation.

Having visited the station a couple of months earlier and been effectively dismissed without a semblance of concern for the issues they had logged, Carl was in no mood to be declaring any pang of understanding regarding this current development.

In the interview room, he glared into the eyes of the inquiring officer, Detective Inspector Benton, who cut a scruffy and uncouth figure as he perched opposite Carl and pressed the tape machine to record.

'Are you quite certain of the date, officer? The fourteenth of July. Wednesday. yes?'

The D.I. nodded without verbal affirmation.

'Well, I can confirm absolutely that we were together at home. We had pizza and rented a film.'

The D.I. did not reply, so Carl continued.

'The film was John Wick. The transactions will show up on my online banking statement. It's all logged on the app on my phone.'

The senior officer grimaced and leaned further across the table.

'*John Wick*?'

Carl was quite enjoying this. He could already detect the scent of potential victory. And he had only been at the station for twenty minutes at most.

'Yes. The movie. John Wick. Keanu Reeves is in it. I recall that night very well because Ash had made it home early for once. Well, about Seven to half seven. So, I ordered pizza about eight and we watched the movie and scoffed. Check out my phone that you've confiscated. I swear on my life that Ashley was with me all night.'

The inspector eyed his colleague guarding the door.

A decidedly tense atmosphere was now descending into the realms of brinkmanship.

Carl attempted to reinforce the message already delivered onto deaf ears by Ashley.

'Look...this Braithwaite person is becoming a big problem. She's had the brush off and wants some form of revenge. She's made all this up. She's off her trolley. *We* made a complaint about *her* a good while back. What she's saying Ashley did...it's all *invented.* I'm telling you she will make fools out of the Police.'

D.I. Benton left his chair and began an uneven shuffle around the interview room.

'You say your phone has logged the bank transactions regarding this date?'

'Yes. On the bank app. Both the pizza shop and the movie.'

The D.I. wasn't quite prepared to accept defeat just yet.

He grimaced at Carl and narrowed his eyes.

'Not really *proof* of anything though is it, Mister Davis?'

Carl found himself on the verge of raging eruption.

Perhaps the game would not be as cut and dried as he anticipated.

'*What*? So, you would believe *her* baseless twaddle against my black and white evidence that I have wilfully and voluntarily brought to the station?'

The inspector rubbed the two-day growth of stubble that decorated his double chin.

'See it from our point of view, Mister Davis. Could she perhaps have any just motive for reporting this? I don't see why she would fabricate the story. Why would she do that to a supposedly respected member of the local community?'

The situation was escalating beyond derision.

Overriding dismay was now Carl's incessant and unwelcome companion.

He had lost patience with the charade but realised that for Ashley's sake he needed to retain decorum.

'Well, that's what psychopaths do, isn't it? Make stuff up to ruin lives? Motives are irrelevant. They just say shit and do shit. She's had Ashley in her sights for weeks. Hey - she even followed *me* into town once and sat beside me for a cup of tea before I twigged who she was! Check our statement on file. It's not pretty reading I can assure you.'

Carl's evident conveyance of antagonism towards his inquisitor was encouraging a distinct and mutual slant of hostility. But he would continue to willingly tread this fine line, despite a warning from the investigating officer.

'Mister Davis…you are not in any position to lecture about the way we uphold duty. Believe you me, at this stage your best policy is to comply with us and oblige our requests. Until we have reached a satisfactory outcome from our findings. Do I make myself clear?'

Carl stared into space. He could not summon the manners to make further eye contact with D.I. Benton.

He ground his teeth and clenched his fists as fury bubbled in his bloodstream.

He took some measured, deep breaths as composure highlighted itself once again as absolute priority.

'Please...inspector...check my phone. Check the food order. If I was alone, I wouldn't have ordered all that lot.'

The policeman reclaimed his seat and placed both elbows on the table.

'You seem to be missing the point slightly, Mister Davis. *Your* activity that evening is not in question. But your friend just along the corridor there...well, his memory isn't as concise as yours. He can't account for his whereabouts. So, you can see where things might get a little sticky?'

Carl's approach altered to a more cooperative stance.

'I'm not surprised at all. He can't remember what day it is at the best of times. What with work pressure and now all *this* kicking off.'

The detective pushed his tongue into his cheek as though presenting his doubt about the authenticity of Carl's story. Trying to evade the plain truth for as long as possible seemed to be the strategy the inspector was endeavouring to follow.

'Mister Griffiths claims that he might have been at his parents' house after work that night. With *you*. Does that not ring any bells?'

'That was some time before. Mid-June, I think. He's getting confused. Like I told you he does. But I was with him when we went to his folks' house. That's bit is correct.'

Inspector Benton once again turned to his assisting officer standing by the door.

'Jenkins...can we get records to do a check on Mister Davis's mobile phone applications please. Just so we might verify his version of events. Bank account transactions for Wednesday the fourteenth of July.'

Carl interjected excitedly.

He was finding the attitude of the Police to be repulsive.

It was almost stinking of a cut and dried fit-up.

'It's not my *version* of events. It's the *truth*! The *actual* events that *actually* took place. It's the Barclays app. Password is four, four....'

The D.I. raised a hand to call for quiet.

Again, he leaned toward Carl dismissing the offer of help.

'We don't need a number, thank you Mister Davis. We have the means to access the sim. But I appreciate your input all the same. If you don't mind, leave the investigating to us.'

P.C. Jenkins exited the interview room, leaving Carl alone with the senior inspector.

'But there is nothing to *investigate* for crying out loud! Ashley was with *me*. He was not with Pauline Braithwaite doing whatever she has accused him of doing. Have you even checked to see if her story holds water? Was she even there *herself* that night?'

'Mister Davis…'

'Well, HAVE YOU? Or do you just take any nutter's word on face value when they walk in here these days?'

There was no reply from the Detective Inspector. He appeared impervious to any expression of heightened emotion from the other side of the table.

Carl could only try and imagine the mental anguish that Ashley was being subjected to. In another room not so far away. Penned in and under duress from supposed law enforcers that would not accept the truth.

He opened his hands and covered his face as if to block out the reality of the situation and the wholly unsavoury environment. The interview room was itself akin to a cell.

Spiritually, figuratively, and morally sparse.

Grey, blank walls. The black topped table. The whirring cassette machine. It occurred to Carl how outdated such equipment looked in the wondrous age of technology. It seemed that Hernwood Police Station had been left behind in the Twentieth Century.

Despite his best efforts to mentally erase himself from the predicament, Carl failed in such a quest.

This latest chapter was further confirmation of the living nightmare that both he and Ashley were firmly immersed in up to their necks.

Completely engineered by a dangerous and vindictive soul who remained at large.

And at liberty to exact any personal whim at any moment of her choosing.

A minute's silence endured before the Detective Inspector decided to recommence his line of enquiry. This time his tone was rather more amiable, as though he was playing the host and Carl was the special guest at the party.

'Are you still comfortable, Mister Davis? Can I get you a drink? The teas and coffees aren't too ugly here even though it is powdered.'

Carl felt extremely patronised.

Carl's patience had snapped long ago.

Carl exploded with fury and jolted forward in his seat.

'Fuck me sideways! AM I FUCKING HEARING THINGS? Let me point something out to you that may have escaped your very limited attention.'

D.I. Benton responded with a placating warning.

'Now, Mister Davis…tread very carefully…'

Carl ignored the advice.

He rose to his feet and slammed both fists down onto the tabletop.

'Ashley and I live together as a couple. A *gay* couple. In other words, Ashley, *your* suspect, is a homosexual. As such, he doesn't make a habit of interfering with women. Let alone women he doesn't even fucking personally know. He isn't interested in women at all. Full stop! Am I painting the picture clearly for you Detective Benton? When are you idiots going to concede that the pieces of your fucking jigsaw do not fucking fit together?'

Despite being adequately prompted to reply with vigour, the inspector remained silent and merely scratched his double chin. Carl was now harbouring extremely grave misgivings about how this whole affair was being handled.

The Police had not conveyed any notion that the information obtained prior to the arrest of Ashley was even reliable in the slightest. This aspect alone was extremely disconcerting. But Carl had also gleaned the impression that all was not going to plan with the intention to charge Ashley. The police seemed to be stalling for time to retreat and perform some much-needed verification.

His emotions might have been fraying, but in his own mind Carl accepted that if his instinct was correct, all he had to do was hold tight, stop screaming, and wait until the ride stopped.

Then hopefully, he and Ashley would be allowed to leave with repute intact, if not temperaments.

*****

He hadn't been able to work out the length of time precisely. Six, seven or even eight hours could have passed since Carl had entered the police station after receiving Ashley's phone call.

The police hadn't even insisted he attend.

And despite not even being under arrest and certainly nowhere near to being charged, Carl now found himself being detained in a holding cell at the station.

But it was Carl's persistent intention to intervene and defend the man he loved from some very negative attention, some very suspect Police inspection work, and a broad attempt at veritable character assassination.

And that was just from the supposed upholders of the law!

But as time elapsed and the horror of the scenario deepened further, despair had finally overcome the spirit of Carl Davis.

Ashley's statement meant nothing.

Carl's alibi meant nothing.

And so, he had resigned himself to sit in his cell.

And wait for nature to take its unpredictable course.

Carl sat on the hard surface of the mattress and stared ahead.

His knees tucked up under his chin.

His heart on the floor along with most of his hopes. The darker recesses of his imagination now bombarded him with the double-edged psychological slant.

Probability versus possibility.

Who could come to their aid if the Police would not?

He previously had every faith in the process of legality, and he believed in the potential for justice to be served quickly and cleanly.

But that was before today's timetable of torment had unfolded.

That was before his own personal interrogation had begun.

Having been subjected to the spotlight of doubt and suspicion for most of the afternoon, he now judged the system to be a derisory, corrupt, and distressing waste of everybody's time.

And now that he was alone, the authentic sense of helplessness encroached with increasing severity.

The vulnerability that Carl had valiantly battled to keep at bay was now looming fully over him.

And in his own mind, he had never experienced such desolation.

Above everything else, it was now the lack of communication that was the truly unhinging factor.

Banished to his cell some five hours ago, he had been told nothing since the metallic clang of the door signified the haunting premise of a damning conclusion to the tale.

Carl knew of Ashley's unequivocal innocence.

Yet circumstances evidently dictated that the enforcers of the inquiry must apply a strain of indecision.

That they should turn a blind eye to facts for as long as they deemed appropriate.

And even then, they retained the power to call judgement.

It was almost like he had been thrown into outer space with no safety tether.

Soundless. Lost. Alone. Adrift.

Sentenced to oblivion.

But the most disheartening factor of business was that Carl himself was perhaps under suspicion of fabricating a false statement.

He too was now deemed untrustworthy by authority.

Absurd wasn't the description that could adequately depict matters.

It had been a snowballing, multi-layered work of fiction from the very essence of its creation.

Yet nevertheless, there they both were.

Locked up.

Firmly entrenched in the hands of fate.

Rightly or wrongly, the game was set.

And unseen players currently had the upper hand.

For Carl and poor Ashley, they hadn't even been made aware of the rules.

They could only hope that destiny might retrieve them from the spider's web.

*****

When the bell tolled it was precisely twenty-eight minutes after seven o' clock in the evening.

Carl heard the footsteps beyond and the jangle of keys.

He sat up on the bed as the viewing portal flipped open and two suspecting eyes of reservation set their attention on to him.

The viewing portal was duly snapped shut, and the turn of the key in the latch was a sound that conveyed neither aspiration nor damnation.

The creaking steel door swung aside.

Detective Inspector Benton carried the expression and posture of a man who had been subjected to a very long and fruitless day.

It was a stonewall guarantee that the two innocent people that had been incarcerated under his jurisdiction were also now extremely weary, and in need of a resolution to this sinister business.

The investigating officer was so full of contempt, that he didn't even bother with the courteous gesture of removing his hands from his trouser pockets as he scornfully observed his prisoner.

Carl glared at the two-and-a-half-day growth of grey stubble on the senior officers two chins, and the tell-tale dark bags under the eyes.

He had little energy left to resist what may be coming his way.

D.I. Benton stood in the doorway, and without the merest hint of sympathy or contrition for the emotionally shredding plight he had given his counsel to, he spoke the words that must have descended from the heavens above.

'Mister Davis. You are free to go.'

Supressing the desire to express any form of response, Carl simply registered what he had just been told.

He straightened his cramping legs and got off the bed.

Mild shock began to encroach as he moved unsteadily to the door.

He was ushered quietly from his cell and escorted by another constable along the dimly illuminated corridor.

Another key unlocked yet another door, and the guided tour continued through to the station reception area.

And as he was shown toward the foyer desk, the vision that greeted Carl's entry immediately availed him in offloading the insufferable and wretched experiences of the previous hours.

Ashley turned to face Carl.

His features weathered.

He looked a forlorn and mentally trampled individual.

Ravaged.

Wronged.

Targeted.

As the waves of relief crashed and saturated the pair, they embraced tightly.

Lovingly.

Longingly.

Their eyes moistened, threatening to betray their feelings for one another in front of their presuming and callous observers.

But they adequately concealed their true instincts.

They had already been forced to surrender so much that day.

The earnest joy of reunion could wait for a private arena.

They would not exhibit their affections in that place of reprehensible oppression.

The bald Desk Sergeant interrupted the moment of intimate reconnection with a bark that resonated through the glass screen in front of him.

'In each of the two trays are the belongings surrendered by the both of you on entry. Please check them against the list provided and leave a signature.'

This was the most satisfying aspect of the entire day of procedural ineptitude and corruptive indecision.

Ashley and Carl pocketed their possessions before taking one another by the hand in readiness to depart.

Detective Inspector Benton eyed the newly liberated couple and offered a final parting shot.

'Thank you for your valuable assistance in this matter, gentlemen. I'm sure your cooperation can be relied upon further should we need to contact you again. Good night.'

Neither Ashley nor Carl saw fit to utter any word in reply.

They did not even look back as the sliding exit door allowed them access into the welcoming arena of the station car park.

Still hand in hand, they shuffled dejectedly into the darkness, through the biting autumn air towards The Falcon's Nest, which was the nearest convenient public house.

The awkward silence restricted both men in starting to openly analyse what it was they had just endured.

In the pub, they sat in the seats of their private snug and stared aimlessly through their glasses of beer.

Having been trapped at the centre of a maelstrom, it was now placating to sit, observe in silence, and keep the world outside exactly that.

They briefly felt untouchable.

Undetectable.

And then eventually, it was Ashley that opted to breach the peace between them, moving his trembling left hand to cover Carl's right as he spoke softly.

'Jesus Christ, Carlos. Whatever it is I've done to upset this woman, I wish someone would let me in on the big secret. She really got me put through the mangle in there. Rinsed out. Good and proper.'

Fighting his volcanic emotions, Carl attempted to conjure something appropriate in response.

'They didn't want to listen to the truth, Ashley. I had the alibi ready and waiting. But they weren't interested in the slightest.'

Both men continued to fix their attention on their drinks.

Ashley continued to report the climax of the day's trauma through wavering vocals.

'They checked your alibi eventually. They did exactly the same as I did after I found out she stayed the night at the hotel. The fourteenth it was. That one, solitary night. They looked at the same CCTV footage I had looked at. They checked the logged bookings for that night. It was all there. On the hotel system. No argument. But eventually they also had no proof or argument about the fact that I *wasn't* there. Even though I was also on film leaving the hotel two hours before! They knew full well they couldn't pin this on me. And the alibi you provided must have been enough. Eventually, anyway.'

Ashley's tears now ran freely.

Carl could only squeeze the hand of the man he loved and listen reluctantly to the torrid release of his partner's inner turmoil.

They had been the ones under scrutiny all day.

Fending off questions with irrefutable facts.

Yet there they were at the end of it all, in the pub, now finding themselves in desperate need for some answers.

Answers it seemed, that were not to be forthcoming.

Carl tried to stem Ashley's upset slightly with a question of his own.

'What did they say to you in the end, Ash? Apart from the fact that you were free to go?'

Ashley looked directly into Carl's eyes through the murky interior of the bar snug.

'Nothing. They didn't tell me *anything*.'

'What...*nothing at all*?'

Ashley shook his head and sampled some beer.

'I asked them if she had been in touch to confess about her total lies. But they wouldn't reply. I don't think they've even spoken to her since she made the initial complaint. And I don't even know when that was!'

Carl decided to throw common sense into the mix.

'Maybe they realised they had no case. Because they had no evidence. Because you weren't ever fucking there in the first place. Just like I fucking told them first thing when I arrived at lunch time. They could *never* charge you, could they? They were never *going* to, either. All a game. Just playing through the procedure. The fucking wankers.'

Now it was Carl's turn to succumb to his natural frustrations.

And Ashley's turn to assist in calming him.

'I don't know where I stand with any of this now, Carl.'

'How do you mean? We are free men. Cut and dried.'

Ashley again sampled deeply from his glass before setting it down on the table.

'Think about it for a moment. Some weeks ago, we lodged a statement about her which basically gets ignored. Then she makes one false accusation, and they are all over me like flies on shit. If it wasn't for you today, I'd be remanded in that cell tonight…I'm telling you now. They wanted easy pickings out of me. And she played them so easily. I could have been in real strife.'

Carl gulped down some of his own drink as he attempted some angle of consolation.

'Look, Ash. Don't overthink it, now. It's over. You'd have done the same for me. Let's try and forget about it. Let's get a taxi booked and get home.'

But Ashley was not appeased in the slightest.

His expression had become a permanent mask of dreadful anticipation.

'But what about next time? And believe you me, there *will* be a next time. What if I can't find a safety net next time? What if there is no alibi next time?'

'Ash. I said forget it.'

'But she seems capable and willing to do anything to bring me down. Could she really be that demented and obsessed? She has the power to ruin me, Carl. I'm telling you now, this isn't the end of it. Mark my words. I think she purposely stayed the night in the hotel purely to set this fucking trick up. And it very nearly worked!'

Carl sustained his fraying composure in the face of Ashley's terrified and justified concerns.

But he also sympathised.

Because he secretly believed that Ashley was correct to harbour such concerns.

Carl too had witnessed their nemesis at close quarters.

Pauline Braithwaite herself, had declared her omnipotence.

Unstoppable, was her claim.

A curse delivered from the horse's mouth.

And Carl was now beginning to quietly understand that it was indeed a valid declaration on her part.

Her crusade was now living up to the billing she had bestowed upon it that day in the coffee shop.

But Carl would not disclose his most potent and despairing thoughts. The priority was to restore Ashley to the realm of reason and routine.

'Look, Ash. It's been a testing, tiring day. Let's get some supper and get to bed. Everything might make a bit more sense in the morning.'

Ashley nodded and checked his phone.

He rang for a cab. But home was not the destination.

'Why are we going to the hotel?' enquired a bemused Carl.

'Cos my car's there. I got chauffeur driven to the station in a bright yellow and orange limo, didn't I?'

Both men could only hope that despite their now deep-rooted misgivings, the bizarre and destructive business with Pauline Braithwaite was perhaps at an end.

But unbeknown to them, their hopes were sadly in vain.

For the demon was still present.

And she remained unrestrained.

Untamed.

Unsated.

From her secluded vantage point under the shadow of night, she observed their departure from The Falcon's Nest and started the engine of her little silver Fiat.

She applied the brakes at the pedestrian crossing, affording the duo their right of way. She watched the two men walk hand in hand over the road to the taxi rank.

Just as, several hours earlier, she had witnessed their arrival at the Police station.

Ashley Griffiths' downbeat appraisal was nearer to the truth than even he could have dared imagine.

Pauline Braithwaite was far from finished with her ominous schedule of gambits.

Ploys that were intended to dismantle the foundations of a loving existence.

In truth, her mission had barely begun.

TWENTY-EIGHT

Despite the intake of half a bottle of white wine after eventually getting home for just after nine p.m., Ashley did not sleep a wink all night. Tossing and turning throughout, he made the decision to rise at four and get ready for work. The intention being that he could be in the office well before six.

He was aware that his attendance had been a little erratic of late. It was time to grab the reins and prioritise once again.

Crouching over the duvet he kissed Carl lightly on the cheek before setting off. Before retiring to bed the previous evening, they had discussed the need for routine to reclaim the usual agenda, as opposed to perhaps allowing negative influences to disrupt it. Ashley's unusually early start at work was being tested as a form of therapy.

He was on the road for five-twenty.

Probably over the limit but he was willing to take the risk.

Yet despite his desire to resume the busy yet ordered lifestyle of only a few short weeks ago, Ashley now felt different.

He now sensed bitterness polluting his bloodstream.

The resentment gnawed away at his conscience with every passing minute.

His continuing state of open vulnerability was a situation that now raised a furious indignation within his core.

Ashley Griffiths was a man who had been badly mistreated.

And he wanted solutions to the issues that now burned at the forefront of his mind day and night.

Due to sickness of the night receptionist, Martine, Mo Ravek had doubling up on his duties. Perched behind the check-in desk, he offered a surprised yet cheery greeting as Ashley strode through the entrance doors.

'Morning, boss. Early for you, isn't it?'

Ashley made it clear he was in no mood for pleasantries.

He tried in vain to conceal the fact.

'Well, somebody needs to keep abreast of what's going on around here, don't they? Have you been on your own all night, Mo?'

The security guard rose to his feet and shuffled around to the other side of the desk.

'Yes, Martine not very well. Been okay here, though. Been quiet. Did you get your paint job fixed on the car?'

The question was innocent enough and borne out of genuine concern and curiosity.

But Ashley's mood suddenly darkened on hearing Mo's query and supplied a curt reply.

'No. Not yet. Haven't had time. I'll be in the office if anyone needs me, okay?'

Mo sensed his manager's air of disquiet and opted to say nothing further as he observed Ashley press the foyer lift panel and disappear through the sliding doors of the cubicle.

*****

His office door was unlocked.

The first port of call was the coffee percolator behind his chair.

Slumping into his seat with his drink he booted up the computer and gazed aimlessly at the various windows that popped up during the process of engaging the hard drive. It took nearly a full minute for his keyboard and monitor to connect and be ready to use.

Having logged on Ashley went straight into the bookings portal and scrolled impatiently until he located Wednesday the fourteenth of July.

And there it was. Plain as day.

Room four-four-four.

One night reservation.

Check-in: nine-fifty-one p.m.

Check-out: five-forty-nine the following morning of the fifteenth.

But Ashley was also aware Martine had updated the records without physically setting eyes on the departing Pauline Braithwaite.

The door card had been left on the reception desktop.

She then saw Lee Pinder outside and gave him the aftershave.

The mystery burned away, enticing Ashley further into its maw.

He ought to have placed the issues to the backburner, but he found himself consumed by an increasingly intensive curiosity.

The experience with the Police yesterday had scarred him mentally.

He wanted to know who Pauline Braithwaite had spoken to on site that evening and what she had said.

He needed to speak to security again and also to Martine the duty night manager.

Ashley could not let this go.

He felt he had been severely wronged.

He wanted as far as possible to redress the balance.

But would it be a wise policy to cast the spotlight on colleagues?

He trusted them to do their jobs.

He carried his authority implicitly and was highly respected for the fact.

And they would be nothing if not totally honest with him.

Any move he made seemed destined to cause unwarranted disruption to a very efficient team.

And yet he could not eliminate the possibility that her one night stay in room four-four-four was the purposed foundation she needed to begin spreading her toxic presence.

Ashley's mindset descended further into its pit of cynicism.

If she could deceive the Police, then she could ably fool anyone.

She had the natural bravado and the twisted will to engage anybody in her illicit game if she so wished.

Maybe Ashley was being manipulated without even realising it.

Could she really possess the power to control his mind?

His thought processes journeyed on varying tangents as he sipped his coffee in contemplation of the recent past.

And then another thought bombarded his unsteady peace.

Was she ever at the hotel at all?

Could it have been an imposter?

A decoy utilised specifically as the catalyst for this trickling, infesting unrest?

Whatever her modus operandi, her invasion of his psyche had indeed been masterful.

And thus far, supremely successful.

*****

'She was outside the front of the house, today. I mean…just beyond the driveway. On the pavement. Standing. Staring right back at the house! Twenty fucking yards away, Ash!'

Carl stood the other side of the kitchen island as he conveyed his earlier discovery to Ashley, who had barely had time to place his briefcase on the floor having just walked in from work.

It was the last news he wanted to be greeted by after an arduous day at the hotel.

'How do you know?' mused Ashley, hoping Carl might have been mistaken.

'I was in the back room upstairs working and got the notification from my phone through the doorbell camera we installed. So naturally, I looked at it as I was expecting a parcel to be delivered. And fuck me! There she was! Just fucking standing there!'

Ashley had spent most of the last twelve hours attempting against all odds to bring a semblance of tranquillity into his beleaguered head.

Carl's revelation had competently obliterated any signs of progress made on that score.

'Okay…so, what did you do when you saw her outside?'

'What do you *think* I fucking did? But by the time I got downstairs and through the front door she had vanished. I ran up and down the road. No sign anywhere. It was like she disappeared into thin air.'

Ashley found his frustrations were now veering toward Carl as a suitably convenient target.

'Jesus Christ. She's really enjoying this isn't she? Why the hell didn't you ring me?' Ashley barked as he removed his suit jacket and hung it on the back of a stool.

Carl's insistence on a new policy of moving forward and putting the past behind them was quickly losing gravitas.

And Ashley was quickly losing his temper.

'Because I'm trying to help us get through this. *That's* why I didn't ring you. You only said this morning that you need to get back on track with running the hotel. What was I *supposed* to fucking do?'

'Okay, okay. So, tell me again…what did *she* do?'

'I'll show you the footage. She was just standing and looking. No movement or expression. It was fucking spooky! Then she walked off. I presume toward the precinct. Or rode off on her broomstick. I wouldn't put that past her, either.'

Ashley pulled open the fridge door and retrieved an unopened bottle of white wine.

He pulled two glasses from the cupboard above his head and began to pour as Carl watched in disapproving silence.

'Don't look at me like that, Carlos. I know I'm overdoing this bloody stuff, but it numbs the pain. Here…tip yours down the sink if you think it will make you feel any better. I'm drinking mine.'

'It won't make things better, Ash …but I'm not wasting it…'

A momentary peace prevailed as the pair indulged their habit.

Both moved into the lounge and attempted to settle on the settee.

Ashley opted to inform Carl of his own day's events.

'My brain has been spinning. First thing this morning I checked the bookings for the date in question. I had already had confirmation that she had stayed when I checked at the time but seeing it in black and white on a monitor made me realise this is not a bad dream.'

Carl didn't respond. Ashley continued.

'I spoke to day security and then night security and the night manager, Martine. She said she recalled our friend arriving and checked her in. Very polite and attractive so Martine says.'

'Nothing untoward said by anybody, then?'

'Nothing out of the ordinary was mentioned at all. Just please and thank you and goodnight. All this is just a ruse. She's an expert in diversion tactics. Talk about pull the wool over people's eyes. If she wanted to put the fear of God into me, she's done it! And now according to you she's staking out the house! Fuck me when does this end?'

Carl emptied his glass and stuttered a reply.

'Not just *you*, Ash. I'm constantly on edge, too. I know I act hard but I'm not. I can't hack this shit for much longer. My work is suffering. I'm struggling to concentrate. She needs sorting out.'

Ashley was suddenly overcome with real concern as Carl's admission registered heavily.

'She'll get bored. It will pass. That's what you've been saying to me, isn't it?'

Carl didn't meet Ashley's worried gaze, instead keeping his attention fixed on the blank TV screen.

'Well, to be honest I'm not sure I'm willing to be patient, anymore. I've missed two big deadlines in the past three days. Serious clients that won't come back if I mess them about. Me being late means they are charged a reduced fee. So that means everyone's pissed off.'

Ashley placed a hand on Carl's shoulder as encouragement to address him directly. The atmosphere had been injected with real foreboding. The infrastructure of their very relationship was now coming under scrutiny.

Ashley's throat tightened as he attempted to lighten Carl's suddenly overpowering despondency.

'You'll pull the time back, won't you? Surely your clients will understand?'

Ashley's genuine plea was met with astonishment from the other end of the sofa.

'It's my *business*, Ash. Just like in your trade…excuses don't cut the mustard. I've got to give people what I promised them and *when* I promised it. If I fail on that then things fail for them at their end.'

'But surely there's scope for some wriggle room?'

'No, Ash. Of course, there isn't! The supply chain runs forever. The thing is, I only get *one* chance with new clients. If I can't honour the agreement, they will go to someone that can. End of story.'

Carl's sudden defeatist demeanour was not anticipated.

Ashley found himself drowning in a myriad of potential negative outcomes to the undeniable dilemmas that had now infiltrated their life together.

Yet this new strand of domestic fracture had caught Ashley on his blind side. It was almost as though Carl's approach to the scenario had altered at the flick of a switch.

And Ashley was at a total loss as to how he might try and remedy the looming disaster.

'Okay. So, what is it you are telling me, Carl? Because I have no solution to any of this mess at this current time. I sympathise with you letting customers down. I get it. But surely you can manage around the problem. Start work earlier?'

Carl was stuck for an instant reply, as Ashley continued.

'Okay then…finish later? Flexibility is key if we are going to get over this hurdle.'

Carl shook his head and stared at the empty wine glass dangling through his fingers via the stem.

He offered yet another, more sinister thought to the table.

'You don't understand, Ash. We are sitting ducks, here. Even though she stays outside, that woman is now within these walls. Every second of every day it's messing my head up. But I can't allow it to mess my business up, too. This environment has been poisoned. Just like the poor cat was! It's almost like she fucking *lives* here with us. In our heads and in every corner of every room. Today really freaked me out. And I'm not too proud to admit it.'

Ashley looked at his partner's trembling hands.

Carl's manner of expression implied that he had already considered the situation in depth and had come to a decision.

Ashley sensed there was a revelation on the horizon.

A revelation that he instinctively did not wish to hear.

'Okay, Carl. You've had time to mull this over. I can see that much. I know you have something to tell me. Just cut to the chase. Please. For crying out loud.'

An agonising period of quiet descended on the room.

Until Carl eventually plucked up the courage to disclose his temporary solution.

'I think it best…in the short term...if I relocate to my brother's and work from there. Just for the time being until I've got work back on track and the shitstorm this end has blown over.'

Ashley's spirit drained away with every syllable Carl uttered.

It was the worst possible proposal coming at the worst possible time.

'I can't work in this house. I'm like a jumping bean every two minutes. I'm in the grip of real mindfuck, Ashley. And I've never experienced anything like it before. For me, a change of scenery is vital and could solve things quickly.'

Ashley was now rocked to his very essence. Carl's standpoint had appeared out of the blue like a thunderbolt. The last thing in the world Ashley has anticipated was desertion by the man he loved with all his heart.

His voice quivered with wavering desperation.

'But…your brother…, he lives fifty miles away. It's silly doing such a journey every day. It's going to cost a fortune in train fares. Please…try and sit it out here with me. Things will be fine, Carl. I promise you.'

Another indeterminable hiatus ensued in the discussion. Another period of uncertain contemplation. Before the resumption of upset. Carl seemed reticent to expand on his plan.

It soon became clear why.

'Well…that's just it, Ash. I won't be commuting. I'll be *staying* at Rob's. He has a spare room I can use for work and sleeping. Just until…well…you know…'

Ashley felt the vexation surge through him.

He knew he would not be able to prevent its immediate release.

Only yesterday Carl seemed to be the saviour.

The knight in shining armour.

And now his true colours were being nailed to the mast.

Ashley stared in shocked dismay at the man he loved.

Who had seemingly schemed in private to depart the scene as a coward and a traitor.

Ashley sat forward. His mind battling a storm of mixed responses.

'You *what*? What did you say? You're *leaving* me? The rat escaping the sinking ship? You're seriously intending to abandon me at the time in my life when I need you by my side the very most? Am I hearing things? Am I still in bed dreaming? Did the last twenty-four hours never happen?'

Ashley's accusatory stance pushed buttons in Carl.

Tempers that had been feasibly prompted yet well constrained during the previous weeks were now well and truly firing.

'Ashley…I've tried to ignore this and carry on with life, but the problem isn't going away as we'd hoped it would do. Its knackering up *my* wellbeing as well as *yours*, you know. It's not just *you* that's suffering.'

Ashley could not retain composure and became angry.

It seemed the seeds of division were now bearing fruit.

'Oh, right? So, your solution is to piss off and leave me with it all? That's *really* going to help me. That's *real* teamwork that is! Well, I'm sorry, Carlos. But your idea of showing solidarity is a little bit out of synch with mine.'

The heated discussion was gently snowballing into an irretrievable exchange of opinion and drawing of lines. Emotions spiralled beyond control, as truths buried just below the surface now flooded forth into the arena.

Carl did not hold back with a cutting assault that contradicted every sentiment he had previously conveyed.

‘We wouldn’t *be* in this position if it wasn’t for that campaign of yours. Mister Big lapping up the bloody attention. You brought this on yourself, Ash. I take no blame for any of it. It wasn’t *me* plastered on billboards all over the bloody county, was it? Your period in the spotlight was obviously going to upset someone eventually wasn’t it. It’s the law of averages that you would find trouble with some idiot or other.’

Carl’s declarations were like knives through Ashley’s heart.

And it seemed, in his back.

‘I really cannot believe it’s *you* that is saying these things, Carl. You encouraged me every single step of the way. *Everybody* did! Everyone said what a great idea it was and how good it would be for me. In fact, I was the only one that *did* have reservations about being the fucking poster boy! Well, my instincts were proved right, weren’t they! Because now I’m pretty damned sure it was a *terrible* idea. But thanks for letting me know how you *really* feel now it’s too fucking late! Thanks, a whole fucking bunch!’

Ashley tried in vain to stem his upset and retreated to the kitchen.

Tossing his wine glass into the sink capably shattered it into a dozen pieces.

Ashley’s watery gaze settled on the evening blackness through the window toward Marjorie’s grave.

His whimpering tone had quickly lost its edge of aggression.

He was now suffocating under the weight of realisation as he sensed his partner’s presence right behind him.

‘Well go on then. Fuck off and leave me to it if that’s your intention. Sounds like the arrangements are in place and I’m the last to know about your sneaky little plan, anyway.’

Carl stood in the kitchen doorframe.

Perhaps enshrouded in guilt.

Perhaps not.

‘I’ve got to ring my brother. It’s not confirmed yet.’

Ashley did not divert attention from the darkened vista of the rear garden.

‘Well hurry up and fucking ring him then! Leave me here to suffer alone. I’ll say this…your timing is brutally shocking. But like with everything else in my life at this moment, I’m helpless to do a thing about it. My hands are tied. Just remember this is *your* choice, not mine. Absolutely fucking charming.’

*****

Carl poked his head into the lounge to observe Ashley curled on the sofa in the foetal position.

Both physically and spiritually, Carl Davis now felt genuinely horrendous.

This was a scenario with no positive angle whatsoever.

‘Ash…Ash…are you awake?’

There was no reply.

Not a glimmer of movement.

Carl was tempted to depart without saying a word.

But he attempted to communicate once again.

He wasn’t sure if his whispered farewell would reach its audience or not.

‘Ashley…I’m off to my brother’s. The train is in twenty minutes. I’ll be in touch. I promise. I’ve got my critical work equipment and some clothes. If I’ve forgotten anything I’ll have to come back for it.’

The crucifying goodbye eventually prompted a response from the desolate figure hunched on the settee.

Ashley stretched off his legs and sat upright.

It was all he could do to offer Carl a cursory glance before hiding his face in his hands.

He attempted to summon one final grasp at resolution as the tears fell freely.

‘Carl…I’m begging you. Please…don’t go. I’m sorry for being angry and shouting. I love you. I can’t do this without you. Please don’t leave me.’

There was no verbal response.

The only indication to Ashley that his wish was not to be granted, was the click of the front door latch as Carl pulled it closed behind him and headed for the railway station.

Leaving a desolate Ashley alone to drown in soul-destroying turmoil.

TWENTY-NINE

The searing heartache cut through Ashley like a razor.

He had spent the entire night downstairs on the settee, staring into the bleak nothingness of his now hollow, empty home.

And as the shifting night invited the onset of dawn and beyond, Ashley knew he would be no use at work.

He also knew that the announcement of his absence would not receive a sympathetic ear.

Every second on the phone to Derek Evans was undiluted torture as each syllable ricocheted around his conscience.

'Derek…its Ashley…I'm afraid I won't be on site for the rest of the week.'

'It's a fairly delicate and personal matter that I'd really rather not divulge at the moment.'

'Not ill as such. But I've got a lot on my plate this end. My mind would be anywhere except where it should be.'

'Yes. I appreciate that Hernwood is on the verge of full occupancy and that it's going to be a frantic few weeks.'

'Perhaps Scott from Denton can double up?'

'He can cope in the interim, surely?'

'Yes, I'm sure he is but he's very capable. Hernwood would be in good hands.'

'I'm not absolutely sure. Its more mental than physical.'

'It's a long story that I don't want to concern you with.'

'No, I'm not being awkward or evasive.'

'Okay…if you really must know my partner has just walked out on me. Okay, happy now?'

'Yes, Derek. I probably could perform a shorter shift. but I wouldn't be in the zone. My head's all over the shop as you might imagine.'

'Yes, I'll contact Jeanette. She won't have an issue, I'm sure.'

'How did you hear about that?'

‘Oh right. Big mouths everywhere aren’t there…’

‘Yes…I perhaps should have informed you, but that issue was also personal to me and didn’t pertain to my role.’

‘Well of course I understand that having the Police on site for any reason creates a negative image to guests.’

‘Believe you me the Police had no authentic motive for wanting to talk to me at work.’

‘I couldn’t really avoid it, could I? Firstly, I wasn’t expecting a visit and secondly, before I knew it, they were escorting me out through reception.’

‘Well, what would you have expected me to do?’

‘Yes of course. Extremely embarrassing. But if you don’t mind, I don’t want to dwell on it any further.’

‘No, I’m fairly certain it didn’t negatively impact on the welfare of the guests. I’ve heard no complaints, anyway.’

‘Believe me, Derek. If I had any inkling of what was going to happen that day you would have been the first to know.’

‘Yes, well isn’t hindsight fantastic. Bloody useless but fantastic.’

‘Look…can we draw a line under it, please? No one suffered except me. A storm in a teacup.’

‘Yes, if I’m honest this period of absence is loosely connected.’

‘Yes, I know I’ve been hit and miss with my attendance, lately.’

‘No, I hope it won’t be prolonged, either. Believe me I would rather be on site than sat here in this house. But I’m too preoccupied.’

‘Yes, Derek. Any changes to the situation and you will be the very first to know.’

‘Okay…and thank you. Ta Ta for now.’

Ashley switched off his mobile phone and placed it on the kitchen worktop. He leaned on the sink and observed the late autumnal scene through the window.

The rear garden looked particularly uninviting at this time of year.

Once more he settled his attention at Marjorie’s resting place, and the upset rose from the depths to drag him under once again.

His tears splashed onto the white resin draining board as wails of anguished despair echoed around the walls of the house.

It was a few minutes before his fragile composure returned, and he shuffled upstairs donned only in his bath robe. It might have been an error of judgement, but he could not resist pushing open the spare room in which Carl had utilised to run his business.

Certain items had been removed, bound no doubt for his brother's house.

The empty desk and chair were symbolic of a former life.

Representative of the life Ashley was now deprived of.

Or should that be, a life that Pauline Braithwaite had caused him to lose.

The moment of shredding emotion passed.

Now replaced by random rushes of fury as he contemplated events.

Why had Carl suddenly decided to run?

Why couldn't he give Ashley the opportunity to talk him around?

Or at least try to?

He reflected on the summer's chronicle of unwarranted malice and sinister torment.

He wanted to vomit; such was the swirling nest of toxic hatred now being nurtured within his gut.

Ashley's life and career had suddenly entered a dark tunnel.

Uncertainty and fear were now his only companions as he travelled through it alone.

How long he would be forced to further endure this sufferance, was now in the lap of the gods.

But there was one crumb of comfort among the debris.

At least hitting rock bottom would ordain the inevitable scenario.

Surely the only way then, was back up.

THIRTY

Derek Evans' typically casual and accommodating demeanour was starkly absent. The unspoken frustrations hanging over the Managing Director of Ultimate Inns were however very detectable to Ashley from the other side of the desk.

Dressed in jeans, trainers and a hooded top, Ashley's attire evidently did little to dilute the tension in the room.

The M.D. eyed Hernwood's Head of Operations for a few seconds before commencing his monologue, though Ashley figured it wouldn't take a genius to guess the gist of what was about to be said.

'I thought we needed a chat, Ashley. And in sympathy towards your current circumstances, I thought it best I come here as opposed to dragging you eighty miles to *my* office.'

Despite the lingering apprehension surrounding the so-called emergency meet-up, Ashley felt inwardly appreciative of his superior's approach. He adjusted position in his chair but knew he was unlikely to establish any semblance of comfort.

'Thank you. Derek. That's very thoughtful of you.'

'Have you spoken to any of your team since your arrival on site?'

Ashley thought the question a little odd, but his answer was honest enough.

'Not really. I parked around the back and came in through the kitchen service door. The breakfast staff have seen me, but we didn't socialise aside saying good morning.'

Derek nodded in apparent relief.

'That's fine. We don't want any unnecessary distractions among the crew. They're fighting to keep the ship steady as it is.'

It was plainly obvious that Ashley's nigh-on three-week period of sickness leave from work was a source of contention for the Managing Director, whose patience was evidently being tested.

How he was going to broach the subject face to face would be interesting for Ashley to witness, to say the very least.

The attempt to be kind-hearted over the phone some twenty days earlier was now about to be eclipsed by a rather different tone from the figurehead of the chain.

Ashley thought he would pre-empt the brewing storm.

'Does this impromptu get together concern my illness, Derek?'

Derek Evans' expression remained unreadable. But Ashley was no fool and could envisage that his prolonged leave could be detrimental to the performance of the hotel, both within the chain and against local competitors.

'I understand you have some domestic issues to resolve. I don't wish you to divulge any personal details, of course. That is your business. But yes, I'm here to discuss *this* business. Especially regarding your attendance of late.'

Ashley felt dog tired. He had barely eaten or slept since Carl's departure. He really wasn't in the mood to talk about any of the current dilemmas that had attacked the very fabric of the existence he once knew and trusted.

But he nodded solemnly in full acknowledgement of the M.D.'s position.

For his part and to his credit, Derek Evans was trying desperately not to read his most prolific site manager the riot act.

Although at a push, it was possibly justified.

'I'm fully expecting a reprimand from you, Derek. I've not communicated effectively over this mess and for that I can only apologise.'

The M.D. rose from his chair and moved toward the window, which offered a bleak picture of late-November beyond the glass.

But Derek wasn't concerned with the weather.

His eyes cast down across the nigh on full car park, which at least served to confirm that trade was in a very positive state.

Pressing the need ever further for the Operations Manager to be back at his post.

Derek turned and opted to exhibit a warm smile.

‘Rest easy Ashley, for lord’s sake. This little chat is off the record. Just between me and you. You’re my top man. I’m worried about you. Business is recovering far more swiftly through the chain than anyone anticipated. Particularly here. But every team needs its leader.’

Ashley felt slightly despondent at the blatant attempt to hook him back into the workplace via flattery.

‘I know. But my mind is all over the shop. I’d underperform and I would let you *and* the side down. It’s too soon, Derek.’

The M.D. faced his most accomplished and admired employee.

‘Ashley…I need you suited and booted and back in that chair pronto. I have no temporary cover anymore. All the sites are under strain and pushing to recruit. We are stretched to the max. I can promise to cover your backside for so long, but not indefinitely.’

Ashley found himself suddenly aggrieved by the implication.

It was as if Derek’s standpoint regarding his private struggles was dismissive and viewed as a second priority.

He was very tempted to respond in kind as he observed Derek Evans shuffle around the carpet. In one key respect, he could perhaps be justified in pointing the finger at his employer for being the initial cause of his troubles.

Ashley now firmly held the conviction that if he hadn’t agreed to involve himself in the promotion campaign, then Pauline Braithwaite would never exist.

He would still have Carl at home with him.

He would still be at work, doing the job he loved.

In short, Ashley could possibly be vindicated in blaming his employer for this entire situation.

But such an argument would not hold water with Derek Evans, who had now finished his contemplative walkabout and had moved back to the desk.

The M.D. loomed over Ashley’s chair.

To most, he typically portrayed a kindly face to those working for Ultimate Inns Limited.

But today, he was very much in proprietor mode. This conversation might have been deemed off the record, but Ashley felt the slap on the wrists, nevertheless.

And sure enough, Derek was quickly closing in on the nuts and bolts of the scenario.

Now the tone of the message was orderly, as opposed to an informal piece of advice.

'Whatever is going on at home, Ashley…get it sorted. And get your priorities re-aligned. If you need a doctor, then see one. We can offer an occupational health assessment if we feel it might be warranted. If that's what *you* feel might help, then I can make the call today. But do we really want to go down that route? I don't think so, do you?'

It was incredibly stifling to adjust to Derek's callous perspective.

He played a hard game. He was a businessman.

There was clearly no leeway for slacking in the ranks.

Especially for the barracks commander.

Basically, resumption of his role was all that was on offer.

And that is what was being demanded.

The irony hung around the walls and ceiling like a thick, syrupy fog.

Not four months ago Ashley Griffiths was being lauded as the saviour of the chain, and it was the consensus that he had single-handedly helped to guide the business out of the gloom that the Covid pandemic had cast.

Now he was being unofficially warned about his employment future.

How times change.

How the memories must be so short.

The element of compassion was gone.

Derek Evans was laying down the law.

Simple as that.

'But if I see a doctor, he will sign me off, anyway. Or the other alternative is medication. I'm not going down that road, either.'

The M.D. clasped his palms together and conveyed an obviously sincere directive.

'So, you take *my* alternative, Ashley. And you come back to work.'

Derek Evans turned on his heel and made for the door.

His visit to Hernwood was short, unsweetened, and barely worth the cost of the fuel.

Sadly, for Ashley, he was already further ensnared into a web of self-pity and this unenviable exchange with the company's owner did little to alleviate the sensation.

Subsequently, sarcasm seemed appropriate to accompany the M.D.'s departure. Ashley remained seated behind his desk as the big chief turned the door handle.

'I'm quite honoured, Derek. You come all this way to see your favourite manager and then proceed to kick his arse. And its only taken you ten minutes to put me flat on the floor.'

Derek glared at Ashley as he pulled the door ajar.

An open display of previously suppressed disapproval was rapidly replaced by a crocodile's smile.

'That's exactly my point, Ashley. You *are* my best! Don't let your standards slip. You're still *way* ahead of anyone else's game.'

Ashley sensed a little pride seeping through the joints as Derek continued with his parting shot.

'But don't get too big-headed. I didn't get in the car *just* for you. I'm doing the rounds. The only difference is, I let *you* know I was on the way to see you. Denton and Hathersham haven't a clue. But its already ten-thirty, so I'd best be off.'

Ashley eventually saw fit to employ some manners and rose to his feet to see Derek out of the office.

The corridor beyond was deserted aside a room maid who had just commenced her shift and was far too pre-occupied to notice the Operations Manager and the Managing Director shaking hands some thirty yards away.

'So, Derek. When would you like me back in the chair?'

The M.D. looked Ashley up and down before leaning closer and whispering.

'How about *today*? But go home and change first. I can't have my site managers loafing about in denims and PE pumps.'

Surprisingly, Ashley identified the strand of humour in Derek's parting comment.

He re-entered his office and closed the door, now accompanied solely by the disconcerting contemplation of what lay immediately ahead of him in the long, dark tunnel.

THIRTY-ONE

Neville and Elaine Griffiths had never envisioned the day when they might see their only offspring weighed down by such distress. Even as an infant, their son would overcome pain and shock with a forced smile and an almost casually stoic attitude.

Tears and upset were never in the child's remit.

Not that he had been raised to conceal his feelings and emotions.

Far from it.

But the notion that he could now, as a fully-fledged, capable adult, ever be caught in the grip of such visible mental destruction tore through their hearts.

For Ashley to suddenly appear at their home and break down before them was unthinkable. For him to kneel on their dining room floor, wailing in agonising grief, presented the torturous image that any parents should dread being witness to.

For the close-knit Griffiths clan, today marked a journey into unchartered, potentially treacherous territory.

No sooner had Ashley entered the hallowed arches of their home, his demons attacked, forcing him into submission, and making him succumb to their torrential and insidious game.

Meanwhile, his mother and father could merely stand by as helpless spectators.

Rendered powerless by their mutual despair and forlorn disbelief at the harrowing sight unfolding before their eyes.

Their only son, now in his fifth decade.

A charming intellectual.

A naturally personable and entrusting character, who endeared himself to all who crossed his path.

Now being gradually eaten alive by a sinister virus that had invaded his recently idyllic existence.

As a son, he was a credit not only to his parents, but also to himself.

As a person, he was cherished by all who knew him.

Whatever their particular association with him might be.

As a professional man his record spoke for itself.

Accreditations galore.

Ambition, experience, commitment, and loyalty had all contributed to his standing as a talented and pioneering leader and respected manager.

He symbolised reliability and security, and the unspoken message echoed to all in earshot that whilst Ashley Griffiths had control of the helm, nothing would be left to chance.

The champion of Ultimate Inns Limited.

And yet, for all these plaudits and inherent qualities, he still collapsed in defeat before his parents.

And he cried unashamedly until the tears ran dry.

As if in a position of prayer.

Or more likely, a plea for mercy.

Neville Griffiths glanced covertly to his wife, whose own observations had exposed her long dormant frailties.

She too had submitted to the wanton upset as she attempted to close her arms around her baby boy.

It was a tragic, courageously pathetic display of a family in despair.

Neville too sensed his emotional defences weakening, but his resolve would hold firm. He would uphold responsibility as his wife and child would expect him too. He would be their rock of dependability.

Painful minutes endured before Neville gestured to Elaine that they might assist Ashley in getting him back up to his feet. Eventually, the family reconvened around the dining table.

But the channel of upset was relentless, and they would not attempt to thwart their son's natural release.

Neville recognised that his son could now descend no lower.

He was now at the bottom of his hideous chasm of disorder.

But suddenly, Ashley wished to speak.

Composure reigned as he wiped his eyes until red raw, but he was ready to confess. His mother and father were aware of the early stages of the downturn.

But their son's chronicle of misfortune and sufferance now had further revelations to add.

They both listened to the latest harrowing chapters.

They held a mutual refusal to accept that human nature could be capable of such vile conspiracy and hatred. How could a woman's mind conjure such a dastardly schedule without true and just motive for doing so?

But the real kick in the gut for Neville and Elaine was still to come.

The announcement of Carl's desertion left them both floundering in a wake of silent, furious bemusement.

The love of Ashley's life.

Choosing abandonment as opposed to unity.

What had been taken for granted by Ashley was seemingly never there in the first place.

And Neville Griffiths struggled to reconcile his personal responses to such explosive and damaging news.

Having initially been the bigot; the doubter; the dismissive judge.

Neville had gradually altered his mindset to embrace the happiness and contentment of his only offspring and the partner he felt might just be in his life for eternity.

Neville had surprised even himself that his previously rigid and belligerent approach to his son's relationship with Carl had mellowed over time.

Neville Griffiths had proved to all that he *could* change.

And Carl had accordingly and swiftly been entrenched as Neville and Elaine's other son.

Part of the family.

Maybe not bonded by blood.

But certainly, by love.

And yet is *this* truly how the faith and optimism are to be repaid?

Neville's adopted sentiment of affection and acceptance faded instantly, to be eclipsed by a despairing inner commotion. The room in his heart that was once occupied by Carl had now been vacated.

The harm was done. Irreparably.

Elaine listened intently as Ashley declared his disabled mindset.

Unfit for clarity of thought or even a vague grasping at rationale.

And as if the scenario was not inconceivable enough already, the parents learn that their son's employer - the seeming root cause of the entire unsavoury saga - has shed no sympathy toward Ashley's plight.

Ironic that Ashley answered the call of duty at a most critical hour, yet as the process gathered momentum and consequence, he began to drown in quiet regret.

And it was this aspect of developments that rankled most with Neville and Elaine.

After all, was it not the sense of devotion to his role that allowed the subsequent unravelling of his life to commence?

Was it not Ashley's unwavering obligation to his position that lit the fuse under this calamitous powder keg?

As is so often the human custom, history is relegated to oblivion in the minds of its instigators.

So, Ashley Griffiths now finds himself to be a discarded soul.

Left untethered, to quiver and buckle in the harsh winds of fate.

Left to prise hope from unimaginable depths of despair.

Left wishing that the uninvited and undesirable elements of the equation had been banished and that perhaps, there may be a shaft of light at the end of this bleak, foreboding road.

And as their son continued to exhibit a pitiful, disturbing example of demolished body and spirit, the mother and the father engaged one another's attentive stares.

As they considered what should be done to remedy this tale of toxic injustice.

*****

It was just after midnight when Ashley roused himself from a fitful period of shallow slumber on his parents' settee.

He awoke and sat up. Rubbing his tender eyes brought into focus the vision of his father who had remained with his son and kept a compassionate vigil in the armchair opposite.

Neville had not slept.

It was not on his agenda that night.

He watched over his offspring through paternal allegiance.

Pure and simple.

'Dad? I'm sorry. You didn't have to stay down here with me.'

Neville moved position and laid a caring hand on Ashley's shoulder.

'Can I get you something to drink, son? There's tea or coffee. Or a double Scotch if that appeals more?'

Ashley swallowed.

He definitely required liquid of some form but plumped for the first and most basic instinct.

'Just a glass of water please, Dad.'

As he drank, he analysed the reasons why he should even still be at his parents' house. And naturally, when reality returned to smack him full in the face, release was needed once more.

'Jesus, Dad. How the *fuck* have things ended up like this?'

Neville Griffiths did not attempt to offer any strand of reasoning or explanation. The act of protective observation sated him for now. He had watched over his boy and kept any further disturbance at bay.

'Your mother and I think it's for the best if you stay with us for a while. Being home alone is not healthy for you. Not the way things are, at the current time.'

Ashley seemed quite surprised by the suggestion.

'I appreciate your concerns, Dad, but I'll only get in the way. You don't need my mess heaped on to your plate. You've got your own lives to lead.'

Neville Griffiths engaged directly with his son's fraught visage.

His tone now carrying a distinctive, fatherly quality.

'Nonsense. You won't cause any inconvenience at all. We'd both be more comfortable having you here. If you were back at work, it wouldn't be so bad. But going back to your house...well, me and your mum think the days will be very long and very lonely for you. Not a good environment at all.'

Ashley once again felt emotion welling in his throat and gut.

'I shouldn't be needing consolation at my age. Christ almighty what is happening to me?'

'All part of life's great plan, lad. The most important thing now is that you don't start blaming yourself for any of this. We all know who is truly responsible.'

Ashley sat back in his seat and sighed heavily as rivulets of saltwater trickled down his cheeks.

'Believe me, Dad. I've tried and tried to weight up the politics of all this. But this woman...this fucking lunatic...she is good at it. Bloody conniving and bloody clever. She's a practising sadist, I swear.'

It was extremely discomforting for Neville to hear the nemesis of his son being held aloft in such dubious esteem, albeit through a cynical and fearful appraisal of her poisonous accomplishments.

But Neville Griffiths was not fazed by the scenario.

Not one iota.

'There is one golden rule I want you to humour me with, Ashley. While you are in my company, you don't mention her name. Not ever again. I ask you to oblige that request for me, please.'

Ashley nodded in contemplation.

'I understand, Dad. I don't particularly wish for the subject to arise in conversation, either. She's occupied more than enough of my brain space, lately.'

Neville threw his son a stern glare in the half light of the lounge.

The discussion fixed itself to another issue.

'How long is it since Carl did a runner?'

The recollection was anguished for Ashley.

'About two weeks, I think. I'm not sure. One day seems to run into the next without me realising.'

'Well, speaking purely for myself…I'm completely devasted by what he's done to you. To this family. But what I think is irrelevant. It's what *you* think that matters.'

'I don't get you, Dad.'

'What do you reckon to the idea of your mother contacting him?'

Ashley's bemusement was growing by the second.

It was certainly an unprecedented offer and not a suggestion that had even entered Ashley's mind.

'Contact him? What for, Dad?'

'Reconciliation. He can't just walk away and expect us to forget about him. He's got responsibilities to you and your mother thinks he's hit the panic button. She wants to try and help if possible.'

Ashley did not take long to respond to his father's suggestion.

'Okay, Dad. I'll talk to Mum about it when I've decided how I feel. I'm not entirely sure myself, yet.'

'Of course, son. But you can count on your Ma and Pa. You know that. We'll help you see all this to a positive conclusion. You've got my solemn promise on that.'

Both father and son rose to their feet and embraced in a meaningful and timely gesture of trust.

Ashley felt suddenly safe and closed his eyes to savour the sensation.

Neville Griffiths stared at the wall over his son's shoulder.

As brewing ferocity began to simmer deep within his soul.

THIRTY-TWO

'He'll refuse, Mum. I just know he will. He's glad he's out of it. And if he really *is* the coward I think he is, then I'm *glad* he's bailed. But until the problem goes away, he's not going to want to have anything to do with me. I'm convinced of that much.'

Elaine Griffiths observed the dishevelled and desolate figure of her son as he munched idly on a piece of toast.

'Let me cook you something, Ash. That toast won't fill you. Please let me do you some egg and bacon, hey?'

She could see he was losing weight. In the days since he began to unofficially reside back with his parents, Ashley's appetite had dwindled further by the day.

In that time, he had barely touched a square meal. He looked gaunt and his cheekbones had hollowed. But she recognised that he was old enough to decide for himself. She felt rather helpless. Force feeding her son wasn't really a viable option.

She attempted to console herself by perching opposite Ashley at the dining table. They were home alone. Neville was out playing golf with his usual Tuesday morning gang.

Today was the annual Christmas Seniors' Medal. At least, that's what he told her before leaving the house. Elaine had no idea about the ins and outs of her husband's golfing competition, but she did pick up on the fact that among the three prizes were a hamper and some meal vouchers.

She had wished him well with fingers crossed.

December was leaning toward an allowance of winter's harshest greeting. The mornings were icy, but scenic. She always thought Neville was bordering on lunacy playing in such cold temperatures, but she couldn't fault his enthusiasm to get out into the fresh air and try and have some fun.

In his opinion, there would be many days to come when the weather would prevent him going to the golf course at all.

He figured while it was clement enough, he ought not to waste the opportunity. Plus, it would hopefully distract him from the domestic troubles of his son.

If only for a few hours, at least.

'Okay, Ashley. Let me put this idea to you. You won't approve, but it's better than doing nothing but sitting and thinking.'

He reached across for the sugar bowl and spooned some into his coffee.

'Go on then, Mum. I'm all ears.'

Elaine took a deep breath as she mentally finalised her proposal.

'If you don't feel confident in talking to Carl yourself, then permit *me* to ring him up and speak to him. Just to see how the land lies with everything.'

The premise of the idea already seemed ridiculous to him.

A grown man in his forties having his mother volunteer to sort out his love life for him.

And yet, as the caffeine began to work its magic on his senses, the concept began to offer some appeal. Even though he had decided not to chase Carl with phone calls and messages, a contact from Elaine might succeed in thawing relations a little.

Like her husband, she too had come to view Carl as a second son.

And in similar fashion, Carl held great affection for his mother-in-law, as he always half-jokingly referred to her.

He might just respond positively.

Perhaps an injection of feminine reasoning might alter the dynamic of his thinking. Perhaps she might be able to lessen his resolve and unearth a solution to this period of unsettling and frankly confusing estrangement.

Ashley drained his mug and set it down on the coaster as he engaged with his mother's enthusiastic gaze. This alone was enough to encourage a long overdue smile to establish itself across his downcast features. If his mother was keen to assist him, then who was he to refuse such an offer?

'Have you spoken to Dad about this? I get the distinct impression that Carl has been struck off his Christmas card list.'

Elaine nodded with honest conviction.

'Your father is naturally protective of you, Ashley. What happened with this Braithwaite woman is bad enough, but to have Carl leave you in the lurch with it all…well its very hurtful for us both to digest. So, yes. Your father is the unforgiving sort. But when it comes to your happiness he will bend with the wind if necessary. But he's very big on loyalty. And Carl's actions make us wonder what's been going on inside his head.'

Ashley fully comprehended the standpoint of his parents.

No one was feeling the confusion and disappointment more than he was. But it was high time to rise from the depths and offer some proactive movement.

'It's a real shame isn't it, Mum. He's let us all down. I'm on your side of the fence with this. You couldn't have done more for us since we have been together. But I love him. And if he's truly scared like he says he is, and there is a chance his head can be turned, then we've got to give it a shot, haven't we.'

Elaine Griffiths wagged a forefinger in her son's direction.

Her eyes widened in readiness for a dispute.

'Err…let me stop you right there, Ashley. As far as we are concerned, you and Carl *are* still an item. And if you truly believe that your future lies with him, then it's got to be worthwhile fighting for what's been taken away. Don't you agree?'

Ashley wiped his moistening eyes with his fingertips.

'Yes, Mum. You're right. Of course, you are. But I just don't want it to interfere with the life you and Dad have got together.'

Elaine's own expression of vigour shed light into the dubious mindset of her son.

Her declaration completely erased Ashley's reservations.

'Darling…this was your father's idea. He was the one that suggested it. We'll get things back on track. I promise you.'

Ashley already sensed excitement welling within him.

'He did mention something vague about it…but I didn't take him seriously to be honest.'

'Well, it was definitely *his* call. But he didn't want to pressure you. Your father and I have spoken about it two or three times since you came back here last week.'

Ashley felt his emotions taking command once more.

He strived to retain composure.

'I don't know what to say, Mum. Apart from…I love you.'

Elaine moved around the table and embraced her son tightly from behind as he sat in his chair.

'And we love you too. And we want to set things right for you again. If Carl has been properly spooked, then I suppose it's understandable. Perhaps he's secretly relishing the thought that we might go chasing him. Perhaps that might just give him his confidence back to return to you so you can deal with things together again.'

The probability that Carl was indeed running away out of genuine fear had not entered Ashley's equation prior to this moment.

He had become so consumed by how events were affecting his own mindset, that he had afforded precious little time to consider Carl's floundering position.

In hindsight, Ashley surmised that Carl's perspective changed completely after he was confronted in the coffee shop.

It was there he bore witness to the physical embodiment of authentic, devious malice.

Perhaps Ashley had been too callous regarding Carl's need to flee.

Perhaps Ashley should have been stronger himself, instead of relying on Carl to be the tower of dependability during this unprecedented period of their relationship.

'I just wish, Mum…I just wish he would have opened up to me and talked about how he felt instead of privately planning his escape route. That hurts more than the fact he actually bailed.'

Elaine smirked wryly as she re-filled the kettle.

She knew exactly how to respond.

‘Men *don’t* talk, Ashley. They run away. Or go and play golf. Women are the ones that do the talking when the tempers have calmed down. That’s why God put women on Earth. To balance out all the stubborn males with a bit of female perception and logic.’

Ashley chuckled at his mother’s gloriously inciteful appraisal of life.

His positivity was now stirring within once again.

The long bout of dismay and darkness was beginning to offer an end in sight. At long last, there seemed to be a morsel of optimism to add to the bleak mix.

Elaine Griffiths switched on the kettle, turned to face her son, and folded her arms.

She glared at him, feigning an inquisitive air and an expression of encouragement.

‘So, Ashley Griffiths…am I doing this match-making gig or what?’

*****

Ashley and his mother positioned themselves on the settee. He was pensive to say the very least. The plan had been agreed upon.

His mother was the chosen purveyor.

He noted the time on the mantelpiece clock.

Nearly twelve-thirty p.m.

Carl usually broke for lunch at around this time.

At least, he used to when he lived with Ashley.

It was a fair presumption that he was still based at his brother’s.

Elaine had insisted on using the home landline to phone Carl. Such things were deemed almost prehistoric in the modern age, but she was captain of the mission and Ashley had little choice but to oblige her authority.

His mother’s theory was that Carl would readily answer the phone through natural intrigue if he saw it was the Griffiths’ house number.

As opposed to potentially disregarding a direct contact from Ashley’s mobile.

The proof would imminently be in the pudding.

With the number dialled in and double checked, Ashley and his mother waited nervously for the call to connect.

Then the ring tone tolled.

Ashley's pulse quickened with anticipation. He entrusted his mother to handle such a task with accomplishment. But of course, it's ultimate success was fully dependent on Carl's disposition.

At least she could assure her son that she would endeavour with the crusade to the best of her abilities.

That was the only guarantee currently on offer.

All Ashley could now do was sit tight and listen to his mother convey the message of mercy.

The wait seemed eternal as the ringtone droned ever onward for second after second. As he fidgeted on the sofa, Ashley gradually began to convince himself that Carl would not be picking up at the other end.

And then, at the very point of his total conviction in the matter, his mother's authoritative voice jolted him back to attention.

Now focusing intently on her side of the dialogue, aspiration enveloped his very being.

'Hello. Carl? Hello darling. Yes, it's your long-lost mother-in-law.'

'I hoped you'd recognise the number and answer.'

'Do you, really?'

'That's good. At least you knew it was me, then.'

'Yes, Nev and I are fine, thank you.'

'Are you on your dinner break?'

'Oh good. Can you spare a moment or two for a chat?'

'Yes. That's right. It's about Ashley.'

'Yes…he's trying to battle on, bless him.'

'We heard that you'd gone to stay with your brother Rob for a while.'

'Yes…we understand. Of course, we do. It's been a horrible time for you both, lately.'

'Well, hopefully the dust has settled now.'

'Well, that's the thing, really. Ashley thinks you have gone for good. That you aren't coming back.'

'He's very upset about your decision.'

'He misses you terribly.'

'Neville and I have told him its only temporary, too. But he's taking some convincing.'

'I don't think he feels confident to speak to you about it, himself.'

'Probably because he's worried that you'll confirm his fears and say it's all over.'

'I know he's being silly.'

'It's unthinkable that we wouldn't see you again.'

'We keep telling him that.'

'I know. It's been a while since you both communicated.'

'Well, like I say, I think he's lost a lot of confidence in himself.'

'Yes. This is exactly why I've offered to phone you see. He would love to speak to you himself but he's under such strain.'

'Yes…he's been signed off work for the past fortnight or so.'

'They wanted him back, but he just can't do it. Not yet.'

'He so desperately wants to see you, Carl. If only for your reassurance that your relationship is strong enough to withstand this little blip and come out of the other side.'

'Yes. Whenever that might be.'

'He would prefer to speak face to face. He figures that you can't hang up on him if you are in the same room.'

'He's frightened about *everything* at the minute. But the idea of losing you is his biggest worry.'

'He just wants to know things will be okay. It's a very strange time for everyone, I know.'

'So, you *would* be willing to meet up with him, then?'

'Oh really? That's fantastic! He'll be overjoyed!'

'Well, he's currently available any time of day or any evening.'

'You'd come to Hernwood?'

'To stay over? Wow! He will be in Heaven.'

'Okay…so you'll do a half day tomorrow?'

'Then you'll be in Hernwood by mid-afternoon?'

'At the house?'

'Yes. Oh, you've made *me* so happy too!'

'I'll tell Ashley to expect you tomorrow then. About three?'

'He'll be over the moon I can tell you now.'

'Thank you, Carl. From the bottom of my heart.'

'Lovely talking to you, too.'

'Yes, darling. Take care, Bye-bye!'

Elaine disconnected the call with her fingertip and replaced the receiver back in its cradle.

Then she engaged with the face of her son, whose expression of earnest gratitude said more than words ever could.

Time to dish out some orders.

'Right then, *you*. My lovely, handsome boy! You're sleeping with your parents here tonight. And then its home in the morning to spruce that house up for your esteemed guest!'

Ashley's voice trembled with pleasured anticipation.

'Did he really say he would stop over with me tomorrow night?'

'He sure did!'

The son fixed his gaze onto the mother.

She broke the silence with humour.

'Am I *good*? Or am I *good*?'

Ashley wiped the tears of relief from his eyes and buried himself in his mother's arms.

He felt eternally indebted to her at that instant.

'Thank you, Mum. This means everything. Hopefully we can draw a line under this horrible chapter and start a new one tomorrow.'

Elaine Griffiths pondered the imminent scenario for a few contemplative seconds.

She hoped against hope that Ashley's agonising sufferance was now about to conclude. Her son's reunion with Carl was a step forward in the right direction.

But tarnishing the moment of euphoria, was the distinctive shadow of reality.

Her head had made the right decision with the phone call.

Yet the instinct in her gut suddenly fought against the inclination in her heart.

And she secretly envisioned more problems lying in wait.

THIRTY-THREE

Ashley had been on tenterhooks all morning. The house had been cleaned from top to bottom. Fresh flowers stood proud in vases in the lounge and kitchen.

His anticipation was now breaching beyond fever pitch.

The mood was incredibly jovial when Carl eventually arrived at the house just after two-thirty p.m.

It was very rare he ventured behind the wheel these days, but he had borrowed his brother's car for the journey to Hernwood.

Carl's smile lit up the hallway as he entered through the front door at number thirty-nine, Harrogate Close.

'I tell you what Ash…you're a real sight for sore eyes when you come off that motorway! That billboard is superb!'

Such a compliment set the tone for the afternoon.

No further time was wasted on small talk.

The physical reunion was consuming, passionate and tender.

Both men held the mutual hope that the tide had finally turned for their relationship to bloom once more.

*****

Danbury's was selected as the ideal place to go and talk about the future. Both Ashley and Carl were keen to revisit the venue of their first ever date just over four years ago.

It was modern bar on the outskirts of the town centre, which attracted ample passing patronage but also a degree of privacy should customers require it.

Quiet segregated snugs with recessed television screens lined the walls, which provided ample opportunity for couples or groups of drinkers to seclude themselves from the core group of customers that tended to gather around the bar in the middle of the main room.

Ashley felt ecstatic just walking back into the place.

There were tall tables around the serving counter too which were mostly occupied, but thankfully tonight looked like being one of the less raucous evenings.

Carl didn't need to ask what the preferred drinks would be as Ashley avidly designated their seats. Despite the domestic choice regularly being wine, he returned from the bar with two pints of premium lager before removing his jacket and sliding his legs under the table opposite Ashley.

They smiled knowingly at one another in the flickering neon half-light. Anticipation was in the air. Yet both agreed that some form of resolution needed to be ironed out as soon as possible.

This was the first chance both had made to discuss the matter of their relationship openly. Awkwardness initially prevailed. Their parting three weeks ago was tense and aggressive.

Neither was sure about where or when in the timeline they should commence the discussion.

Fortunately, after a minute or two of inexplicably nervous drinking and uncharacteristic aversion of eye contact, it was Carl who opted to take the reins on the exchange.

'I know you think I've totally over-reacted to what's been happening, Ash. That I've been over-cautious, perhaps. Selfish and uncaring. But taking myself out of the problem seemed to be the only sure-fire way of dealing with it at the time.'

Ashley gazed lovingly at the man sitting across from him. The pub's music feed provided a fitting, even calming backcloth.

But the semi-darkness of the snug failed to conceal the unnerving demeanour that Carl had adopted during his absence. His disposition as an individual had certainly changed.

He was visibly shaken by matters. And earlier in the afternoon he had commented on Ashley's loss of weight due to the stress of the situation.

Both parties had endured more than enough. It had been an unprecedented period for their union.

But the one crumb of comfort for the couple arrived in the knowledge that at least now they had overcome the initial hurdle of not communicating.

The barriers they had recently erected were already showing signs of buckling and perhaps even being smashed down with swift glee.

Their decision to meet had offered honesty a vital conduit. They were shoulder to shoulder once again. Physical proximity had worked wonders for earnest evaluation.

The table was between them.

The cards needed to be laid on it.

Ashley greedily sampled his pint as he mentally conjured a response to Carl's opening gambit. He found himself sympathetic to his partner's motivations and reasoning. The frustration and upset he felt just a couple of weeks ago had dissipated somewhat.

Reflection on the subject would not prove healthy, but it had to be done as part of the process of reparation.

'Carl…I get it. I really do. I've been with my parents' every evening mulling things over. I've been avoiding the house, too. Today was my first visit there for nearly a fortnight. Staying away helped a little. It reduced the horrendous feeling that I had lost you for good. But I'm not going to lie. I miss you like crazy. I can't survive this on my own. I need you back. We need to pick up the basics again. Back together. Back at our home. As one.'

Carl now looked slightly aggrieved.

His attention flitted briefly to activity at the bar area before he leaned across the tabletop wearing a stern mask of irritation.

'You miss the real point of this, Ash. This isn't my problem to fight. It's *yours*. And I know how awfully cold-hearted that might sound, but that's how I genuinely feel. We tried a united front. And police laughed at us as we walked out of the station. And then when you get arrested the same happens all over again. Look what attempting a joint defence did to us. It *crippled* us!'

Now it was Ashley's turn to experience frustration.

The recent sense of strangeness between them seemed to be attempting a comeback. It suddenly felt to him that four years of intimate commitment counted for nothing.

As though their mutual history was being steadily erased by current events.

'But I still struggle to understand why you would just up sticks and leave me. Out of the blue. No chance to discuss it. I felt abandoned.'

Carl smirked wryly as he studied the remnants of his beer.

'*Abandoned*? Bit dramatic, isn't it? I tell you what I struggle with. Keeping my fists in my pockets. Because I felt like hunting her down and doing some very regrettable things, I can tell you. And I wouldn't have battered an eye lid doing it, either.'

Ashley's temper was verging on simmering.

'Is it dramatic to say I felt abandoned? Is it, *really*? I couldn't abide the situation any more than you, but I was left totally alone with it, wasn't I?'

Tension was unavoidably asserting itself between them.

Carl opted to change the subject just slightly.

'Whilst we are on the subject of being left in the lurch, have your bosses not accepted responsibility for any of this mess, then?'

Ashley contemplated his half-empty glass as he muttered a reply.

'The hotel doesn't really know what's gone off if I'm honest. I've tried to keep a lid on it. Personal problems quickly become tittle tattle in the workplace, don't they? The M.D. had me about my absence and tried to lay the law down. So, I thought fuck the lot of it and got signed off.'

Carl appeared mildly shocked to hear of Ashley's standpoint with his job.

'How long you been off sick then?'

'Pretty much since you packed your bags, I suppose. I don't know. And frankly I'm past caring about the place at the minute.'

'Jesus, Ash. You need to get your arse back into work.'

'Yes…I know. But I can't face it. My head's been all over the place. What with you, the M.D. and of course not forgetting that psychotic bitch.'

Carl drank deeply and emptied his glass.

'What do your folks make of the business with her?'

Ashley now felt pangs of embarrassment and guilt.

It was an angle on the scenario that he had not truly considered until now.

'They're worried about me, I think. And their door is always open to me. They've been brilliant. But I feel ashamed that a man of my age still goes crawling back to Mum and Dad when he's upset.'

Carl observed Ashley drain his own pint jar and place it on the table.

'But they are still supportive of you?'

'Well, of course. They're my *parents*. Ironically though I think I've shed far more tears in front of them about *you* as I have about the other issue. *You're* my only priority, Carl. Mum volunteered to contact you because I convinced myself it was all over between us. I thought you would just ignore me if I tried to talk to you.'

Carl simply shook his head. It appeared they were both at loss as to how their splintered bond could be fixed quickly and effectively.

He hauled himself from behind the table and picked up their empties.

'I'll get us two refills. It's your round but who's counting.'

Ashley smiled and touched Carl's hand as he went to get served.

The room was becoming gradually more vibrant, and the music volume had been turned up a notch. As the effect of alcohol began to settle him, Ashley was starting to feel a little more comfortable about the evening's potential.

He gazed at other couples scattered around the bar and sensed pangs of mild envy. Every partnership has its squabbles, he supposed.

It would be nice to think that his and Carl's were behind them.

Carl returned promptly with a tray.

Two beers; two single malts; two shots of absinthe.

'Here, get this lot down us and we'll be away. You haven't got work in the morning so no reason *not* to get smashed, is there?'

'Haven't you got to drive back to your brothers in the morning, though?'

'No rush, Ash. He's fine I've got the car. He doesn't need it.'

For the first time in what felt like eons, Ashley smiled as Carl re-positioned himself opposite.

Ashley felt proud to exhibit a broad, genuine expression of happiness. A long-awaited acknowledgement that his perpetual dark tunnel was now revealing a tantalising glimpse of an exit.

The aniseed shots - as per tradition - were sunk in one eager, celebratory gulp.

The pair lifted then raised their pints of lager and touched glasses.

Carl mastered the ceremony with an evolving mood of joy and a firm proclamation.

'Here's to the end of *her*. And to the resumption of us.'

It was an unequivocal delight to witness Carl saying such words.

'Hear! Hear!' concurred Ashley, now truly believing that the devastating period of uncertainty between them had been officially declared as at an end.

The whiskey chasers soon worked their magic. Ashley sipped his Scotch and again absorbed the activity around the now busy main bar area. He briefly recalled the night of their first ever date in the very place.

Such winsome thoughts made the malt taste ever sweeter and the company ever more alluring.

But more prominently than anything else, Ashley was relaxed.

It was a physical state he had not been privileged to enjoy of late.

And it was soon necessary to replenish the empty glasses once more.

*****

Ashley's optimism overflowed from every pore. Snaking through the crowd of revellers, he returned to the table with a tray adorned as before.

Setting the drinks down, he slid opposite Carl on his backside and again the shots were downed with a hopeful statement.

'To a belated reunion and a very successful date.'

'Indeed, Ash. To us!'

Thimble glasses were once more replaced by single malts, and they barely lasted a minute before the lagers returned to the fray.

The earlier apprehension between them had all but evaporated.

The conversation had been casual but old style.

Just talking like they used to talk not so long ago in time.

Ashley ventured an unplanned extension to the evening's agenda.

'It's only eight-thirty. I could book us into Antonio's. My treat! You know you can't resist the calzone!'

Now for the first time that evening it was Carl's turn to display a broad expression of contentment. His handsome features were quickly adorned with a movie-star smirk.

Rugged yet clean. Inviting, yet denying.

Ashley was falling in love all over again as he sat transfixed by his man's half-shadowed profile.

'I still get butterflies when you look at me like that. It takes me back to the early days when I went in deep for you.'

Carl simply gulped his drink in response. His own exhibition of pleasured contentment did not falter as pink and green neon highlighted the contours of his face.

'Hey, Ash. We are still *in* our early days. Everyday should be a honeymoon day for you and me. And I'm so sorry, okay? So very sorry for putting you through more worry than you already had.'

Ashley's stomach knotted with yearning and regret. His heart thumped against his chest, in a rousing beat that uniquely complimented the track blaring from the speaker system.

Faith was being renewed in that snug. Both men sensed it and felt free to wallow in their newfound intimacy.

Carl was enjoying his gradual inebriation and gestured regarding Ashley's earlier suggestion.

'I tell you what. You ring the restaurant, then. I am getting hungry. Table for nine-thirty would be great. Gives us a while longer in here doesn't it.'

Ashley could barely contain his excitement as they both quaffed the remnants of their latest intake.

'Okay, Carlos…it's my round. So, I'll go to the loo. Then I'll get the drinks. Then ring Antonio's. You sit tight and don't go anywhere!'

In a moment of welcome spontaneity, Carl leaned across the table and gently kissed Ashley on the lips. It sent shooting spasms of coyness and anticipation through Ashley's very being.

One incredible thought prevailed in Ashley's conscience as he left his seat.

It was working.

This summit that had instilled so much trepidation and doubt was actually having the desired effect. Minds and souls were intertwining as one. Relief did not seem a big enough descriptive emotion.

Ashley sidled through the drinking lounge enveloped in relentless contentment. The thought briefly caressed him that despite the positive contributions of himself and Carl in rekindling their partnership, one other person needed much earned acknowledgement.

Pushing open the door to the gents' toilets, he silently pledged to ring his mum first thing tomorrow.

*****

Ashley wavered amusingly over the urinal and checked his watch. Twenty-five to nine. His smile was now unrestrained and maybe carried a hint of recklessness to the casual onlooker. But the feeling inside was fantastic.

Especially as he had convinced himself not so long ago that this kind of elation would never be his to sample ever again.

He reflected at leisure on the last few hours.

He was back with his man. They had made love. They had sat and communicated.

Any unpleasant issues had been forced to one side so that the arena was reserved solely for them and them only. Mutual concentration on finding one another once more. And mutual appreciation for allowing each other to emerge from a shell of self-imposed preservation.

Despite Carl's perceived selfishness and Ashley's understandable fears, it seemed at that moment that their future together might well have been salvaged.

He just hoped that the plan for Carl to stay the night was not a case of running before they had tried walking. But he would willingly take the risk. The renewed joy of discovery lay ahead.

He needed and wanted Carl back in his life - lock, stock, and barrel. Tonight had presented them with a most valuable foothold that Ashley required no hesitation in utilising.

Once outside the toilets, Ashley scanned his phone in the half-lit corridor. He located the number for the restaurant and made the table reservation for half an hour's time. Then it was back to the bar for a final tipple or two. Two more pints. Two more chasers. Going for glory. And why not? Was this not a glorious occasion?

Gingerly supporting the tray of drinks, he weaved an unsteady path through the buoyant throng before relocating their snug in the mid-distance.

As he got closer to the seats, the first thing that struck him was that the side of the table Carl had occupied all evening was now vacant. Ashley suspected nothing unusual as he set the tray down on the tabletop and slid into his own seat.

It was only when he apportioned Carl's pint and tumbler from the tray that he noticed another anomaly.

Carl's coat had vanished. No longer in the seats opposite where Carl had placed it when they arrived. But again, Ashley was not unduly puzzled. It was a chilly night and Carl must have fancied a smoke.

He didn't often touch the fags these days, but the mood must have encouraged him. He had taken to using a vape dispenser, but he always claimed he missed lighting up a proper cigarette.

And why shouldn't he?

As per the established tradition of the evening, Ashley opted to leave the whiskey alone until Carl returned so they could toast one another once again. After all, the night had evolved into a cause for celebration.

It was only correct that they acknowledged this together.

A couple of minutes elapsed. Carl had not yet reappeared, so Ashley took the opportunity to idly study his online profile feed with a view to posting about the fantastic evening he was experiencing.

Losing himself in the minutiae of other friends' threads, it eventually occurred to him that he had been alone at the table for nearly fifteen minutes. Even by Carl's standards this was a long smoke break.

Ashley decided to check outside to tell Carl his drinks were ready and that they had about ten minutes to sup up before the Italian restaurant beckoned them.

Beyond the front entrance of the premises, Ashley passed the doorman before scrutinising the gaggle of smokers and vapers that gathered a few yards along the pavement.

It became quickly evident that Carl was not among them. He walked closer to the huddles and scanned the faces that hid behind garlands of tobacco mist and foul-smelling mist.

Bemusement now encroached as Ashley confirmed in his own mind that Carl could not have ventured outside for a cigarette after all.

Again, he squinted up and down the High Street.

Carl had apparently vanished.

Now confused but far from disgruntled, Ashley returned to the interior of Danbury's and instantly commenced observing the many faces in the crowd. Still Carl remained untraceable.

He made his way back though the merry scores of drinkers and swiftly checked the gents' toilets.

No clue. No sign. No Carl.

It was on returning from the toilet that Ashley spied their table through the flashing shadows and unleashed a nervous sigh of gratitude.

In the half-lit distance, he could see that Carl was back in his seat.

Ashley approached the snug out of Carl's eyeline. Rather than make him jump in surprise, he opted for humour and still a few feet away, he raised his voice to carry over the lively music track.

'Thank the lord for that! I thought you'd done another runner on me!'

Ashley's giggles were instantly halted by the terse response.

And the subsequent revelation that the person in the seat, was not in fact Carl.

'He *has* done another runner on you.'

Realisation clattered into Ashley's recently shored fortress of emotional stability as he rounded the table and reclaimed his chair.

Abject horror secured its prey as his conscience registered the vision positioned opposite.

The figure displayed a familiar smile before removing her hood.

The words she had uttered immediately conveyed full and frank explanation for Carl's sudden absence.

He felt the foundations of his world sway and then shake under gravitational seizure, as Pauline Braithwaite lifted one of the tumblers of Scotch between thumb and forefinger and gestured to him.

'Cheers.'

Nonchalantly, she necked the short and gently placed the glass back down on the tray.

Ashley wanted to speak.

To shout.

To scream.

Yet his mind had become a defenceless void as the phantom before him flourished with its own sinister omnipotence.

He grappled desperately for some reasoned logic to what was transpiring before his very eyes.

Some grain of rationale.

Yet she had effortlessly expelled all channels of sensible thought from his mind.

It briefly occurred to him that he was hallucinating.

Seeing a ghost. A work of evil and psychological fiction.

But he was definitely not imagining the nefarious presence just four feet away.

She was there, wallowing in all her perverse glory.

All-consuming and very real.

Her stare never averted from Ashley's as she openly relished his obvious evolving panic.

Yet her tone remained incredulously controlled and contrarily soothing, as she emitted some conveyance of satisfaction.

'Lover-boy decided not to hang about once I showed up. I assured him his drinks wouldn't go to waste. All in a good cause, eh?'

Fully engaged with Ashley's rampant disbelief, she then sampled from one of the pints of lager, pretending to analyse the taste as she sipped.

'Not my usual tipple, but I appreciate the generosity, Ashley. I knew that we'd get our date, eventually. And well, well! Here we are!'

Ashley's initial wave of disbelieving trepidation had now conceded the passage to a pulsing fury, as he slammed a fist heavily onto the surface of the table, causing the glasses on the tray to jump to attention.

He wanted to whisper to evade any unwanted passing scrutiny, yet his voice was now competing with the emotional pull that had been triggered, and his opening salvo was issued with considerable volume.

'What the *fuck*...do you think you are doing here?'

She raised the pint jar a little higher.

Unperturbed, she willingly baited him.

'Just having that drink that we never arranged. That's all. No harm in it, is there? Bottoms up!'

Keeping eyes firmly fixed onto Ashley, she lifted the glass to her lips and swigged heartily.

He was staggered by her fearless arrogance.

He was also considering a foolish course of action that would be construed as a serious error of judgement.

Ashley clenched his fists as instinct urged him to become aggressive, but thankfully he held true to his albeit fraying facility of common sense.

'Where is Carl? What did you say to him?'

Again, she exhibited her striking yet woefully deceptive smile.

'I just told him that two's company…three's a crowd. You should have seen his face. It was a picture. A bit aggrieved, you might even say!'

Ashley stared blankly at his uninvited adversary.

A myriad of responses consumed his mind and body.

She appeared so serene as she orchestrated the wanton destruction all around her. Yet she was still strikingly attractive, even when administering such a level of completely unwarranted penance.

Ashley reined in his faltering composure.

'What…do you want?'

She pursed her lips and slowly shook her head in mock dismay.

The intermittent neon and shadow of the bar room gave her profile a malevolent hue, as she upheld her facade of complete indifference.

'I told you what I wanted. I told you many, many weeks ago. I want *you*. I want *us*. Not too much to ask, is it? Especially at Christmas? Looks like Santa came early…if you'll excuse the uncouth phrasing…'

Pauline Braithwaite chuckled into the top of her glass before tasting more beer.

Ashley vacated his seat and closed in on the enemy.

His patience in avoiding a public confrontation looked to be unravelling into oblivion.

He detected the scent of her perfume as she rested her elbows on the table.

'You are fucking with people's lives. What pleasure can you honestly derive from this? You are one sick woman!'

She tilted her head back and rolled her eyes before re-engaging with Ashley's wilted grimace.

'I told your feeble boyfriend I couldn't be stopped. Nothing and nobody will stop me. I know you've been to the police. In their eyes I'm as pure as the driven snow. A shame for you, eh? Mister Hotel Celebrity of the Year.'

Cackling once again, she reached across for the other whiskey.

'A lager and chaser. Goes down well in these testing times of ours. Good choices, Ashley.'

Now beside himself with vexation, Ashley considered submitting to temptation and physically assaulting her there and then. But that was a dead-end road. There would be only one loser. He had to resist such a perilous whim.

'You shouldn't be out on the streets. The public aren't safe with you in their midst.'

Pauline Braithwaite laughed loudly and literally in the face of Ashley's proclamation.

'Of course, they are! Don't be so melodramatic, darling. I'm very choosy, you know. I don't just select targets at random. Whoops! That was a very incriminating thing to say. Hope you're not recording me. But then again, I'm only sitting here having a quiet drink with an old friend.'

Ashley was drowning in desperation.

He glanced around the vicinity.

Surrounded by people yet rendered in complete isolation aside from the monster in glorious disguise that perched beside him.

'I had my hair done especially for you this evening but wearing that hood has messed it a little. Do you like it? Not that it matters, really.'

Ashley found himself transfixed with the motion of her pulling a bobble from her handbag and bunching her bob into a small ponytail.

'My God. You really are insane, aren't you?' he murmured.

Her smile returned, accentuated with a pointed forefinger.

'Not officially. But I reckon I'd tick most boxes. Practice makes perfect, as they say.'

Ashley struggled to reconcile her alluring physical frontage with the fact that she had no scruples or moral compass.

Her principles were from some other world.

At that moment, her momentous claim to be unstoppable carried true conviction.

He had literally no idea how he might try to extricate himself from her venomous grip.

She had nearly finished the pint of beer as well as both double Scotches. He couldn't tell that she'd even had a drink.

'This is nice. Just the two of us. And you're wearing the aftershave I bought for you. I'm very impressed that you made the effort. I've noticed you've not been at work much. Or at home much, for that matter. Is everything okay?' she gleamed.

Ashley placed both palms down onto the table and leered into her.

'You could have ruined things for me and Carl. Just when we were getting back to a good place, again.'

Her bravado defied belief.

'Oh, stop fooling yourself, Ashley dear. He's not for you. Total mismatch.'

Ashley couldn't comprehend the relentless conceit being employed. And she continued to taunt him.

'Look, darling…you must have surely worked it out for yourself? When the going gets tough his answer is to jump out and look after himself. That is no foundation for a relationship.'

It was incredulous to listen to.

Yet still Ashley's composure held fast.

'Yes. Because of YOU! But *why*? Why *me*? What I have *I* ever done to you?'

Pauline Braithwaite emptied her glass of lager.

Her smile faded quickly. Her green eyes narrowed and drew his attention fully into her.

The customary deflective humour and sarcasm in her approach were eclipsed by a presumably earnest declaration.

'*You* let me in, Ashley Griffiths. *You* started this. *You* put yourself on my radar. *You* wanted to play the game. And so, play the game we shall. Until it is concluded. Until there is a winner. It's too late for sorrows. This is all *your* fault.'

Ashley shut his mind off.

Exchanging dialogue with her was futile and extremely unnerving.

He had to locate Carl as soon as possible.

Retrieving his coat, he began to make an exit.

He did not look back as he neared the door at a frantic pace.

Marching aimlessly along the High Street he pulled his mobile phone from his jacket pocket and vainly attempted to ring Carl.

Yet the stirring realisation now overshadowed his every step.

Despite her rehearsed posturing and illicit notions, there was one of Pauline Braithwaite's statements, that now pounded with crucifying resonance in his conscience.

Carl had run away. *Again*.

Knowing full well that Ashley was once more stranded alone with this ongoing problem.

Indicating once more, that maybe he wasn't the true soulmate he purported himself to be.

Perhaps Ashley was indeed totally alone in combatting the evil presence that was Pauline Braithwaite.

And if he should begin to succumb to her wrath, beyond being able to deploy an able measure of self-defence, then where now might he find an ally to match her?

Or eventually overcome her?

Ashley's heart screamed and his tears fell, as he wandered alone into the unforgiving dead of night.

THIRTY-FOUR

Neville and Elaine Griffiths studiously watched their son as he sat on the edge of their settee staring vacantly into the fireplace.

There was no longer the outpouring of emotion.

No conveyance of his innermost feelings.

No expressive fear.

Just a silent, prevailing numbness.

Ashley's elbows rested on his knees.

His fingers on either cheek, pulling the skin downwards from his eye sockets, fully exposing the spent, raw windows to his now hollowed soul.

His parents did not need him to confirm what they could witness for themselves.

Ashley's fortitude had been completely dismantled.

No longer was he the tour de force of legend.

Once a powerhouse of a personality.

The light in the room. The leader. The champion for all causes.

The fighter to accomplish any quest set before him.

He was now a mere remnant of a character that once thrived.

No longer possessing his customary zest.

A trampled spirit.

A will crushed under the might of an untouchable foe.

His mother and a father gazed to one another clutching for some morsel of respite for their son.

They too were stranded on the unforgiving ocean with their only child.

Drifting with no discernible direction.

No anchor to offer them security.

Their once welcoming domain, now fully occupied by the infesting pain they shared with their offspring.

Finally, Neville Griffiths offered a proclamation.

'The offer stands as before, Ash. Stay with us. For as long is needed.'

Elaine concurred with a pledge of her own.

'If you think it will help, Ashley, we would both much prefer you here. Not home alone. Not this time of year.'

Forty-eight hours had elapsed since the disastrous encounter at Danbury's. Carl was not answering his phone. He had presumably driven straight back to his brother's having been ousted by the appearance of the enemy.

How he managed to keep the car on the road was a blessing, considering he must have been dangerously over the limit.

Being neither seen nor heard appeared to be Carl's automatic defence mechanism. Off the radar and untraceable.

Ashley was not privileged to enjoy the luxury of concealment.

He had barely spoken a word since returning to his parents' house yesterday morning. Yet today, with a clearer head and space and time between events, he felt the need to include his mother and father in the mystery that had elapsed.

Still stunned by the episode, his revelations remained composed and concise.

'Honestly…things were going so well. We were getting on. We were getting drunk. We were going for a pizza. He was happy to stay the night. Then when I came back with more drinks, he was gone. Vanished into thin air.'

Neville was an astute man. But it didn't take much detective work to understand the process that had transpired.

'She's obviously watching your house, son. Watching every move you make. It's the only explanation. She's probably outside watching *our* house now as we speak.'

Ashley nodded in fiercely reluctant agreement.

'It's too much now, Dad. It's like being followed by a ghost. I can't cope with the tolerance of it anymore. Something's going to give pretty soon. I can sense it coming. If this doesn't stop, I'll just take myself out of the equation. That's the only way the game will end as far as I can see. I'd rather be out of everybody's hair than be the cause of all this grief.'

Elaine put her hand to her mouth in horror at hearing her son's thinly veiled diagnosis.

She couldn't believe such a sentiment could come from him.

'Now don't talk like that, Ashley! That is an absolutely *awful* thing to say. Tell me now that you don't mean it. Tell me it's just your frustration talking.'

Ashley felt compelled to engage with his mother's fearful expression and instantly felt remorse concerning his last statement.

'I apologise, Mum. I didn't mean it. But it's how I feel. I'm so alone with this. My relationship seems fucked. My homelife and career are very much in the balance. Everything I've worked for could go up in flames, and all because of *her*. She's crazy enough to want to see me finally drown in all this. You should have seen her gloating when I first laid eyes on her in the pub. In Carl's *seat*! Drinking *his* fucking lager! Preening herself about her success in sending Carl running yet again. She's a maniac. A proper authentic, nutjob. And I can't do a damned thing about her.'

Neville scratched his head as he contemplated any strand of positivity to extract from Ashley's ongoing dilemma. He squatted to his haunches in front of his son to gauge his full attention.

'You said you went to the police didn't you, Ash?'

'Yes, Dad. Many moons ago. After we lost the cat. That was when Carl began to lose it, I think. And when he realised the police weren't going to help us. He's obviously not up for the long haul with me, is he? So here I am. Battling away on my own once more.'

Once again, his father strived to conjure an upbeat contribution.

'And you say she won't respond to reasoning? That you've been polite. Shown no malice or threatened her in any way?'

Ashley smiled half-heartedly.

'Come off it, Dad. I'm scared of my own shadow. I've been completely patient with her. I lost it a bit in the pub. But it had no effect whatsoever. She just sat there grinning at me. Like she knows that there's nothing that can justifiably be done to stop her.'

Neville shuffled closer and placed a hand on Ashley's knee.

He had another iron in the fire but felt somewhat reticent about offering it up for family scrutiny.

'So, all you've done is say thanks but no thanks back in the summer. And you explained your reasoning? But she won't accept it. And now you've reached a dead end?'

Ashley nodded and buried his face in his hands once again.

'Yes, Dad. In a nutshell, that's it. I'm up the creek without a paddle.'

Neville and Elaine were themselves becoming impatient with the perpetually sinister torment that their son was being subjected to. They could see that the fabric of his life had been pulled apart, thread by thread.

Elaine observed the steely determination in her husband's eyes.

She was fully aware of the plan that he wanted to broach. As she stared hopefully, he nodded to her as a prompt to unveil their proposal.

She swallowed in caution and kneeled next to Neville.

'Ashley…I know this might sound totally ridiculous…but there is a possible way out of this.'

Ashley lowered his hands from his face and offered his mother full focus. His eyes were bagged and pink with the worry and fatigue, yet Elaine detected a brief flicker of light in them as she continued.

She took both his hands in hers and squeezed them reassuringly tight. She employed a soft, maternal whisper to ease the passage of the forthcoming suggestion.

Doubt and trepidation consumed her, but her husband nodded with more conviction this time and encouraged the proposal to become public.

'You know…when I was a little girl and growing up, my parents had a theory about school bullies. A theory that they truly believed in.'

Ashley's curiosity was aroused.

He had not considered the fact that Pauline Braithwaite might be termed as a bully. And at his age, it wasn't something that would have readily crossed his mind at all.

She was a tormenting, dangerous individual.

That much was obvious. But a bully?

'And what did Granny used to say about bullies then, Mum?'

He continued to listen to his mother's delicate sermon.

'That they could be killed with kindness…'

The room fell quiet as Elaine's words resonated in Ashley's conscience.

He had listened to her and heard the words she had spoken but had little idea how practice might marry up with such a noble policy.

'Keep talking, Mum. I'm hooked so far. You're taking me to last chance saloon by the sounds of it.''

His father opted to take the reins from his wife in projecting some form of enticing explanation.

'This is going to be difficult for you to swallow, son, but your mother and I think that as a final resort it might well be worth a crack. Desperate times need desperate measures, yes?'

Ashley did not hesitate.

'Okay, Dad. I'm still on board. Hit me with it. I've got nothing left to lose, have I?'

Now it was Neville's turn to pause and consider the plausibility of what he was about to say.

'Try looking at this problem through *her* eyes, Ashley. She is infatuated with you but is bitter and twisted because you've told her you're not available. So…why not change your tactic?'

'Now you're losing me fast, Dad. But I'm hanging on to your coat tails. Go on…'

'Give her what she wants. Arrange to meet her for the date she so craves. Give in to her and don't fight it. Offer her the sense of victory. Let her think that she has finally worn down your resistance.'

Justifiably, despite his willingness to hear his parents out, Ashley sat in a state of abject disbelief at what had been suggested. Especially when coming from a crusty, inflexible, and old-fashioned operator such as his father was. Ashley ran his fingertips over a very furrowed brow as his parents waited with bated breath for his initial reaction.

'Let me ensure that I've got this right before I laugh out loud. You mean…I should *encourage* her? That I should let her think that after all that's happened, that I actually *fancy* her? Pretend I'm somebody other than who I am, you mean?'

Neville fully anticipated a wholly prickly response to the idea.

But he was far from deterred in his belief that it just might work.

Nor was Elaine, who swiftly reinforced the logic of the plan.

'More often than not bullies operate in their own minds, Ashley. If you trick her into thinking she's got what she wants, she might sit back and enjoy the triumph. Then get bored and leave you alone.'

Ashley stood up and moved to gaze at the grey and unwelcoming view beyond the bay window. The familiar street and houses outside were a snapshot of his childhood. Everything was so reliable and comforting back then. So different to adulthood and the demonic reality he was currently submerged in.

He didn't want to overtly dismiss his parents' input out of hand. Perhaps it warranted consideration. After all, it was the only offer of a solution on the table at that current time.

But nevertheless, as he turned away from the window to face them both again, he was struggling to find even a remotely sensible mental handhold with which to embrace the concept.

'Okay…say I play along and perform the charade. At some point I'm hoping to shake her off, yes? And when she won't let go…just as she won't do now…what then? What do I do *then*?'

Neville opened the palms of his hands as a gesture of concession.

'Then son, you won't be any worse off than you are at the moment. Will you? But at least you can say you gave it a go.'

Ashley rubbed his eyes again and began to pace the room as his parents reverted to their seats. They recognised that the premise would not sit well initially. It needed a period of digestion. But at least the seed had been set. It was up to Ashley to derive the necessary enthusiasm.

However, his expression of bemusement didn't lean toward embarking on the scheme any time soon.

'So...Mum, Dad...the aim is to bore her to death. That's the theory? That we must hope she gets fed up with me, eventually?'

Neville jumped in to confirm.

'Yes, Ash. If it doesn't work, we'll just have to rattle our brains again, won't we?'

Ashley was overcome with a mix of responses ranging from abject dismissal to profound intrigue.

He reclaimed his own seat with a heavy sigh of indecision.

'Jesus Christ! Life was far less complicated when we only had Covid to worry about, wasn't it.'

Elaine and Neville laughed with relief that their son's dry humour was still capable of producing glimmers of the old touch.

Ashley observed the mantelpiece clock. It was only just before eight a.m. Yet his mind and body were craving sleep.

He turned appreciatively to his mother and father.

'Look. Let me think about this strategy of yours. Is it okay if I crash for a while first? I'm totally bushed.'

His mother did not conceal her delight at the request.

'Of course, love. The spare room is already made up. Do you want a cuppa bringing up?'

Hauling himself wearily back to his feet, he embraced his parents, before kissing his mother on the cheek and then hugging his father.

'No thank you. I don't think I'll take long to drop off. Fingers crossed. I'll hopefully wake up with some decision on your crazy plan.'

Neither Elaine nor Neville's expression altered from a sternly insistent glare as Ashley exited the lounge.

'Okay, love. Try and sleep well.' whispered Elaine.

Ashley couldn't have been more thankful for their presence.

'Love you both. See you in a bit.'

*****

Unsurprisingly, Ashley slept for nearly twenty-four hours and was still in bed when Neville Griffiths placed himself at the table for breakfast the following day.

He smiled appreciatively at his wife as she placed a plate before him containing poached eggs on toast.

'Have you got golf today, love?'

'Yes, if the rain stays off. Last round before Christmas. Not that it feels much like Christmas.'

Elaine poured her husband some tea from the pot.

'Okay. I've got to nip into town for a couple of bits. Could you drop me off?'

'Yes, love of course I can.'

Neville proceeded to grind black pepper onto his eggs as Ashley entered the kitchen donned in a pair of his father's pyjamas and a bath robe.

His mother's cheery greeting was encouraging in helping him face another day. He perched at the table opposite his father.

'Morning Ashley, love. Can I get you something to eat. You've had absolutely nothing in your stomach for nearly two days. You'll be poorly.'

'No thanks, Mum. I'm fine. I've no appetite. Just a cup of coffee, thanks. Then I'll be out of your hair for the day.'

Neville glanced across to Ashley on hearing the last statement but did not query it. Instead, he proceeded to sample his eggs in silence.

A silence that did not endure for very long.

'I take it you slept well?'

'Yes, Dad. Better than of late. On and off. You know.'

Ashley sensed the anticipation emitting from his parents as he added sugar to his mug and began to stir. Elaine joined them at the table and began to apply butter to some toast.

Suddenly the peace was disturbed as Ashley decided to announce his feelings.

He did not sense the need to dress up his conclusion.

‘Well…I’m going with your suggestion, folks.’

Elaine and Neville ceased chewing their food simultaneously. They stared at their son in wide-eyed admiration. Ashley engaged with their loving gazes before retrieving his mobile phone from his bath robe pocket.

Switching it on, he opened his messages account. Having located the relevant conversation, he passed the handset to his father for scrutiny.

‘Here, Dad. It’s a short exchange but it looks as though my proposal to meet up has hit the right note with her.’

Neville studied the message and nodded in approval before passing on to Elaine.

She squinted at the tiny screen and pursed her lips as she read, before focusing on her son with only a hint of doubt in her heart.

‘It’s arranged, then? Today at one o clock?’

‘Yes, Mum. The Bistro out at Fendern. Thought I’d show off with a bit of style?’

Neville swallowed some tea before declaring his appraisal.

‘Good thinking, son. Sounds like she snapped your hand off, too.’

‘Like taking candy from a baby, Dad. I just hope for my sake that I know what I’m getting into.’

Neville chuckled as he pushed a forkful of toast into his cheek.

‘You’ll be fine, Ash. Everything will go to plan. Like your mother says…you need to kill her with kindness.’

Ashley wanted to convey some strain of genuine enthusiasm as he drank his coffee. Yet the weight of expectation was subduing.

In his heart of hearts, he didn’t think for one second that Pauline Braithwaite would be fooled by the performance. But then again, her behaviour until this point had exhibited a complete absence of any typical law of reasoning.

Perhaps there could be an outside possibility that she might just get sucked in unawares.

And that his perennial nightmare could soon be over.

*****

The Griffiths clan were dressed and preparing to leave the house. The hopeful embraces were warm and meaningful.

The apprehension in the cold air was tempered by a fuelling sense of imminent success.

The trio made toward Ashley's car. The crass etchings on the boot lid still required attention. He had pledged to book a respray with the garage at least ten times over the previous weeks.

Neville prompted the eleventh.

'Keeping it as a reminder, eh lad?'

Ashley glanced at the offending mural gouged into the red paint.

'I'll sort it. One of these days. Goes without saying I'll let you know how things pan out this afternoon. Thanks for being here for me, Mum. Thanks, Dad. I must want my head testing for going through with this. But on a serious note, you're both keeping me sane. And I'm not joking.'

Neville placed a hand of reassurance on his son's shoulder.

'Just be yourself. Charm Wit. Elegance. Win her over. And watch her crumble with surprise. Once she realises you're interested, that will be the end of her. Trust me. She only wants the unattainable. She only craves what she can't have. When she gets it, her game is up. Have faith in yourself, Ash.'

'If you say so, Dad. If you say so. Right, I'd better get home and spruce myself up for the big date, hadn't I.'

His father called after him as he was about to get behind the wheel.

He was puzzled as he walked back up the driveway.

'What, Dad?'

'Just one other thing, son. Take a photo...of you both at the pub...for me and your mum. And send it us. Please.'

The plan was getting wilder and more bewildering with every turn.

'You mean you want a *selfie*? *What*? Of me with the monster from the black lagoon?'

Neville did not smile.

'Yes, please. Don't forget to send it to us as soon as you've taken it. It's important.'

'Christ, Dad. I don't know who's more round the twist. Lady Braithwaite or *you two*! I'll do my best. See you later.'

Neville and Elaine observed their son buckle himself into the driver's seat and head back home to Harrogate Close.

Neville eyed the coarse vandalism still very much in evidence at the rear of Ashley's car as it turned the corner and disappeared.

Two loving and loyal parents did not need to exchange further word, as they got in their own car and headed to town.

THIRTY-FIVE

The Bistro at Fendern had acquired a very positive reputation in a very short time. Formerly known as The White Swan, the canal side premises were completely renovated and re-badged by the brewery to attract customers into experiencing a more contemporary and memorable experience.

At least, that was the promotional jargon printed on the front of the menu. But at that precise moment as he sat alone and stared at the pub's rather flimsy Christmas tree, Ashley Griffiths could not have felt more discomforted by the surroundings.

His current predicament was even reaching beyond the realm of a fantasist's imagination.

Meeting with Pauline Braithwaite was in principle a very risky notion and distinctly unadvisable.

Yet advised Ashley had been.

And that advice he had willingly opted to embrace.

The prospect of the encounter filled him with rabid anxiety.

Now placed into the physical reality of the chosen arena and the liaison pending any moment, the immense trepidation was in danger of overwhelming him.

But he would not retreat. Running away was not an option.

He was here because he had already reached the end of reason.

At a total loss for a practicable solution in dealing with her.

This summit was strictly the final throw of the dice.

If this plan of action failed, Ashley would readily accept being pulled over the proverbial cliff edge. No more hanging on by fingertips and hoping the demon would desist. He no longer possessed the wherewithal to buttress his own psychological collapse.

Pauline Braithwaite may or may not have been aware as she parked her silver Fiat in the forecourt of The Bistro, that despite the motive for being there, she still held all the cards and was still playing the game according to her own rules and design.

So far as she was concerned, Ashley Griffiths remained totally at her disposal. Defenceless, desperate, and nigh on suffocating under her command.

It was nearly one-fifteen when she eventually strode through the entrance doors of the public lounge and made straight for the bar. This would afford her the best vantage of the whole room and those who occupied it.

On swiftly spotting Ashley at a window table overlooking the wintry deserted beer garden, she wasted little time in announcing her arrival.

Ashley's sixth sense detected her approach, yet he nervously maintained his nonchalant posture, until she appeared in his eyeline.

Light footed and svelte, she wilfully posed before him.

She was dressed to impress despite the frosted air outside.

She smiled radiantly and her green eyes engaged brightly as she beheld the vision of Ashley.

His instantaneous and yet perverse reflexive thought was to appreciate the attractive woman standing beside his chair. Although not inclined to be so acknowledging, he could not help but be affected by her cosmetic efforts.

But Pauline Braithwaite was a striking individual in any company and the look on her face suggested she was at long last relishing playing out the role of the cat that supposedly got the cream.

'Well, well...fancy bumping into you. Do you come here often?' she giggled, whilst clutching a small handbag with both hands.

It was completely against Ashley's instinct to feign authenticity, yet for the sake of his own existence, he needed to ensure that the current course was maintained. However stormy the waters might become.

Yet he was already inclined to predict resounding failure.

Too many events had taken place.

Too much upset had been caused.

And Pauline Braithwaite had ably proved her tenacity and intelligence.

Surely, she was not so blinded by her conviction in winning Ashley's favour, to see she was already being played by him?

Surely, this erratic scheme was doomed for nothing less than abrupt calamity.

Ashley conformed to expectation and like the gentleman he was, he rose from his chair and offered her a seat across the table.

They shook hands. A gesture that to him aptly defined the fogged perception of his own mental balance.

'Hello, Pauline. Can I get you a drink?'

She displayed all the signs of a woman enthralled by her present moment. She removed her long black coat and hung it over the back of the chair. She laid her clutch bag on the table as Ashley observed her figure-hugging short dark grey dress.

Then she made a contemporary move.

'I'll get them. Soft drink, is it? I presume you're in the car. Being as it's parked outside in the car park. Or are you going to risk a pint of your favourite German lager?'

He avoided falling into the trap of timely sarcasm.

He would refrain from mentioning the act of vandalism she had scratched into his boot lid that keenly identified it as being his vehicle.

'Just lemonade, please. With ice.'

'Sure thing. I'll be back in the blink of an eye.'

Ashley observed her feminine gait as she moved to the bar counter. There was no obvious indication that she possessed any salient traits of the average psychopath, but it was unlikely that such individuals complied with any standard photo fit or personality criteria.

Besides, he presumed that the truly wily madwomen of the world were surely clued up enough to capably hide the signs.

Concealing any unsavoury tendencies must be the obligatory policy for the unhinged, or the game would be up relatively quickly.

Pauline Braithwaite disturbed his train of thought as she returned to the table and placed Ashley's drink in front of him.

Seating herself opposite, she held in her hand what looked to be a small coke.

The urge to commence with a quip swiftly overpowered his inclination to resist as he felt himself compelled to display a smirk.

'What's in that, then? Triple vodka?'

She giggled and fluttered her eyelashes as if displaying coyness.

The atmosphere was almost as if this was a genuine first date.

'Not whilst I'm driving, Ashley. Even *I'm* too sensible to risk getting points on my licence.'

Ashley carried the false confidence of a pilot flying blind-folded into no man's land. Immersed in foreign territory and nothing rehearsed.

His next gesture seemed incredulous and considering the history between the pair, it felt highly inappropriate. But he would maintain the charade for now as he lifted his glass.

'Cheers, Pauline. Here's to us.'

She reciprocated the move and flashed her broadest smile.

'And to you, darling.'

They sipped their drinks as the conversation stumbled once again.

She maintained her unyielding stare and would not let her eyes off him for a second.

Thinking on his feet, Ashley was almost relieved when she finally offered to stimulate the dialogue.

'Well…I must say…this is very nice. And completely unexpected. You can only imagine my delight when I opened your message and read it. I've been so excited I can't begin to tell you. Us meeting up here is a dream come true. It really is.'

Ashley felt the murmurings of unease beginning to awaken in the pit of his stomach. For him this was a vomit-inducing scenario on so many levels. But he had to see it through.

One way or another he had to persevere with the mission.

'Well…you know…I thought that I'd avoided the issue for long enough. I'm obviously so irresistible to you. I felt guilty for denying you the pleasure any longer.'

Pauline Braithwaite rolled her green eyes in mock disapproval, accentuating the mascara she had applied.

'Six months it took you to decide! And I bet you haven't bought me a Christmas present either, have you? It's only next week. You've still got time, you know!'

Ashley unwillingly manoeuvred further toward the centre of the spider's web.

'Well, your methods of persuasion were shall we say, unorthodox, but I got the message eventually. Better late than never.'

She glanced round the room at the other nearby occupants. Perhaps to check that no one was in earshot. Her eyes narrowed as they focused back to him.

'Well, if that's how you view it. But you see, the thing is I'm used to getting what I want without begging. The word *no* isn't in my vocabulary. I'm not very well acquainted with the concept of refusal.'

Ashley swallowed more lemonade to alleviate his parched throat. He was aware of treading very cautiously. She was very articulate and quick on the draw. Qualities that belied the fact she was a socio-maniac.

Even though he was supposedly playing an equal role in the duel, he knew he had no control over the direction it might drift. Yet for now he was content for her to stay in control of the helm.

Then he recalled his father's last request.

He duly removed his phone from his coat pocket.

'Come on, Pauline. Selfie time. For posterity.'

She willingly moved next to him and leaned forward with her cheek next to his, offering a teasing glimpse of the top of her modest cleavage. The gold neck chain that settled at the base of her throat was a convincing tool in drawing a casual gaze.

Once more the crocodile smile was exhibited as she queried him through a low, supposedly seductive hiss as he took the photograph. She reclaimed her seat as he deftly delivered the shot to his father's phone.

'So, Ashley, what was it that finally persuaded you to take up my offer?'

Ashley had no response ready in the barrel. But any wording he utilised needed to appear plausible.

Uncertainty was now his only ally at that table.

The falsehoods were making him feel ill.

'Well, I suppose curiosity got the better of me. You are persistent and you wore me down. Typical old-fashioned romantic method on your part. But here we are. It worked.'

She sat back in her chair and laughed out loud, perhaps now to purposely turn heads in the vicinity.

'Romance? Do you honestly think that's what this is all about? Love is a mythical creation, Ashley. A figment of imagination. There is no such thing as romance. What we have, Ashley…is *chemistry*! Pure and simple.'

Ashley found himself to be suddenly intrigued by her use of such a ridiculous term.

'Chemistry? As in the sexual kind, you mean?'

'Any way you decide, darling. Primitive…sexual…animal. It's all about the mutual electrical response to one another, isn't it. You finally caught up with me. We're singing from the same hymn sheet at last. God knows I tried hard enough to flag for your attention.'

Quite rightly, Ashley found himself becoming increasingly angered by her overly casual references to the destructive and heart-breaking methods that she had deployed.

She had wittingly attempted to inflict great harm on to major aspects of his existence. Her campaign of ruthlessness was unrelenting.

Her time was surely coming.

Somehow.

Whilst he was there under extreme duress, it occurred to him that perhaps she too must also be playing this meeting out as an act?

Surely Pauline Braithwaite herself must privately acknowledge that she wears the mantle of the monster in all possible forms?

With his demeanour now significantly altered, Ashley attempted to steer the exchange into potentially unfriendly territory.

'You've caused me a lot of pain and upset, Pauline. I can't begin to relate to you how much you've put me through.'

Her condescending smile was permanently fixed in position now. Her continuing flippancy served only to increase the level of antagonism that had already begun to simmer between them.

'Oh, by that you must mean your so-called boyfriend. I thought I put you right on that score. He was never in tune with your needs. Showed his true colours again in the end, didn't he? Bailed out on you yet again with the last parachute. Believe me, you are well shot of him.'

Her callous and self-serving arrogance was beyond anything Ashley had ever experienced in anyone. He convinced himself she too was across the table simply for the sake of this stupid battle of brinkmanship.

He was a willing audience, and she could not resist the chance to take the stage.

He attempted to call her bluff.

'Despite what you might think…Carl loves me. And I love Carl. We were happy together. We had history and we had a future. Until you came along. You destroyed all that.'

Once again, she cackled dismissively, threw her head back, and drained her glass down her throat.

The atmosphere between them was souring rapidly.

'There you go again. That word. *Love*. It doesn't exist, Ashley. It was *never* part of your life. Whatever you thought your relationship with him was founded on, it wasn't that. Love is a fable for the masses to believe in but when it came to the crunch, did love prevent him from walking away? No. He was gone. Like the mists of time. As if he was never there in the first place. You must acknowledge that, now?'

Ashley was flailing amid a running contest to keep his temper.

He was aware that this undertaking would be a stern trial of mettle, but his undiluted hatred for Pauline Braithwaite was in danger of seeping through the cracks. He had entertained his parents' scheme with the best of intentions, but it was already proving to be an unwarranted waste of time and energy. He was no longer certain of withstanding her presence without the suppressed feelings of hostility brimming over.

He placed his forearms on the tabletop and leaned as close toward her as possible to avoid being overheard by the other diners nearby.

'For a woman who purports to be attracted to me, you offer little concern for the fact that you've demolished a solid domestic relationship. My homelife is in pieces. My career isn't much better off. Not to mention my state of mind. You have single-handedly crushed everything I held dear to my heart. Even my poor cat. And whilst we're on the subject…what the fuck was the point of that? What in the world could you gain from such cruelty to an innocent animal? Tell me? I'm desperate to know.'

Pauline Braithwaite had now adopted her other, less hospitable sheen. Her smile had vanished, replaced by a line of distaste directed at the opponent sitting across from her.

The pouting princess perched only two yards away was about to be eclipsed by her own sadistic mania.

'It wasn't just *any* innocent animal, though Ashley.'

'What do you mean by that?'

'It was *your* innocent animal. That was my only motive. Easy, isn't it? It got your attention, didn't it? I was getting frustrated with the civilised approach. Being nice to you was getting me nowhere.'

He watched her expression alter into a mask of thorough disdain that projected a sinister flickering hatred. In Ashley's mind, it was now an indisputable fact that Pauline Braithwaite was indeed in need of some form of medical intervention.

Yet her softly spoken and matter-of-fact manner of conveyance was the most disturbing facet of the whole picture.

It was obvious even to the casual observer that she felt fully justified in accomplishing her checklist of insidious deeds.

With animosity once again openly blooming between them, the level of the exchange deepened once again.

Instead of the curious cross questioning and rallying of responses, there was an encroaching mutual acceptance of one another's true standpoints.

Bizarrely, Ashley now felt ready to abandon his original ploy of diplomacy in favour of re-escalating the war.

He was powerless to restore the damage she had inflicted.

Similarly, she held no remorse over her conduct.

The stalemate between the protagonists had been reached rapidly.

Perhaps because of the futile scrutiny centring on the recent past, maybe Ashley's thoughts might be better served if focused on the immediate future.

It appeared that Pauline Braithwaite had reached the very same conclusion.

And now suddenly her artillery was openly drawn.

Cocked and ready to fire his way.

Who might be quickest on the trigger was yet to be unveiled.

'Okay. So, Ashley…all things considered and, in all sincerity, what the actual fuck did you hope to achieve by meeting me here today?'

She now spoke with abject venom lacing every syllable.

The malice between them was almost tangible.

Ashley's reply stuck gamely in his throat.

The essence of the man convulsed with wanton fury and inner anguish.

His spirit all but vanquished, he grasped at the remnants of the original plan, knowing full well that such a flimsy veil of authenticity would not fool her.

'I thought we might at least get to know one another a little better.'

The manner of her address switched instantly once more.

The sultry smile was back.

The seductive look in her eyes.

She utilised her looks superbly.

Lord knows how many weak souls had succumbed to her spell in the past.

A natural beauty; now disguised and demonised beyond recall.

'Oh really? So where do we go from here then, Ashley? How quickly and efficiently would you like to get to know me better?'

The surreal and abrasive nature of the conversation was not obvious to the passing onlooker. Witnesses would be forgiven for acknowledging them as any ordinary couple having a relaxing drink together.

Yet the palpable malevolence between them continued to gather intensity. Nobody would have been able to suspect the lady companion of her atrocious effect on the life of the man sitting opposite.

Yet there they sat. At the window that overlooked the damp, cold and deserted beer garden beyond.

Continuing to dance to the unpredictable tune of their unrehearsed production.

And Ashley still clung by his fingertips in trying to avoid the precipice of complete failure.

'I suppose I hoped that today we could get along okay, Pauline. Perhaps become friends. Perhaps you might then be persuaded to stop the campaign of abuse.'

Pauline Braithwaite's instantly mirthful reaction echoed around the walls and ceilings of the pub lounge. As the laughter subsided, she gradually reverted attention to him.

The game was up, now. He had blatantly shown his hand. He had fallen over the one tripwire that he should have been smart enough to detect and evade.

Her amusement at the fact only served to compound his regret.

'Ah! So *that's* it! Soft soap me and then *beg* me. That was your intention, was it? Butter me up and hope I walk away quietly? Oh, dear oh dear, Ashley. I'm so disappointed that you underestimated me to such an unflattering degree. I really am.'

Ashley clenched his fists and stared back into her pitiless visage.

He had nothing to lose now.

Plan abandoned. Mission aborted.

A psychological red alert alarm began to pound in his conscience.

'Pauline…I'm out of answers. Tell me what it would take to get you out of my life for good.'

Her features contorted into a furrowed image of frigid detachment.

'But Ashley…I'm not *in* your life. I'm not *allowed* to be in it. *You* have decided that much. That's correct, isn't it? Or have I misinterpreted the signals?'

He despised the very existence of her.

He wanted to banish her from the world there and then.

This evil creation that taunted him was a curse upon his despairing soul.

'You've been fucking around with me for months. There is no common ground here. I am the victim of your sick mind. I have become your entertainment. All I can ask is that *you* end what *you* began. Peacefully. So that no one comes to any further harm.'

The dynamic shifted yet again.

She adopted the air of someone who might have had a chink in her armour exposed for the very first time.

She now carried the look of the Devil himself.

'Are you threatening me, Ashley? Because that sounded very much like a threat. And I don't take kindly to being threatened.'

Ashley had now passed the point of composure.

Long beyond any concern about consequence.

His voice contained an element of wild displeasure as he welcomed the imminent prospect of public altercation.

'And I don't take fucking kindly to having my life ruined through a hate campaign started by a fucking *lunatic*.'

Her exhibition of indignation was briefly accompanied by a raucous shout of protestation.

'Hate campaign? That's a stern allegation. One that I wager you wouldn't be able to substantiate with hard evidence.'

His thoughts were taken back to the first visit with Carl to the police station. She was quite correct in her presumption.

He had no ace up his sleeve.

She was enjoying the visible acceleration of his sufferance.

She relished watching him plead with her for leniency.

The immorality of her very being swarmed around him.

It wasn't enough for her to have her quarry ensnared.

Her genuine pleasure derived from spectating on its subsequent and frantic fight to survive.

Yet contrarily, Ashley's character had evolved through the horrendous realisations whilst being held in her company.

His quiet defiance had transformed itself into willing an acceptance of what fate may bring. Pauline Braithwaite could inflict no more misery on him than she had already done.

Her reservoir of covert spite and open vindictiveness must surely be close to exhausting itself.

Ashley took confidence from this possibility to the point whereby he no longer projected the inclination to protract the fight against her.

Yet within himself, he conjured up one last ditch attempt to appease her nastiness. One last grapple to allow decency to overcome corruption.

He remained at ease and collected, knowing full well this could well provide his parting shot.

'I have done nothing to deserve your hatred. If you persist, then there is little I can do about it. But every dog has its day. You *will* slip up. You *will* overstep the mark. One of these days you will bite off more than you can chew. And that day I will fucking be on to you quicker than you can say my name. Nobody is *that* clever. You haven't covered *all* the bases. It's impossible. Your downfall is nearer than you know. Mark my words.'

Her bravado responded, yet the acute smile she displayed was perhaps tinged with reservation. Arrogance was her dearest weapon and it duly stepped forward to defend her against attack.

'Wow! Very deep and philosophical, darling. I'm very impressed with your insight into my future. But believe you me, I have every angle covered. It's what I do. Nothing…can…stop…me. I shall continue to obey my whims and wonts. And if you stand in my way, then the consequences will be yours to face.'

Having heard more than enough of her diatribe, Ashley rose to his feet and stared down at the enemy.

A sensation of liberation abounded. It flushed his veins. It cleansed his mindset. He had tried reason and he had tried aggression and he had tried hope. All virtues had failed him.

So be it. Destiny would claim final authority.

'As you wish, Pauline. I'll see you on the other side, then.'

Ashley left the table and strode through the lounge room.

Accompanied by a blossoming self-righteousness, he exited the main doors with a distinct bounce in his step.

He held conviction in the belief that his scruples had put him on the high ground for the final round in the gladiator ring.

There was the feint possibility that Pauline Braithwaite's next decision would be a cessation of hostilities. Did she possess the necessary amount of charity in her soul to submit to embracing humility?

In his heart of hearts, Ashley knew it was highly unlikely.

But for some unspoken reason, he also now sensed that some form of conclusion to matters was pending on the horizon.

Starting the car engine and finding reverse gear, he exited the car park and departed The Bistro at Fendern, with the firm notion that her reign of terror would be coming to an end.

Sooner, rather than later.

How this might transpire was yet to be determined.

But for the first time in a very long time, Ashley Griffiths felt totally assured of his instincts.

His priorities were now renewed and twofold.

Go back to his home where he belonged.

Go back to work where he was needed.

*****

Pauline Braithwaite sat in contemplative solitude for a few minutes.

She stared blankly through the window at the seasonal dimness beyond the glass.

Now completely pre-occupied in her own twisted avenue of thought.

Her immediate requirements were also now twofold.

Renewal of her mission, and infinite self-preservation.

Finally opting to leave The Bistro, she rose steadily from her chair.

Donning her long black coat and clutching her handbag, she floated with apparent confidence through the exit doors and down the steps to the car park.

An untouchable statue of cold, contradictive femininity. A woman who found herself and her actions to be fully justified. And having seen her target convey his empty and desperate warnings on departure, she might have felt more empowered than ever.

Under the presumption that she had no authentic challenger, she held her head high on approaching and unlocking the little silver Fiat. With precision and an element of almost male suave, she slid behind the wheel and started the engine.

Yet despite the ill-placed sense of credence in her cause, and the sly doggedness with which she reinforced it, Pauline Braithwaite had failed to notice that she was no longer the sole omnipotent overseer.

For she was now under scrutiny herself.

From a discreet position not five metres from her own car, her observers patiently studied their person of interest.

Just as they had done when she had first arrived on the premises.

Completely oblivious to the fact she was being followed as she departed the scene, Pauline Braithwaite navigated a path to the main road and joined the scant flow of traffic.

Her self-appointed aura of autonomy had been given true sustenance during the previous hour. Yet she was also completely unaware that she was on the verge of making her first, pivotal, catastrophic mistake.

Home was where she was destined.

Her secret fortress.

The inner sanctum.

Where her crooked inclinations were born.

Nurtured and harboured and exploited.

And this was surely the setting where she would be rendered most vulnerable.

The observers remained concealed, unknown, and anonymous as they followed behind in their own car.

Back toward, and possibly beyond, Hernwood.

But ultimately, to the sacred, previously unchartered personal domain, of Pauline Braithwaite.

Where fate would duly unveil its final decree.

THIRTY-SIX

On entering his parents' hallway, Ashley was quietly thankful that they were not yet home. He figured that his mother would get the bus back from the town centre unless she had arranged to be collected when his father had finished at the golf club.

On the face of it, his partially competent attempt to resolve the situation with Pauline Braithwaite had ultimately gone with prediction.

Yet Ashley Griffiths did not feel like he had failed.

On the contrary.

He had somehow channelled a strong element of vigour from the exchange at The Bistro. He had reached the bottom of his personal well of despair. He now felt his ascent was imminent.

His mentality had been liberated due to confronting her directly.

She no longer seemed to be the ogre that stalked him in the dead of night.

Some intangible elements to the dynamic had dramatically altered the lie of the land.

The feud appeared now different in nature and design.

The psychological shackles that bound him so tightly up until that afternoon had been overcome.

He was now absolved. He felt motivated to finally take those positive steps that had instilled such reluctance in him before.

No longer cowering. But now intent on defeating the shadows that had loomed so large over him for so long.

He thought about making himself a coffee but didn't want to delay further. His mind brimmed with hope and belief.

No longer running. No longer hiding.

But now standing firmly at his ground and developing the inclination for wilful resilience.

And he would start by erasing the unsavoury chronicle of upset and replacing it with a series of healthy events. Beginning there and then with a light trot up the stairs to his parents' spare bedroom.

He pulled his holdall from under the bed and began to fill it with the belongings he had brought with him.

He was now fixated by the mission to reside back at his house on Harrogate Close. He didn't wish to be a burden to his mother and father any longer than was necessary.

He glanced through the bedroom window at the diminishing daylight beyond. The dull grey air lay heavily upon the static and lifeless estate. But he would ably illuminate it with his suddenly revitalised spirit.

Normality was calling.

He would reclaim the broken building blocks of his life.

It was time for resumption of duty for Ashley Griffiths.

And the premise fuelled him so.

As he loaded the car boot, pangs of guilt began to assault his conscience. Departing his parents' abode without giving them prior warning had left him feeling rather inconsiderate.

But he pledged to himself that a phone call later that evening would more than suffice.

In any case, they would likely be sated by his altering demeanour.

As a gesture of gratitude, he scribbled a short note to inform them of developments and left it in the centre of the dining table where they were bound to see it.

Locking the front door to his mother and father's house was symbolic of his emancipation from the mental trauma that had plagued him for weeks.

He even felt a flush of glory as he embraced the return to the Ashley Griffiths of old.

The Ashley Griffiths that he knew and loved.

The Ashley Griffiths that many others knew and loved.

The resistor.

The leader by example.

Unflappable and unswayed by circumstance.

He sat behind the wheel of the car and the elation began to flow forth within his veins.

The first leg of his mission would soon be accomplished.

The second leg would also soon be tackled, as he pledged to make the phone call to Derek Evans and inform his employer that he would be returning to work the very next morning.

Engaging the engine, Ashley even found himself smiling in earnest as he lifted the clutch and headed for home.

*****

'Yes, Mum. Yes, I know you would rather have seen me off.'

'Well, I guess I felt the time was right after meeting with her today.'

'There's really nothing more to say about it.'

'No, it was a complete waste of time.'

'No, Mum. But you see I'm honestly not that bothered anymore.'

'Yes…yes I do mean that.'

'I'm happy again. And it's about bloody time!'

'Mum…don't cry, please.'

'Don't get upset, Mum. I can't hug you better over the phone.'

'I'll be round again quicker than you know, anyway.'

'Just want to settle back here for a few days.'

'Yes. I've phoned work. I'm back tomorrow.'

'Yes, Derek was delighted.'

'Yes, especially as the Christmas functions are in full swing, now.'

'No nobody else knows at the hotel. Will be a nice surprise for them!'

'Did you have a nice afternoon anyway?'

'Oh, great. Did Dad not go to the golf club then?'

'Okay. Well, I'm glad you both got things done.'

'Honestly, I'm fine. Anyway, you both deserve your own space back.'

'I was in the way. I've got to stand on my own two feet, haven't I.'

'No. I know you don't…but that's how it felt to me.'

'What's Dad doing now?'

'Cleaning his clubs? Oh, he's playing tomorrow instead, is he?'

'Oh right. Just readying them for the New Year, eh?'

'Look, I'll leave you be for now.'

'Okay, yes.'

'Love you both. Send my love to the old man.'

'And thank you both. Lord knows what state I'd be in if it wasn't for you two.'

'Bye Mum. Speak soon.'

THIRTY-SEVEN

The psychological relapse hit Ashley within hours of his re-establishment at number thirty-nine, Harrogate Close.

The vulnerability.

The shadows.

The fact that Christmas was around the corner and the fact that he would be alone in the house.

The fact that he desperately wanted to talk to Carl again but saw little scope in trying.

The fact that Carl had made no attempt to contact Ashley only deepened the emotional wound that had not even begun to heal.

The fact that despite his upbeat declaration to Derek Evans earlier that day, he had already resigned himself to the knowledge that a return to work was still out of the question.

The bravado he had conveyed to his mother and father was a fabricated sheen of optimism.

And he knew they weren't likely to be fooled by his sudden apparent desire to face his issues alone.

Parents are never fooled. They know the game and they know all the signals in their offspring.

The inflation he detected within himself after the episode at The Bistro had now completely dissipated. Indeed, his primitive fear of Pauline Braithwaite was now at its most acute.

And she had discovered him once more.

Back at his own house.

He had seen the clear black and white footage from the doorbell camera.

She had paid him two visits.

In the dead of night.

Standing. Staring.

Motionless. Emotionless.

He was a prisoner once again.

And he had no comprehension of how he might now begin to conceal himself from her evil attention.

Or her evil intentions.

His thought process crucified him. Leaving hints as to what he might find waiting for him outside should he ever develop the courage to venture beyond his own front door ever again.

Yet the gods of fate were speculating.

Conclusion would soon be upon him.

*****

December. The twenty-seventh. Monday. Eleven a.m.

Neville Griffiths tensed as the sound of his wife's distress resonated through the lounge.

He listened intently to her side of the conversation.

It was heart-rending to digest.

As it would be for any loving father and husband.

'Come back to us, Ashley. Please, darling.'

'I can't believe you spent Christmas Day on your own in the house.'

'We phoned you. We messaged you. You ignored our knock at your door.'

'I know. We haven't felt like celebrating either.'

'But at least we would have been together.'

'So, what have you been doing if you haven't been to work?'

'Oh Ashley…this isn't good.'

'No…I'm really worried about you.'

'I bet you've not been shopping, either.'

'This is tearing me and your father apart.'

'You have got to be joking.'

'Outside the house?'

'Even on Christmas Eve?'

'The police need to know, Ashley.'

'And what did they say?'

'Not enough officers?'

'Oh, my baby. This can't go on.'

'Don't talk like that.'

'That's the worst thing you could ever say to your mother.'

'Don't ever mention it again.'

'Of course, people will miss you.'

'But think about me and your dad.'

'You are in a very bad state of mind. You need help.'

'I know you have, darling.'

'They just don't want to know, do they?'

'She's broken no laws, I know.'

'You mustn't think along those lines.'

'Right…me and your father are coming to get you.'

'Now. This minute.'

'Have you been drinking?'

'Well then. Stop it! Stop talking like that.'

'Ashley don't cry my love. I feel so helpless.'

Neville wiped his eyes and gestured for Elaine to pass him her mobile phone. He cleared his throat as he observed his wife flee the room under the weight of relentless emotion.

He addressed his son calmly and concisely.

'Ash. I will ring you back in a minute. I need to talk to your mum first.

The response from Ashley was a mumbled affirmative.

Neville Griffiths disconnected the call and entered the kitchen to find Elaine inconsolable.

Detecting her husband behind her, she turned to face him and recognised the expression he now carried.

They did not exchange further words.

Destiny had finally decided.

It was now out of their hands.

THIRTY-EIGHT

New Year's Eve. Friday. Nine a.m. The unyielding knocking at the front door echoed dimly around Ashley's estranged psyche. He didn't want visitors.

He couldn't handle company of any kind.

The tears of his mother during the phone call from four days ago still pricked sharply as a reminder of the upset she carried too.

It was no surprise his father didn't ring back.

He had other priorities in attending to his wife.

Ashley's personal desolation was now all encompassing. The only crumb of comfort was that he had abstained from alcohol as a method of soothing his anguish.

There would be no refuge found in the bottom of a glass. Any attempt to search for a solution through the bottle would only add to his mountain of problems.

From his position on the sofa, he squinted across the lounge to ascertain that the bay window blinds were closed. Consoled that nobody could see inside, he curled up even tighter.

The pounding headache had reduced to a gradual numbness but nevertheless remained despite the plentiful painkillers he had absorbed.

Yet the resonant banging continued.

The front door seemingly bearing the brunt of a repeated and purposed pounding.

Louder and firmer.

Firmer and louder.

Ashley unwillingly leant his ear to the muffled voices that suddenly began to converse beyond the lounge window.

Curiosity compelled him to alter position on the settee and attain a better interpretation of who the voices might belong to.

It didn't sound like his mother and father.

Derek Evans didn't typically make house calls, but in current circumstances he may have made an exception.

But Ashley had withstood a predictable and obvious lack of sympathy from his superior.

His immediate U-turn regarding resuming work duties was the second such occasion in the space of a month.

Outside, the hammering and the talking did not relent.

It was highly unlikely to be Carl. That ship had sailed.

No contact during the Christmas period pretty much assured Ashley that the coffin lid was nailed on their relationship. There was no other way to interpret the situation so far as Ashley was concerned.

The persistent clattering vibrated through the hallway.

The visitors were evidently intent on being received.

Ashley strained his hearing amid his silence.

Then a booming tone bellowed through the letterbox.

A male voice. Gruff and determined.

A request to know if Ashley Griffiths was at home.

This question was followed by a revelation.

The callers were not belated carol singers or even Jehovah's Witnesses.

It was the Police.

Ashley's heart skipped a beat at learning the identity of those seeking his counsel. Contrary thoughts echoed and ricocheted around his mind. Panic bombarded him and then collided with calm.

His previous communications with the local constabulary had supplied nothing but negativity. He didn't suppose this particular visit might garner anything different.

It was ironic. When he did want to consult with them about his concerns, they didn't wish to listen. Yet when they need to talk to *him,* it's deemed to be the most urgent of matters.

Dealing with the law seemed to be a one-way street.

He continued to listen as the activity beyond the front door had appeared to have lessened. He wasn't interested anyway. He had nothing further to say to them.

His maltreatment at their hands had left a bitter memory.

He would not answer to them.

They would have to resign themselves to surrendering their quest and retreating. In any case, Ashley felt in no state to communicate with anybody on any level.

He was happy to see the New Year in just as he had Christmas.

Alone in his own company.

He was sick and tired of the games people felt inclined to play.

He was sick and tired full stop.

The odds were never with him in any scenario.

Always against him.

Always pinning him down. Always incurring defeat.

He would play by his own personal rules from now on.

Fuck the Police.

They were neither use nor ornament as far as Ashley was concerned.

And then came the violent thud.

Intrusion to the property was enforced with an explosive crescendo of sound.

The battering ram did not require a second attempt to achieve its purpose.

The front door latch fixings immediately conceded to the mightier force. Swinging on its hinges it crashed unceremoniously into the console table in the hallway, in turn knocking over a small potted cactus.

Ashley was quickly stirred and sat nervously on the edge of the settee. Whether he was up for the game or not, the Police were evidently intent on ensuring he participated.

He heard loud authoritative voices shout vibrant instructions.

Heavy-booted footsteps swiftly accessed upstairs and searched the bedrooms and bathroom. Strange voices confirmed no one was present on the upper level and the situation was cleared.

And then without warning, the lounge door was kicked open.

Two impressively armed and fully armoured officers entered the room and lodged the barrels of their semi-automatic rifles in Ashley's direction.

He sensed his bowels becoming severely disrupted as he followed the barked command to remain seated and place his hands on top of his head.

Feeling disconcertingly vulnerable dressed in just his pyjamas and bath robe, Ashley eyed the two policemen who had trained their weapons on him with considerable enthusiasm.

They were an intimidating sight in bullet proof vests and sleekly designed headgear.

Then a third armed officer entered and walked through to check the kitchen.

Thankfully he utilised the locking mechanism on the back door, negating a repeated employment of the battering ram. Ashley was briefly inclined to offer a quip about the preferable ease of using handles to open doors, but in considering current circumstances he resisted temptation.

Neither officer looked to be in a mood ready for comedy as they squinted at their quarry with trigger fingers at the ready. The cost of replacement of the front door was a strangely prevailing issue in Ashley's mind as he gazed through the kitchen window and observed the third armed officer inspecting the rear garden.

A walkie-talkie hissed into life and a croaking tone confirmed that the occupant of the residence was indeed alone. A few seconds of very uncertain silence evolved into a minute or more before another gentleman, this time dressed in plain clothes, walked casually into the lounge.

It wasn't too difficult for Ashley to ascertain that the latest entrant was superior in rank to his colleagues. Attired in dark suit and trench coat, the middle-aged officer sported greying hair and a day's growth of stubble, stood to the side of the armed duo and commenced proceedings with a barely moving line of a mouth and black soulless eyes.

'Mister Ashley Griffiths?'

The response was somewhat reluctant and mumbled, disguising a bubbling fury.

'I am, yes. Can someone explain why my front door is hanging off?'

The officer in the long dark coat proceeded to retrieve his I.D. badge from the inside pocket.

He allowed Ashley only a brief inspection of his credentials.

'Detective Inspector Neil Huntley. I am the controlling officer assigned to lead this investigation.'

Ashley's indignation was now combined with a hefty dose of confusion. He felt fully assured in requesting some elaboration.

'I'm sorry...I don't understand. What are you investigating and who exactly are you looking for?'

The D.I. could see that Ashley offered little in the way of posing a potential threat and gestured to the pair of gun-wielding guards.

'Relax boys. I can't see any issues with this one for the time being.'

Moving closer to Ashley and pointing his forefinger to the ceiling, the senior officer instructed him to stand up.

Another officer in a constable's uniform then appeared magically from the hallway and promptly manoeuvred Ashley away from the sofa and to the centre of the lounge.

He then produced a set of handcuffs.

'Jesus Christ, not again. We've done this once before, haven't we?'

Ashley's arms were duly secured behind his back as the D.I. began to shed a little light on matters.

'Just a precaution, sir. That's all. We don't want you getting in a temper, do we?'

Ashley shook his head and almost chuckled in disbelief as anger pulsed through his veins.

'Well, it's a bit late for that, I think. Now, is there a danger of you letting me in on the reason for gate crashing my nice quiet party?'

Inspector Huntley casually placed his hands in his trouser pockets and squared up closely to Ashley as if to intimidate him.

'Mister Griffiths...can you confirm that you are an acquaintance of a Mrs. Pauline Braithwaite?'

Ashley exhaled as inevitability crash landed into his existence once again.

It was perhaps justifiable that he already felt nothing but abject disdain for the Police Inspector standing before him.

'Yes...I know her. Unfortunately. What am I supposed to have done *this* time?'

The D.I. glanced to his uniformed colleague who had applied the cuffs, before turning his full attention back to the man wearing them.

'Well, Mister Griffiths...that is what we would dearly like to establish. We thought that as you were the only link to her on our database you might have something of interest to discuss with us.'

Bemusement quickly eclipsed Ashley's rumbling disgruntlement.

'I'm sorry. You have me at a complete disadvantage here. Whatever she has told you I can guarantee it's all lies. You always know when she's lying because her lips move.'

The senior officer pursed his mouth and again exchanged a brief look with the cuff dispenser.

Ashley was now in great danger of losing his patience.

'Unfortunately, she isn't in any position to tell us *anything*, Mister Griffiths. Because your friend, Pauline Braithwaite...is *dead*.'

The premise of bowel movement that hinted earlier was suddenly shifting gear to prompt an immediate evacuation.

Ashley's head began to spin. He suddenly felt feint as his brain attempted to register the last statement of the Detective Inspector.

He looked at the expressions of the surrounding police officers as if expecting to see one of them crack and give the game away.

'I'm sorry...is this some sort of sick joke? She's *dead*? You've come to my house and vandalised it? To tell me that Pauline Braithwaite... is *dead*?'

The D.I. could not refrain from displaying a very inappropriate half-smirk at Ashley's supposedly feigned surprise.

'Yes, Mister Griffiths. Deceased. Beaten to a pulp. Beaten so badly that we only barely identified her through her injuries. You are claiming no knowledge of this development, I take it?'

The realisation now dawned.

The situation was potentially disastrous for Ashley.

Was this to be her final act of malice?

Her decisive parting shot?

To engulf Ashley into suffocation with the damning process that was about to unfurl?

He observed the disparaging glint in the eyes of D.I. Huntley.

Ashley had been hung out to dry.

No doubt the chief suspect.

No doubt the only suspect.

And the next words he anticipated from the senior officer were already crashing through his mind. He was once more about to be thrown into a bottomless well of horrendous scrutiny.

Rendered completely vulnerable.

The sitting duck, indeed.

Defences already annihilated.

'Ashley Griffiths…you are being placed under arrest on suspicion of the murder of Pauline Braithwaite. You have the right to remain silent. Anything you do say may be taken down and used as evidence in a court of law. You also have the right to legal representation. If you do not have a solicitor, one can be appointed on your behalf.'

After months of strife, and struggle, and strain, and fighting the rumoured oncoming tsunami, the foundations of Ashley's world finally conceded defeat and succumbed to submersion.

The D.I. stood aside as Ashley was ushered from the lounge into the hallway. An armed officer formed a disheartening escort.

At the bottom of the stairs, Ashley turned to the sergeant who had secured the wrist restraints. He then fixed attention on the D.I.

His resulting words were a genuine inquiry, issued through the withered voice of a man who had now completely conceded to the whims of fate.

'Now what do I do?'

Detective Inspector Neil Huntley smiled yet again.

The handcuffs were duly removed from Ashley's wrists.

The senior officer carried the demeanour of someone who was relishing generation of possibly the easiest ever conviction in the history of the Police Force.

'*Now*...Mister Griffiths...you will go upstairs with two of my colleagues...and you will get dressed. *Then*, you will be going into custody at the station. Let's hurry it up, eh?'

THIRTY-NINE

Ashley stared straight ahead at the featureless grey wall of the cell. As a minimalist diversion tactic, his eyes traced the painted lines of interlinking mortar from floor to ceiling and then down again.

This was just about the only activity that his brain could ably accommodate at that moment.

Hunched on the edge of the sparse bed, he rubbed his eyes of raw fatigue. He had no more tears left. His emotional capacity had been rinsed totally dry many days since.

His spirit having long deserted him, he even considered prayer for the first time in his life. If only he knew of one.

But even the simplest words of salvation eluded him as he sat alone in his suffocating void of captivity.

But such a concept seemed futile. Nobody would hear him.

Deserted and destitute, he desperately evaded contemplation of what lay ahead for him in the next few hours and days.

His predicament seemingly totally beyond retrieval.

A *murder* suspect? Indeed, he was, yes.

The severest indictment a man could suffer.

Accused of taking the life of another.

The most effective method of eradicating one's established character and reputation.

Ashley was cornered.

No respite from suspicion. No room to breathe. No space to move.

A damning verdict possibly already being determined beyond that thick, cold, steel door.

Dark, terrible thoughts were winning the battle against wish and chance.

The confounding dilemma thickened around him like a choking fog with every passing minute.

That he was personally innocent of any wrongdoing was not in doubt within his own conscience.

He was steadfast and assured in his own knowledge and conviction in this argument.

Yet such adamance might count for nothing.

A stoical loyalty to his own truths may not be enough to impress the authorities that now secretly presided over his future.

Ashley's dictum now followed thus: if they flung enough mud, then some was bound to stick, eventually.

After all, he had been ensnared into such turgid territory before. Yet it remained a complete mystery as to how and why he was previously liberated from the shackles that the law so enthusiastic threw upon him.

A retraction from the plaintiff?

He would probably never know.

One thing was certain within this current drama.

Pauline Braithwaite's demise ensured she could not act either as persecutor *or* saviour.

Neither plaintiff nor redeemer.

For all intents and purposes, Ashley was cast adrift of any moral foothold or rational mitigation.

Only two things were now defined as absolutes.

She was deceased.

And he was in the frame.

He had only been in solitary confinement for little over ninety minutes. A 'cooling off' period, claimed the desk sergeant as he slammed the metal into the hole and turned the lock.

Yet it had already seemed like a year and a half as opposed to the damning reality of an hour and a half.

Once more his concentration centred itself on the minutiae of his immediate surroundings.

Once more around the mortar line. This time wall to wall. Around the simplistic combined toilet pan and basin. The small strip bulb overhead encased in its protective cage, shed little light of inspiration.

Only the humming shadow of dread.

This could already count as a final and posthumous triumph for the enemy.

He thought he could hear her laughing from the heavens where she had undoubtedly cheated the gatekeeper to gain admission.

Yet the confounding irony prevailed.

Ashley had no semblance of an idea as to what had truly transpired regarding Pauline Braithwaite's fate.

Yet the officers of the law believe he knows every single detail.

Ashley's memory strived to venture back in time.

To a point not so far back in his personal history.

When love, work and wellbeing were competing with one another to ride atop the crest of his ever-growing wave. And the more expansive and unpredictable that wave became, the more adept he became at riding it.

Back in the days when he was invincible.

When nothing could de-stabilize him.

Until fortunes changed irrevocably.

Until Pauline Braithwaite entered the fray.

Once more he counted the bricks in the wall of the cell.

Once more he combatted past dreams with current nightmares.

Why was he chosen to be her victim?

Why not somebody else more deserving?

The conundrum had plagued his existence for many weeks.

Now it seems it would cost him his freedom.

The spider's web specifically woven for him and him alone.

And the more he wriggled, the more tightly entwined he became.

Yet still he struggled to reconcile the news of her death.

If this truly was her inglorious farewell, then Ashley supposed she would have had plenty of opportunity to fabricate evidence that implicated him as her killer.

He had recently been in very close contact with her.

Clues to his presence would surely be on her person somewhere.

DNA is an intrinsic tool in modern crime solving.

Surely his fingerprints left on the glass at The Bistro in Fendern would be amply incriminating in the eyes of any detective worth their salt?

Ashley now anticipated nothing less than a ruthless and calculated attempt by the Police to bring him to justice and put him away for life.

And she had found it so simplistic to achieve this aim.

And she would undoubtedly find it so pleasurable.

The twisted mind of a madwoman would have no parameters of morality.

Ashley presumed he was already up to his neck in it.

And that it was now only a matter of time before he would be smothered once and for all.

And she would undoubtedly have employed all in her power to ensure such an outcome.

Despite being confined within his persistent self-pitying outlook, Ashley's attention was briefly diverted to potential activity beyond the cell door.

Outside in the corridor, another guardian of law enforcement was escorting some other misguided soul into incarceration. The new arrival voicing opinion through a trail of profanity-laced objections, before the protestation was abruptly halted by the familiar sound of metal clattering into doorframe.

It would offer no advantage whatsoever for Ashley to convey such remonstration.

The fact that he had committed no crime had not prevented him from being hauled into custody.

In the eyes of the Police, he was the chief suspect.

Whether guilty or not, they had their man in custody.

As such, there was no leeway for an innocent man to explore.

Yet his mindset fought to uncover a strand of positivity among the doom-laden implications.

Those now sitting in judgement had brought the onus on themselves.

Ashley's logic demanded a reversed appraisal of the scenario.

If they wished ultimately to convict him, they would need a trial.

For a trial to transpire, they would need a charge.

And they could not charge him without concrete proof that Pauline Braithwaite had died at his hands.

The requirement on that proof then being conclusive and indisputable.

Could she truly accomplish meeting such pivotal criteria from beyond the grave?

Did she really feel so wronged by Ashley Griffiths that by willingly stripping herself of her own life she would in turn cause such collateral damage to his?

It was an inconceivable possibility, but could she have staged the beating that apparently took her last breath?

Was suicide seen by her as the fitting penance in order to accomplish her demented aims?

The wild rush of conspiracies clawed at his soul as he hunched on the cell bed. The voice of objection along the corridor had suddenly found new volume and reiterated the bemoaning and bellowing of earlier.

As he listened to the fellow captive vocalise his thirst for rebellion, Ashley had already accepted that fate was in control for the both of them now.

Acceptance of destiny's call was the only option available.

He could fight no more.

He would fight no more.

*****

Several hours had elapsed when Ashley was suddenly awoken by the rattling of the porthole in the cell door. He stirred swiftly but missed the eyes placing him under scrutiny as the small hatch was shut again.

The insertion and turning of the key alerted him to an entrant.

He almost felt a sense of privilege as his stomach cramped with expectation.

He rubbed his eyes vigorously and sat up on the mattress as the desk sergeant was escorted into the cell by two uniformed constables, one of which duly handcuffed Ashley with his wrists bound at the front over his groin.

The sergeant grimaced as he made his declaration with all the practised charm of a gallows attendant.

'The D.I. would like a word, Mister Griffiths. Follow me, please.'

FORTY

'This is the warrant for your arrest. I do apologise for not producing it earlier.'

Detective Inspector Neil Huntley duly offered the document for scrutiny, not that Ashley was overly interested as he stared with disdain at the tabletop.

'I think that horse has bolted. Don't you, Inspector?'

The D.I. did not respond to the mild hint of sarcasm and took the seat opposite Ashley's.

'We will need a signed affidavit from you very soon. You really do need a solicitor, Mister Griffiths.'

Another layer of procedural necessity just to add to the rest. The Detective Inspector studied Ashley's sorrowful expression as another officer entered the interview room and closed the door.

Ashley thought he had all justification to uphold his right not to speak. Yet the vibe in the room did not strike him as being appropriate to a murder enquiry. The atmosphere was almost too casual.

Perhaps an indication that the Police felt they had an open and shut case. Ashley's presumptions were equally strong, but for reasons to the contrary.

'We won't concern ourselves with using the tape recorder just yet, Mister Griffiths. Not until we've had a little chat and you are sure of how you wish to proceed. I'd like to keep things informal for the moment. If you are agreeable to that?'

Ashley considered the senior officer's words as he continued to maintain focus on the surface of the table, on which he now rested his bound hands.

Something was amiss, but he couldn't put his finger on it.

Was he a murder suspect or was he not?

Things were a little too amiable for his liking.

There was a bitter taste on his palate which prevented any willingness to conjure a reaction to the D.I.'s ad hoc prompts.

‘You’re obviously aware that you have not been charged, yet I repeat, you *will* need legal counsel. If only for the preservation of fair process. Do I make myself clear, Mister Griffiths?’

Ashley’s involuntary numbness in response to circumstances continued to prevail. He felt no inclination to offer a defence as an innocent man.

Whilst aware that such a policy was extremely naive, he felt the Police should uphold full responsibility and put their cards on the table.

If they had any cards.

But then a change of tactic suddenly dawned.

Perhaps it would prove to be a wiser investment if he *did* talk to them? After all, it wasn’t as if Ashley was withholding vital information. He was only aware of what the police had told him.

It fell to logical presumption that Pauline Braithwaite’s body was perhaps in a state of serious disrepair. The thought occurred to him that unless he drew some details from the inquiry, he wouldn’t be able to assess his own standing in the matter.

And so, he u turned.

He would relinquish his right to silence.

Ashley himself needed some answers.

His first question perhaps carrying most pertinence.

‘Inspector…you say that Mrs Braithwaite has died. Can you explain what this has to do with me? Why am I sitting here under your scrutiny?’

The D.I. smiled wryly as he picked up on Ashley’s change of approach to the situation.

‘Were you…or were you *not*…a friend of hers, Mister Griffiths?’

Ashley pressed his lips together and shook his head.

‘Hardly! More like arch enemies. She had been hounding me for months. She was off the charts. A fruit loop. It’s all in the statement I made in the summer with my then partner. And there were more problems afterwards which I didn’t bother reporting.’

The D.I. noted Ashley’s shift in the tone of expression.

‘Given the circumstances it seems rather bizarre on your part to claim that you were enemies. You have also said previously that you hardly knew her.’

‘I knew *enough* about the woman, believe me. I only met her face to face four times. My judgement derives from experiencing her actions toward me…not her background or her personality.’

The Detective Inspector rose from his chair and as per habit placed his hands in his trouser pockets. He commenced a steady sidle around the room as he spoke.

‘How *was* her personality, Mister Griffiths? From your limited knowledge. How would you have summed up her state of mind?’

Ashley rubbed his furrowed forehead with both sets of his tethered fingers.

There was no going back now.

He had no alternative but to convey the facts that he knew.

‘We first met at my place of work. The Ultimate Inn here in Hernwood. I’m the Operations Manager. I think I still am if I ever manage to walk through the front entrance again. It’s been a while since I set foot in the place because of all this trouble.’

‘Ahh, yes. The billboard boy. You have quite a presence around town.’

‘Don’t remind me. Mrs Braithwaite got the idea in her head that I might be up for a romantic dalliance.’

‘But you weren’t, I take it?’

‘I explained to her that I’m a homosexual and in a settled relationship. So, on those two fairly decisive counts, I figured she might get the hint. I’m off-radar where women are concerned. In terms of intimacy, anyway. Christ, I feel like a stuck record going over this again.’

The D.I. continued to waltz solo across the floor as he encouraged the conversation to expand.

‘And how did she respond to the fact you were off limits?’

Despite his better intentions, Ashley was now becoming very bored with raking over the same old coals.

This absurd latest chapter really was beyond fiction or fantasy.

'Look, Inspector. All this is in the statement you already have from me from last September. Or it could have been earlier I can't recall exactly. It's all on record. That's why I'm here in the first place isn't it? Because I'm the only bloody link on file that might help you lot find out what happened to the woman.'

The D.I. stopped his graceful stride and leaned to Ashley's ear.

'Please humour me again, Mister Griffiths. I repeat…how did she respond to learning that you were off limits?'

Ashley calmed himself and resumed a sense of cordiality.

'To my face…she seemed absolutely fine. Behind my back…she started to stalk me. From about the middle of July last year. Until the day she died.'

Ashley sincerely hoped he wouldn't be asked to go into detail.

The senior officer folded his arms and with an index finger he began to play with his lower lip as his thoughts engaged him.

Ashley felt a compulsion to press once again for the reasons he was being held at the station.

'Let's cut to the chase, Inspector Huntley. Are you going to charge me with her murder?'

The Inspector appeared surprised by the direct nature of Ashley's interest.

'Patience, Mister Griffiths. This is a delicate case. We need to weigh up all potential scenarios before we decide how to move forward. You are quite correct. We have made the link to you because of your previous complaints. And the fact that you are the only friend on her social media account.'

At last Ashley sensed progress.

'Great! So, you'll know about our last meet up? A few days before Christmas. The Bistro at Fendern. That's the last time I set eyes on her. I *left* her there. She was *alone*. It was a last-ditch attempt to talk her round to sanity, but she was totally fixated on the campaign to ruin me.'

The Inspector came in with an unexpected side swipe.

'So, when your kind and considered words failed to stop her, you thought a more stringent remedy would put an end to her fun and games. Is that how it happened, Mister Griffiths? Are you telling me you resorted to violence in the end?'

Ashley slammed his fists on the tabletop.

The D.I. was taunting him and having some success.

'No, officer! Absolutely *not*! I might have been at my wits end with the woman and detested the sight and sound of her. But I tell you here and now…I'm no killer.'

The D.I. was willing to accelerate the emotive debate further.

'Perhaps you didn't *intend* to kill her? Perhaps you hoped a good beating would be enough to finally get the message through to her? Desperate people sometimes employ desperate measures, Mister Griffiths. It would be understandable given the scenario you were in.'

Ashley smirked inwardly on hearing the repetition of his father's philosophy. He purposely extended the smile in open mockery of the inspector's ludicrous deductions.

Perhaps another angle on the discussion was called for.

'Inspector…you said she was beaten to death? Where exactly was the body found?'

'Discovered at her home address by a concerned neighbour. Three days after Christmas. The twenty-eighth. But that doesn't necessarily infer that she was killed there, does it?'

More satire from Ashley served to sour the atmosphere in the room.

'Well, unless you have some footage, or a witness that saw me dragging her body through the front door, then I'd say you're backing a loser with me. Wouldn't *you*? Besides which…I have absolutely no inkling of where her house is. I only met her at the hotel and the pub.'

The senior officer was now visibly frustrated.

'You could have had help, Mister Griffiths. Her address details are on record at the hotel from the booking she made in the summer. The information was available to you should you have decided to use it.'

Ashley's patience was also steadily evaporating.

He now figured that losing his temper would do no more harm than keeping it in check.

'Oh, Jesus Christ Almighty! Look…my life is a big enough cock-up without going down for murder as a finishing touch. I had made my mind up to ignore her. Not wipe her off the planet!'

'So, you've never been to her home, then?'

'Never in my life, Inspector! She had enough wild ideas in her head without me fuelling the damned fire. The meeting in Fendern was my last gasp attempt to impart some sympathy into her. Hands up! I failed miserably.'

Detective Inspector Huntley resumed his pacing of the room's perimeter. Ashley maintained his gaze at the closed door as silence descended. He had rescued a sliver of positivity from the last few minutes. It was no surprise that the Police obviously had no shred of proof to link him to the victim.

He almost relished spectating on the challenge the Police had set for themselves, knowing their chase would fall at the first hurdle.

As Ashley's perspective gained solidity, so did his bravado,

He observed the meandering senior detective, who appeared increasingly more puzzled and desperate, to say the least.

Ashley's manner remained controlled and forthright.

'You *know* I didn't do it, *don't you*? You have rightful grounds to believe I *could* have done it, but the truth is, there is absolutely *nothing* connecting me to this case. That's why you aren't recording…isn't it? That's why I've not had to make my statement, isn't it? You're flying blind, aren't you, Inspector Huntley? No leads…no clues…no trail. Nothing. All I've done is confirm what you already knew anyway. You started at a dead end with this…and the way I see it, you're stuck there.'

Neil Huntley's mood became mildly aggressive.

Ashley had knowingly pushed buttons in him.

But the game was not quite over yet.

Now it was the D.I.'s chance to throw a curveball.

'Where did you go after leaving The Bistro in Fendern, Mister Griffiths?'

Ashley wanted to smile but concealed his satisfaction.

He had to deal with the change of direction the D.I. has instigated.

'I went to my parents' house to collect a few things. Then to the shop for a couple of bits. Then I went home.'

'Home being, number thirty-nine, Harrogate Close?'

'Correct. Check my doorbell camera. I would have got home about…say…three or four-ish. And that's where I stayed all over Christmas. Until your kind people picked me up earlier and then locked me up.'

The Inspector closed in toward his suspect.

His eyes narrowed and the volume softened as though he smelled an opportunity to prise fresh information.

'Do you have an alibi for this?'

'For *what*, exactly?'

'That you were alone and didn't leave the house over Christmas?'

'Only my doorbell. But that would prove that I didn't go out again.'

'So, there's nobody at all that can vouch for where you were these past few days?'

Ashley was suddenly feeling rather smug about the fruitless way the inquiry was heading. He was gaining the upper hand while the police continued to clutch at more straws.

'My mother phoned the day after Boxing Day. She was upset I was on my own. But I didn't feel like company. That's not a crime, is it?'

Detective Huntley clenched his fists and placed both hands knuckle down on the tabletop. The veins in his forehead were visibly bulbous. His annoyance was obvious, but still he persisted.

'So, besides your mother, you didn't contact anybody after leaving Fendern or then your parents' house? You have seen no one for the better part of a week? Is that correct?'

'Hang on. Yes. I phoned my boss. Derek Evans. He will confirm. I was supposed to be returning to work but couldn't face it in the end. But apart from that…I kept myself to myself.'

The D.I. chuckled as he stood over Ashley.

Cynicism was creeping into to the exchange.

'So says the guy plastered across every motorway junction in the southwest. For someone who likes to lead a quiet life you have a very public profile, Mister Griffiths. For saying you're supposedly a private man, you must have foreseen the attention the hotel posters would have given you?'

Ashley sported a knowing grimace.

Now digging for a possible motive, the Police were evidently scraping the barrel for a concrete link.

'Yes, I can see where you might like to head with this angle, Inspector, but I can assure you I did not encourage the attentions of Pauline Braithwaite in any way, shape, or form. Quite the opposite! Now…I'm a patient man but I'm fraying a little bit at your futile and empty questioning. Either pin something on me that will hold…or let me go. Please.'

D.I. Huntley displayed a mask of contempt toward his one and only suspect as he knocked on the interview room door to alert the guarding officer outside.

He turned to Ashley as the door duly opened.

'I think some more time in your cell might encourage your memory to revive itself a little.'

Ashley's frustration was also on the verge of spilling over.

But he also knew he held the high ground in this issue.

'Well, if you haven't anything on me now, I can't see you advancing much further by the time my twenty-four hours is up.'

Neil Huntley exhibited no hint of concession as they passed one another in the doorway.

'Mister Griffiths…I must remind you that despite the inconvenience to your good self, this is an ongoing murder case. I've put in for ninety-six hours to keep you here. You're not going anywhere any time soon.'

Ashley could have retaliated but opted not to.

He gritted his teeth on entering the outer corridor.

Despondency and silence were his two accomplices as he was led back to the cells.

Then bemusement also followed him as he sat on the bed and listened to the metallic clang of liberty being further withheld.

It seemed that no one knew anything regarding the demise of Pauline Braithwaite.

That she was no longer alive appeared to be the only certainty connected to the entire investigation.

But Ashley pledged to himself that he would administer patience.

For as long as was necessary.

FORTY-ONE

'How was the grub?'

Ashley gazed forlornly at the custody officer. The cheeseburger and fries were a welcome if brief diversion from the situation, but reality soon enclosed him again.

'Fine. Thank you. I was hungry.'

'Don't worry…we didn't spit in it. Not everything you see on TV happens in real life, you know.' sniggered the constable.

Ashley nodded idly. He was dog tired, if now nourished. He squeezed his eyes tightly shut before attention aimlessly settled once again on the wall of the cell.

It had been several hours since the so-called informal interview with D.I. Huntley had been suspended.

However, Ashley's prospects were no bleaker.

He figured the Inspector was stalling for time as the case remained stone cold. He optioned the opportunity to converse with the custody sergeant who shut the cell door and spoke through the port hatch.

'How long have I been in here?'

Two brown eyes peered back at Ashley through the peep hole.

'Just over twenty-six hours since initial admission, sir.'

'I don't suppose you have any idea how long this farce is going to go on for have you?'

There was no further reply from the custody officer.

The latch closed and was pinned shut.

The waiting game it was, then.

*****

Thirty-seven hours and six minutes had elapsed since Ashley had been arrested and incarcerated.

And still the hollowness of developments lingered in the air.

No one had been back to speak to him.

He was getting hungry again. He couldn't fathom why the police should wish to detain him yet not interrogate him.

It seemed to be such a dismal exercise in protocol.

Maybe they hoped that Ashley would concede under the weight of his enforced solitude and disclose the name of the killer.

But he had no name to confess.

In fact, he was now becoming more intrigued and mystified than the investigating officer probably was.

The enemy was no more, yet the cause still evaded disclosure.

Ashley's thoughts were briefly diverted to the hotel and its staff.

And Derek Evans.

Christ Almighty.

What would his colleagues be making of all this?

A career likely in tatters and a reputation in the gutter.

Quite a leap, their manager being absent through stress to being absent through being framed for a suspected homicide.

This latest episode was too ridiculous to earn contemplation on any rational level.

No doubt he was the subject on everyone's lips.

A source of relentless conjecture and suspicion.

The vultures would already be swooping with their declarations of judgemental scepticism.

I told you he was iffy.

No one could be that squeaky clean.

I bet it was a one-night stand.

His partner left him because of it.

It was that final thought that brought Carl back onto the psychological horizon. If the Police had a warrant for Ashley's arrest, then they would likely have a warrant to search the house.

If the search had taken place, then it had done so without his consent or knowledge. But he supposed that with a murder inquiry the police were granted autonomy anyway.

They were in command of everything.

And he was obliged to sit tight and comply.

They had also confiscated his phone.

So, they would be aware that Carl had not been contacted for several weeks.

Perhaps they had analysed Ashley's I-pad and laptop too. If so, they would be disappointed with the lack of fruitful information on them.

But Carl would also surely be a suspect by default?

Why had he too not been hauled in for scrutiny?

Surely any bona fide inquiry would cover these bases?

But Carl presumably knew nothing of the latest events.

He bailed out long before the Fendern meeting with Pauline Braithwaite and the subsequent fallout of emotional debris that it caused.

A pertinent consideration then entered Ashley's mind as he pondered the recent past.

What if Carl *had* heard about the latest development?

What if he *had* opted to return to the trench and fight covertly alongside his partner?

But without Ashley's knowledge?

Highly unlikely; however possible.

Carl had twice proved himself to be disloyal.

Unworthy of Ashley's deep-rooted affections.

He wouldn't stop to help a friend in need.

More likely to cross the road and plead ignorance.

So, it stands to reason that he wouldn't be prepared to extinguish the life of any foe.

Not even for Ashley's sake.

*****

Nearly three days attained in extended custody.

Three orders of cheeseburgers and fries.

Three bowls of cornflakes.

A gallon of tap water.

And not a single question asked by the head of the investigation during the previous forty hours.

Yet still Ashley resisted accommodation of his rising frustrations.

Still, he tolerated the illogical absence of the inquisition.

The Desk Sergeants came and went as their shifts changed and converged.

Beady eyes of suspicion peered through the view hatch at regular intervals of the day and night but offered not the slightest clue as to the progress of matters beyond the cell door.

Ashley's polite request to know the time was greeted by dull silence and the resounding slam of the porthole.

A plea to perhaps take a shower was refused outright.

Soap, a toothbrush and a towel were provided for use in conjunction with the basin facility in the cell.

It was clear that the staffing of the station was a world away from the cutthroat mechanics of a murder inquiry.

The only certainty was that the Detective Inspector had full authority over Ashley's current predicament.

No other officer was privy to carry any other duty aside preserving the health and wellbeing of the chief suspect.

Neil Huntley was the only person that could bring this to an end.

Until then, Ashley would have to endure the continual personal soul searching until the Gods on high decided to endorse his immediate fate.

He had accepted that this was the way of things.

He had accepted the solitude.

Accepted the segregation.

These were positives, and in his view the longer time ticked on, the more readily his freedom would likely be restored.

The Police could ask no further questions.

They had nothing left to ask.

They could talk to Ashley…about nothing.

And the game must play on.

*****

Seventy-one hours and thirty-two minutes.

The top door hatch opened.

Ashley presumed it to be delivery of another meal.

Whether it might be burgers or cereal he could not decipher having lost track of all time.

Ashley was standing over the stainless-steel urinal pan when the custody sergeant declared that there was a visitor.

Completing attending to nature's call, Ashley then washed his hands. As per practiced procedure, he stood facing the far wall of the cell with his nose pressed against the grey-painted brickwork, whilst the door was unlocked allowing entry of two uniformed officers.

The handcuffs were predictably applied.

Judging by the fragrance of perfume it was a female officer that employed the wrist restraints. His suspicions were confirmed when she instructed him to turn around.

An attractive lady of mixed-race origin glowered at him in the line of duty. The female sergeant disturbed the quiet with words that inflicted both relief and trepidation into Ashley's core.

'Detective Inspector Huntley would like to speak with you. Same room as before. No tricks or tantrums, please. You've been a very good boy so far. Be a shame to spoil it.'

It was very difficult to determine, but Ashley sensed that the sergeant's wording implied finality was upon him. Whatever had been discovered, or had remained undiscovered, warranted discussion. For him to be requested for further engagement was a pleasant change to the status quo.

On entering the interview room, Ashley wasted no time in taking a chair. His cuffs were removed and replaced. With his hands again now bound at the front, being seated was less encumbered. The female officer then took up position across the table, directly opposite Ashley.

After several seconds of unblemished inactive quiet, the D.I. entered the fray and nodded to the second constable present, who duly stepped into the corridor and closed the door.

The Inspector placed himself next to the female officer and attempted to evaluate the almost serene disposition of his one and only suspect.

Neil Huntley still looked to be a man without cause or direction.

'I hope your prolonged stay as our guest is proving hospitable, Mister Griffiths. As a man in the trade, I'm sure you'd be the first to pinpoint any lapses in the quality of service?'

If that was an attempt at humour, then the D.I. had selected the wrong audience to try out his new material.

Ashley's expression did not alter. Nor did he offer a reply.

As a completely spent force, he now just wanted the ordeal to end.

He hoped that the senior investigator would soon cement this wish.

'I understand that you have had no offer of the singular phone call?'

Ashley shook his head slowly, largely disinterested in the topic of conversation.

'I can tell you that we have had no external enquiries about your welfare, either. My, my. We aren't very popular, are we?' smirked the D.I.

Why did the Detective Inspector insist on confirming what everybody already knew? It was a strange habit. As if he was yet again stalling for time and striving for a valid reason to communicate.

'The ongoing inquiry is still at its very early stages, Mister Griffiths, but is very intensive. I would have liked to have spent more time with you, but unfortunately, I haven't found the opportunity…until now.'

Ashley finally relented and opted to join the discussion.

'What you *really* mean, Detective Huntley, is that you've kept me here for three days whilst desperately turning over every stone and looking in every nook and cranny so you can find something solid to hang on me. But you've not found anything, have you?'

Neil Huntley was far from enamoured by Ashley's façade of smugness. His own visage became slightly contorted with annoyance, but he maintained a level of professional decorum.

‘Indeed, Mister Griffiths. My team has been exhausting every conceivable avenue. And yes, at this moment it does appear that we may yet have more work to do to uncover the truth here.’

It came as a shock for Ashley to hear a guardian of the law confess to being confounded in the search for clues. A highly irregular scenario, in fact. The D.I. sat back in his chair and stifled a yawn.

He had more to say yet seemed strangely reticent.

‘You see, Mister Griffiths, until I have evidential reason to mount a charge, I cannot ask you to make a statement in a formal interview. And you were justified in avoiding employment of a legal rep. You know the score here. I’ll credit you for that. However, things may well change considering the events of the last eight hours.’

The tangent of the conversation had adopted a most unexpected slant. Ashley was receiving very mixed signals from the leader of the investigation.

‘I’m a little confused, Inspector Huntley. You say in one breath I am not a suspect, yet in the next breath you’re advising I might need a solicitor? What’s happened in the last eight hours, then?’

Neil Huntley leaned forward and placed his elbows on the table. There was the merest flicker of accomplishment in his expression. His tone of voice even carried a slight strain of sympathy as he observed the puzzlement emerging across Ashley’s features.

The next statement from the senior inspector hit Ashley as an authentic shock.

‘At this juncture in the procedure, you are free to go, Mister Griffiths. I can’t justify holding you here any longer.’

The words echoed around Ashley’s mind.

Did he just imagine what thought he had been told?

Free to go?

No reasoning?

No notice?

The ball and chain removed. Without explanation?

This was not a satisfactory outcome for Ashley Griffiths.

The police needed to provide more than a cursory farewell.

As a former chief suspect in the murder of Pauline Braithwaite, he felt fully entitled to know what had recently transpired and why it should have been valid enough to enable his return to civilisation.

D.I. Neil Huntley had read Ashley's mind.

Indeed, a revelation *was* imminent.

FORTY-TWO

Ashley remained at ease in his seat. His attention fixed firmly on the senior investigating officer positioned opposite.

Fighting a pending state of disorientation, he strove for clarity of thought.

Three days of confinement and no charges brought against him.

Circumstances of the inquiry now smacked of being remiss.

The D.I. looked slightly flustered. The atmosphere had altered considerably during the previous minutes.

Whatever was being concealed from Ashley required airing.

Yet it seemed to be highly surprising that he was now the one requesting information, as opposed to the typical Police custody process.

But Ashley was compelled to uncover whatever it was that was being withheld.

And this tenacity was not borne out of anger, but from a genuine interest in how the deceased had met her end.

'Are you informing me that I am no longer the chief suspect in this investigation?'

Even Neil Huntley's considerable experience seemed to have left him in the lurch in terms of dealing with the mysterious latest development. He appeared uncertain in formalising his response to a very earnest question. The D.I. was duty bound to reveal nothing, yet his manner suggested that he might wish to make a declaration of sorts.

'You are to be released on conditional police bail, Mister Griffiths. And until the investigation deems otherwise, you will remain as a pivotal figure for our inquiries. But for now…you may go.'

This was nowhere near good enough.

Ashley demanded further detail.

'What does the bail thing mean? Explain it like I'm three-years-old, please.'

'Quite simply, Mister Griffiths, you are still very much a person of interest in this investigation.'

'But I can walk away?'

'I do not possess sufficient grounds to charge you and as such I cannot hold you in custody any longer.'

The waters were still very muddied.

Ashley persevered for clarity.

'Okay. So, when I leave the station today…what are the conditions of my release?'

It was clear that the senior officer was incredibly reluctant to divulge any more information than was deemed absolutely necessary. And it was specifically this undue mode of secrecy that was beginning to infuriate Ashley.

In his eyes he was fully entitled to be made aware of the full scenario if it was carrying the potential to affect his future welfare.

'It's nothing too stringent, Mister Griffiths. It's an agreement to comply and cooperate with us should we need to contact you again. And you must oblige the discretion of the investigation whilst it is ongoing. No discussion on the matter with *anybody*. No discussion with *any* potential witness. You may have your mobile phone returned to you today on departure, but the other items will remain under our jurisdiction until twenty-eight days after the one-month bail period has expired. And you must surrender your passport and stay in the country until further notice.'

'*Witnesses*? What *witnesses*?' balked Ashley.

The D.I. raised a hand of caution.

'I said…*potential* witnesses, Mister Griffiths. Loose lips sink ships. We don't want this case compromised. It's complicated enough, already. But in all honesty, I don't think you'll be considering doing a runner.'

The plot was thickening by the second. D.I. Huntley was being very circumspect with his contributions to the dialogue. There was more going on behind the scenes than was being admitted to.

'So…I'm on Police bail for a month. Then what?'

The D.I. left his chair and knocked lightly on the door. The guarding constable duly answered the call and allowed the senior officer to exit.

Ashley's impatience began to burn at the display of ignorance.

'Inspector! If you don't put me in the picture, then how do I know if I'm playing by the rules or not? What is going to happen to me when my bail expires?'

Neil Huntley glanced briefly at his female colleague who had remained at the table with Ashley. Again, he deliberated a cautious response as his attention focussed on his former prisoner.

'By that time, we should have determined if you are an accessory, or whether we can possibly eliminate you from the inquiry. But at this stage there is a strong potential that any subsequent arrest may involve you being remanded by the courts.'

Ashley was now completely dumbfounded. The more the inspector told him the less he understood. But it was the information still being withheld that was Ashley's bugbear.

'*Accessory*? Did you say…*accessory*?'

Neil Huntley nodded without reply.

'So…you have apprehended another suspect, then? So, you now think this killing was maybe somebody else's effort, then?'

The D.I. hovered in the corridor, undecided whether to divulge the current situation.

'We are now fairly certain you are not directly responsible for the murder of Pauline Braithwaite, Mister Griffiths. We just need to ascertain whether you were in allegiance with those that *did* commit the killing.'

Ashley rose to his feet alerting the reflexive responses from the female sergeant opposite.

She placed a hand on his shoulder as a warning to refrain from following the D.I. out of the room.

She offered her dutiful instruction.

'Remain here for the moment, sir. You will be escorted to the reception desk soon enough. Your bail paperwork is ready to sign.'

Ashley obeyed the command as he observed the sergeant consult with her superior in the corridor. She covered her mouth to prevent Ashley identifying any aspect of the exchange with Neil Huntley.

‘What are you thinking, Guv? He’s a bit riled in there.’

The senior investigator scratched his forehead.

‘I need to see the Chief Super immediately, Rose. In twenty-three years as an inspector, I’ve never known a case like this one. What is your take as an impartial?’

She offered Ashley a brief glance as she conjured an answer.

Sergeant Rose Washington had been privy to the bigger picture. Yet her view on the way forward was no more decisive than her superior’s.

Although she did offer a slightly different perspective on the arena.

‘If the new suspects have already made sworn statements that preclude Mister Griffiths’ involvement, then he’s off the hook, isn’t he? And judging by his current manner, I’d also say he has had nothing to do with it whatsoever.’

‘I need the nod from the top floor if we are going to tell him what’s developed. But my feelings match yours, Rose. He didn’t kill her. And it’s obvious even to the untrained eye that he hasn’t a scooby-doo who *did*. Keep him in here until I’ve had some guidance on it. Another half-hour won’t ruin his schedule.’

‘Okay, Guv. What do I tell him, though?’

‘At the moment we tell him *nothing*. I’m sure it will be a big enough shock when he does find out, anyway. I’ll be back down soon enough.’

FORTY-THREE

'What's your experience telling you on this, Neil? How would you see fit to play it?'

Chief Superintendent Peter Dickinson had been kept fully abreast of developments regarding the investigation into Pauline Braithwaite's death.

He understood the dilemma now facing his Detective Inspector and sympathised with the difficulty of the highly untypical situation they now faced.

'I just said to Rose downstairs…this is something I've never dealt with in nearly three decades in the job. That's why I need some guidance, Sir.'

The Chief Super scowled at the slate grey scene beyond his office window.

'It's a new one for me too, Neil. To suddenly inform the chief suspect that he isn't going to be charged is disparaging enough for the Force. But this? I don't think the rulebook covers such a predicament.'

D.I. Huntley declined the offer of a seat.

He needed clarification on the issue.

The way forward was unchartered.

'The thing is, Sir, Ashley Griffiths has portrayed himself as innocent from the word go. He seems to be a man of impeccable character. We've spoken to some colleagues of his. His credibility has never come into question. I believe he is the genuine article. He was the first obvious port of call for the inquiry…but we're barking up the wrong tree with him. Have been since the get-go.'

Superintendent Dickinson narrowed his eyes and focussed sternly on his D.I.

'Now Neil…We can't run a case on instinct. Only fact. Just because Griffiths comes across as a nice bloke doesn't assure his innocence. Assumption doesn't appease the CPS.'

The D.I. persevered in depicting the lie of the land.

‘Sir…we have no evidence connecting him to *anything* regarding the victim’s murder. The problem is that now he knows he’s likely off the hook he is desperate to find out who is taking his place. That’s the aspect of all this that I’m not clear on how to handle. Ordinarily, murder suspects would never have cause to communicate. But how *this* is supposed to play out, I’ve no idea.’

The Chief Super digested Neil Huntley’s last statement. His grimace was accentuated by a forefinger extended in the direction of his most senior detective.

‘Off the *hook*…did you say? Not bloody likely. The prosecution will fight tooth and nail to bag him too, whether guilty or not. I’m sorry Neil but you need to alter your perspective. The events of the last few hours link Griffiths to the murder ever more directly. It will never wash with a jury that he didn’t get his hands dirty, too. Think of it on those lines and the whole investigation presents itself in a rather different light don’t you think?’

Detective Inspector Huntley shook his head despairingly.

‘I’m well aware of how this might look in court, Sir. But without proof I’m not getting too excited about taking Griffiths down with the sinking ship. Facts are needed, you just said. Well, the fact is, so far as I’m concerned, he’s *clean.*’

The Super leaned forward in his chair.

Deliberation etched across his features.

Neil Huntley continued.

‘The suspects that came forward are being held at Borton nick. Our follow-up on them has been throwing evidence at us left, right and centre. Prints, swabs, weapons. Made it easy for forensics. The security camera footage from Mrs Braithwaite’s property is crystal clear. You name it it’s all in there. Irrefutable. Open and shut. That’s a done deal for the crown. But if the prosecution wants to claim Griffiths in the same net, then they’ve a very tough call. There is no chance in the world he was an accessory to this. He’ll be released on conditional bail. That buys us a month to tie him in. But I just can’t see it happening.’

Superintendent Dickinson rose to his feet and paced slowly around the desk.

He looked to have yet another spanner to throw in the works.

'I don't envy you, Neil. I really don't. But think on this. If the new suspects are as cut and dried as you claim, then it could be interpreted that they are covering for him. And he will be dragged into court to prove his innocence, anyway.'

'Yes…of course. Quite correct, Sir. So maybe I don't have to work very hard to keep him in the mix. Is that what you are saying?'

'Bailed or not…he remains a major cog in this investigation. Unavoidably so. Especially now.'

'Okay…cutting to the chase, Sir. Do I have your permission to disclose recent developments to him? He has a right to know and will find out soon enough anyway. Damage limitation for us, perhaps?'

Superintendent Dickinson did not take long to decide.

'Yes. You do have my blessing. Sign him out for his twenty-eight days. It's a guarantee he won't be straying far. But forget about being blinded by his amiable character, Neil. He is a person of interest. And until we say otherwise, he remains a key fixture in all this. Get him escorted out to Borton if you wish. Satisfy his curiosity and put him out of his misery.'

FORTY-FOUR

'Apologies for keeping you waiting, Mister Griffiths. I've assembled the necessary paperwork for bail.'

D.I. Huntley entered the interview room this time displaying the semblance of a smile.

Ashley's previously abrupt mannerisms had flattened out to a weary acceptance of whatever might come his way. He pretended to read the documents placed on the table before him. He signed his name in the relevant fields and took the carbon copies for his own reference.

'So, Inspector Huntley...I take it I am now bound to a curfew?'

'Ordinarily you would be under a strict timetable, yes. But I don't think it's necessary in this case. All we ask is that you cooperate should it be required.'

Ashley was ushered from his chair and had the wrist restraints removed.

'I hope the new suspects are offered better communication than I've received. Your concept of explanation leaves a lot to be desired I can tell you. Its mediaeval! Locking folk up when they've done nothing wrong. I don't know how you get away with it.'

The D.I. did not rise to the bait.

He had other pressing matters to address.

Then Sergeant Rose Washington gestured for Ashley to reclaim a seat.

'Christ alive...*now what*?'

Neil Huntley attempted to venture something substantive for the confusing nature of the previous three days. Ashley picked up on the sudden slant of tension across the table.

The D.I. appeared troubled and hesitant.

He was lacking the customary steel of a senior inspector.

His aura was far from akin to that of such an esteemed rank.

'Mister Griffiths...you must understand that because you were on our file as a complainant, and had an association with the deceased, we were duty bound to apprehend you as the most significant person of interest at the outset of this murder investigation.'

Ashley nodded and leaned on his elbows with fingers clasped.

'Yes, Detective Huntley. With hindsight I accept all that. But I am *innocent*. Her death is nothing to do with me.'

Neil Huntley closed his eyes and took a deep breath.

'I do believe you are telling the truth, Mister Griffiths. There is no discernible connection between yourself and the murder scene. We have established this whilst holding you here at the station. And even without your provision of a reliable alibi, we have no reason currently to doubt your recollection of your whereabouts during the afternoon in question.'

'Okay…so we have reached common ground and have a mutual understanding at last. So why the bail conditions? And why am I still being held?'

'Mister Griffiths…during your period of custody there was a significant shift of focus regarding our inquiry. Our attentions were unexpectedly diverted towards the acknowledgment of other potential suspects.'

Ashley stared intently into the eyes of the Inspector.

He still had no clue as to what had transpired beyond his cell door during the previous three days.

And he now found his desire to be consulted all-consuming and infuriating.

'So, I take it I wasn't the only one she stalked and haunted? These other suspects got the same treatment, did they? Sounds like they snapped. I was damned close to losing it, I can tell you. And can I presume that you have more than a shred of evidence connecting *them* to her death? And that they are locked up in a cell somewhere. Just like I have been?'

The Detective Inspector glanced at his female colleague before nudging himself nearer to the precipice of disclosure. It was a tough examination of mettle for any experienced officer. And for Neil Huntley, each passing second added unwanted pressure to the task.

‘They are under arrest, yes. And they are in custody. But not at this station.’

‘Oh? Why not here? Where then?’ Ashley gasped.

‘They are being held at Borton. It was deemed to be the sensible decision that you weren’t all held under the same roof.’

‘I’m still muddled, Inspector. How many other suspects have you lifted for this murder?’

D.I. Huntley paused for thought. The air was already laced with distinct unease. He suspected that the next stage might well be all-out hostility.

As the senior Policeman continued to stall his reply, Ashley’s desire for answers only became more vigorous.

There was no avoiding this.

Extreme displeasure was inevitable.

Finally, the truth was divulged.

‘We are currently holding *two* suspects at Borton station. They were arrested I would say around eighteen hours after your period of custody commenced here.’

Ashley’s intrigue was now rabid. With every morsel delivered by the investigation’s leader, he became immediately hungry for the next. But he could see that the head of the inquiry seemed very unsettled about something. Yet again it struck Ashley that such trepidation seemed most odd for an officer in charge of a murder case.

‘Are they known to you, D.I. Huntley? Did they know Pauline Braithwaite, then? Old enemies that finally caught up with her. That’s how it plays to me.’

The Detective Inspector folded his arms and continued down the path he would rather have avoided.

‘She wasn’t previously acquainted with the new suspects, no. Not in the typical sense, anyway. But the suspects targeted her, specifically. They’ve left no room for any doubt about that.’

Ashley was almost beginning to feel like he was part of the investigative team himself.

The D.I. at this point was beginning to wish he definitely *wasn't*.

'So? What happened? Were they burglars she caught red-handed? I'm having to presume that the attack took place sometime after our date at The Bistro. You say she was beaten up?'

'I really shouldn't be discussing this with you, Mister Griffiths. But circumstances are exceptional. Yes. Repeated blows to the body and head with a blunt weapon. Critical external and internal injuries.'

Ashley would not relent in his pursuit of detail.

'Jesus…she *must* have sprung them red-handed. These youngsters are vicious bleeders these days. They don't think twice about violence. Must be a generational thing.'

The D.I. stared at Ashley.

The moment of harsh reality was almost upon them.

Still in two minds about the wisdom of proceeding, Neil Huntley opted for honesty.

'They weren't youngsters, Mister Griffiths. The two suspects in the cells at Borton are a male and a female. They are both in their late sixties.'

Ashley was completely taken off guard by the latest revelation.

'*What*? How did you find out what had happened? Did a neighbour report it?'

'They arrived *here*. Whilst you were in custody. Voluntarily. And openly confessed to their crime.'

Ashley found himself immersed in disbelief.

Bemused now, as well as brazenly curious, he ventured the one final question that would prove to be to his eternal detriment.

'I don't get it. Why would an elderly couple team up and kill her if they hardly knew her? This is *too* weird, this is!'

Detective Inspector Neil Huntley said nothing more.

He silently engaged with the understandably perplexed visage of Ashley Griffiths.

And he maintained focus on his former prime suspect, as the dawn of realisation slowly began its emergence from the shadows of confusion.

Ashley's brain computed the facts that had been conveyed.

And with each passing second, the emerging, brutal, inconceivable picture became all too clear.

The senior officer studied Ashley's features as they altered rapidly.

His jaw tightened as his eyes widened.

The solution to the puzzle had now finally presented itself, in all its demoralising, emotionally shattering glory.

He wanted the ultimate knowledge.

And when the knowledge was bestowed, it did not sate him.

It crucified him.

Ashley's gaze wandered from the tabletop and up toward the apologetic figure opposite.

The D.I. cut a solemn yet sorrowful silhouette as Ashley stuttered a response to his horrific personal discovery.

'You mean...God no...please tell me I'm completely wrong, Inspector Huntley. Please, I beg you. Tell me I'm in the middle of another nightmare. Tell me this isn't real. It can't be...'

The senior officer was almost relieved that the burden had been off-loaded by Ashley's instinctive, yet devastatingly accurate summation.

D.I. Huntley now had no option but to declare the scenario as it stood at that moment.

'Mister Griffiths...your mother and father are being held at Borton station. They are now the chief suspects in this investigation. They both made a full, signed confession thirty-six hours ago. I'm very sorry to say this, but it looks like Pauline Braithwaite was murdered in cold blood...by your parents.'

FORTY-FIVE

January; Twenty-Twenty-Two. Friday; the twenty-first.

Two weeks had elapsed since Ashley's overdue release from custody at Hernwood station, albeit under the conditions of Police bail.

The most supremely discouraging fortnight of his entire life.

His emotional reaction to developments had floundered on a daily basis. Veering frequently between a dismally paralysing refusal of acknowledgement, and almost empathetic pride in his parents' actions.

Up until today, the Police operation supervising the investigation had presented Ashley with an outright refusal to communicate in any way with his mother and father.

Despite a conveyance of albeit diluted sympathy from the officers involved, procedural restriction had negated any opportunity for Ashley to have any form of access to his parents.

But eventually the human touch prevailed, and the mutual request for the family's wish to convene was ultimately granted.

At one p.m., Neville and Elaine Griffiths would engage in a supervised exchange with their one and only son.

But it had been made clear to all parties that this would be no typically tactile reunion.

The Griffiths were justifiably now regarded as priority one killers.

Each had presented full confessions, and each had pleaded accordingly at the hastily orchestrated arraignment.

The representatives of the Crown Court Judiciary heard two charges pertaining to two counts of first-degree murder.

And two accompanying pleas of guilt.

The subsequent decision displayed little hesitancy, in ordaining them both to be remanded in prison custody until a trial date could be confirmed. Most surprisingly to all involved, Neville and Elaine were not to be segregated whilst awaiting trial.

The location for their remand was however declared as confidential.

So much of the inquiry had broken new ground.

Accommodating arrangements was pleasingly smooth.

The judge deciding that due to both statements comparing as nigh on identical, and as both suspects were fully compliant in their mutual admissions, he saw no need to separate them.

It was his view that the defendants being held in custody under the same roof would present very little detriment to the ensuing inquiry and subsequent trial.

However, Ashley's permitted visit *would* entail his parents being temporarily moved to a neutral venue.

The officiating QC, Mister Simon Reville, had also made the court's position very clear during the arraignment.

So far as he and his consulted colleagues were concerned, this was far from an open and shut case.

Far from black and white in nature.

In no way symptomatic of a foregone conclusion.

Despite Ashley's apparent ignorance of matters directly related to the act of murder itself, the Crown was not yet convinced of his complete vindication in the matter.

Both the counsels for defence and prosecution had been awarded a burden of proof to establish unequivocally that the confessions of Neville and Elaine Griffiths could not be interpreted as ambiguous.

When Ashley requested explanation of Mister Reville's phrasing, it was put to him in simple layman's terms.

If it were possible to determine during the trial that Ashley Griffiths had any role whatsoever in his parents' wrongdoings, then Ashley himself would be arrested, remanded, and would himself face trial as an accessory to first degree murder.

But as D.I. Neil Huntley further explained, the physical and forensic evidence would likely exonerate him from any involvement.

So far as the head of the investigation was concerned, he had his true killers already, and he did not seem overly concerned to loop Ashley into the ring with them.

He also expressed a gut feeling that any jury would also dismiss the possibility of the chief suspects conspiring in a cover up for their son. By default, a murder trial was purposed to conclude whether the defendants were guilty or innocent.

It stood to reason that if the police suspected Ashley of partaking in the very same crime, he would certainly not be enjoying the comparative luxury of bail.

The likelihood of such a dramatic prospect was viewed as absolutely minimal, by the legal professional that Ashley had briefly consulted.

It was accepted that Ashley had no prior knowledge of his parents' plan and that it was purely of their own invention.

It had also been established and reported back to Ashley that his mother and father had behaved with extreme stoicism at their arraignment.

They had steadfastly maintained that their actions had not been motivated or governed by any outside influence.

That the mission was not to merely impart harm.

That the mission was a formalised and purposed attempt to kill.

And that the mission was purely of their own making.

That they exhibited absolutely no remorse for the deed whatsoever.

Ironically. the collateral from events was most damaging to Ashley.

His greatest ever allies were now behind bars.

And he was now completely alone in confronting whatever the future might bring.

*****

H.M.P. Stenton was approximately sixty miles from Hernwood, but Ashley would have driven to the end of the Earth to make today's privilege become a reality.

He pulled the car to a stop at the security barrier and confirmed his identity to the guard on duty by exhibiting his official visitors' documentation.

The lodge officer eyed the paperwork with customary suspicion, and subsequently eyed the driver who had presented it to him.

The seconds passed under the weight of an unforgiving hiatus.

Ashley's heart thumped erratically as he stared ahead through the rain-spattered windscreen. The only sound was that of the wipers performing their intermittent task.

Finally, the guard acknowledged authenticity of the appointment.

He withdrew to the security lodge in order to elevate the barrier.

As per the predictably gruff instruction, Ashley stationed the car in visitor's lot number seventeen, before nervously wrenching on the handbrake and disengaging the engine.

He temporarily immersed himself in the pleasantry of solitude as he awaited the arrival of Detective Inspector Neil Huntley, who had personally volunteered himself for the task of overseeing the temporary reunion between the Griffiths family.

This would be Ashley's first communication with his mother and father for over a month, which in itself felt quite odd even when compared to their temporary estrangement during both lockdowns.

Yet in current testing circumstances the situation was completely bewildering.

Ashley's brimming anticipation at setting eyes on his parents was overshadowed by the darkly imposing locale. Tall brickwork expansions loomed all around him, with their windows barred, reinforced, and razor wired for security purposes.

Intimidating wasn't the word as he alighted the car, and with a quickening heartbeat gazed upward at the facade of the main prison complex. As things stood, it was already a bleak enough late January afternoon without the anguish imposed by his current location.

One thought prevailed in Ashley's mind as he awaited the arrival of the D.I.

The same thought that had plagued him for weeks.

How could the very fabric of his life have unravelled so rapidly and relentlessly?

How could events have conspired to demand his incidental immersion into such a demeaning and depressing environment such as this. The surrounding vista was a stark symbol of the dismally tragic predicament the Griffiths family now found itself in.

And yet, a crumb of comfort might be gleaned from the daunting shadows of such an oppressive setting.

The authorities had seemingly taken an unusually lenient stance when deciding whether today's meeting should even be taking place. Let alone the direct restrictions that they might wish to impose upon the family.

Ashley had been offered no detail on what was to transpire over the next couple of hours.

But dubious contemplation on the matter would no longer be necessary as he observed a familiar figure striding across the tarmac to greet him.

Smiles seemed wholly inappropriate, but the gesture was mutually reflexive from both men as they entered proximity and shook hands.

Detective Inspector Neil Huntley looked fatigued, and Ashley could not afford to underestimate the extremely precarious nature of what was about to take place.

'You found us okay then, Mister Griffiths?'

'Yes, Inspector. Straight up the motorway really. No problem.'

'Okay, then. Let's go.'

A blustery wind accrued increasing force as Ashley walked with the D.I. toward a glass fronted entrance way, where two armoured prison officers offered glares of earnest disgust at the visitors' approach.

Having navigated their way inside, the perfunctory physical search was performed. Ashley had only his car keys and mobile phone on his person. Both were surrendered to the admittance office and procedure was quickly obliged with a lanyard sporting Ashley's name in a laminated card.

They were permitted through another door, which then slammed unceremoniously behind them. Finally, the senior officer opted to disclose some detail on what lay ahead as they marched along a steel lined corridor.

'You're lucky. Sometimes those body searches can go on for a while depending who is on duty. Unavoidable when you walk into places like this, I'm afraid.'

'It's no problem, Mister Huntley. I was expecting it. What happens now?'

'Well, you fall under my supervision today whilst on these premises. They've afforded us the privilege of a private consultation room as opposed to the visitors' hall. You should feel honoured.'

The pair entered a small office and Ashley was told to take a seat.

'Tea or coffee, Mister Griffiths?'

'No, neither. I'm fine…thank you.'

'Right…I'll go and check the state of play. I won't be long.'

No sooner had D.I. Huntley departed the office, a warden appeared at the doorway and stood at ease. He carried a grimace that appeared to convey an abject distaste for Ashley's very existence.

He also carried a suitably sized baton, just to reinforce the point.

All part and parcel of the prison experience, Ashley thought to himself, as he centred his attention on the smattering of crime prevention posters adorning the office walls.

A bit late in the game for sporting such literature, perhaps.

Then a mildly amusing consideration flashed through Ashley's mind.

That this was the stuff of soap operas.

A script to a ridiculously plotted TV drama. The nightmare that never ends. A reality show with a distressingly foregone conclusion.

How on Earth had his family become embroiled in such a plight.

More minutes ticked by as Ashley continued to await the senior detective's return.

He contemplated the pending conversation with his parents.

He had already been informed that he was allowed a duration of thirty minutes in their company and no more.

It seemed to be a wasted opportunity should Ashley pump questions at his mother and father that he already suspected he knew the answers to.

Their notion to commit such an act was perhaps noble in principle.

Yet all three would already be aware that the consequences would be life changing.

And it was this soul-destroying conviction that crashed through Ashley's frail conscience, as Detective Inspector Neil Huntley suddenly appeared in the doorway of the office.

This time, there was no accompanying smile from the head of the investigation as his eyes bore deep into Ashley's.

'Okay, Mister Griffiths. Ready when you are.'

*****

The interior of the building served Ashley with a sensation of abhorrence as he was escorted by the D.I. along a maze of intertwining gangways and corridors.

Ultimately, they arrived at another office.

To sit at another table.

Opposite two empty chairs.

'I won't be present in the room, but I will be listening in via intercom and watching on CCTV. Your parents will each be afforded a guarding officer who will remain for the full half hour.'

Ashley was suddenly overcome by a cloud of solemnity.

'Thank you, Inspector Huntley. I appreciate your help.'

'And for what it's worth, Mister Griffiths, bear in mind this might well be the last chance you ever get to be in the same room as your parents before the trial is set. No physical contact. Stay seated. Or the privilege will desist and be withdrawn immediately. I'll leave you to it.'

Minute after minute elapsed in soundless isolation.

It was an uncanny period of dreaded uncertainty for Ashley, which was ridiculous considering who he was about to be reunited with.

Upset verged as he overthought the scenario.

But the emotions instantly subsided as he detected movement from the other side of the door over his shoulder.

Ashley's body became rigid as he stared straight ahead, strangely fearful of the imminent appearance of his parents. He heard the door open and then the scuffing of feet on tiled flooring.

It was confirmed that he had company.

As predicted by D.I. Huntley, each was accompanied by a prison guard, though it was a blessing to see they were not handcuffed to their chaperones.

Still glaring at the far wall, Ashley was content to allow his mother and father to shuffle fully into his frame of vision in their own time.

Finally standing before their only son from across the other side of the table, Neville and Elaine Griffiths were instructed to be seated.

Their attention never averted from their son's.

Watery, dumbfounded stares preceded any inkling to speak. Ashley observed their matching orange prison fatigues as they slowly sank onto the appointed chairs and simultaneously slouched toward him.

A dual portrait of undying loyalty.

A desolate indictment of a terrible, wilful mistake.

Now banished to the confines of Hell for their deeds.

Words did not come freely.

Awkward seconds of noiseless indecision passed them by.

Ashley was transfixed by the damning concept of his flesh and blood being responsible for the death of another. He studied the lined faces and the grey hair of the two people that had brought him into the world and were now destined to leave him behind within its fold.

The very cornerstones of his existence.

His flesh and his blood.

His heart and his soul.

His safety net and his anchor.

Mum.

Dad.

It suddenly struck him as grossly inconceivable that such a moment of tenderness and intimacy should be subject to unwarranted scrutiny by the hardened array of wardens and policemen.

To say the very least, the presence of authority's generals was automatically inclined to inhibit honesty and any authentic conveyance of sentiment.

Not that either side of the table had the slightest idea how to commence the exchange.

Silence and stares.

Stares and silence.

Mother to son.

Father to mother.

Son to father.

The hiatus in communication was eventually unbearable.

Mournful.

Despairing.

And then, a tentative voice could be heard.

Screaming above the buckling tranquillity.

Neville Griffiths opened the dialogue in a clear, yet almost reticent tone.

'If you came here to receive an apology, son, you may as well get up and leave now.'

Ashley found himself caught up in a three-way response.

Humour, anger, and desperation fought for prominence.

Finally, he summoned a reply for the ears of his beloved mentors.

'Being sorry is irrelevant now, Dad. I understand your motive. I understand why you proceeded with the secret. I don't need an apology.'

Elaine Griffiths felt compelled to offer a first contribution.

'We did it to protect you, Ashley. That's our first and only instinct. We knew that if we talked to you about our intentions, then you would be an accomplice. And you would be going on trial, too.'

Ashley watched as his mother wiped her moistened eyes with her forefingers and continued with her explanation.

'It was our ambition to free you from the problem, Ashley. Not dig a deeper hole for you.'

Ashley nodded and retreated into his conscience once again, hoping to pluck the relevant questions from his beleaguered brain.

Frustration enveloped him as he spoke.

'So...Mum...Dad...did you have it all mapped out? From when you suggested I met her for a date? Was your scheme in place from that point?'

Neville assessed the gnarled facial features of the prison guards who stood with their backs against the wall. Whatever was said now was highly unlikely to incriminate anyone further.

The deed was done.

Their fate was sealed.

'Yes, Ash. We followed you to Fendern and waited outside The Bistro in the car. We watched you leave. Then we watched her leave. That's why we requested the photo. To be sure who she was. And then we followed her to her home. To make sure that we would know the house when we went back. It was the day after Boxing Day. After your mother called you. We paid her the visit. We tricked our way inside. Then instinct took over.'

Ashley struggled to reconcile the almost casual revelation from his father. It was akin to listening to the reminiscences of an East End gangster.

'So...when you phoned me...you had already committed yourselves to doing it?'

Once again, his mother offered supplement to Neville's simplistic account.

'Yes, son. And then when we saw on the local news that there had been an arrest, it spurred us to confess. We were always going to volunteer ourselves to the Police. That was the whole point of the plan. To ensure your freedom. In exchange for ours.'

Ashley could not believe the selflessness of his parents.

Neville took the reins from his wife once again.

'We instantly signed declarations of guilt, Ashley. No detail was spared. We felt no reason to hide anything. Our eyes were wide open going into this. We have no regrets about doing what we did. We did it because our only son was suffering. And because *she* deserved it. Any parent would do the same.'

It was dumbfounding.

Ashley staring across the table at the two elderly figures.

The whole scenario was like a remnant from the recesses of his worst nightmare.

And still he could not recognise that his mother and father were capable and willing murderers.

Surely, there must be a mistake somewhere.

He felt an episode of time had passed him by as he strived to make connections between the people that raised him and the people that had willingly engineered the demise of another life.

'But what about the sacrifice you've both made? Effectively bringing a halt to your own lives to give me a chance to continue with mine. It's too much to take in. It's not real. It can't be happening.'

Neville leaned forward in his chair, mildly alerting the attention of both wardens standing by the door.

'Consider this, Ashley. *You* were the only suspect. Your mother and I knew full well that the police would hook you in before anybody else. Like your mum says...we were always going to come forward and confess. If we hadn't, the murder would have been pinned on you. And we couldn't let that happen. The way we see it, the problem is now resolved. Your life can carry on, now.'

The inglorious image suddenly occupied Ashley's imagination.

His parents wielding weapons. Standing tall over the apparently defenceless victim. These weren't the civilised, law-abiding individuals, whose grounded sense of logic and wondrous morals he had taken for granted for nearly five decades.

In the eyes of the public and the Police, they were now nothing more than senseless killers.

Right there in the flesh.

Positioned just feet away from where he sat.

'Tell me, please. What did you do to her?'

Neville's expression carried the merest hint of glee.

'We bludgeoned her.'

'Yes…but how? What with?'

The husband glanced across to his wife before settling his focus back to his son.

'I used my nine-iron. Your mother used the eight. Or was it the seven?'

'Seven.' chipped Elaine

The nonchalance of Ashley's parents was astounding.

Almost perversely amusing.

'Golf clubs? You killed her by hitting her with *golf clubs*?'

'Sure did. They were quite adequate for the job, too.'

Now his mother emanated a glint of satisfaction as she reflected on the recent past.

Both of them together projected an air of triumph.

As though they had nurtured real accomplishment from the crime they had committed.

Jointly they conveyed a simmering detachment.

Neville described the scene with paternal pride.

'Yes. The clubs were in the boot, anyway. The Police said she was virtually unrecognisable when they arrived at the property. The next-door neighbours called them, apparently. I'm surprised they heard any noise to be honest. The first strike on the back of the head stunned her and she was there for the taking after that. She couldn't put up much of a fight. We made sure of that didn't we, darling?'

Ashley found himself descending into a horrifying realm of dismay.

This was borderline pantomime.

Had his parents conceivably lost their minds?

Neville rubber-stamped his personal approval on matters through a thinly veiled mask of pleasure.

‘The general idea was to make minimal fuss. It happened pretty quickly from start to finish, really. But the main thing is she won’t be stalking you anymore. That’s the *main thing*. Mission successful, eh?’

Ashley shook his head as the pieces of the insidious jigsaw fitted themselves together.

Abject disbelief ensnared him.

‘But Mum…Dad…you said to me to try and kill her with kindness, didn’t you? What happened to that theory?’

‘I know we did, son. But your mother and I couldn’t wait for that. Besides, such a theory would never have worked. She was a certifiable lunatic. And there’s only one way to stop a certifiable lunatic.’

Ashley’s stomach turned at the referencing from his parents.

This was no ordinary day in the life of the Griffiths clan, yet his mother and father exhibited precious little notion of the fact.

‘Have they told you when the trial is likely to be taking place?’

Neville shrugged his shoulders.

‘Who cares? Me and your mother certainly don’t. It’s all out of our hands, now. We’ve done our bit.’

The contented lack of awareness in his parents was bemusing.

They held no remorse for the past or indeed trepidation concerning their future.

‘But they’ll throw away the key, Dad. Does that probability not worry you both? Because it is frightening the bloody life out of me.’

Neville observed the steadily rising emotion in his son. It was understandably unpleasant for a child to see his parents in such a predicament.

Yet their demeanour retained a thick strand of optimism. Why this should have been the case was a complete mystery in the circumstances.

Elaine suddenly reached across the surface of the table with her right hand.

Ashley replicated the gesture, knowing full well that if there was any physical contact then the meeting would be shut down instantly. He found himself at a total loss as to where the conversation should now be directed. He was most grateful that the burden was taken off his shoulders by his mother.

'Ashley…your father and I…we so love you much. Please don't judge us for our sin. We couldn't just stand by and watch you get trampled further into the dust. You had become a different person because of her. A shadow of your former self. Just promise us that whatever has been taken from you these past few months…you will do your utmost to reclaim it. Don't leave us thinking we acted in vain, son. Pledge that you'll make all this mess worthwhile. Rise again, Ashley. Rise again.'

Ashley's tears fell on to the table without restraint or indeed any attempt at concealment.

He so wanted to hold his mother's hand but dare not take the chance.

And yet then, in an instantaneous turn of approach, he grasped his mother's fingers and squeezed them tightly as he openly wept.

And authority instantaneously lurched into action.

Bringing an end to the family reunion.

And as the prison wardens predicably pulled their hands apart and called time on the occasion, Elaine stared deeply into the eyes of her only son and mouthed a temporary farewell.

'Thank you, Ash. We love you. Never forget that.'

Speechless through a disarming and misplaced swell of admiration, Ashley watched as his parents were ushered to their feet by the prison officers.

They had wilfully re-written their destinies for him.

This ethic alone warranted his eternal gratitude.

Yet as he watched his mother and father be promptly escorted to the opposite doorway, overwhelming sorrow was the only sensation that now engulfed him.

It was his father that offered a parting word of wisdom as their separation loomed.

His message was sheathed with a determined, paternal tone.

‘Go and get your life back, son. The time for stress and strife is gone. Grasp the opportunity now it’s there. And don’t worry about us. We’ll be just fine.’

Ashley dried his eyes with his coat sleeve and found himself to be under orders. A uniformed police officer requested he vacate his chair and leave the room via the door behind.

His departing glimpse of his parents filled him with pride.

Yes, they *would* be fine.

They felt only self-assurance.

No distress.

No remorse.

No contrition.

How wrong were they to feel this way?

As parents and offspring were manhandled through doors on opposite sides of the office, Neville managed to shout out one final question to his son.

‘ASH!’

‘Yes, Dad?’

‘Come and see us when things are settled. After sentencing. We need to see you happy again. Just do that one thing for me and your mother. Will you promise to let us see you happy again?’

Through a watery gaze, Ashley nodded sullenly.

‘I promise. On my life. And Dad?’

‘Yes, son.’

‘Thank you. Thank you both. I get it. I really do.’

Ashley did not look back as he finally exited the room to the echo of metallic door crashing into the frame.

And the steady realisation descended upon him.

The next time he would set eyes on his mother and father, would be in Crown Court.

*****

Detective Inspector Neil Huntley did not utter a single syllable as he chaperoned the visitor back through the maze of steel doors and dimly painted corridors.

And likewise, Ashley felt no compulsion to communicate with the senior officer. The picture was now clear enough for all concerned. Words would be meaningless.

Within minutes, Ashley had been checked out of the building and was at liberty to leave the premises.

Once back in the solitude of the car, his mental maelstrom finally caused the floodgates to open.

With a wrenching gut and a broken heart, he repeatedly and deliberately butted his forehead against the steering wheel. The wintry rain was now incessant. The wails resonating from the driver's seat could only be detected by one person.

And that one person was Ashley himself.

The emotional vortex rinsed him and rendered him a weak and quivering wreck. He clenched the wheel in his fists as the relentless tide of torment crashed around the jagged rocks of his ravaged essence.

Until eventually, he passed through the storm.

And calm resumed once again.

Red, raw, salt-stung eyes stared at the dishevelled reflection in the rear-view mirror.

The face of a once broken man.

A once fearful man.

Now ready to repair himself.

To be reformed.

To be empowered.

To oblige the one and only wish of a doting mother and father.

FORTY-SIX

September; Twenty-Twenty-Two. The sixteenth. Friday.

Two-fifteen p.m.

Eight and a half months after being initially remanded in custody.

The trial of Neville and Elaine Griffiths finally reached its conclusion.

The judicial process endured for a total of just ten days.

Twelve members of the jury returned two unanimous verdicts.

Those verdicts being, that Neville David Griffiths and Elaine Susan Griffiths were equally guilty of murder in the First Degree.

Q.C. Simon Reville offered no leniency toward the defendants.

The indifference they had displayed toward the deed was no act, either. As such, they were awarded the due and fitting penance for their crime.

Each receiving a minimum sentence of twenty-five years in prison.

Both were strongly advised against appealing the decision unless they wished to invite a harsher term.

There would be no eligibility to apply for parole until they had served at least fifteen of those twenty-five years.

As the one and only link between the victim and the killers, their son, Ashley Griffiths, was duly obliged to take the stand on the second, third and fourth days of the trial.

The sole mitigating party to an unfolding chronicle of incidents that had led to jeopardy of mesmerising proportions. Into which Ashley and his parents had become unwillingly and unwittingly entwined.

Ashley's innocence in matters was established with relative and unexpected ease. There was no iota of aspersion cast upon his position or his account of events under oath.

Character witness statements were provided most enthusiastically by Jeanette Morris and Derek Evans.

Indeed, the judge, Mister Simon Reville, and jury foreman, Mister Raymond Baxter, exuded an unspoken sense of genuine sympathy toward Ashley, in consideration of the upheaval his life had been forced to accommodate for the previous fourteen months.

Yet even as the appointed head of the court sessions commandeered that the convicted be sent back to jail to continue serving their sentences, Ashley stared at his mother and father's placid demeanour as they were led downstairs to the waiting security vehicle.

They were unwavering in their adamance at having just cause.

They displayed no expectation of impunity. Far from it.

And just at the very last second before vanishing into the depths of the courthouse basement, they looked to their son. A dual glance of hope and of optimism. And Ashley needed no translation of its meaning.

The counsel for the defence openly admitted their presence in court was merely perfunctory. The counsel for the prosecution had never administered with such overriding certainty.

Indeed, the ease of process was unprecedented.

Irony surrounded the disclosure of the two verdicts.

Ironic because Neville and Elaine Griffiths were effectively sent down as victors in their own minds. They fully embraced the punishment. It was nigh on an acknowledgement of their triumph.

Theirs was a madness embraced. The perception of success was their accompanying balm, even as they were driven back to prison.

Their concession being that they had relinquished the likelihood of ever being able to sample civilian life again.

In order that their only child might be able to reclaim such a privilege.

And so, it played out as it was ordained to be.

Liberty was restored for the son.

Incarceration was assured for the parents.

A twisted, previously uncharted tale of paradox.

Now on public record.

For one and for all to view.

*****

Ashley departed the court building with a heavy heart. The only strand of positivity gleaned being that the verdicts and subsequent judgement were fully anticipated.

His parents had already informed him that when the time came, he would be legally declared the sole benefactor to their estate.

Their planning had been reckless yet so meticulous.

In every way, Neville and Elaine Griffiths had made provision for their son's regeneration.

Ashley himself was no longer submerged by quandary.

He had long since returned to his duties at work.

He had fronted out the whispered discussions and the shadowy speculation that had inevitably transpired beyond earshot.

He had retained the trust of his public and colleagues alike. Most felt desperately sorry for him. And as relations warmed after the extensive period of his absence, he found himself gradually enabling a renewal of faith in fellow man.

But he was already missing the ready and reliable presence of his mother and father. His guiding lights. His foothold.

He had inherited his principles from them.

Maybe they had delivered the ultimate sermon in enforcing their son to finally fly solo.

In tribute to their sacrifice, he would do just that.

*****

As he strode dejectedly toward his car at the rear of the courthouse and activated the central locking, Ashley did not detect the covert observer hidden from sight some yards away.

He pulled open the driver's door and slid behind the wheel, completely oblivious to the fact he was under scrutiny.

The concealed spectator continued to study Ashley's vehicle as it manoeuvred from its space, before exiting the court site and joining with the main flow of traffic.

The chance was gone.

This time, seemingly, forever.

Carl Davis had afforded himself multiple opportunities to open communication with Ashley as the trial progressed, having attended every day from the seclusion of the public gallery.

Yet he had decided that his presence should have consistently and wilfully remained anonymous.

The fragile courage that he hoped would bolster the possibility of personal engagement with Ashley, had repeatedly deserted him each day.

Especially this day.

This most critical of all days.

And as he contemplated his own personal burden of regret, and perhaps wayward sense of moral responsibility, he felt resigned to never being able to speak with Ashley about what had happened to their relationship.

He had tried to cope with the phantom of Pauline Braithwaite.

He had tried.

And he had failed.

Indeed, he and Ashley had stood shoulder to shoulder initially.

They had endeavoured to repel her diseased invasion of their lives with hard hearts and stern unity.

But now it was all over, Carl Davis could no longer envision the wondrous reacquaintance with the man he thought he once loved with all his heart.

And by his own private admission, it was this perpetual and overriding doubt that had been the death knell for their relationship.

That he might not have loved Ashley Griffiths enough, was the true catalyst for failure of their life together.

It was not the fault of Pauline Braithwaite.

Her temporary intrusion was merely the event that served to highlight issues that Carl had always sensed creeping over the horizon.

Nevertheless, a shroud of guilt was Carl Davis's singular and uninvited companion, as he departed the courthouse premises to catch his train.

Guilt that he anticipated would hang over his head for the remainder of his days.

And so, whilst he would walk away with a certain reluctance, he would bear the conclusion just as unwillingly as he had envisioned it.

Though his head and his heart were now finally in unison.

And together, they had already dictated that Carl Davis would not cross paths with Ashley Griffiths ever again.

EPILOGUE

December. Twenty-Twenty-Two. The fourteenth. Wednesday.

Twelve-forty-five p.m.

'Have you had a lunch break yet, Jeanette?'

The Head of Reception looked up from her monitor to see the Head of Operations standing on the other side of the check-in desk.

'No. Ashley. But I'm not hungry. I don't need a break, anyway. I thrive on adrenaline.'

'Okay. I'm going to take some air for twenty minutes. Ring my mobile if you require me to return forthwith.'

Jeanette smiled.

His sparkle was slowly returning in brief glimpses.

But it was still very early days.

'I think we can cope without you for twenty minutes.' she chuckled, as Ashley feigned indignation.

'You're getting cheekier in your old age, Mrs. Morris!'

Now it was Jeanette's turn to convey offence.

'And *you're* not too old to get put over my knee. Now go and get your walking done. You've used up two minutes of your twenty already. I'm counting, you know!'

Ashley portrayed his broadest grin as he zipped up his coat.

'I won't be too long. It hasn't got above freezing all day. Proper December weather isn't it. Just need a change of scenery. See you shortly.'

*****

The Head of Operations and sometime sampler of celebrity cut a lonely figure as he ambled through the centre of Hernwood's shopping precinct and made toward the outskirts of town.

His destination was pre-designated.

A calling from the depths of his own psyche, perhaps.

Yet it was a signal he felt obliged to obey.

His concentration fixed directly ahead as he strode.

His senses acknowledged nothing amid the pre-Christmas hustle and bustle of market day.

The traffic; the shoppers.

The weavers and the duckers, laden with carrier bags.

Onward he marched with a determined poise, as the chill of the wintry air bit into his cheeks.

He was focused and clear in his mission.

Yet simultaneously, dazed and confused.

The town's main exit road was duly located, but the Hernwood Hotel Head of Operations and sometime champion of its publicity campaign still had further to wander.

Beyond the boundary of Hernwood he moved.

His hands locked in his trouser pockets.

His mind struggling for an anchor amid a diminishing yet sorrowful hurricane.

Passing the industrial estate.

Skirting the retail park.

Ever closer to his target.

The last outstretched fingers of a residential pocket adjoined to the main traffic junction of the town.

The trunking artery that fed and connected the community.

Whilst also enabling departure and disconnection from it.

A spider-like arrangement of A roads, B roads, footbridges, and the overpassing motorway.

And finally, after a journey on foot ghosted by clinging uncertainty and dubious motivation, the Hernwood Hotel's Head of Operations brought his trek to a gradual halt.

Looking upward, first into the watery slate sky, his attention then centred on the steel-framed billboard.

The same billboard that had sported his image for eighteen months.

The depiction was of a supposedly carefree, perhaps even a happy man.

An image conveying warmth, they said.

An image conveying honesty, they said.

An image, they said, that would leave the public in no doubt who the man in the poster was, and what he represented.

And how right *they* were.

About all the things *they* said.

He stood to attention on the pavement.

His expression deforming into a grimace of wanton disgust as he continued to scrutinise the forced display of rehearsed positivity within the poster.

And the disgust fused with the shadows in his memory to form nothing less than acute nausea.

A living, breathing, tangible hatred for the charlatan in the hotel blazer, with his hands outstretched and his teeth pearly white. And his hair perfectly coiffed and his fingernails flawlessly manicured.

A depiction of lies.

A portrayal of hollowness that ably turned his gut.

If only the passing public knew of the reality behind the façade.

If only the passing public knew that the mood of the man on the pavement contrasted starkly with the perceived mood of the man stretched across the billboard.

Indeed, the Head of Operations cut a very unsettled figure as he contemplated his photograph and contemplated his losses.

Losses that he could never be compensated for.

He still viewed it as inconceivable that what commenced in earnest, had concluded in calamity.

He calmed his breathing to restrict the rumbling onset of emotion.

His upset might yet breach the surface and become visible.

But he hoped not.

Still, he stared at his own image, with the full knowledge of the destruction that it had invited into his existence.

He privately wanted that bastard of a billboard burned to ashes.

So that nothing remained but a pile of dust.

To be caught on the breeze and relegated to the annals of long forgotten history.

But, of course, it would always be too late.

The price had already been paid.

The cost had been detrimentally high.

And that bastard of a billboard remained standing.

With everything he once cherished and coveted now relegated to a mere nothingness.

The injustice of it all pierced his conscience with every single beat of his shattered heart.

For such torment, there would be no remedy.

*****

The minutes passed as the Hernwood Hotel's Head of Operations continued his private phase of desolate reflection.

Despite the freezing wind he was unmoving.

Yet so moved.

So immersed was he within his personal deliberation, he did not identify the cautious approach of footsteps.

A curious soul, who had bravely decided to seek the company of the solitary male figure on the pavement.

The voice that eventually resonated was feminine, gentle in tone and possibly kindly in nature.

'I thought it must be *you*…it is *you*…isn't it?'

The Hernwood Hotel's Head of Operations digested the comment and reacted with a slight turn of his head to assess the source.

The woman was attractive and possessed a striking expression of vigour atop her thick scarf and beneath her woollen hat.

This ignited a personable response from the subject of her wonder, as Ashley performed in his most hospitable guise.

'Yes…unfortunately…I am he. The poster boy…in the flesh. For all my sins.'

The woman chuckled and moved closer to the Hernwood Hotel's Head of Operations.

Together they stood in a mutual pondering silence as they both observed the gregarious image that loomed high above.

Then the woman broached an extension to the conversation.

'Ever since that poster went up last year, I've always thought how handsome you are. But now I'm actually next to you I can see that you're even more of a dish in real life.'

The Hernwood Hotel's Head of Operations panicked internally, yet somehow conjured a repost of appropriate modesty.

He forced a smile and played along with the charade.

'Don't be silly. You're making me blush!'

The middle-aged woman shifted position to gain better vantage of the Hernwood Hotel's Head of Operations.

She stared intently into his eyes, forcing him to do likewise into hers.

An instinctive shiver screamed down his spine and the hairs on his neck rose, as if to offer an acute warning.

In turn, she pursed her lips and fluttered her eyelashes.

As a devastating mask of sincerity formed across her delicate features.

'Oh, I wasn't being silly. Far from it. In fact, I'm being deadly serious…'

ACKNOWLEDGEMENTS

I wish to thank the following people for their invaluable expertise and support in helping this book gain wings:
Samantha Thornton; Hannah Bliss; Charlotte Wilson; Robbie Wilson; Carole Thornton, Chris Bliss; Charlotte Bliss; Jeanette Taylor Ford; Sue Hayward; Ford Wood; Beverley Latimer; Yana Z, and last but certainly not least, David Slaney for his superb cover design.
I couldn't have done it without any of you.
I am forever indebted.
RJT

Also Available on Amazon
by Richard John Thornton

thrillers

DELIVER US FROM EVIL
AT HELL'S GATE
THE SWANS AT CLEARLAKE
WITHIN THESE WALLS
A PRAYER FOR MARTIN

the 80s trilogy

LAST OF THE OLD SCHOOL

Printed in Great Britain
by Amazon

25472956R00209